I0647191

The Rain
That Touched the Sky

Manoj N Premal

ZORBA BOOKS

ZORBA BOOKS

Published in India by Zorba Books, 2018

Website: www.zorbabooks.com
Email: info@zorbabooks.com

Copyright © Manoj N Premal

ISBN Print Book - 978-93-87456-38-9
ISBN eBook - 978-93-87456-39-6

Zorba Books Pvt. Ltd.(opc)
Gurgaon, INDIA

Printed at Repro Knowledgecast Limited, Thane

Dedication

With love to Joanne and Dhruv

ACKNOWLEDGEMENTS

We express our primary indebtedness to the divine supreme consciousness for blessing us with direction, thoughts, and courage to do what we needed to do when we needed to do it.

Sincere thanks to our family and friends for their insightful guidance and constructive criticism that helped in shaping the story. We are immensely grateful to Sreedevi chechi for her inputs, encouragement, and editorial suggestions. Our heartfelt gratitude to Father Aniyil Tharakan for critical inputs that gave a direction to our efforts.

Many thanks to Revathy for her support and to Priya for the book cover design. Sincere thanks to Deepankuran for the music and Bharat for the trailer. Immense gratitude to our friend Ajaya Mishra for his guidance and encouragement on this long journey.

Sincere thanks to our team at Zorba books for holding our hands and guiding us into the world of publishing. This would have remained a dream without them.

Our heartfelt thanks to our families and dear friends who have helped us and supported us through thick and thin. And finally, we bow in gratitude to you for supporting us by purchasing this debut novel.

Perspectives

Some people are born with tornadoes in their lives,
but constellations in their eyes.
Other people are born with stars at their feet,
but their souls are lost at sea.

- Nikita Gill

PROLOGUE

*M*ore than the brunt of time, the door appeared bruised by recent violence. The shoe prints on the door looked fresh. It must have taken several kicks to break it down, but it seemed firmly in place.

Is she safe?

Are we late?

With trepidation and doubt, AK glanced at his friends as he deliberately pressed the doorbell.

No sound!

He knocked on the door.

No answer, he knocked again. No answer again.

The trio stood in silence hoping to hear her approaching footsteps. Impulsively AK pushed firmly on the door and it opened slowly creaking at the hinges, and a hinge fell off, the top of the door now hung out like a dislocated limb. This door had been pulled back into place.

Clothes torn and strewn across the room, a broken photo frame nearly falling off the wall, a broken table and chair and a destroyed almirah greeted them. The almirah door had been broken with a sharp object. There were some old newspapers and utensils lying on the floor. The unwelcome sight of her house showed on their faces. They passed a quick restless glance at each other.

They slowly sauntered into the kitchen and the bedroom. Violence reared its ugly head everywhere. The blood stains on the walls made their insides turn. AK's trepidation burst from within and he couldn't contain himself. He rushed to the main door followed by his friends to check the surroundings, hopelessly praying that she might be safe hiding somewhere outside. He

1

nearly stumbled over the broken chair on the floor and a glint caught his eye, as the first rays of the sun pointed it out to him.

Picking it up, a tear escaped him. It was the broken half of the pendant he had gifted her. He looked up into their eyes imploring silently- *is she safe?* His friends looked at him helplessly, the burden of his question weighing them down. Without uttering a word, shaken they walked towards the door.

As they neared the door, their eyes fell on a grapple hook that lay on the ground smeared. They knelt down to examine it closely. Someone had desperately tried to hold on to the grapple hook but was wrenched away. Arising, AK noticed a fuzzy palm print on the wall adjacent to the broken hook and his eyes widened in horror. It was her blood stained palm print!

CHAPTER 1

Akashan Krishnakumar Menon, AK to his close buddies, like any typical happy-go-lucky Malayalee NRI lad had the fun part of his life well planned out. First, get a driver's license soon after his eighteenth birthday, which was just half a year away from now. Then plead, beg, and grovel in front of his dearest mom to request his strict dad for a Ford Mustang- even a second hand would be perfectly fine. It would be an ideal way to be a part of the "in-crowd". Being a dark, 5'11" wiry built teenager donning popular brands like Reebok, Tommy Hilfiger etc., the long hours of grooming, offered no help where it mattered. He never scored with girls. He had never had a girlfriend! How could he? Having studied in a boys' school, his degree of nervousness was directly proportional to their beauty and grace.

These issues, although minor to others, were rather magnified and pertinent to AK. *The only solution to this* mused AK, *Was to get a girlfriend!* Joining his friends at the University of Wollongong in Dubai, upon returning from his holidays in India, would ease him into this much needed social therapy.

However, unknown to AK a few things worried his dad. Apart from the challenges of business, his paternal grandmother's frail health meant she needed to be relocated from their apartment in Dombivli, Maharashtra to their native place near Thiruvananthapuram, Kerala where Mr. Krishnakumar's sister and her family could look after her.

That fateful day, 15th May 1998, would forever remain etched in AK's memory. His parents, sister, and he had happily boarded the Emirates flight from Dubai to Mumbai.

Brimming with the eagerness and enthusiasm of first visiting family and friends in Mumbai, and then travel to Udupi, a few weeks later, to drop his younger sister Akhila to boarding school. The final leg of the trip would include sojourning with relatives in the idyllic locales of Kerala. Everything had been perfectly planned.

Upon taking their seats in the flight, a stewardess requested the family for AK's cooperation. Ah! when the immaturity of age and willingness to charm a superior beauty rushed in , how could he refuse? In keeping with his polished appearance and polite mannerisms, AK happily exchanged his seat with a geriatric lady who preferred to sit on the aisle seat. So she could periodically stand and stretch her legs to relieve her recently operated knees. Now sitting two rows behind his parents and savouring the taste of his first Heineken beer, discreetly gifted to him for his kindness by the same pretty stewardess. AK smiled and relished the taste of his first foray into adulthood. He was THE MAN! The first one gave him the courage and machismo to ask for another beer, and the beautiful lady obliged. The beers were worth being away from his parents in that short trip.

Akashan, fondly called Akku by his mom, a nickname well past its prime, often made him the butt of his friends' jokes, had a surprise awaiting him. Upon landing at Mumbai airport his mother remarked, "Akku, your Dad and I think it is best for you to study here, in some good college in Mumbai!" AK was too baffled to protest. Surely, he hadn't heard her correctly. Probably the beers were already working on him. After a while, he clarified with her again. She answered affirmatively with the same nonchalant air as before confirming that he would be spending the next three years of his life in Mumbai! His Ford Mustang sped off from his dream! and the "in-crowd" vanished! He was baffled at first and soon indignant at both of them. He couldn't believe that such a life altering decision could have been made high up in the air.

On the way to their apartment in Dombivli, a sulky AK was mentally marking points like a lawyer to base his arguments in favour of studying in Dubai. However the courage to place those points in front of his father was never to trickle in.

He was not new to Mumbai. AK was born in Dombivli and had studied there until the sixth grade before relocating to Dubai with his family. He was so habituated to Dubai and its comforts that although familiar, Mumbai felt strange to him. Was it the fear of the unknown and unexplored? Or the fear of change? Perhaps a mix of all this worried him. It was only when his best friend, Sanjay Ramanathan Iyer passed on his wisdom of Freedom did AK see the true light of life.

"Yaar, you don't get it, do you? This is your chance at freedom!! Something that fellows like me and so many guys only dream of but never get! FREEDOM!! Away from parents!! There is a whole new world waiting for you to explore. Dumbo, don't miss this golden opportunity" said Sanjay, slapping AK's shoulder in excitement.

And so in that momentary excitement AK agreed to his parents' decision to stay back and study in Mumbai.

Marks were an issue both in Dubai and Mumbai. The Central Board of Secondary Education announced the results of the HSC board exams by the end of May, 1998. AK had procured only 65% marks, a bare aggregate compared to the super teens vying for admission into the colleges in Mumbai. Had he diverted some portion of his grooming time on studies probably he could have done better. On hindsight that's how he consoled himself.

"Yaar, You are OC - Open Category. You need to get at least 95% only then your name will make it into the first list. If you get into the second list you are lucky, let's hope" said Sanjay. AK was dejected to hear this at first, but the rejections from several colleges meant he would soon be back in Dubai.

The deep rumble of the Ford Mustang's engine was now sweet music to his ears and the old familiar smile returned on his lips.

Valour to confront his father trickled in. The moment had arrived! And the stage finally set at the dinner table! Braving that cold stare from his father, AK hinted that probably his destiny was to study in Dubai. "You are studying here in Mumbai," his dad asserted with a finality driven by his furrowed brows. Thus closing the topic even before it had been opened. A giggling sister and a mother who pretended to not hear a word were all AK had for support. His courage sped off faster than his red Ford Mustang.

AK's parents persisted in their search. After two weeks of running around, he managed to secure admission in 4 colleges. They chose the best out of the lot--K J Somaiya College of Arts and Commerce, in Vidyavihar. The college was roughly an hour's commute, by train, from Dombivli. He was now fated to be in Mumbai.

The following week his father dropped AK's sister off at her boarding school in Udupi, and continued the journey to take their grandmother to his aunt's house in Kerala. While his mom helped AK settle down in their apartment in Dombivli. Uncle Mahesh, his father's younger brother who was still single, agreed to stay along and look after AK. And so the family trip to Kerala was cancelled.

Several weeks passed and soon, it was time for his parents to head back to Dubai.

With a heave AK placed the heavy suitcase onto the trolley. He turned around to see his mom dissecting his uncle's head picking his brains and stuffing it with details of all the food he loved, should have, and must have. While his uncle patiently made mental notes and kept reassuring his sister-in-law.

As far as his Dad was concerned, for the umpteenth time, he took him through the never-ending labyrinths of financial planning. He was given a long list of do's and don'ts--How to stay in control? how to spend judiciously? what to spend on? The list never ended.

"Akku, please take good care of yourself, be a good boy, don't fall into bad company, no unnecessary friendships, study well .. and no unwanted interests or habits. There's time for all that later on" his mom said, her voice choking with tears. She hugged him tight and kissed him goodbye. All his worries melted away and, he merely nodded.

His dad hugged him and kissed his forehead, "Take care son, be good. Mahesh please take care of him ok. And let me know if you need anything" said his Dad. *Well, behind that steely exterior, he does have feelings and that is nice to know, but he probably does not know how to show it,* AK sighed within.

He watched them push the trolley and enter the airport. His parents turned and they waved at him. He saw them disappear into the departing crowd. They would see their daybreak in Dubai.

Unexpectedly he felt bad. *I feel bad…that I don't feel sad that they are leaving me here and going back.* He mused, a smile broke through, contentment, and that made things even worse. How could one feel content inside and show sadness outside? Did he need some emotional rewiring inside his head? He wondered. *Ah! Freedom is a heady cocktail! Here I come!* He bit his lips to suppress his smile.

They were into the first week of June and monsoons were yet to bless the city. AK and his uncle hailed an auto from the Chatrapati Shivaji airport to Ghatkopar station.

The train creaked to a stop in front of them and before AK knew a stampede was pouring out of the compartment in front of him like a dam bursting at the seams. Someone pulled him back and held him to the side for the rush to subside. He turned to see, it was his uncle and he was grateful for him just being there.

On getting aboard, he suddenly realized with dread that his uncle might not have gotten into the train. AK breathed a sigh of relief on spotting him. There was another problem with Mahesh Uncle. Being short and a bit plump in nature, standing at just 5′2″, he had literally drowned out of sight.

The train started its movement and was surprisingly picking up speed even before he found the space to land two of his toes. He was literally standing on someone else's feet.

I think I know now why Mumbai is considered the melting pot of all cultures. One, I am melting now…and two, the train is one place where everyone rubs heads and shoulders with each other…only to finally step out smelling like others. And yeah, I also feel like I am in a pickle jar now! He sighed as he mused. He rued having to take the train.

As the train halted at the next station more people squeezed in and soon the train moved. Suddenly he felt a crawling touch on his butt, slowly feeling him up. *This can't be happening!!!* He was shaken. *NO NO NO noooo I am going to get raped by some dirty leech in the train!* Enraged and helpless, he wanted to scream for help but the fear of being laughed at, prevented him.

He tried to turn around and see. He couldn't. He tried again. He merely managed to catch a glimpse of a slightly longer mane. He was confused and repulsed. He could feel the warm breath on his back but the fingers did not feel strong or thick. He jolted when he suddenly felt a pair of soft yet tantalizing mounds pressing against his back. He was shocked!

I am getting groped by a lady, he thought. *What the hell? Which decent woman would be doing something like this? And why? Is she a hooker or something? Or is she in so much heat? What an embarrassment! Good god!* He lamented.

She was literally groping him up…and although he hated to admit it…it felt great. A weird mixture of anguish and excitement that made him guilty with pleasure.

The constraints created within his jeans, between his legs, due to this act of treason and embezzlement of modesty was proof enough that he enjoyed it after all.

As in, it's not often that one gets groped by a woman, with her breasts pressed against his back while her tantalizing fingers are playing delightful tunes of desires around his nether regions, and that too in a train. This strange yet delightful episode made him sweat more with excitement than embarrassment, and although it lasted for 10 minutes, it seemed to have lasted merely for a few seconds. He realized that his mysterious admirer had stepped off when he suddenly felt the fingers retreat. He looked around to note that it was Mulund station. It was always in Mulund where around forty percent of the crowd got off.

Thane, the next station was where, normally, half the crowd would leave. He regretted that he couldn't get to see his groper's face. *How did she look? Was she good looking enough? Was she fair? Or was she a black beauty? Her Venusian mounds felt firm and proud*, he sighed, wishing he had seen her.

Anyway, after Thane surely, he would get a seat to safeguard his rear from prying hands. But a fleeting thought did cross his mind *Maybe…just maybe…she found me attractive!* He blushed. AK couldn't stop smiling, and well, the thought was a confidence builder. He did have scope in Mumbai after all. At the age of eighteen, even the smallest act of touch, smile or look from a beautiful member of the opposite sex, was a confidence booster for a guy, making him soar above all human creations. He sat down with a smile. The train moved on.

Time flew, and before long, "Akku, come on…next stop is ours," his uncle said, getting up from his seat.

AK followed him to the footboard.

"Uncle please don't call me Akku…it's weird" he said in a hushed embarrassed tone.

Uncle smiled nostalgically and said, "You used to respond only to that when you were a kid."

"I am not a kid anymore," he retorted as the train entered the station.

Alighting, they were greeted by a huge commotion, near the canteen, on the platform of Dombivli station.

Usual profanities, punches and kicks flying on the face and body of what looked like a slightly built man, in his mid-thirties, with a slight paunch in a white t-shirt, grey trousers, and sneakers. The frenzied mob had the poor soul writhing in pain and disgrace on the ground, begging for mercy, being hammered by the angry mob.

"*Mujhe maaf kardo…chodd do mujhe please ghar pe biwi bacche bhukke hain.*" (Forgive me…please spare me, my wife and kids are starving at home) The body of pain pleaded and begged for mercy.

They continued trashing him like a punctured ball and hurling the choicest abuses at him. Apparently, he had been caught stealing from a senior citizen and the angry mob was now punishing him mercilessly. He saw two constables approaching the mob.

One of the two constables asked him in Marathi, "*Tujha naav kai?*" (what's your name?)

"La…. Laxman Das," he responded, while crying uncontrollably.

"*Haath pudhey kar,*" (Show your hand) said the other constable.

The man extended his hand, only to get spanked by a *lathi*. He cried in pain.

"*Chala chala saguley… kaay tamasha laavlaay ikde… aplya aplya ghari chala! hyala amhi chowkit gheun jatoy!*" shouted the constable (Okay, now all of you leave…Off you go to your homes now, we'll take him to the station… it's no free show running here…come on, move on!).

The crowd dispersed and the two constables took the battered culprit away.

"Akku, don't worry! Such things happen here," Mahesh Uncle said. AK was shaken by the violence that he had just witnessed.

They made their way over the footbridge, past the cacophony of the railway station and the chaotic chorus of roadside hawkers at the foot of the overbridge.

All the while he wondered what an eventful evening it had been. *The crowded train, the grope, which brought a twitch of shameless pride and smile to his face again!* He felt like a sex symbol.

An hour into the flight Nandini, AK's mom, jolted up from her sleep, her maternal instincts pricked her with an uneasy feeling. Before she could turn to see her sleeping hubby, the plane was suddenly shaking mid-air. The warning signs went off. The captain assured them this mild turbulence would soon pass, and it did. She looked at her husband and marvelled at his ability to sleep peacefully throughout the flight.

Amidst all this, her thoughts drifted to her son and she prayed for him. Her instinct told her something was wrong, but she resolved not to let anxiety get the better of her. She would call him as soon as they got home.

The auto rickshaw made its way through the narrow road, littered with hawkers and occupied by vendors. The homeless, stray dogs, and abandoned cattle were donated a mix of fresh and leftover vegetables from the market, at the close of day. It was good to see some vendors and hawkers were indeed humane. These sights, smells and sounds would be a part of his life until he finished his graduation. Suddenly, AK realized that life had changed.

They reached below the building.

"I'll get that uncle", AK insisted on paying the fare,

"Ok, *chutta hoga*?" (Ok, got change?) he enquired on knowing the fare as he reached for his wallet.

He slipped his hand into his denim's back pocket and his fingers jutted out from the bottom of the pocket. He felt for his wallet again. Surely, it must be there.

"Oh NOOO! My Goodness! Bloody Hell! I got screwed!" He broke into a cold sweat, forgetting the fact that his uncle was nearby.

His blue denim's back pocket was cut at the base and his wallet GONE.

"What happened?" his uncle enquired, bewildered.

"My wallet got flicked," he said, crushed and hurt.

The auto driver looked on with apathy. He naturally saw this reaction everyday many number of times!

"It's ok, I will pay him," his uncle said and settled the fare.

"I had Rs.300 in that," he said, feeling lost.

"What about the money that your mom and dad gave you in the morning?" his uncle asked with concern.

"It's at home. I didn't carry much money with me. But the wallet was a new one that mom got me…as a present."

His mind started on a rewind mode tracing back, where it could have happened.

The airport, the station, when he was with the crowd…the train…OH NO! It was the lady…damn it… She was not feeling him up… Oh God! He had been robbed and he helped her do it!

And that too by a lady. How could he even tell this to anyone? He could not believe it happened to him.

groped away by a
his genitals rather
as he could ever ha
    He freshened u

The doorbell rang
    "Hi Akash! C
said, unlocking th
up, Akash is here.
voluble tone.
    Ramanathan u
during their first
became   friends.
Subbalakshmi, hi:
friends since then
Aunty, Sanjay's mc
and kind. Her dem
feel welcome and
always felt at hom
glasses, and Sanjay
worried   mother c
laziness.
    AK smiled and
will wake him up."
within, thinking o1
    Sanjay and AK I
They went to the
school till sixth gr
while Sanjay conti1
    A wheatish cc
and felt he looked
He often wore jea1
the typical know i
touched, including
arguments, on and
status – Single! He \

How was he going to survive in Mumbai at this rate? It had barely been over two hours since his parents had left and he had already messed up.

"It's ok. Look at it this way. It could have been worse, imagine if you had your college ID card and ATM card in the wallet. To make a duplicate would have been a headache. You would have had to file a police complaint and create an affidavit, which is not necessary now. Besides this has happened to me too…a long time back," said his uncle, trying to pacify him.

He nodded at his uncle in silence.

How could he be consoled? He had lost the wallet his mom had got him. What hurt him more was that it was a nice black expensive *Hidesign* wallet, and HE HAD HELPED THE THIEF FLICK IT. He now regretted not trying to stop it and not trying to see the woman at all.

So much humiliation, excitement and embarrassment all packed into too few minutes. *Phew!*

They got to their apartment, which was on the third floor of the building. Climbing the stairs another disturbing thought hit him. What if she pricked him with a HIV+ needle like in the stories he had heard.

He quickly undressed, panic-stricken, checked for any needle marks on his bottom. Relieved to have found none, he put on his night clothes and quickly hit the bed but could hardly sleep, and for the first time realized how the deafening silence could be so loud. He suddenly missed his mom and dad's banter.

ncle Ma
as an ele
plant visits at tl
throughout the
informed him of
and that he wo
With a drowsy h

Within minu
crash back into l
of an ISD call. H
mom.

A few secono
peaked.

"Really, there
say and you are
firmness in her v

For mothers
now THAT was a
that no matter h
and thoughts, th
you out aloud ri

Being drowsy
and after some n

Placing the r
was heavy. He m
about the wallet
definitely tell he
fifteen days. The
and to know tha
enough, but lyin

Anger began
was he ashamed

to his ignorance of that fact. But the losing competitors slyly rumoured that like his eloquently waxed speeches, he also waxed his face. Thus Sanjay's *Achilles Heel* was his sparse facial hair that showed no signs of developing despite shaving daily.

On coming out of the room, they were welcomed by the aroma of ghee and *dosa*. Lakshmi aunty was an excellent cook and her *dosas* were irresistible. They had the right crispiness. The taste and aroma of ghee and the way the *dosa* melted in the mouth, made one drool for more.

AK did not need much cajoling, the temptation was a bit too high. He agreed for one but had two, and ended up licking his fingers with glee.

Over the week, they played some gully cricket with Sanjay's friends. AK was introduced to several of them.

Of all the friends he met, Pratap H Kulkarni and Mukesh K Shah spent quite a lot of time with his childhood friend and they had been with him from his under-graduation days. The trio went to the same coaching classes in Dombivli.

Mukesh and Sanjay were classmates in IT engineering at Vivekananda College in Sion. Tall, at 5'11", with wavy hair, Mukesh was on the chubbier side and often attired in jeans and thick striped shirts. Fair complexioned, his ruddy cheeks had minor pimples camouflaged by a mild stubble. Concerns from relatives over his recent stoutness were stiffly countered by his stating that he was just a bit short for his weight and was confident it would be sorted, as soon as he grew taller. But his will often lost to his sweet tooth. He was very popular amongst his guy friends for his sense of humour and for being the *'Jugaad'* (fix it) guy.

Pratap, on the other hand, was pursuing chemical engineering at Kelkar's college, in Mulund, and he attired differently from the rest. He was often seen in anti-fit denims with half sleeved short shirts. The most striking feature on his face was the distinct slim goatee with no beard or moustache. His straight hair fell sideways finishing just above his eyes. At 5'6", fair complexioned, he carried the uber cool look with élan. The other two usually made Pratap the butt of their jokes often teasing him with Nivedita.

Within days, AK was happily a part of the former trio.

The academic year began for his engineering friends, bringing their daily cricket and meet ups to a halt. To kill boredom AK had only two hobbies, listening to rock music and reading. Being a fan of bands like--Metallica, Guns N Roses, Aerosmith, Bryan Adams, Bon Jovi and Def Leppard, their music often played on his stereo from the start of the day.

In between the hours of the day he read *The Bourne Identity* by Robert Ludlum.

His uncle called from the office reminding him of a few errands, especially paying off the utility bills.

On returning from his errands, as he entered the 'A' block, which was on the ground floor of his building, he was tenderly interrupted. The aged, frail, stooping figure stood smiling at him with the warmth of grandmotherly affection. AK remembered her from his early childhood days. Age had caught up with Mrs. Sulochana Bhonsale, fondly known by the children in the building as Sulu *aji* (*aji* means grandmother in Marathi).

Her husband had passed away a few years back and her stay-at-home maid lived with her. *Aji's* children were settled in the US. She reminded him of his own grandmother. She enquired with AK in Marathi about his father's mother. He replied to her in the best of his broken Hindi that she was now in Kerala. After some brief courteous talks, she requested his help to check the letter box on the wall. Owing to their short stature neither her maid nor she could reach it. AK checked it and handed over a letter in her name. AK promised her he would check for her letters and drop them through their latticed door. He checked the mailbox once again for any letters that may have come for his parents, uncle, or him. There were none.

AK rushed down to meet his friends, Sanjay and Pratap- the birthday boy- who was treating some close friends. AK had been informed the night before of this birthday treat but he had dozed off after lunch. Had it not been for their phone call, he would have missed it. AK happily wished Pratap and apologized to them for the delay.

As they made their way to New Modern Café, he could not help noticing the long queue of people waiting to buy *vada pav* (it was akin to a spherical vegetable burger made of mashed potatoes, deep fried in oil, and served sandwiched between two square buns, with smears of garlic and chilli powder with mint chutney – a very popular traditional snack in Maharashtra) from the fast food joint *Tridev Vada Pav Centre*. People sang praises of their *vada pavs*, but AK was yet to try one.

Chatting, they reached outside New Modern Café. There, they were met by a group of people who, after greeting Pratap, were introduced to AK as Kartik and Vijay.

As they engaged in light hearted banter, an auto rickshaw pulled up in front of them and two girls stepped out. AK couldn't call her pretty, but above average. She wore a brown *kurta* with cream embroidery and a matching *salwar*. She had a small *bindi* on her forehead. She looked as if she had spent some time and effort in prettying herself. The smile on Pratap's face said it all, Nivedita had achieved her goal.

groped away by a lady thief who made him think with his genitals rather than his head, made him feel as low as he could ever have felt in his entire life.

He freshened up and headed off to Sanjay's place.

The doorbell rang at the Iyer's residence.

"Hi Akash! Come on in," Subbalakshmi aunty said, unlocking the outer latticed door. "Sanjay, wake up, Akash is here…it is almost noon," she spoke in a voluble tone.

Ramanathan uncle and his mom were colleagues during their first job and with time they eventually became friends. She got along very well with Subbalakshmi, his wife, and they had been family friends since then. Subbalakshmi aunty, aka Lakshmi Aunty, Sanjay's mom, was a gracious host, affectionate and kind. Her demeanour always made her son's friends feel welcome and at ease. She was so motherly that he always felt at home with her. She was petite and wore glasses, and Sanjay looked a lot like her. And like every worried mother complained to him about her son's laziness.

AK smiled and soothed her, "Don't worry aunty, I will wake him up." *Are mothers all the same?* He wondered within, thinking of his own mom fondly for a moment.

Sanjay and AK had been best friends since childhood. They went to the same nursery and were in the same school till sixth grade. After which, AK left for Dubai, while Sanjay continued in the same school in Dombivli.

A wheatish complexioned Sanjay stood at 5'9", and felt he looked mature and manly only in formals. He often wore jeans, pairing them with shirts. He was the typical know it all geek who aced every subject he touched, including debates. His victory in debates and arguments, on and off stage, against girls ensured his status – Single! He was unperturbed by this, primarily due

15

to his ignorance of that fact. But the losing competitors slyly rumoured that like his eloquently waxed speeches, he also waxed his face. Thus Sanjay's *Achilles Heel* was his sparse facial hair that showed no signs of developing despite shaving daily.

On coming out of the room, they were welcomed by the aroma of ghee and *dosa*. Lakshmi aunty was an excellent cook and her *dosas* were irresistible. They had the right crispiness. The taste and aroma of ghee and the way the *dosa* melted in the mouth, made one drool for more.

AK did not need much cajoling, the temptation was a bit too high. He agreed for one but had two, and ended up licking his fingers with glee.

Over the week, they played some gully cricket with Sanjay's friends. AK was introduced to several of them.

Of all the friends he met, Pratap H Kulkarni and Mukesh K Shah spent quite a lot of time with his childhood friend and they had been with him from his under-graduation days. The trio went to the same coaching classes in Dombivli.

Mukesh and Sanjay were classmates in IT engineering at Vivekananda College in Sion. Tall, at 5'11", with wavy hair, Mukesh was on the chubbier side and often attired in jeans and thick striped shirts. Fair complexioned, his ruddy cheeks had minor pimples camouflaged by a mild stubble. Concerns from relatives over his recent stoutness were stiffly countered by his stating that he was just a bit short for his weight and was confident it would be sorted, as soon as he grew taller. But his will often lost to his sweet tooth. He was very popular amongst his guy friends for his sense of humour and for being the *'Jugaad'* (fix it) guy.

Pratap, on the other hand, was pursuing chemical engineering at Kelkar's college, in Mulund, and he attired

Next to Nivedita stood a voluptuous lass.

At 5'3, in a body hugging green and white *kurta salwar*, Nivedita's friend was a delight to look at. She had long, slightly wavy hair which curled at the ends, falling below her shoulders. AK found it difficult to take his eyes off her. *Phew!* He mused, nearly gasping.

"This is my friend, AK," said Sanjay interrupting his thoughts like an unwanted speed breaker. "AK, this is Tanya."

"Hi," said AK clearing his throat "How are you?" he asked, trying to appear normal.

"Hi...fine," she replied, and looked away. It was Pratap's birthday and so he was naturally the centre of attraction. Everyone had their eyes and ears only for him, including Tanya.

AK knew that the feminine species by itself had to be dealt with differently. The want to prove his masculinity, coupled with the need for recognition put him into a quandary where he was unsure of what to do next, and how to impress her, and be called "Her kind of MAN!"

The only interaction he had ever had with the female variety happened to be his sister, his cousins, mother & aunts, in front of whom pretence was not required as there was no way they would call him a "MAN". For them, he would always remain "that kid".

AK could easily speak to the guys in the gang, but the ladies were making him self-conscious. He envied the smooth talkers.

The restaurant had a separate section called "AC Hall". Pratap whispered to the waiter and he signalled an usher to lead the group inside. Packed with more people inside than out, with the temperature just right and cool, with boys cracking jokes, girls giggling, some conspiring and first-time lovers being shy, holding hands and just being lovers, this was every teen's paradise.

Two large tables were joined to accommodate the birthday party gang. They ordered food. Since the hotel was vegetarian, he had resigned his fate to the general consensus that all had on food.

AK thanked his lucky stars as Tanya sat next to him. But the very next minute, he cursed himself because he realized that he could not even start a conversation with her, let alone look at her, partly because they were not sitting face to face. He felt embarrassed as he realized how easily he was attracted to her. *Was it her looks, or her proximity, or her perfume?* He wondered.

It's the whole package! He concluded.

He gave her a sideways glance, once...twice... thrice... *She is so blessed at the right places...what am I thinking? Ok, let me start talking to her,* AK thought. He was already ogling the girl!

"Hey Tanya, hope you met Akash," asked Sanjay, pointing towards AK. He just wanted to hug Sanjay and shower his thanks. He was so glad that his best friend helped break the ice.

AK and Tanya greeted each other.

"Pratap, would you like butter *naan* and *daal tadka*?" asked Nivedita

"How come you know that's his favourite dish – *daal tadka*?" Sanjay teased her.

"I don't know, I just asked him...that's my favourite too," she replied, rather sternly, to the giggles and teasing that ensued.

"Akash, so where do you stay?" asked Tanya turning to him.

"Very close by!" he answered.

He felt so embarrassed talking to her. He just couldn't pull himself up to look at her eyes and talk. She looked at him as if expecting to say something more.

"Er...I stay close by, just behind the Tridev vada pav centre," AK ventured forward.

"Oh, I stay in the west, near Bharatnatya Mandir," she responded.

"Oh cool! Nice," he replied. *Gosh, was that all I could say? But where is that place?*

AK fumed within himself, plummeting blows after blows within him and cursing his DIVINE self for not having prepared him with a boot log of how to deal with the feminine world.

"So, what brings you here from Dubai?" she asked.

Oh! So, it looks like Sanjay has told the entire world I am from Dubai, he mused. AK was just about to answer her when they were interrupted by the waiter asking for the order.

All of them gave their orders from the menu.

He quickly agreed to have what Sanjay was having. Now fully turning all his attention to Tanya, he asked her "Yea, where were we?" he gathered a lot of courage to speak to her.

"Well, we were…in Dubai," she said, raising her brow as if to remind him.

"Really, you too?" exclaimed Akash. Alas experience speaks, and as expected he did not get the cue.

She shook her head, giggled, and pointed to him. *Of course, she was referring to where I left the conversation,* he chided himself.

"Ah yeah," AK felt floored. *Well at least I am able to make her smile.*

She certainly seemed to be enjoying his company and her behaviour was putting him at ease. "I came here to join UG studies. I have joined B. Comm at K J Somaiya College of Arts and Commerce," he said.

"Oh! Ok, why? Aren't there any colleges in Saudi?" she enquired. *Well, point proven that she didn't know the difference between Saudi and Dubai,* AK thought, amused.

"I really don't know about Saudi but in Dubai colleges are just coming up and they are quite expensive. Moreover, universities here are much better," he replied, keeping a straight face not wanting her to feel insulted.

"Do you have any siblings?" she asked, hastily realizing her mistake and changing the topic.

"Yea," AK replied, obliging. She raised her eyebrows, it was the 'please complete the sentence' look again.

"I have a younger sister," he added.

"So, I take it that your entire family has shifted here since you are studying here now?" she asked.

"No, only me," he replied.

Sanjay was looking at him as if he wanted to say something but AK could not figure out what it was.

"What about you? Do you have any siblings?" he asked Tanya.

"Yeah, I do, I have a brother," she said

"Oh!" AK gasped, the worried look on his face was inescapable.

A slap and a kick from a burly 6-footer is the last thing a guy wants, and worse is when it happens in front of the girl to whom the proposal is given destroying the miniscule RESPECT she MIGHT have had for him. And what's even worse is when the burly 6-footer happens to be HER brother, hence destroying every right to retaliate even. His mind wandered to the probabilities of being beaten up, or being alive, or being somewhere in between.

"Why? What happened?" she asked, sounding surprised. Akash came out of his action movie and saw Tanya still smiling at him, and on checking realized that he was still in one piece.

"Nothing, just asking. Is he older or younger?" he asked, rather tensed.

"He is doing his 8th grade now," she replied casually.

"Oh! That's great!" AK replied, he just couldn't stop smiling from the relief that flooded in.

"Okay, but what's so funny...and great?" she asked.

"Eh...nothing," said AK happily.

"Ehh...then why are you smiling?" she asked, amused.

"Well, I was just happy that you have a younger brother and that will not be a problem," he replied back without even thinking.

Suddenly Sanjay coughed and AK saw his face was turning beetroot red. Sanjay was glaring at him, the look said it all – What in the world do you think you are doing!

AK stole a glance at Tanya and she had that look on her face too. You know...the *'God save me from this loser' look.*

He was fuming.

Gosh, I should have just kept quiet, he thought. *How does one make an ass of himself, please everyone...please look at me...am I not an amazing example of how to be a complete idiot? Damn! How could I be so incredibly stupid!* AK plummeted blows after blows on himself.

In that AC room, he was the only one reaching out for a handkerchief as beads of embarrassment formed on his forehead.

"*Arrey*! Have any of you seen SATYA?" asked Sanjay, a bit loudly, diverting the attention that AK was getting from Tanya.

"Yea, I did, today's noon show...I thought the movie was terrible, it was too violent," replied Tanya. Soon, the rest, except AK, chipped in with their views.

As they were speaking, a chocolate cake with a lit candle was brought by the waiter. Since Pratap had his back to the waiter he did not know till the cake was placed on the table, but then his eyes were literally glued on Nivedita. It seemed to AK that she was trying to avoid his gaze.

The waiter placed the secretly ordered birthday cake in front of Pratap.

Pratap's face shone with happiness.

"Wow...thanks a ton guys!" Pratap exclaimed, obviously stunned by the surprise.

He blew the candle and did the honours, and pulled out a piece amidst the chorus of 'Happy birthday'. His face clearly portraying the confusion whether to offer the piece to Nivedita or not?

The impending embarrassment and jokes that might crop up from that offer made him gobble it.

Tanya pulled the plate to cut the cake and hand over the pieces to all, when Sanjay, Vijay, and Kartik dug out small pieces of cake and applied it all over Pratap's face.

"Happy birthday mate. We can't give you birthday bumps here so this is the least we can do," remarked a very satisfied Vijay after going through his handiwork.

Pratap looked very comical with a cherry on his nose tip, trying to lick the pieces off his own chin, and that made everyone laugh.

Though he did not know all of them well, AK was having fun. They were a cool crowd to hang out with and he was happy.

Tanya handed Pratap the neatly wrapped gift, while Nivedita goaded him to open it.

Pratap happily tore open the wrapper to find a nice black shirt with white pin stripes.

The festivities were interrupted by the waiter, who served the food. They had their fill amongst some more banter, and soon it was time to leave.

AK wished the birthday boy again and he split from them. A question popped up in his mind, but he chose to ignore it for now – *Why didn't Mukesh come? Was he not invited?*

CHAPTER 3

After a disconcerting train trip to Joshi & Bhatt CA classes in Ghatkopar, AK returned home. The single train trip made him miss Dubai and its comforts the most. Soon, after reaching home, AK happily freshened up and rushed to his friend's house for lunch as agreed. He was so famished.

He was certain that Lakshmi aunty probably made the most delicious, finger-licking sambar in the entire Mumbai, as he poured more onto his plate while Sanjay sat along watching TV.

Sanjay enquired about his day.

AK ended up detailing about his frustration and dismay with the crowded trains and the travel time. After hearing him patiently, a slightly annoyed Sanjay scolded him, "Really! Don't you think you are over reacting *yaar*? Everybody travels by train here, such things happen to many people."

"I mean...seriously I wish I was, but I guess I will get used to it," AK answered, not knowing how to put it more plainly and make Sanjay understand the culture shock he was experiencing.

"Look *yaar*, AK...you are not in Dubai for your higher studies...your parents decided to leave you here for a good education...maybe because they could not afford higher education for you in Dubai... whatever the reason...but now instead of crying over it you have to adapt to your new place...you are not Akku agugugu anymore. You are in Mumbai now for the next three years. So, it's time to act matured now," said Sanjay, in a slight rebuking manner.

AK wasn't sure whether he was being blunt or diplomatic, but he was effective. He was right, AK needed to adapt and that too, soon, at least before the college opened.

Further banter was interrupted by the doorbell. It was the maid. AK sat back contemplating on all that Sanjay had said.

"*Yaar*, you will be spending much of your time travelling...so adjust...and I hope you will find time to study," said Sanjay, interrupting his thoughts. AK nodded.

On his way back home, AK observed a queue of people building up at the Tridev vada pav centre. The shop was at least 16 x 16 feet and also served other vegetarian food items, "No frills, just good veg food," as his friends told him. It had a separate area with a shorter queue for buying other cooked vegetables and *chapatis*. There was a separate queue for their famous *vada pavs*. On an impulse, he joined the '*vada pav*' queue. He wanted to uncover the truth for himself. He hogged a *vada pav*. The hot *vada pav* covered in fried batter, containing boiled mashed potatoes, green chilies and red chili and garlic powder was an explosion of flavours. Sweet! Spicy! Tingly! YUMMY!

Everybody around him was burying their heads into their own books. The questions and answers kept darting to and fro between the professor and the students in the CA coaching classes. The start-jerk was abrupt and it had left him unsettled. To add to his woes, the knowledge flow incessantly increased. Reaching a tumultuous ascent, the strength of the waves just kept getting alarmingly Bigger, Meaner and Stronger. Every problem of differential calculus bit him like a shark, drowning him in painful slow death.

All problems looked identical and confusing. He gathered some courage to look around the class and saw all the other students buried in their books taking notes, and asking genuinely intelligent doubts to the professor, each of which was adding on to the already long list of life's mysteries he couldn't understand ever since he was a child.

He rolled his eyes upward in a feeble attempt for a breather and was greeted with darkness inside his head as his eyelids closed. It felt like he was staring into the back of his own head trying to make out IF there was an organ called the BRAIN that he could use. Or rather, did God forget to leave it there? He couldn't comprehend the ferocity and ease with which others around him were gobbling up the math equations. It jolted him like lightening from a clear blue sky, that maybe, he was not cut out for Math...EVER! He felt a shudder pass through him. He immediately refocused his attention back to the class, the attempt was futile and he groaned within.

He remembered his dad's 'silent' words, "If you want to get ahead in life you should be good at Maths and an engineer, or else..." and that silence spoke more volumes today than any other day. His dad would often start calmly and end on a high pitch that would nearly rattle his ear drums. But today he was rattled by silence, the silence of speed and sincerity with which the rest of the students completed the maths equations.

The bell rang, and the Math class for the day was over. *Phew! One day down, how many more to go?* he wondered.

A week had passed, and he felt like five years had gone by. He was struggling both with studies and *book-mates*. Well, he couldn't call them classmates as he couldn't gel with them, at least not yet.

"Side please," said a scrawny pale guy next to him.

"Sorry?" responded AK, forcing him out of his tryst with contemplation on fate.

The short scrawny guy gestured that he wanted to step out of the bench they were sitting on. AK obliged, getting up from the bench. AK immediately noted that for some in Mumbai 'Side Please = Excuse me'. *For all the math and studiousness, some of these Mumbaites were usually rough around the edges when it came to conversing in English,* he mused as he made his way out of the class room.

A tap on his shoulder shook off all his thought-clouds. He turned around to see, it was the same scrawny guy.

"Myself is Bhavin Bhanushali," he introduced himself extending his right hand for a handshake.

Well for one, that answers the query! The guy didn't know English, which also meant that he didn't mean - 'move out of my way'! AK mused. On first impression, Bhavin seemed like a nice chap, with his oiled hair, neatly combed and partitioned on the side. Bhavin was as *Gujju* as they come, with his typically printed *Gujju* shirt. With a pair of glasses to go, he appeared very studious - the perfect accountant geek.

"Hi! I am AK. Nice to meet you," he replied, shaking his hand.

"Eh, which coolleage?" he asked.

"K J Somaiya...you?" asked AK.

"Same," a smile lit up Bhavin's face, "I see you bephore today in Accounts class. I hear your Ingliss very very good, your doubt ask sir," he added in the best of his English.

"*Mujhe Hindi aati hai,*" (I know Hindi) AK replied gently and forgivingly, wanting to ease the guy's trouble with this foreign language.

Just then another guy came to him and started speaking to Bhavin in Gujarati. A few giggles and a sweet voice distracted AK and he turned to look for the owner behind him.

And there she was, like a blooming rose in that sunny afternoon talking and giggling with her friends in the corner. Time stopped as he lay eyes on her. She wore a figure hugging crimson red *salwar kameez* which finished just above her knees and her silky red *dupatta* glistened with a shimmer of silver stars, swaying lyrically in the breeze. Her skin seemed so soft and tender, her cheeks with a hint of pink and she had innocence in her eyes and a smile that could melt hearts. All these, further enhanced by her creamy milky complexion and her hair which had tinges of brown and golden hues, flowing straight and curling at the ends. *WOW! Who is she?*

"Ahem heh...koff koff," the artificial coughing spasm successfully shifted his vision off the beautiful living sculpture and into the eyes of a demure wheatish lady with plaited hair, around 5'4", with short heels. Her petite form covered in a pastel green *salwar kameez* was gazing at him strictly "Don't make it so obvious," she said in a soft tone.

"WHAT? What? Excuse me!" he asked, flabbergasted. He couldn't believe he got so carried away admiring the angelic beauty that he failed to notice how others around him had begun to feel the intensity of his unwavering attention.

"Hi! I am Nehal Vora," she smiled and extended her hand.

"AK, hi!" he replied with a sheepish smile, trying in vain to save himself almost shaking his head sideways to say NO, but failing at it. "I was not looking at her," he added, and pushed his hands inside his denim pockets.

"I never said it was her…it's ok…hmm…I know you were staring at her…and ehh…if I didn't interrupt you, the others…" Nehal gestured with her raised eyebrows to a group of girls on her left, "They would have thought that you were very nobly just looking at that girl," she added, again raising her eyebrows and gesturing at the pretty angel AK was smitten by.

"What rubbish? I was not looking at her but that bike on the side," he said defensively, trying again in a futile attempt to save himself.

"Oh, you know a lot about bikes?" she asked with a smile so sly, it was clear that she did not believe him.

"Yea I do, all guys do, it's a guy thing," he said with such confidence that even the late Soichiro Honda would have saluted him from heaven.

"Ok. Then let's bet. If you tell the make of the bike correctly, I'll owe you a sandwich else you would owe me one. So which bike do you think it is?" she asked earnestly.

This was the time when he could sincerely use some divine intervention like Mr. Soichiro Honda entering his head and whispering the answer, or maybe even human intervention would do.

He looked at Bhavin, who seemed engrossed in a vividly animated conversation in Gujarati with his friend as if they were tasked with preparing the upcoming Budget. *Uh Oh...no help from him!* he sighed within. He looked into her eager eyes and nodded his acceptance.

"That looks like a Honda," he said, trying to sound casual.

It was an old black bike and the name was not visible from where he stood, and the paint on the bike had faded. *Well, it was worth a shot!* AK decided, after all it was a question of his respect.

Bhavin joined him by then. If Functional Derivatives went over his head by a mile then Bhavin's broken English was going over his head by light-years.

He turned to find Nehal was talking to the pretty lass. He was petrified for a brief moment. He fervently hoped that Nehal was not telling her about him staring at her. *I am thinking too much! She won't say that!* He hoped.

Just then the Economics professor walked by and it was time for AK's favourite subject—ECONOMICS.

He could, however, barely concentrate in class, his mind was constantly hovering around Nehal and the new damsel he was smitten by. He was dying to know what they had conversed about. A tinge of worry and a bit of nervousness welled up inside.

Did Nehal tell her that I was staring at her? No way, but then...probably she did, and maybe the girls were deciding on how to pass jokes about me after the class. Let's see! he thought, *maybe she has a boyfriend! Come on AK! You are being too silly! Be positive! She is single!* He smiled, changing his thoughts.

The economics lecture finished after an hour. His watch showed 4 p.m. There was a ten-minute break between each class. There were four classes in a day, each lasting an hour. 4 p.m. was the snack break and this lasted for 20 minutes. AK stepped out during the break. He found the benches very inconvenient. AK was easily around 6 feet in height with shoes, and he felt clearly broader than most of the guys he saw in the classroom.

On an average, most guys looked like their shirt sizes would be either 'S' or 'M' and were not taller than 5'8", while AK looked and felt manly.

Bhavin was undecided whether to approach AK or not. Last time he had a conversation with this chap, it failed to take off due to interruptions. His response was however surprisingly polite, for a burly, silent, serious guy like him. So, probability of him being a good guy was higher. Bhavin walked up to AK who did not realize Bhavin was right behind him.

AK's demeanour seemed very different and likeable. He came across as a polished and refined guy. He felt that AK's face was just a mask, and the inner guy was very different. It seemed to him that AK may not be from Mumbai at all.

Bhavin decided to test the waters. "Hi, AK!" and AK turned around. But before AK could respond, Nehal quickly introduced herself to Bhavin, "Hi! I am Nehal," she said, smiling.

"Hi!" Bhavin replied, pleasantly surprised. They continued their conversation in Gujarati.

AK looked on at their conversation, he was hoping they would stop soon, their language barely decipherable. He managed to conceal his spiritedness in seeing her again. Well he was curious to know what Nehal had spoken to his angel earlier.

AK's patience was wearing thin, time was not a luxury he had and their Gujarati conversation never seemed to end.

"What did you think of the economics lecture?" AK butted in. It was a vain attempt at accentuating one's presence to others. Even AK had to admit that to himself, but he wanted to divert the topic and talk to her.

"*Bapu aa toh gayu*!" (This man is a goner!) she said in Gujarati to Bhavin. He smiled.

They both looked at him. She flashed a naughty smile at AK. She again said something to Bhavin in Gujarati, and turning to AK, "Hey, I won the bet. It is a Yamaha. You owe me a sandwich mister!" she said, grinning victoriously.

"Ohh…ok, so where shall we get that?" he asked, embarrassed at his disgrace.

"There is one opposite the road in that corner. Lakshmibai sandwich centre, we'll go there," she replied.

"Now?" AK asked, suddenly unsure.

Hmm, first of all, he had never taken a girl out for anything. Secondly, his angel was still around. *What would she think?*

"Cut the drama AK," she said, "Of course, now."

"Alright, after you," AK said resignedly. After all, being in her good books was essential and so was keeping her in good humour, given the fact that she knew something more about his beauty queen.

She led the way. They crossed the road and walked around 20 feet from the institution. On reaching the *char rastha* (intersection), they took a left turn and there in the corner was the small shop. There was some crowd there, mainly school students, and a few guys from the classes. AK was surprised by the strategic location the sandwich centre was in.

The shop was just big enough to accommodate two individuals, while five would crowd and halt traffic.

Apart from people crowding for sandwiches, traffic slowed down adjusting to the comparatively narrow width of the lane.

She placed an order for two veg sandwiches.

"So, tell me...." said AK.

"You lost the bet!" she said, laughing.

AK looked at her with exasperation. "Oh really! Thanks for telling me. I thought I was being charitable and trying to feed a hungry girl child."

Don't these females ever understand the matters of the heart? AK almost rolled his eyes but with great difficulty managed to keep a straight face.

"Hey! You are crossing the line...." she said, her voice stern. AK jolted in surprise at her reaction.

"*Bhaiya, order cancel kar do,*" (Brother, cancel the order) she said angrily, looking at the sandwich guy.

"*Nahin*(No)…no, please, we need the sandwiches," AK said, turning to him.

"*Ready ho raha hai saab…pleaje, ek minute* (It's being prepared sir...please give me a minute)," he said, hastening the preparation lest he also cancel!

"I am sorry dude…ok, tell me, what did you talk to her about?" AK asked casually as though trying to change the topic.

"Now, you are toeing the line," she said smugly.

AK looked at her in amusement realizing that she had being taunting him all along and he had fallen for it. He didn't want her to have the upper hand, but yet these women knew to act when men least expect them to.

"Shikha Dubey, that's her name," she said, after a minor pause.

"Hmm…you are one cunning fellow," she chuckled, "I brought you here so that we could discuss this freely. Does Bhavin know about you wanting to stalk her?" she asked naughtily.

Impatience was reaching a crescendo to burst, but he checked himself. *Did she really have to go all over the place?* He kept quiet and kept looking at her. *Keeping quiet was the wisest option,* he affirmed.

"Shikha studies in S K Somaiya College," Nehal cut into his thoughts.

AK was thrilled to hear this. "Awesome! That's damn cool. I am in K J Somaiya, her college is right next to mine."

He tried to hide his excitement.

"Gosh! Look at you. You are like a two-year old who just got some candy," she said, giggling at his frank display of emotions. AK never quite understood the immaturity he displayed.

Their sandwiches were ready and handed over.

"Ok, now listen," she cleared her throat, and dug into the sandwich, and after a small bite continued, "She stays in Kurla West, has an elder brother, works somewhere in Fort, Mumbai. Her mom is a housewife," She took another bite and munched on while he waited, eager to know more.

"That's all?" AK asked eagerly, hoping for more, wishing she knew EVERYTHING about her.

"Do you want her telephone number?" Nehal asked, with a sincere questioning look on her face.

"WOW! Are you kidding? Of course! Give me, wait, let me take out my pocket dairy," AK was overjoyed, and he proceeded to pull out his tiny telephone dairy from his wallet. This was like winning a lottery. Nehal seemed to be the best thing that had happened to him after getting to the classes. She got so much information in a few minutes. He considered himself very lucky.

"Nehal, you are superb and simply awesome! I underestimated you," AK gushed, taking out a pen to note down the number. "Tell me, Nehal," added AK.

"Ohh…underestimated me, eh? Ok, write it down."

AK was ready to jot it down.

"Ok, I will give you clues, you have to find the number," she stated.

"Eh…come on dude, please, just give it, why all this drama?" he requested.

Paying him no heed, she proceeded, "77340105."

"Hey, thanks a lot pal! You are AWESOME," he said happily, "More sandwich?"

She shook her head. AK paid the sandwich maker.

He quickly rushed over to a nearby phone booth, popped in a 1 rupee coin, and keyed in the phone number. "This number does not exist. Please check the number and dial again." The female voice replayed this message again in Marathi and Hindi. He was not discouraged, after all, there may have been some error on his side. He redialled, same response again, not to be easily discouraged, he tried again. Same response again. *Damn it! Either I got it wrong or...or...damn! It was Nehal who took me for a ride!*

He looked around but he couldn't find her. She was standing with her friend, a tall girl, and talking to Bhavin. He quickly walked over to her and asked her to step aside, she refused.

"It's ok, ask here," she said politely.

"Eh, this number...er, I need to check with you again…I think I missed something," he replied, politely concealing his resentment.

AK handed over the pocket diary to her.

"Of course, you did not cross check with me!" she said, shrugging as she shook her head. She borrowed his pen and made minor modifications to the number 5 and 1 and handed it back to him. Bhavin and the other girl burst out laughing.

AK was baffled, he couldn't make out what she had written. Bhavin, who was still laughing, took the tiny pocketbook and turned it around. It read 'GO TO HELL'.

The three of them laughed. AK was dejected.

"She is very naughty…don't mind her. Hi, I am Dimple Chheda," she said. He greeted her back half-heartedly. He noticed her dimpled smile. She was fair, tall, and slender, at around 5'5", in a brown salwar suit, with straight hair in a pony. Nehal got up and walked to the side and gestured him to come over.

"Who do you think I am? What do you think of yourself?" she asked sternly.

AK sensed something was wrong, "Ohh, okay… chill, please calm down," he gestured with his hands.

She hushed down her volume, "Did you take me for some kind of an idiot who will go and make a fool of herself for another fool?!"

Public ranting by a girl drew public attention for one, but luckily for AK she was using hushed tones. He realized that Nehal was a total stranger after all and he was gullibly running along untrodden paths without bothering to know the danger points that could elicit this kind of a reaction.

I don't understand how asking for Shikha's number could be such a preposterous thing? He wondered.

"Nehal…relax. Tell me what happened," AK asked with all the humility he could muster.

Nehal took in a deep breath and said, "AK! AK! I barely know you, I don't even know what AK stands for but at least in her case I know her first name…so basically, that's how much you both know about me. Today was the first time I spoke to her, and you know we are not even in the same college. It would not feel right, you know. Basically, you know what…it is funny that I have to explain these things to you, like you were born yesterday."

"Oh I…I did not think of that," he replied, recognizing his folly.

"Ok, take your time and you can try asking her tomorrow maybe," he added hopefully.

"Uff! Arrogance! Stupidity!" she snapped, with her hands on her hips.

"Ohh, you mean she is arrogant?" he asked, curious.

"Look, whatever A and K that you are…I thought you were a nice chap, but I did not know you are so stupid.

You did not say 'Sorry' to me yet, you did not say 'Please' yet," she responded, shaking her head in disbelief.

Realizing his idiocy, he hoped no prying eyes and sharp ears had caught their embarrassing repartee. He promptly apologized and requested her with a restrained and concealed 'please'

He decided to be bolder, because internally he knew some things have to be done the right way.

Women are complicated, he mused *I shouldn't have rushed! That's what ticked her off!*

"Enough, leave this now, we will talk tomorrow," she said, irritated.

"What? Are you a TV show or something? Talk tomorrow? Eh...talk now," he said, with a sheepish smile.

She glared back at him. He stretched out his palms in total surrender. She turned around and walked to her friend and Bhavin who were chatting away in Gujarati.

Language does play a very important role when it comes to communication. But when you tend to grasp only half of it every time it's spoken, the idea of communication becomes a herculean task, making one feel like a fish out of water. That's exactly how AK felt. He recognised the language but never understood Gujarati.

Confounding this further, a man from the administration came and announced something to all in Gujarati and Hindi. It was neither audible nor understandable for AK from the far corner where they were standing. To add to his woes, what little he did catch, he didn't have the slightest of idea. Bhavin went over to the crowd that gathered around the man. He spoke something in Gujarati and the crowd started to disperse. AK grew curious.

"Bhavin?" Nehal called and spoke to him in Gujarati.

He replied to her in Gujarati. They were happy with whatever he said.

37

"Guys, what happened?" AK asked, seeing the excitement.

"Class is over for the day," Nehal replied helpfully.

"The law professor is absent today," added Dimple helpfully.

"Meaning we are off for the day, YAY! Let's go somewhere," said Nehal, excited.

These last few words hardly fell on his ears. His eyes were arrested by his fair angel. She stood there at a distance. Suddenly, he reminded himself how last time, Nehal had averted his glance treks on her. He tried to exude an image of a serene hermit, and he honestly believed he did till Bhavin tapped him.

"You in looking tension...bhut why?" asked Bhavin with genuine concern that made AK feel puny in his attempt.

Nehal looked on at AK, irritated. Dimple, chuckling, nudged her. Nehal sighed, "You are hopeless!"

"AK? What is AK?" Dimple asked him, smiling. Her dimples made her smile cute.

"Akashan Krishnakumar...boring name so...the cool one is AK," he replied casually.

"Why Akashan? Why not Akash?" asked Bhavin earnestly. *This guy asks questions at the right time!*

"In Kerala people add *'an'* to every name," AK replied.

"Then why is Krishna Kumar not Krishnan Kumar or Krishnan Kumaran?" asked Nehal.

"Stop pulling my leg," he retorted. Meanwhile, Bhavin caught up with Dimple and the two began chatting in Gujarati. While AK and Nehal continued their conversation.

"Hey!" she said, slapping his arm, "I am seriously asking," she added.

"Ok, I don't know but don't do that ever again," he said.

"Do what?" she asked.

"This," he raised his hand to hit her on the shoulder and she turned in quick reflex. He missed. And she laughed. The other two laughed with her.

Damn, she is quick! He broke into a smile.

"Your parents gave you that name...it is a nice name," she said, "See, you are talking to us now very casually and coolly now...you should talk to her the same way, you know."

AK pondered.

"Cut the arrogance with me and cut the guilty feeling of love towards her...by the way, you are horribly infatuated." She giggled.

Dimple and Bhavin caught up with them. He wanted to change the topic.

"Hey, I forgot to ask...where do you both study?" he enquired.

"Oh, so, finally? His highness wants to know!" remarked Nehal smugly.

AK was amused by her witty retorts.

Dimple laughed and jokingly nudged her.

"Dimple, where do you study? I mean which college?" he quickly asked, wanting to avoid conversing with Nehal.

"We both are in SNDT – Ghatkopar," she replied

"Ah nice! My mom studied in the Churchgate one."

"Hey, listen! Are you both joining us?" Nehal asked, interrupting into their conversation.

"No, not today. Thanks for asking though...but some other time...really," said AK before Bhavin could answer.

Nehal and Dimple were both strangers, and he was yet to feel comfortable with them, before they could socialize further.

"Are you going home now?" Dimple enquired.

"Yeah," Bhavin answered.

"We can drop you off on the way," Nehal volunteered.

"Don't bother. I live in Dombivli," answered AK, genuinely touched by her concern.

"Ah ok...that's where you stay? Where is it actually?" Nehal enquired.

AK felt a twinge of surprise that she did not know of it, or was she mocking him again?

"It is en-route to Kalyan," AK answered.

"I really don't know where that village is?" said Nehal, rather loudly, with a smug look on her face.

"Hey, it is NOT a village," AK retorted, *Oh! This female could really pull at times!* AK cursed.

"Ok, it's up to you…see you later…bye," she said, waving at him as she giggled.

"Bye," said AK, waving back, and quickly ambled towards the station.

"*Tu nahin…jaa…raha unke...saath?*" (Are you not going with them?) asked AK to Bhavin as he caught up with AK.

"*Nahin, mujhe ghar jaana hai, thoda kaam hai* (No, I have to go home, I have some work)," Bhavin replied.

"Ok your wish…I mean, *theek hai,*" said AK "By the way, *mein bhi…ghar jaane wala…hoon,*" (I am also headed home) added AK.

"Wehr you staying?" Bhavin asked.

"Dombivli," he said.

"Ohh, Dombivli!" exclaimed Dimple from right behind him. The boys turned around in surprise.

"It's after Thane…Diva *na*?" asked Nehal.

AK nodded in agreement.

"Diva is a village. Dombivli is also a village?" asked Dimple tilting her head, he caught her sarcasm.

Dimple and Nehal were giggling away.

"I get it! This is why Akashan tries to be cool with AK! Because this villager is running away from his reality," Nehal was poking fun at him. He smiled at them.

Bhavin laughed. A stern gaze from AK subdued it to a mere smile. Unknown to these boys, Dimple and Nehal had been walking behind them for a while.

Dimple suddenly remembered something and spoke to Nehal in Gujarati. The girls insisted they had to rush home, bid the boys bye and left in an auto rickshaw from outside the station.

Turning to AK, "*Mera* uncle, my mummy berother stay Dombivli West," said Bhavin smiling.

"Oh, so you know the place?" AK asked with relief as he climbed up the stairs.

"Yes, yes.…" he said, nodding and oscillating his head in a typically Indian fashion, which was more like your head oscillating 180 degrees in both directions, just like the pendulum in an old clock. It was a combination of a "Yes" and a "No". This was the typical way of replying that he had observed amongst most people after coming to India.

"*Kya soch raha hai*?" (What are you thinking?) asked Bhavin curious, "*Tu beech mein kahaan kho jaata hai, yaar*?" (Where do you get lost sometimes?) he continued. AK shook his head.

"*Toh phir phrom wehr*?" asked Bhavin with his right hand, gesturing in a way that looked like him holding an imaginary glass from the bottom with all the fingers pointed upwards and shaking it from left to right and back. AK was feeling the culture shock take over again.

AK's mind was already reeling with the 'Mumbaiya Hindi -Marathi' that was hindering his ability to learn the finer nuances of this nationally unifying language. And to top it, Bhavin's innocence and questions only made it worse.

AK told Bhavin all about himself.

"Dubai! Wah! But why here?" exclaimed Bhavin, "*Yaar, tera English bahut acha hai* (Your English is very good)," Bhavin added in admiration, "*Tera bolne ka style bhi acha hai, main woh tujhse seekhna chahtha hoon* (Your style of speaking English is excellent and I would really like to learn it). I istudied Gujarati medium, I nahin no English. I…"

"I got it…it's alright," gestured AK with a thumbs-up and placed his arm over Bhavin's shoulder immediately, interrupting him, and assuring him politely with a smile.

Chatting, they reached the railway station. It was time for AK to go home. Before leaving, Bhavin insisted they converse in English only.

"Alright buddy!" agreed AK, "I have to get going. Time to go home. It will take me an hour to get to Dombivli if I take a slow train," AK spoke slowly to ensure that Bhavin grasped what he was trying to tell him.

"*Toh phir fast train lena yaar,*" said Bhavin *(Take a fast train buddy)* "Yeh (This) 'buddy', what is it?" asked Bhavin, curious.

"Chill...it means 'yaar', just like friend. You know just like 'mate', 'pal', like that," explained AK.

"Ok, ok...good…thank you," he said, pleased. Bhavin appeared genuinely happy.

"Next time say thanks…sounds better, know what I mean," AK replied and right then, after a long time he finally felt he had found his comfort zone in this chaotic land because Bhavin made him feel comfortable. After all, it is ok to not be perfect. It is our imperfections that make us human and make us perfect.

"Thenks buddi," said Bhavin. His English sounded improved, although it was sprinkled rather generously with a Gujarati accent.

They parted at the railway station. The 6:31p.m. Kalyan local slowly trudged into the station. He rushed into the compartment with the vigour and tenacity of a champion Rugby player. People alighting hurled abuses at him, he didn't give a damn. He finally negotiated his one square foot space to stand in the train. Gone were the thoughts of humidity and chaos as he stood engrossed in Shikha's thoughts.

He felt that very soon Shikha would be beside him. He blushed at the thought. Her angelic image, her feminine frame made him blush again. AK felt like God had shown Shikha to him, he felt a certain assured calm within himself that Shikha was destined for him and he for her. He could not wait to share this exuberant feeling with Sanjay.

But hey, what about Tanya? He wondered.

CHAPTER 4

everal attempts at planning met with failure as their luck hinged on AK. Nearing the end of his patience, Sanjay jumped in joy when he got the good news. Luck shined on them unexpectedly! AK's uncle had to leave town urgently for work. So, Mahesh uncle and Lakshmi aunty agreed that it was best AK didn't sleep alone. Hence, Sanjay would go for company.

Sanjay quickly informed Mukesh and Pratap.

After all the plans were in place, Sanjay rang AK to tell him that he was coming over, but with some surprises. AK was disinterested, he did not fall for the hype. For him, a surprise would be if Tanya were coming over.

Within minutes the two were at his apartment.

"Pratap, welcome to Akku's crib," Sanjay said, with a gleam.

"Akku eh…interesting nickname," Pratap said, acknowledging it.

Pratap sauntered around the house, which AK found a bit weird. He never looked the nosy type. He had this cool, casual style about him with his tiny goatee which made one feel like he would say something witty all the time. On the contrary, he was a quiet observer. Sanjay, the IT geek, was mostly in formals and he preferred 'his look' in that manner because according to him that made him appear more manly and intellectual while AK considered him to be a noisy librarian. *Ah! The impressions that appearances create!* AK mused.

"*Yaar*, don't be fooled by the looks of this flat! His Pappa is loaded but only Akku gugugu baby is poor," he chuckled, mocking him in a baby voice.

"Come on mate! Who bothers with such things?" responded Pratap calmly.

"I have told this idiot Sanjay several times not to call me that…call me AK," he replied indignantly.

"*Yaar*, see, you are this dark, tall macho looking guy, with a childish nick name," chuckled Sanjay.

"Yea, think about it…Stallone being called Sue," added Pratap, and images of his iconic *Rambo* action hero was replaced by a picture of Stallone in a pink baby suit. AK shuddered.

Like a playful gentle slap, in one instant he was served both a compliment and criticism. Confused, he thought, *maybe…just maybe…going to the gym in Dubai was worth it!*

"Please guys, only call me AK," he literally pleaded.

"AK, *yaar*! Forget that…I'll tell you something that we actually came here for," said Sanjay glancing at Pratap.

They told him of their plans.

"Hey, that's a great idea. I am cool with it," he replied.

"I knew you would not say NO! Mukesh will join us soon with the stuff," Sanjay replied joyously.

"Ehh…what stuff?" he asked, with some trepidation.

"What else *yaar*?" said Pratap "Girls, booze, and drugs!" he completed coolly.

"What the hell man! No, I cannot accept this. I was not expecting this," AK said feeling lost, "Girls and booze are fine…but no drugs, *yaar*! How am I supposed to be okay with drugs? What if someone OD's and dies?"

"Forget it, *yaar*! What's OD?" asked Sanjay curious, pushing up his spectacles with his middle finger.

"You don't know OD means OVERDOSE?" asked AK, with his eyebrows raised. It was his turn to embarrass his friend.

Pratap couldn't control himself. He burst out laughing. The doorbell rang, and the phone rang too, but with a distinct ISD ring.

His parents called to check on him as usual. They enquired about his college, classes, and overall wellbeing. His overbearing Dad warned him about his callous attitude towards studies.

"Listen Akku, I trust you. Please study well, and take care of yourself, be a good boy...don't hang around too much with Sanjay...he is good but he is too mischievous, he will study well and do well, while he will keep disturbing you," said his mom.

"Yea ok, mom...I am not a kid anymore...so please, don't AKKU me ever again," AK replied trying not to sound condescending. *Gosh! I AM A MAN! Why can't they get it?? And...Sanjay and studious? Not to mention his friends?* AK smiled within. They soon finished the call.

He could hear some chatter and laughter. He quickly hopped to the mirror. Check looks, looks are ok, check dressing, that's ok too. All done. AK stepped out into the room wondering *Who rang the bell? Which chick walked in? Tanya?*

"Hey, Mukesh! You?" exclaimed AK

"You are not happy, eh?" laughed Mukesh, as his eyebrows shot up.

"Hey, nothing like that dude...I am...it is a pleasant surprise," he replied.

"Dudes! We are here to PAARRTTTYYY! So, let the poisons flow," Pratap shouted, punching the air.

In a jiffy Sanjay set up the table.

"Guys, welcome to Rascals da Dhaba!" he announced excitedly.

Sanjay explained to a curious AK that 'dhaba' was the name given to popular truck stop eateries by the highway. These were often run by Punjabis and the food was always delicious.

On the table were twelve bottles of Kingfisher, a bottle of Imperial Blue, a bottle of Old Monk, and four large packets of Kurkure and Haldiram *namkeen*. They also had at least a dozen disposable plastic cups and plates. By the looks of it, these would be more than enough for all.

AK's eyes fell on the other black polythene bags on the dining table. He took a quick peek – it had Debonair, Playboy, and Penthouse magazines. He rummaged through the bags again.

"Yaar, that bag is too big to hide any chick! So, we thought we will get one to come through the door," Sanjay said.

"Hahahaha! Very funny! I am looking for something else," replied AK mockingly.

"So, sad?" said Pratap "Nothing to snort," chuckling.

AK smiled back in relief. "Thanks dudes! Really! I am ok with drinks and girls but no drugs! Really, no way!"

"Good to know you are very liberal *bhai*," said Mukesh patting AK's back. "But why be so biased against drugs? Poor things also need your grace," AK shrugged it off as a poor joke.

"*Yaar*, Mukesh how did you get out of the house and what did you tell them?" enquired Sanjay.

He explained that he used group study at Pratap's house as the perfect excuse. Pratap was worried about Mukesh's parents calling to check on them, as he recalled his phone had been dead since the last week due to technical reasons.

"Cool it *bhai*, (brother) don't worry about it. I know I remember you telling me that. The point is nobody should pick the call. I already told them, the phone in your house is not working. I already phoned my mummy from the pay phone nearby and told her I reached your place," replied Mukesh gleefully.

"Forget aunty, what did your papa say? How did he let you go?" asked Sanjay, surprised.

"He was on the phone, and I slipped out. Besides, I am sure my folks are thinking wow, *hamara beta padhai ke baare mein bahut serious ho gaya aajkal*," chuckled

Mukesh (Wow! Our son has got really serious about his studies recently.)

"Well, you are not bad at studies, so why are they so worried?" asked Sanjay.

"Well, they wanted me to become a CA, which I so hate, anyways," said Mukesh.

"Shut up fellows! It's my belated but actual birthday celebration! Open the bottles yea," announced Pratap, interrupting Mukesh and rubbing his hands in anticipation.

Everyone quickly grabbed their beers and opened them.

"Okay, Pratap, please step into the centre, and everyone form a circle around the birthday man," ordered Sanjay. Pratap obeyed and they all encircled him. Mukesh held a bottle of beer in his hand.

"Alright dudes! Our friend Pratap has walked this earth for all of 18 years. Since long we have known him. He has been a great friend to us all and of course we are sure that he will continue to be so in the future, cheers!" toasted Sanjay.

"CHEERS! HAPPY BIRTHDAY PRATAP!" they all said in chorus.

All were eagerly waiting to get HIGH in spirits. AK was enjoying the tempo and he was sure so were all. Everyone took a bottle each, and the river of liquor flowed freely down everybody's throat. Adding to the mood, Def Leppard played on the stereo.

"To Pratap and the rest of the rascals!" cheered Mukesh.

"Aye captain!" cheered AK.

"From now on you can legally drink at any bar out here," claimed Sanjay.

"Yea, your mouth is no longer a virgin!" said AK "I mean, you have tasted alcohol now," he added quickly, correcting himself.

"Yes, absolutely, and you can elope too! Ehh…I think," said Sanjay, Mukesh chuckled. Pratap showed him the finger.

"Ah…that reminds me…like they say you can also pop your cherry now," said Mukesh, with a beaming smile.

"And you will not be jailed for it!" said Sanjay laughing. AK was puzzled over the last sentence, noting to ask Sanjay about it later, he did not want to risk embarrassing himself. *What's the big deal about a shoe polish or the fruit after crossing 18?* He mused.

AK sipped his beer, the slightly bitter taste of cold beer with its fizz, fizzling down his parched throat created a cool sensation both within him and in his head. A smile of satisfaction played on his lips as he felt the happiness of touching the forbidden again, this time with "THE RASCALS". And enjoyed the cooler feeling when it reached the pit of his stomach. *AAH! That felt really good!*

Macho was the word that played on his mind. The bitterness of the Barley water felt sweet. He felt like a man – like a macho man.

"AK, now if you could come back into reality, you could dig into the side dish," said Sanjay, waking AK out of his dream world.

"Friends! let us all thank our host- AK!" announced Mukesh.

AK grunted casually with a shrug. "Sorry…AK, thanks a ton mate! Really, we owe you. Besides, man, we have been wanting to end the drought for a really long time," said Pratap gratefully.

They pulled out the chairs and sat around the dining table in the hall.

"So *yaar*, tell me *na*, which is your favourite beer?" asked Sanjay.

"Heineken," AK boasted without batting an eyelid, recalling the brand he secretly had in the flight.

"I hear that's a good one. One of the best," remarked Mukesh.

"When would you be going to Dubai next?" asked Pratap "Get me a crate from there," he added.

What left him wondering was the innocuous manner in which people in India assumed that once you exchanged names they had the liberty to ask favours from you. What he didn't realize, and something he would know later on was that, the same liberty could be applied back to them and the same was assumed. Love and friendship were exchanged without pretence in this country and he was to soon enjoy and experience it, making him a changed person for life. But when would that change occur…only time would tell.

The discussion veered around petrol being cheaper than water in Dubai. By then AK was getting high and higher steadily. "Of course, Petrol is cheaper than water! Besides anything from there is the BEST," he remarked. Mukesh chuckled.

"Man, that is crazy! Petrol is cheaper than water," exclaimed Pratap in disbelief.

AK kept praising Dubai as the discussion veered towards malls, luxury cars, sports cars, and super cars.

"Which car does your Daddy drive?" asked Mukesh, curious.

"His own," AK replied and chuckled, the rest smirked. "Toyota Land Cruiser V6, dune bashing is awesome with that," he added.

"I am sure your papa never goes for that," said Sanjay confidently.

AK agreed, they laughed again. The beers were almost finishing with only a quarter left in each bottle. "So *bhai*, which school did you study in Dubai?" asked Mukesh.

"The Indian High School. It's CBSE," he replied.

"And you?" he asked for courtesy sake, not that he knew the schools around.

"Manjunath Vidyalaya...you've probably never heard of it," Mukesh answered.

"So, were there Arab locals in your school?" Pratap asked curiously.

"No mate. It's an Indian school, especially for Indians only," AK replied gesturing 'Indians' with quotes.

"I see, but hmm, how many such Indian schools are there?" Pratap asked.

"A few actually. There's my school, the India school, then there's Our Own, where my sister studied."

"Your folks run a school or is the name of a school "Our Own"?" Pratap asked, clearly amused.

"That's the name of the school, I know it sounds weird, but it's a well-known school," AK replied, grinning.

His tongue had begun to feel heavy. He felt light on his feet, having his second bottle of beer. He was having difficulty in gulping more of it.

He wondered if he should leave the second bottle of beer at that...*Damn!* It was only his second bottle of beer and he couldn't gulp it down. *I would look weak in front of my friends!*

Mukesh suddenly stood up and placing his left leg on the chair announced, "Friends! Brothers! Countrymen!"

They all looked at him with rapt attention.

"Now that I have your attention...Let's drink bottoms up," he added.

No sooner had he said that AK's imagination went wild.

Damn, am I DRUNK? AK thought and shook his head.

Everyone stood up. AK decided to just mirror their moves.

"What are you mumbling to yourself?" Sanjay asked AK, looking amused.

AK looked at him. Sanjay appeared a bit unsteady. *What a dude! Can't handle his drink?* AK thought with a smirk on his lips.

Everyone held their bottles, ready to gulp.

"Alright *yaaron*! Go," said Sanjay. AK gulped his beer down, he could feel the taste as it gushed through his throat, but he could hardly savour the moments as he kept shoving the drink down his throat trying to gulp it down as soon as possible. When he lifted the bottle off his lips he was greeted by the sight of all those around him patiently standing by waiting for him. *What the HELL! They are fast!*

His stomach felt like the glass - the one people say is full half with water and the other half with air…but in his case, he felt full - half with god knows what and the rest with beer. He gave a long disgusting belch, it felt good…AWESOME!

"AK…eh, you ok?" asked Sanjay, concerned after seeing the conflict of emotions shooting back and forth all across his face.

"Buddy, trust me I have never felt this good," AK replied.

"Yea I am glad, you really are enjoying the party mate!" Pratap exclaimed.

AK felt a dull throbbing in his temples.

"Here *bhai log* (brothers)! Come on, we've hardly finished," Mukesh opened the Imperial blue and poured whiskey shots in each cup and added soda.

"Here you go," Mukesh said as he handed AK the whiskey. He grabbed it and gulped that down too. He felt a trail of fire erupt within him. Starting from his mouth, scorching its way down. The effect didn't get confined there, rather his eyes erupted and water surged. He was temporarily blinded and left choking. But then he had to get a hold of himself. He couldn't be the weakling that his friends would perceive him to be. He grabbed the bottle from Mukesh and poured some more into the glass and took a sip.

He headed to his room. The throbbing had become a dull pain and he couldn't afford to ignore it anymore.

AK excused himself. He stumbled into his room, and reached for the drawer, pulled out a strip of painkiller tablets and popped three pills. He washed it down with the balance neat whiskey. *Now that should completely take care of my headache!* AK thought.

He walked back to the hall and joined the rascals. He had to admit he started to like that name. 'THE RASCALS', there was a wolfish grin on his face as walked back to the raucous happening in the hall.

CHAPTER 5

*A*K opened his eyes as he felt the tremors, the ominous rumble made him tremble. He raised his sleepy head and his eyes widened in horror. He found himself lying on a rail track, and a train was hurtling at him with reckless abandon. He tried getting up but couldn't. Just then, something weird happened, the horn didn't sound like it belonged to a normal train. He struggled, yet he couldn't get up. He started sweating, he called out to Sanjay – no response, Pratap - no response, Mukesh – no response. The train was getting dangerously close and it honked again, as though asking him with total disdain and lack of empathy to get out of the way. The horn exploded into his ears and it jolted him awake.

Just then the phone was thrust into his ear, "What? Where? Hello?" said AK, waking in a rush of panic. Bleary eyed, he saw Mukesh holding the phone signalling him to answer it. Instantly, he was relieved that it was all just a dream.

"Hello," he answered, trying to sound as sober as possible, although he was far from it. His morning voice now deep and throaty.

It was his uncle who called to inform his return would be delayed by two days.

"Hello uncle, good morning," AK mumbled.

"Good afternoon, you were having an afternoon nap?" he enquired.

AK quickly looked around and saw it was almost 3 p.m.…*GOD! I can't believe it!* He mused, slapping his own forehead.

"Yea I was…I had an early lunch at at…" Sanjay gestured to himself, "Lakshmi aunty's place," AK replied, trying hard to sound all freshened up despite his morning voice giving away. After some more banter his uncle hung up.

Hanging up the phone, he flopped back like he woke up with the weight of the world on his head. His belly hurt like he had swallowed stones and been to a boxing match. He glanced at Sanjay and Mukesh and he looked around, *yup this is my room!* Yet, he felt weird. He just couldn't figure out what was wrong. He rubbed his eyes and arched up on his elbows, and finally pushed himself to sit up.

"The legend awakes! *Bhaisaab*, you were *khatarnak*! Dangerous!" remarked Mukesh, smiling, his head oscillating in admiration.

"*Yaar*, you are one crazy psycho bugger," said Sanjay exclaiming, "Any idea what you put us through last night?"

There was suddenly too much happening and he was yet to grasp the fact that he had woken up and the party was over; on top of it his friends were passing weird comments. *Oops! Coming to think of it, what did happen yesterday?* He tried remembering and he found his mind going blank. He recollected entering the bedroom and popping the tablets and joining them back in the hall. All goes blank after that.

And now his body hurt like he had been rammed by a truck.

He looked around slowly coming to his senses. His room looked ok, his eyes drifted down to his bed, and his eyes WIDENED IN SHOCK. He was nearly in his birthday suit!

"Where are my jeans?? Where are my clothes?" AK asked, all rattled up and wide awake, though his throat was coarse. He was shocked to find himself only in his briefs.

Sanjay threw him a towel, "Go freshen up first, and don't act like you don't know."

"And you should be belted for what you did last night," he added, to AK's perplexity.

Mukesh chuckled.

His head hurt, and he needed to freshen up, and feel good. An unwelcome whiff hung in the air. "Where are my jeans and what's that smell?" AK asked.

"Inside the washing machine," replied Sanjay, "And only you should go and open it."

"We couldn't find the soap powder…so…eh," Mukesh muttered, Sanjay nudged him and he kept quiet.

AK threw water into his eyes, washed his face again, again, again and again.

"And please wrap the towel around," added Sanjay. AK hadn't realized that it had unwrapped on his way to the wash basin. He wiped his face, and wrapped his towel. He staggered to the top loading washing machine and opened the lid. The odour turned into an awful stench. He couldn't even recognize his jeans; it had some yellowish stain all over. He could also smell a bit of his perfume.

"What's all this?" he looked at it, confused. "Why can I smell my perfume around?" He checked himself. It was certainly not on his body.

"Eh you accidentally broke the perfume bottle, so we poured a bit of that inside it," said Sanjay casually.

"What?" AK exclaimed.

"Aaah *yaar*, all of it, actually at least whatever was left of it," shrugged Mukesh.

He leaned over to the garbage bin. He was shocked to see the broken bottle of Versace.

"Oh God!" he groaned.

"Where is the soap powder? We'll put this to wash now," said Mukesh, trying to be helpful. AK silently pointed to the shelf in the kitchen above the washing machine. Mukesh opened the shelf and AK pointed to the PET bottle that contained TIDE. Mukesh took the washing powder from there and just dumped almost half of it into the machine.

"Put some more…that wouldn't be enough dude!" exclaimed Sanjay, "After all, our gunner was shooting all through…from everywhere." They both laughed and high fived.

"What? My head still hurts, what happened last night?" AK sincerely enquired. The phone rang. AK answered the call. It was Pratap, he called to enquire about him and was relieved to know he was ok.

Pratap asked for Sanjay. He promptly handed over the phone. They spoke briefly and hung up.

"Freshen up *yaar*, you'll feel better!" suggested Mukesh.

AK went and showered. He felt wide awake and all freshened up but couldn't shake the ominous feeling of something being wrong. His head still felt heavy.

He quickly changed into his regular grey t-shirt and dark blue denims, smoothed his hair with his fingers, and stepped out.

"So finally, how do you feel now?" Mukesh asked.

"Lot better, thanks, but honestly speaking, dudes what happened last night? I mean it is all fill in the blanks and gaps, I can't put a finger on it," said AK, wanting to know what happened, but not wanting to show his frustration.

"Alright Mr. AK 47, refresh your memory and tell us till what you exactly remember" said Sanjay. Mukesh chuckled and nudged him. AK liked the new nickname 'AK 47', a reference to something that powerful, he must have surely rocked the night.

He retraced his steps.

"Well, I remember that we drank here and we were all talking and then I had a headache and I popped in some pills," He explained to them, "Panadol for headache."

"You what? Pills? While having alcohol? Are you crazy?" retorted Sanjay, shocked.

"Who in their right mind would have medicines when they are having alcohol for the first time?" asked Mukesh, slapping his forehead, appalled at what he had just heard.

"How many?" asked Sanjay curiously.

"Just…three," AK replied innocently.

Sanjay shook his head in despair and slumped his head on his hands and sat down on the chair.

"I didn't think it would do any harm," replied AK unconvincingly.

"Yea, right! We saw it…you were so cool last night," remarked Mukesh, grinning devilishly.

"Really!" AK exclaimed, unable to control his excitement anymore.

"Damn *yaar*! I don't believe this guy…he had pills like they were chewing gums" said Sanjay slapping his forehead, "Entire Dombivli knows your name now," he added laughing.

"Tell me about it!" exclaimed Mukesh, thinking that AK was still fooling around.

AK realized that it was time to keep his mouth shut and listen to what his friends had to tell him because their remarks were confusing him.

"But guys apart from drinking what did I do? I mean nothing happened, I'm fine…I mean…" he looked down at himself and looked back at his friends, "Look at me… ok, I woke up late, but that's all."

They both looked at each other, eyes widening with realizations that hit them like tight slaps making their jaws drop.

"YOU DON'T REMEMBER!" they exclaimed in chorus as they turned to look back at him.

"You remember that we had drinks at your place last night?" asked Mukesh starting again.

"Yea, beer and whiskey, and other snacks arranged by us all," added Sanjay.

"Yea I do remember that and I too had drinks with you all," AK replied earnestly, wrinkling his forehead in a vain attempt to remember anything at all. He raised his hands in surrender and said, "And…after that…what did we do?"

"It's not what we did, it's what you did. After you got drunk, you told us how you were groped by a tranny in the train and she massaged your arse so well that you happily gave your wallet," laughed Mukesh and Sanjay uncontrollably.

AK's face paled. He couldn't believe he had blurted out his well-guarded secret. *How could I have been such a fool?*

"NOO! No such thing happened!" he protested in shock. His friends were holding their sides and laughing away. Given their reactions, he accepted defeat and feared the worst.

"It was a girl...er...woman, I am sure!" he said meekly.

"Come on AK *bhai*! Which girl will enter a crowded gents compartment! and in peak hour! No way! 100% tranny – eunuch," said Mukesh, shaking his head in between his laughs.

"There are many discoveries that are accidental!" laughed Sanjay, "You can bat front and back," he added, laughing hard.

"This is one of them," added Mukesh chuckling, "You have just discovered the cheapest truth serum *bhaisaab*!"

What the hell! More like making an ass of yourself serum! He chided himself.

"There's more," continued Sanjay, just when AK was hoping what he heard was the end of it.

"When Pratap was talking about Nivedita, you butted in and told him that you are ok with him dating her as long as he is not dating Tanya," chuckled Mukesh.

"Ridiculous!" shot back AK in disbelief. "No way, I would never do that. Why would I want to know anything about her?" AK tried to protest but in vain.

"You did, you have not changed a bit," said Sanjay in amazement. "I saw how you were sticking to Tanya that day," he added enthusiastically.

They added that he explained about his loneliness to them and how he missed having a girlfriend.

"No way, I am not upset about it," AK protested defending his tattered reputation.

"*Bhai*, you shouldn't be, it should be Tanya or any other chick who should be worried," interrupted Mukesh, chuckling at AK's justifications. "Control AK! Control!" suggested Sanjay, laughing away.

"Dudes, please let me speak," AK pleaded desperately.

Mukesh, chuckling, raised his hand and gestured zipping his lips, which silenced AK.

"*Bhai*, don't trust us...fine, ask Pratap," said Mukesh raising his palms in surrender, still not convinced that AK didn't remember.

"*Yaar*, you even asked, Pratap to get you Tanya's number," Sanjay added, "you kept on insisting."

"No, pleaded," corrected Mukesh.

"No, begged," corrected Sanjay.

"Yea...actually *bhai* you are right," affirmed Mukesh, "We told you a few things about her! Hope you recollect that," laughed Mukesh. Sanjay said chuckling, "She will dump you faster than you can blink."

AK sat down slowly on the bed mortified by all that he heard. He wore the look of a man who found out that he actually stood nude in front of a reflective glass tint, confusing it with a mirror, and gave the public hearty laughs.

The worst part was he couldn't believe that he would plead about Tanya, though honestly, she would keep coming in and going out of his mind for most part of the day, mostly in, because of which he finally begrudgingly had to agree, maybe there was some truth to all that they were saying but he hoped it was their exaggeration.

"Okay, AK, I am really very sorry," Sanjay said, feeling genuinely sorry for his friend.

"Me too, *yaar*," added Mukesh patting him on his back as he sat on the chair.

They genuinely understood what he was going through and felt sorry for him. They passed an assuring glance to each other and decided to go easy on him.

Mukesh couldn't resist, "But *yaar*, please don't be so desperate. You will land any hot chick! You are NRI *na*," he chuckled. Sanjay too laughed.

Desperate! The mild stress on that word sent deep tremors in his mind. He learnt it the hard way. Perception is more dangerous than harsh truths. It was best to keep quiet now. *My luck sucks!* He mused.

"You went to the door and checked a few times," sighed Sanjay, looking at AK.

"Why?" asked AK curiously "Maybe somebody rang the bell?"

"You were expecting Tanya," replied Mukesh surprised.

"Enough! You guys are bullshitting me! Come on, I would not have been this dumb! You are all lying to me," said AK shocked.

He glanced at his friends, waiting for them to just blurt out that they were joking, but they kept laughing.

"*Yaar*! I wish we could have recorded you last night," replied Sanjay. "You were a LEGEND boss!" he added, still chuckling.

Calm down AK! Keep calm! They are all pulling your leg! That's all there is to it! AK consoled himself.

"*Bhai*, you were very upset, desperate and a lot more…So, Pratap's idea was to take you somewhere for a good time," said Mukesh.

His imagination was now running wild with all that they were saying. He hoped and didn't want to think where they went as he waited with dread.

I woke up in bare briefs! Shit! Did something happen? and I don't even remember it? AK shuddered. Many questions raced through his mind. Had he lost his virginity? Did they take him to a prostitute? And what made him feel even worse was the fact that he didn't even remember it! *No way, my friends can't be that crazy? But they call themselves 'Rascals'.* He was worried.

His mind was a whirlwind of questions and he felt his blood pumping in his ears with the news intake he already had! *I feel like I have lived through a nightmare!*

Mukesh began, "So, we left your flat in a rick…and halfway along the route…you wanted to piss and puke so badly I thought you would do it in the rick itself, even the auto driver got worried. So, we pulled over by the roadside," said Mukesh.

"And here comes the best part, I have to admit, I've heard people say that men become brave after a few pegs. There were these two guys who stepped into a bar which was just on the opposite side of the road. They got off a jeep and a bike, by a lamp post and for some strange reason known only to you, you walked right up till there, as in went right under the lamp post, where their vehicles were parked, and you tumbled and fell on the bike. Man, you knew where you were headed and still you went ahead to just puke all over the seat and onto his helmet too. You, being the brave hero, unzipping your jeans and pissing on the Sumo's wheel, *baap re*," said Sanjay.

"*Haan bhai*, girls says that men are like dogs but you proved it. Your aim at the Sumo's wheel was perfect, *yaar*," interrupted Mukesh chuckling. (Yes, brother)

"Get lost! Idiots! You are all lying," AK shot back timidly.

"Hey you were like emptying the building's water tank! Now comes the worst part. We were headed to you as you were unleashing your glory under a lamp post light, and right then, a car came over and stopped by. Some jerk in the car told you the things that certain kind of women roaming on the streets at that time of the night would love to hear. Do you want to know what that was?" asked Sanjay incredulously.

AK looked disinterested, but he was trying to hide the upheaval inside. He shook his head.

"He said, 'hey bugger, nice booty, fancy coming along, I could show you a nice time?' and do you even know what you said?" to which AK vigorously shook his head with shock, surprise, scare and anticipation unable to even retort as he felt his tongue turn into a knot by itself.

Mukesh continued, "You said, 'Yea, hell I don't see why not'," he burst out laughing, almost literally rolling on the floor.

They are exaggerating! No way! He mused as his face paled.

"Wait till you hear what happened next," chuckled Sanjay.

AK felt shivers shooting all over his body as he tried to prepare himself over what he would hear next.

"We feel ashamed to say this...but to save you...I had to say you are with us," said Sanjay, shaking his head. "Trust me, AK, last night you didn't make any sense whatsoever. In fact, you were the bestest idiot I have ever seen," Sanjay said with disdain, wiping his forehead, laughing and rolling his eyes.

AK was appalled, but then he consoled himself. He deserved it for the kind of ride he gave them! But he fervently hoped he didn't end up giving his chaste virgin butt to some gay guy!

Mukesh, sensing AK's discomfort, "Don't worry, Pratap and I jumped from the auto and ran to save your sorry arse...imagine what would have happened," Mukesh paused for effect, and to see the toll it would take on AK who looked gutted. "That gay man hammering your sorry arse for whatever it was worth." Mukesh and Sanjay burst out laughing.

"Yea and since we came after you...the bloody auto guy who was already watching all this crap got scared and decided to scoot. The guy didn't even charge us for the ride!" Sanjay exclaimed.

"Oh! And then we came back home, right?" AK asked, hoping the ride was over and wanting to do away with the conversation and the limelight he felt uncomfortable in.

"*Bhai*, if errors are comical, you are the king of them all!" proclaimed Mukesh.

"Now comes the shocker *yaar*. When we went closely and looked at the Sumo and that bike, we understood why the auto guy ran for his dear life, Sanjay paused and drank a cup of water making AK impatient, "Because you gave your autographs on police vehicles! Thanks to you we all had to run for about 10 minutes to the railway station and then get an auto from there," Sanjay said, laughing and slapping his head with exasperation.

"Pratap was half dead with all that happened…he is a paranoid nut case anyways…man, I swear, running in the middle of the road at the dead of the night…we lost our high. All because of the supreme idiot that you are," added Sanjay.

"So, we got away from the place safely?" AK asked. Mukesh nodded, still chuckling.

"Then we finally got an auto and we reached there," replied Mukesh with a devilish grin, enjoying the uncomfortable shudder he noticed pass through AK.

"Where did we go guys?" AK asked softly, expecting another shocker.

"We finally reached our destination, and our mission was to induct you in the group. And for that there are certain rituals to follow, before you become a part of our frat pack," Mukesh continued, ignoring AK's question and going at his own pace.

"This is a joke?" AK said, trying to sound as nonchalant as possible, wanting an end to this humiliating saga.

"Hey *bhaisaab*…sorry like you say…" gestured Mukesh raising his hands and folding his middle and ring fingers with his thumbs and stretching out his index and little fingers in a rap star stance, "Yo bro! No…I am not kidding. I am serious!" exclaimed Mukesh, surprised at AK's demeanour change.

63

"Oh! But, no…I mean what kind of stuff…I am sure I wouldn't have done anything insane," AK replied, worried.

"Please don't underestimate yourself *yaar*," Sanjay replied.

"Anyways, let me continue the story," Mukesh retuned back to his never ending, dignity-and-modesty robbing, misery fuelled story that had AK in the limelight.

"We finally reached Pratap's place. And we decided to fulfil your first wish."

"And what was that?" AK interrupted him, not able to contain his anxiety and impatience.

AK kept cursing himself, how could he not remember anything at all. With these thoughts, he reverted his attention to Mukesh.

"*Yaar*, Sanjay, you say," Mukesh nudged Sanjay, with that devilish smile spreading across his face again.

"No, you say it," said Sanjay, with an equally sinister smile.

"Ok, nothing much, we got a top call girl for you," Mukesh said casually.

"WHAT? SERIOUSLY?" AK exclaimed, stunned.

Sanjay burst out laughing and said, "Of course not *yaar*…he is joking."

"Guys, please, that better be a joke. I am freaking scared of that HIV shit," AK said, relieved. The relief had the impact of a shock. He put up a brave effort in keeping his wits together.

"Oye *bhaisaab*, chill *yaar*! We could not get you a call girl so we got you a porn cd for you to learn and for us to enjoy,", replied Mukesh, pointing at themselves with a grin.

"Damn it! And I don't remember anything. That's not fair," AK felt irritated with himself now.

"Frankly, you, my friend, are the eighth wonder of the world," said Sanjay.

AK looked at him and knew more was in store but he didn't want to know anything more.

"I think it was what like…two minutes or so…right? and everything happened," enquired Mukesh.

AK just couldn't contain himself, "Okay…okay… what happened? Where else did I screw up now?"

"Well, that chick in the porn just barely got out of her clothes and you came in your pants," laughed Mukesh.

"WHAT! Oh god.…" AK groaned, but these guys could barely hear him…his protests were drowned in the cacophony of their roaring laughter.

"Impossible! You guys are bullshitting! These are all lies!" protested AK.

"Come on, *yaar*, AK, you woke up in your underwear," replied Sanjay.

"AK, you are unbelievable man…the stain was there and of course it can't be urine coz you emptied your urine tank on police vehicles. Man, you shot like you were a soldier at war and instead of a gun, whatever was stored in you for the last several years came out in seconds, hence your name new code name," said Mukesh.

"AK-47! Damn! You came like a hundred times but for friendship sake I'll keep it to 47. Besides, your name is Akashan Krishnakumar so AK sounds perfecto," said Mukesh with such pride, beaming, that AK suddenly pictured him as a sly, corrupt jail warden branding a new thug in his prison. AK was aghast! AK-47, a title that powerful and dangerous would make its owner feel proud…but for him it was anything but that…and he knew just then that its origins should be kept unknown and a secret from the rest of humanity for eternity, else he would not be able to show his face ever again, or worse he would most definitely have to change his very own name. AK resolved to get them to take an oath right then. Sanjay and Mukesh couldn't control themselves and were laughing on.

"Actually, *yaar*, Mukesh, his name is Akashan, that's how Akash is pronounced in Kerala," said Sanjay, laughing on.

"Ohh really?" asked Mukesh.

"Yea unless they don't add an 'an' and 'g' instead of 'k' they can't make their famous tea!" exclaimed Sanjay chuckling.

"So there bursts his 'cool dude' bubble!" exclaimed Mukesh, gesturing in air-quotes.

"Guys...GUYS! NO ONE...no one can ever know this happened...EVER. My life, my reputation, everything I worked for depends on it," AK pleaded with folded hands, desperation showing on his face.

They both looked at AK and burst out laughing uncontrollably all over again.

"Oh yea...your reputation..." Mukesh said grinning, "You gave it away to a tranny and almost to a homo! We forgot about that!" He burst out laughing again.

"I AM SERIOUS! DAMN IT!" AK lamented, just thinking about the embarrassment this would create. *Damn, I would never even get a girlfriend...I would never even get laid. I would probably never get married, ever, never have a family, die of old age and all alone.* People would make fun of him "AK 47". AK consoled himself, *there is more to life than all this...hell no...my name is ruined....*

"Calm down *yaar*, you are not the only one who has had goof ups, there are equally bad ones around...you had only puked in your pants...that's all," said Sanjay, patting him.

"But hey you are the only one we know who is so trigger happy," interrupted Mukesh and they both burst out laughing again.

"Damn!" AK was feeling all let down.

After a while, Mukesh left. Sanjay waited for AK to get ready. A famished AK needed to gorge on some delicious food.

While getting ready AK thanked his luck. *Phew! At least I did not say anything about Shikha!*

He took the keys and they stepped out. As he closed the door, Sanjay turned to him and in a soft tone asked, "Who is Shikha? You were murmuring that name in your sleep."

"Oh shit!" exclaimed AK, nearly biting his tongue as he went pale.

CHAPTER 6

AK picked up the one rupee coin, turned it over once, twice, thrice, again and again ensuring that it was indeed a proper two sided coin. *Okay…Heads – Shikha, and Tails – Tanya.* He flipped the coin up in the air, everything was happening too fast—Shikha, Tanya, Tanya, Shikha, Not Tanya, Shikha, Tanya, Not Shikha, Yes Shikha, Yes Tanya. He caught the coin in his palm, clasped onto it tight. It was wedged between his fingers.

In the stillness of his room, he could hear his own heartbeat. *Take deep breaths, inhale, exhale, inhale, exhale, inhale.* He regained his calm and composure. He flipped again, up, up it went, caught the coin, opened his palm - same result. He nominated different sides for both the damsels, he flipped again. The result was the same as the previous two attempts. Cursed by confusion, and indecision, he slipped the coin back into his wallet and got ready.

Bhavin finally found the notice of significance to him and AK, the young man he admired. 'First Year B. Comm Induction commences on 22/06/98. Students are requested to assemble at the hall at 10 a.m. Students are also requested to bring four passport size photographs.' On another notice board, the names of enrolled students were listed under each section and displayed. Bhavin's eyes scurried through several sheets and he was delighted to find that AK and he were officially classmates.

Bhavin's dream was to become a successful Chartered Accountant, and if he did that he would be the sole person in his family to have achieved this feat. He came from a Gujarati family, where they valued family honour, traditional family values, and above all else to be 'your own boss', meaning – set up your own business.

As his father would say, 'If you are a Gujju', as most Gujratis are fondly referred to, 'then to do business is in our blood. And for that one has to be brave and fearless, education is good but not as important as courage and the willingness to take right decisions'. Bhavin, on the contrary, wanted to study more and more. He wanted to work as an auditor with Ernst & Young, after all, it was counted amongst the big five audit firms in the world. There were a lot of things Bhavin aspired for but being a businessman was not one of them. He wanted to improve his personality, speak good English. He wanted to develop a more positive outlook towards life, which his current interdependent milieu failed to nurture. He was strolling across the hallway, along with his thoughts, when his new friend appeared.

"Hi! You? Here…now?" said Bhavin happily on seeing his friend.

"Hi! Didn't expect you!" greeted AK and he was relieved to see a familiar face amidst this unknown crowd.

"I told you *na*, I come to college and then classes, and I tell the date college istarts," said Bhavin excitedly.

"Really? When?" asked AK in astonishment, "By the way the accent still needs a bit of polishing but your English sounds improved…you are getting better, yea," added AK quickly finding words of encouragement for Bhavin.

Bhavin smiled, "Fhorget it now. Come see notice board," they both walked over to the notice board.

"Cool! That's good. What about books and stuff?" asked AK.

"Huh! iSStuff?" enquired Bhavin.

"Stuff means like things…like books and stuff meaning, books and other stationery," explained AK

"Ok…" Bhavin nodded his head, enlightened.

"*Haan*, yes, yes, yes…it will be a nice walk, then I will take you to Joshi bookstore buddi," Bhavin replied happily.

"Listen dude…" AK looked around the campus, an idea struck him, "Let us walk around the campus for a while. This is my first time here. I want to check the place out, don't you?" asked AK.

"Ok *yaar*, whatever you wish," said Bhavin with a smile. He was more than happy to comply with his new friend's wish.

Sauntering around the campus, AK was bewitched. In this clustered, urban Mumbai, the sprawling lush green, sixty-acre campus of Somaiya group stood like a utopian dream. The neatly laid out footpaths on one side, with benches nestled underneath trees, were aesthetic and quaint. Facing these benches, two lanes apart was a huge playground where students played cricket. AK was amazed to see so many boys and girls in this sprawling campus.

Like they say - A thing of beauty is a joy forever! So was the beauty of this campus. It held the power to charm every moment into a treasured memory. Bhavin informed him that the entire campus housed more than thirty institutions. AK was impressed. *My folks made the right choice I guess!* He mused.

"We go to Nescafe café and have cold coffee there. It is very very good," replied Bhavin, hoping that AK was not bored of his company. His friend had been quiet all along. Bhavin did not have too many friends since he was always surrounded by books, relentlessly pursuing his quest for academics. Bhavin felt AK was not a poser like others he had known before because AK didn't try to avoid him despite his shortcomings. He could tell instinctively that AK had a certain air of honesty about himself. There was a lot he could learn from him and Bhavin knew it.

"AK...this way," said Bhavin, pointing to the lane on his left, *"Tum kahin khoaye hue ho,"* he added further. (You are lost somewhere in your thoughts)

"No dude, I am just admiring the campus. It is so huuuggee!" said AK in amazement.

Bhavin smiled, and he informed him that nearly all of Vidyavihar was occupied by the Somaiya group. He also informed him that he completed his 11th and 12th in S K Somaiya. AK quickly recollected Shikha was in S K Somaiya. *Only if she was around!* He hoped.

They took a left turn and entered a narrow stony pathway. Nestled in that foliage of trees and bushes was a clearing of roughly 600 square feet, by the right-hand corner of the café's entrance. The buzz of the place immediately appealed to him. It was akin to a sophisticated tea-shack, sprinkled with a hint of nature's ruggedness, in the interiors of a remote tropical island. He knew at that very moment, that he could be marked absent for the lectures, but never here. This would be their favourite joint or *adda*, as such places were popularly known amongst friends in Mumbai lingo.

Bhavin ordered cold coffee for both of them, AK paid him his share of the money. Bhavin went ahead to place the order, while AK went to catch a spot for both of them. There were no chairs or tables in this café, people stood at their chosen spot for a while, had their fill of tea, coffee, tomato soup, Maggi noodles and gossips, jokes, and flirtations to their heart's content and left.

AK was not used to seeing so many damsels in a day—most of them petite, shapely, and pretty. It made him uncomfortable and conscious of his behaviour in such surroundings. On such occasions which were becoming rather frequent, he seldom spoke or started a topic.

He looked up at the increased chirping of birds on the trees, worried; the last thing he wanted was birds pooping on him. He moved from under the tree to a clearing, and he turned to see Bhavin was standing near the counter and talking to another guy. AK realized Bhavin knew many people here. AK's eyes wandered off towards the entrance of the coffee shop and his eyes fell on three girls whose backs were facing him. One of the girls accidentally dropped what looked like a handkerchief, the silhouette seemed vaguely familiar. She bent to pick it up, she turned to her right side as she got up.

"Shikha!" AK muttered in astonishment and looked away. He glanced towards her again. That was Shikha! And all those feelings he denied, he suppressed when Tanya came into the picture, burst through his heart into his head confounding him completely. At that moment, he realized he longed for Shikha's companionship.

At the same time his heart desired Tanya so much that he felt a passionate surge destroying his moral compass each time he thought of her. Dreams of entwining with Tanya were something he enjoyed without guilt occasionally. But whenever he thought of Shikha, he couldn't figure out why he felt guilty trying to imagine her that way at all.

Yet again he couldn't decide. He knew it would be challenging to pursue the girl of his dreams and win her over, the joy of such sweet victory and the love of it would be spellbinding. A smile escaped his lips. He looked around to see if someone noticed. *What's wrong with you AK? Why are you so confused?* AK couldn't decide between Shikha and Tanya.

AK looked for Bhavin, he was still engrossed in a conversation with the same guy near the counter. Refocusing his attention on Tanya and Shikha, he knew he had to quickly come to a conclusion. He pondered, *Tanya stays in Dombivli and so do I. What I know of her from 'The Rascals' is that she is single and will easily mingle and yea I will prove them wrong! Shikha stays in Kurla, definitely not in Dombivli, that is good... good, because Tanya in Dombivli will not know about Shikha in Kurla…ah come on! Shikha is single! Or must be having a boyfriend, and in all probability, she is blissfully unaware of my existence…hmmn…focus AK, focus.* AK pondered, *what if Shikha doesn't have a lover? I could be losing a heavenly opportunity. Since she is in my classes, I can pursue her too. Of course, I can. What if it doesn't work out with Tanya? I could stand to lose both of them. Either way, Tanya wouldn't know…and neither would Shikha. Even the coin tossing was a tie…thrice. Hmm!* His smile widened, as he knew what he had to do. Evaluating the pros and cons, he prepared for an adventure and a thrilling chase.

His self-confidence was soaring faster than the Mumbai mercury. He mused, *I could pursue both these girls and most likely one of these relationships would work, either with Shikha or with Tanya. If both work then…it would be impossible to live,* he couldn't suppress his smile. *No, not impossible but it would be a challenge to maintain both the relationships if they worked.* Then it clicked, like an idea bulb from his dearest Economics subject - OPPORTUNITY COST! He was confident of being an exception to that rule. He recollected the tied result of the tossed coin *Aha! No wonder even luck is on my side!* He mused smartly.

Bhavin walked over to AK with two cups. He was happy that his friend had taken some time to get their coffee.

AK tasted the coffee. He loved it. He knew he would be having this regularly for the next three years of his academic life.

"That girl, same girl you ghoor ghooring in classes all time na," added Bhavin sincerely with a smile. (That same girl you keep staring in classes all the time)

AK choked on his coffee. He couldn't stop coughing. Bhavin had again put him in a fix, AK could neither laugh nor hide, pitying himself. He had foolishly assumed no one noticed his regular admiring glances at Shikha. He prayed that no one had heard Bhavin.

"I am leaving now. Got to get to classes and walking will not get us there on time. I am catching an auto," AK said, turning to Bhavin.

He paused, he was annoyed but he didn't want to leave Bhavin behind.

"Please come, we'll go together," AK said placing his hand on Bhavin's shoulder. Bhavin nodded.

Air-conditioned rooms of the CA classes were a major motivating factor, but first came Shikha, then the classrooms and other subjects. Math was nowhere in the list. The day's first lecture was Math, and it would be over in an hour thankfully.

Bhavin and AK were discussing the insurmountable challenge known as Math, and as to how apart from serving an eliminating purpose it never really helped a Chartered Accountant. There were a handful of students in the class. Shikha, Nehal and Dimple had not arrived yet. The door opened and the Math professor walked in. He marched straight to the board like a zamindar without acknowledging the presence of students sitting there like peasants waiting for their day's chores.

"Boys and girls, today there is good news for you all," he said smugly. His face serenely lit up by his gold rimmed glasses and his grey trimmed beard, the tube light reflecting from his bald head forming an artificial halo of brightest ingenuity imaginable, "Today, since all the other lecturers are absent I will be teaching you Math the entire day," he added. AK's gasps and shocks of 'No' were drowned in the cheers of jubilation by his classmates.

He took the marker and wrote 'Integral Calculus'. AK turned and looked at Bhavin, "I am Integrally screwed." For two hours AK bore the onslaught of Calculus.

Finally, the chapter was 'Matrices', which gave AK some respite, this chapter seemed manageable. The eager front benchers convinced the professor that 'Matrices' was child's play and goaded him to teach them 'Functional Derivatives' instead.

AK's face turned pale at the sight of the first equation on the board, suddenly the bell rang. Everyone stepped out of the class. AK and Bhavin too followed suit.

"*Yaar*! It is very tough for me also *na*," said Bhavin trying to console a harassed AK.

"How am I supposed to feel better with that?" quipped AK.

"Huh?" Bhavin looked perplexed.

"Never mind," said AK, "I think it's difficult for me to pass CA Foundation exams at this rate, even if I pass in others, I will surely flunk in Math," added AK in despair.

"Flunk *maney* fail *na*?" asked Bhavin (mean). AK was getting irritated with Bhavin, then he checked himself. He knew his helpless situation with Math was frustrating him constantly, it was pointless taking it out on Bhavin. The solution--ask Sanjay for help. Sanjay's favourite subject was Math and being an engineering student, he would definitely know these chapters well.

"Dude! I was never good at Math even in my school days, it was always Math that pulled my grades down. And here it is like this humungous Mt. Everest blocking my path. GODDAMNIT!" said AK, clenching his fists in frustration.

"I also not do Maths in my 11th – 12th, but I am having *pakkko viswaas* I will do it. And I have *pakkko viswaas*, you do also." (complete belief) said Bhavin with confidence. AK smiled at his friend's simplicity and endearing encouragement. Bhavin was happy that he was able to create a smile on AK's face.

"Hello boys!" said Nehal interrupting their conversation.

"What happened? Why do you look like the weight of the world is on your shoulders?" asked Dimple. They all greeted each other.

"Because it is," said AK with a shrug, and brushed away imaginary lint from his shoulders "It's gone now!" he smirked. Dimple and Nehal chuckled. AK often observed Bhavin gazing and talking to Dimple fondly, but he didn't tease Bhavin about it yet.

Bhavin explained their predicament. Dimple suggested combined studies to help each other. Nehal and Bhavin liked the idea.

"Hello, we are not trying to learn Gujarati but Math! Do you have any idea?" responded AK sarcastically. Nehal slapped his arm playfully.

"You are so negative about Math! Uff!" shot back Nehal in huff, and folded her arms in defiance.

"And about Gujarati too!" added Dimple nudging his arm playfully.

"He is only positive about Shi-"

"Please man!" he interrupted Bhavin, snapping his fingers. He was in no mood for any joke, knowing where it was headed. He could see Shikha standing in a cosy corner with her friends.

Nehal sat next to him "AK you will be able to do it. We will do combined studies and we all can win this. Have at least that much confidence in yourself," she said.

AK nodded, hiding his trepidation.

"So, when do we start?" asked Bhavin eagerly.

CHAPTER 7

*H*eavy rains lashed throughout the early week of July disrupting railways and traffic. AK's uncle couldn't go to office for two days. And with the unabated downpour, it was not worth the risk. Life in Mumbai and its suburbs had come to a standstill. Monsoon had finally blessed Maharashtra!

Many Mumbaikars loved rains, except a few, one amongst those few was AK. He despised the rains, as he wouldn't be able to wear his favourite Reebok sneakers for the next three months. It would be difficult to hang out with friends in such weather! The roads would be filled with muck and unavoidable potholes. Embarking on a journey to any place would be daunting, at least for AK, while the other residents were habituated to the monsoon and her debilitating effects.

His enthusiasm for combined studies for Math were drained temporarily. His three friends, however, favoured by proximity were meeting at Sarvodaya in the evenings post class hours to study Math, while AK remained out of reach and out of touch from all, due to the monsoons and his dead phone connection. His parents were worried since AK had been unreachable for over three days, but a call to Lakshmi aunty soothed their frayed nerves and they soon spoke to him at her apartment.

The weather--great! The drive--good! The company--fun! Welcoming the monsoon with a long drive and a few drinks was an impulse 'The Rascals' gave in to.

"Mukesh, please drive a bit slow pal," requested Pratap. The roads were still wet, with the heavy downpour now reduced to a faint drizzle. Mukesh obliged. They enjoyed their drive, listening to Bryan Adam's best hits.

The Omni drove into the driveway of their new haunt 'Pravin da Dhaba', nestled in a cosy foliage beyond the outskirts of the city, along the highway.

Each table was inside an open-door hut. They took their table near the main counter. Their conversation veered towards Pratap's love interest - Nivedita. It was soon directed at AK, since Pratap did not want to be teased, but it veered back to Pratap.

Sanjay and Mukesh insisted to Pratap that he propose to Nivedita soon.

"*Bhai*, please do it before Raksha Bandhan eh…else she will really make you her *bhai* too," joked Mukesh with a wink. Sanjay playfully smacked Mukesh at the back of his head. He didn't like being reminded of that. Raksha Bandhan is a popular Indian festival mainly celebrated by Hindus and many others. Traditionally, it was a day when sisters ritually professed 'bond of protection and love' towards their brothers with prayers and by tying a *rakhi* made of ornate threads resembling an amulet. In return brothers promised them a life-long vow of protection and care. Now, in this modern era many pretty young lasses smartly used this festival as a weapon and sweetly tied unsuitable young men into brotherhood. These unsuitable candidates who had an inkling of their pending doom went into hiding on that festive day. Unfortunately, Sanjay was one such candidate.

Pratap looked on in silence for a while. Sanjay goaded him out of it. AK remained the mute spectator wisely concealing the hope of being teased about Tanya.

Pratap replied concerned, "I think I missed the bus. I feel that she is in love with someone else."

"*Yaar*, chill oye! Even if you think you are friend-zoned…you still have a chance…as long as you are not bro-zoned," replied Mukesh with a smirk. Sanjay took a peanut from the plate and threw it at Mukesh in jest.

"I have *pucca* belief…she loves you…and if you feel that she is in love with someone else…then it might be some plot cooked up by Tanya," said Sanjay, "Maybe to get you jealous," he added further. (pucca – sure)

So, her name is finally dropped, mused AK suppressing his inner smile.

"What do you have against Tanya?" asked Pratap, curious. He had not expected this suggestion from Sanjay.

Mukesh chuckled, "Not against, for," he said.

"Oh no, nothing at all," said Sanjay.

"Of course, *bhaisaab* wants a *rakhi* from her too," said Mukesh, looking at AK. "After all, anything for *dosti*!" (Dosti – Friendship)

Sanjay showed Mukesh the finger. They all burst out laughing.

"Talking of that female…please get him her number, or whatever…if that doesn't work out he will find some other girl *yaar*," Sanjay added.

"I don't have her number pal and it is best that she calls AK," said Pratap.

"Guys, it is ok, relax," said AK.

"Hello mate, you take it easy. We have a very good idea about you now, yea," said Pratap, chuckling. They all laughed except for AK. Whenever AK tried to recollect that night, it was still vague.

The waiter, meanwhile, arrived with their beers, cigarettes, ash tray and matches.

Pratap opened the cigarette pack offering it to Sanjay and AK. The boys helped themselves, lit up their cigarettes and puffed. Sanjay and Pratap coughed a bit. AK did not. He continued to puff like a seasoned smoker.

"Are you sure this is your first time?" Sanjay asked AK, interrupting Pratap in between.

"Yes, of course," said AK gesturing to Pratap to narrate his eventful details, and meanwhile, side dishes arrived. Pratap and AK went for the non-veg food while

Sanjay and Mukesh preferred veg food. Pratap finished telling them his version.

"Look *yaar*…I am sure you got this whole thing wrong," said Sanjay.

"*Arrey*! She tells me about every guy she knows and she shows me all birthday cards before she gives them off to her friends. Only this time, she didn't…why?" said Pratap, evidently stressed. He suspected that she had lost her heart to the new guy in her college – Abhay.

"You could have simply asked her more about this guy," said AK. The trio shook their heads in disagreement.

"I understand your situation *bhaisaab*…I do," said Mukesh sympathetically, trying to console Pratap. After all, Mukesh too had his share of heartbreaks, though one-sided.

"*Yaar, Pratap mujhe pucca belief hai ki* she is completely in love with you only and no one else. I am sure there is no Abhay. Even if there is she is just friends with him that's all," insisted Sanjay confidently. (Mate, Pratap, I firmly believe that she is in love with you and no one else.)

"The writing is on the wall Sanjay. True, indeed she does love me as much as a friend would love his or her friend. That's all. I used to love her a lot before, but now I am sure I'll only be friends with her. I am never going to be her man, or live an amazing life with her. It's over… that's all," said Pratap. He gulped down more than half the bottle completely. And one day…one day we will part as the best possible hi-bye friends."

"You are high," remarked Sanjay.

"Yea full on drunk now. *Waah*! Best possible hi – bye friends. First time I am hearing such wisdom," chuckled Mukesh, with a shrug and palms open.

Wow! He really thought so far! mused AK about Pratap.

He turned to AK and said, "*Yaar*, I've given your number to Nivedita, she will pass it on to Tanya and she will definitely give you a call. Promise me…promise me that you will not call her till she calls you first."

"Definitely dude. Of course, Yes. You have my word. And thanks buddy," said AK relieved, suppressing his smile. He counted his blessings. He was certain in his previous birth he had done some good deed to be blessed with a friend like Pratap.

"Ok, fine…enough of this…you are too upset and *bhai*…ideally, one should rise in love with love. I hate this whole idea of saying 'falling in love' like it's something negative, something like a crime you know. Pratap in my heart of hearts I feel that she will be yours… really, I do," said Mukesh.

Patting AK on his shoulder, he added, "I am sure he does too." AK nodded. AK genuinely felt that after knowing someone for three years, there would definitely be some sparks on either side.

The discussion went on till their beers finished. The debate was inconclusive. AK felt like the typical confused viewer sitting in front of an Indian soap that perennially went on for years without any definite conclusion.

Sanjay suggested, "It is best to wait and watch." Pratap looked on like a dejected fatalist.

"Or act," said Mukesh, ever the confident go-getter, "Go tell her what you feel," he added, punching the air. The three glanced at AK. Caught off guard, he said, "I think, wait for two days and then tell her…but it is getting late, shall we?" He added quickly. Confused, he couldn't take a side.

"I have loved her for over two years, and I've loved her so much that at times I get tongue-tied, I don't know what to tell her. I cherish her company and friendship. I feared losing her friendship, that's why I never proposed to her. My heart would break to a thousand pieces if she were to ever reject me. Mate, I love her enough to let her go for her happiness. And I love her more than anything in this world to have her back even if I am the last love of her life. You know what they say love is like a bird, set her free; if it is meant to be it will come back to you, if it doesn't, it never was yours," said Pratap lovelorn, his eyes turning moist.

AK growled with anger on seeing his friend's state, "Let's find this guy, Abhay, and beat him up without anyone knowing and show the world that nobody can play with the Rascals."

Pratap was touched by AK's outburst, while Mukesh was amused, and Sanjay sighed.

"Pratap *bhai*, please don't let that expensive beer come out of your eyes now," Mukesh chuckled.

"Calm down, *yaar*, calm down…chill…chill, please," Sanjay spoke, laying a hand on AK's shoulder, calming him down.

CHAPTER 8

July is the wettest and slowest month of the year, given the slow pace of trains and work. AK would usually miss the evening study sessions with his friends, and Bhavin, Nehal, and Dimple were unhappy by his absence. Bhavin recently confided to him in college that he had a 'likeness' for Dimple. AK knew his absence would be a good opportunity for Bhavin to get closer to her. At times, AK would admonish himself for subjecting himself and his friend to such distractions.

Today, he decided to bunk college but he felt it was his moral duty, and bound by the oath he gave his mom to attend the CA classes. These, he never skipped.

At home AK was studying accountancy and economics. After an hour he had to get ready and leave for his CA classes. Happily, he was able to focus well, and was close to finishing when the phone rang.

"Hello," he answered in an enquiring tone.

"Hello, *kya Akash hai ghar pe?*" enquired a husky feminine voice. (Hello, is Akash home?)

"Yea he is…I mean…*haan, main Akash bol raha hoon,*" he stuttered (Yea, I am Akash speaking)

"Hi! How are you? I am Tanya here," said Tanya in her husky voice.

"Hii…Tanya," he waved his hand, only to realize foolishly he was on the phone with her. "It is nice…I mean…I am fine…how about you? Eh, call me AK, my friends ca…call me that," said AK, overcome by relief and trying to control his stuttering at the same time.

"I am fine, thanks for asking," she smiled. He paused, clueless what to say next.

"Ehh AK…am I…" Tanya went on

"Thanks for asking me earlier too," said AK interrupting her. He almost bit his tongue since he realized he was wrong to interrupt her and it was moronic to interrupt her with something like this.

"You are welcome. So, AK, tell me what do you do in your spare time?" she asked trying to steer away from an awkward conversation.

"To be honest…I really don't get much spare time…I am also studying for CA," he said, beginning to find some composure.

"Ah! That's nice…so what were you doing?" enquired Tanya.

"I was just doing some studies…you know…just going through my notes that's all," he replied.

"Ah scholar! I hope I am not disturbing you…you know…it's ok, we can talk later," she said.

"No not at all…it was a welcome disturbance…I finished for the day…I have to get ready for my classes," said AK, only to realize that it was a very dumb thing to say. *I could skip Math – first hour!*

"You are very kind…anyways, AK tell me what do you really do in your spare time?" she asked. *I dream about steaming with you.* He blushed, musing.

"Well nothing much really…I spend time with my friends, chit-chatting, you know how guys go about their free time," replied AK casually.

"Ok, so who are the people you hang out with? I mean Sanjay and Pratap must be them, right?" she asked

"Yea, and Mukesh too," added AK enthusiastically

"Ohh okkayy," she said, surprised

"Which college do you go to?" he asked

"I have joined B. Comm at MCC," she said

"That's great! By the way I did not get your college's name," he remarked.

"MCC – Mulund College of Commerce…hmm… the weather is crazy! I don't like going anywhere in this weather," she said, dismayed, "You know *na*…clothes don't dry up and everything gets dirty soon, then there are muddy roads, pot holes, and all of that," she added.

"Yea! I know…even I hate monsoons. I love winters though. I love cool weather," he said. AK couldn't help but imagine her in rain drenched clothes. He quickly snapped out of it.

"Me too…same pinch," she replied, only to realize that was a childish thing to say but a nice way to flirt.

"Which college are you in?"

"K J Somaiya for B. Comm," he replied.

"Yea of course, duh! You wouldn't be doing CA otherwise," she giggled. AK loosened his guard.

"True…very true," he replied with a shrug. He was enjoying their conversation.

"Where are your CA classes?" she asked.

"Ghatkopar, Joshi & Bhatt Commerce Classes. You must have heard about them, right?" he said.

"Oh yea! They are quite famous, but both your classes and college are quite far. Don't you get tired with all the travel?" she asked.

"Well, I keep sleeping off in the train. So, I feel refreshed later," he replied, smiling. He glanced at the clock and knew it was time to hang up, but he did not want to leave.

"So, when do you leave for your classes?" she asked.

"I have to be there by 1:30. So I have to start getting ready now and have lunch and rush you know," he said politely.

"Oh I am so sorry…please carry on, ok then, bye," said Tanya hurriedly.

"We could catch up later you know. I will be back by 8 in the evening. Take care," said AK, dejected at the abrupt end of their delightful conversation. *Dumbo! Don't act desperate!* He scolded himself.

"Bye…you take care too," she giggled and kept the phone. Before he could ask her for her number she hung up. He regretfully kept the phone, showered, and got ready. No matter how hard he tried he could not stop blushing. *She finally called! Thank you, Pratap and Nivedita!*

Bhavin was sitting inside the CA classroom, intermittently looking towards the door. Their second Math class would start in ten minutes and there was no sign of AK. He saw Dimple and Nehal sitting together in the second last row, near the door. They smiled at him, he smiled back. Nehal gestured at the seat next to him. She lip-synced 'AK'. He shrugged. Just then the door swung open and AK walked in, followed by the Math professor. Bhavin moved to the next seat and AK sat next to him.

"*Yaar, tu sau saal jiyega,*" Bhavin said smiling. (Mate, you will live a 100 years). AK chuckled "I wouldn't really mind." AK reluctantly sat through an hour of the class.

During the break, Nehal spoke to him and told him she would introduce him to Shikha today. He enjoyed Nehal's company, she seemed to be a nice, friendly and helpful girl. *Shikha here and Tanya there. I am THE MAN!* AK thought, his heart swelled with pride.

"The only thing…I have not seen her today. I don't think she came in," said Nehal. They both stood facing each other. AK was well acquainted with her naughtiness.

"Hmm, forget it, we'll think about it when we see her," said AK nonchalantly.

Nehal looked at him curiously, "What happened Mr. AK, everything okay? You lost interest or someone more interesting happened?" asked Nehal with a mischievous smile.

"Look, to be honest…I am here to study CA, career is more important, so everything else is secondary," replied AK, determined.

He could not reveal to her that he had just spent time talking to his voluptuous vixen earlier in the day. *What would Nehal think of me? I can't tell her, at least not yet,* he mused.

"Hey, there she is…" said Nehal, and AK quickly turned around to check. Dimple and Bhavin were coming over from across the road.

"Ha! Caught you!" said Nehal.

"Look I thought – "

"That it was 'her'," she interrupted, gesturing 'her' in inverted quotes with her fingers, and she pouted to him playfully.

He sighed. It was pointless to argue with Nehal. He blushed.

"Oh, there she is," said Nehal, her eyes lighting up. she nudged him to look over his shoulder. AK knew this was another joke. He could see the Economics professor coming.

"Listen, the Eco professor is here. I will see you later," he said, ambling away.

"Hey, wait…" said Nehal. AK walked away into the class, shaking his head. He knew she was fooling him again. He looked behind just before he entered the class and Nehal was indeed talking to Shikha. *Darn, opportunity missed,* he thought. He moved inside and Bhavin sat in the aisle seat this time. *Opportunity LOST!* He cursed.

The Economics class lasted an hour. After the class finished they all stepped out for the scheduled break.

"Do not you think that this Eco sir is talking in fast ispeed?" asked Bhavin earnestly.

AK smiled, he understood his friend's concern, "*Yaar*, I don't feel so, but he is very thorough on the subject and he loves Economics."

"What is it that you love?" asked a feminine voice from behind, interrupting their conversation. He turned to look, he knew this mischievous one.

"You always have this habit of eavesdropping on other's conversation? We were talking about Economics, by the way," replied AK playfully.

"Relax mister, I was only pulling your leg," said Nehal, raising her hands.

"Nehal, AK, I will be back in a minute," said Bhavin, excusing himself for a short break.

AK turned his attention towards Nehal and observed that she had oiled her hair and tied them in a plait. It looked weirdly funny. She looked like a complete *behenji* (typically, Gujju sister types).

"So now you are looking at me, eh?" she asked him.

"Nothing, you look nice today," AK said covering up, chuckling.

He liked her sense of humour. She amused him and was unpredictable.

"Eh...wait, so you mean I wasn't looking nice the other day?" quipped Nehal her eyebrows arched up.

"No, you weren't," responded AK with a smirk.

Nehal jabbed him "You are so mean."

"Hey, there she is..." he said looking in Shikha's direction, who was talking to Dimple. He quickly asked, "Look I hope you didn't tell Dimple about this. I mean, I hope you understand."

"I didn't tell her anything. I promise on my parents," she said, looking straight into his eyes.

"Alright, I trust you," he replied. Nehal waved to Shikha. Dimple and she started walking over to AK's side.

He was nervous, and was fidgeting with his fingers behind his back. He took two steps back and bit his lip. He thought, *calm down AK, keep it cool AK, breathe in, breathe out, you can do this. Oh! You are so damn nervous. Calm down, calm down.*

Shikha walked over to their side, wearing a pale pink kurta with bright blue embroidery and matching blue denims. AK's heart skipped a beat. Bhavin, who had joined them again, smiled and waved at her.

"Hi Shikha, how are you?" asked Nehal.

"Fine dear, and you?" asked Shikha.

"I am fine too. This is our friend AK," said Nehal introducing him.

"Hi Shikha, so how do you find the classes?" asked AK quickly.

"Easy...since they are here and do not move at all, you know," replied Shikha, and the girls giggled. AK looked on, clueless for a brief bit, and then caught the joke and laughed.

Do you have a lover? AK instantly shot down this thought. *Wrong timing!*

"You were not here for the first lecture, right?" asked Dimple.

"No, I got held up at college and I was a good half an hour late. I didn't want to end up irritating the professor, so I thought I should sit this one out," she said guiltily.

"Don't tell me you were sitting outside in this weather," said Nehal.

"Oh, no way, I was inside the office," said Shikha winking at Dimple. The other two girls giggled too. AK was clueless and so was Bhavin who, through his thick plastic spectacles, appeared perennially clueless and geeky too. They both exchanged blank glances at each other.

"He is so cute *na*," Dimple blushed.

"Our lady has a huge crush on him," said Nehal pointing at Dimple.

"Really? Who wouldn't? Those cute dimples," said Shikha, giggling.

Curiosity was getting the better of AK, and he did not want to sound envious and intrusive.

"So, who is it?" asked Bhavin. *Thank you Bhavin FINALLY,* AK mused.

"*Arrey*, that guy, Pritam, the office administrator,"

"That fellow!" exclaimed AK, trying to hide his surprise. *Agreed! He is a nice guy, but why a crush on him?* AK was horrified. *Not only was Pritam as dark as the night but his pockmarked cheeks had more craters than the rural Indian roads.* He reflected. *He checked himself. Am I feeling jealous? No, I am not. I am just stating fact.* They went on to describe how cute the guy was. *How could Shikha even remotely think Pritam looked cute? Maybe it's just a crush.* He felt crushed by that very thought.

His friend Bhavin was a much better-looking guy than Pritam. He looked at Bhavin who was listening to

Shikha without batting an eyelid. *Damn!* thought AK, *Bhavin is staring at her.* He would have to tell Bhavin about her before he begins to have a crush on her.

"*Arrey*...Accounts Sir is here," Bhavin announced. They all moved into the classroom and to their seats. He couldn't get Pritam's much loved dimples out of his head. *I am feeling jealous of a man who looks ugly! This is too much, it's too much to handle,* he thought. Bhavin nudged him, gestured him to take down the notes. AK quickly came out of his contemplation and complied. The next break, the girls were chit chatting. AK was in no mood to join them, Bhavin proceeded towards them. AK stopped him.

"Bhavin, come with me...I need to go buy a notebook," said AK

"Ok," smiled Bhavin.

As soon as they were away from the vicinity of the classes he asked, "Bhavin, do you really think Pritam looks good? I mean, his face is like village roads, filled with pot-holes?"

"Eh...I not seen Pritam...I seen him from far, so I don't know," replied Bhavin puzzled.

"Look, please don't try and be diplomatic, be honest with me. Do you think he looks good?" asked AK, feeling agitated.

"Can I ask something?" asked Bhavin

"Shoot," said AK.

"No, really, I only want to ask?" said Bhavin innocently.

AK sighed, "That's what I meant."

"Do you like Nehal?" asked Bhavin.

"Duude! I mean NO...only as a friend," he replied, a trifle impatient. He did not know where Bhavin was going with his questions.

"Why did you ask me that?" asked AK, "Do you have feelings for Nehal now? Not Dimple?" he added.

"No *re*...I will tell you later," Bhavin said, returning to his thoughts. AK was least bothered.

"It cannot be Dimple, so then it has to be Shikha that upset you. Right *na*?" asked Bhavin aloud in his Gujjuish English accent.

"Yea you are…look, I really like her…I know it sounds silly…but I think I have a huge crush on her," replied AK.

"You mean to say you like her, like you love her a lot," Bhavin affirmed.

"No, no, no. Look, it is like this. Yes, I do like her a lot but I don't love her. I don't know her enough to love her."

"But I think Nehal likes you. I see her looking you sometimes, and she ispeaks to you lot," said Bhavin.

"No dude…see, I told her that I like Shikha, and she said she'll get me introduced to her and she did that today. So, I don't think she looks at me that way, you know," said AK without a doubt in his mind.

"Hmm ok. Listen, but please give such things time," said Bhavin.

"Yea…I get what you mean," smiled AK.

"You think we both would look good together? I mean Shikha and me of course," asked AK, smiling.

Bhavin smiled and didn't reply back. AK asked him about his fascination for Dimple, he dismissed it as a mere passing crush and nothing else. He liked her as a good friend now. Conversing, they walked till the railway station where Bhavin pointed him towards a hawker selling notebooks.

"So, you don't want to buy book I think?" Bhavin asked.

"Hmm, I'll need to buy one for the college," said AK

AK bought the book and they rushed into the class and quickly settled down.

Soon after the last lecture finished, AK and Bhavin met with Nehal and Dimple, while Shikha was busy chatting with another girl.

Shikha waved bye to them. They waved back, AK too waved back with a smile. *Today is my lucky day!*

His friends took him to Sarvodaya in Ghatkopar West, it was an aged complex that housed a hospital, school, and a temple in the same vicinity. They sat down on the floor of the vast corridor and began going through Math.

They started with Matrices, AK found this chapter easy. After about an hour they all decided to leave. It was past 7:30pm.

As they walked out of the complex, it began to drizzle and soon it began to rain heavily. AK looked back. Dimple and Bhavin were sharing an umbrella. Nehal quickly pulled out hers from her bag and she held it over AK's head.

"Hey, thanks!" he muttered with a smile. "Don't catch a cold now!" she said, smiling. He could see her straining her neck and arm holding it up for him. He took the umbrella from her hand.

"You are tall!" he teased her. In a reflex, she quickly stepped aside and slapped his arm, getting lightly wet in the process. He chuckled and pulled her back under the umbrella, by the shoulder holding her close to him, and their eyes met for a brief moment.

"You have brown eyes…light brown…pretty eyes," he whispered softly. She blushed and looked away. "Eh, you should compliment. Occasionally, it is nice, you know."

"Hey, thanks for today with Shikha… and for Math," he added quickly as they reached the auto stand. She returned his smile. Bhavin and Dimple too caught up with them. The girls caught an auto and left for home.

CHAPTER 9

A boring Saturday greeted AK as he entered past the gates. There was hardly any crowd in the college. He made his way to the classroom where Bhavin introduced AK to a new classmate, Hiten. He seemed an affable young man. At 5'8", attired in black denim and an ivory white full sleeved t-shirt, Hiten was slender and very fair, so fair that AK mentally noted him as Mr. Snow White. However, strikingly, his attire was unlike most Gujjus and unlike other boys in college. Hiten seemed to focus more on sophistication, noted AK.

After the third lecture, cravings for samosas and Cola took them to the canteen.

Thankfully, self-service was not the norm. Upon taking their seats, a young enthusiastic waiter rushed over to take the order and promised to serve them soon. Aroma of hot samosas caught their attention as he approached their table. He quickly got three Coca-Cola bottles and popped them open.

"Talk about service? That was super quick," remarked Hiten, taking a sip from his bottle. AK and Bhavin nodded, biting into their hot samosas.

Hiten indulged in small talk. He told them he helped out in his family business of stock brokering. The duo was impressed. Hiten enquired their whereabouts.

"I am at Garodia Nagar," Hiten said, biting into his hot samosa which turned his cheeks rosy pink. Bhavin coughed and paused for a bit.

"L. B. S. Marg," said AK, pointing to Bhavin and then pointed to himself and said, "Dombivli." He bit into his second samosa.

"Ah, Dombivli eh!" remarked Hiten. AK expected to hear some mocking over Dombivli like Nehal did.

"It would be some coincidence if you know my cousin, Mukesh, a robust, tall fellow, stays in Dombivli East," he said. As they kept discussing, it became certain that they probably knew the same Mukesh. He told Hiten they had a common friend, Sanjay.

AK noted that unlike the other Gujarati students he came across, Hiten spoke good English without any influence of his mother tongue bearing on it. They finished, and as they were about to leave after settling the bill, Hiten decided to head home. Bhavin and AK too decided to head to their CA classes. The trio ambled together, chit chatting, till they reached a parking spot where several cars were parked.

A metallic blue Maruti Esteem stood under the shade of a tree. Hiten unlocked the door and threw his bag inside. On the back seat lay a big book titled 'Palmistry'.

"You really read hands or learning?" asked Bhavin curiously.

"I am no expert...can say I know a bit," he replied.

"Read mine now...please, it will be a good time-pass," requested AK. Sudden showers forced them inside his car. AK and Hiten sat in the front. Hiten pulled out his magnifying lens from the glove box.

"Oh man! I thought you said you know only a bit...expectations are high buddy...your fault," said AK, smiling. AK geared himself up to hear his glorious destiny. AK stretched out his right palm. Hiten pulled the other palm too.

"I thought right is for men and left is for ladies, right?" enquired AK.

"Nothing like that," muttered Hiten, intensely looking into AK's future through the lens. He looked hard for about a minute.

"Hmm, you think a lot...quite a lot," said Hiten looking surprised.

"Eh…well everyone does so that's nothing new," responded AK. *'Think a lot! Yea right! Who doesn't? Anyone with a brain would,* thought AK.

"What I actually meant is you think over a lot of unnecessary things…I meant you think over every small thing and complicate your life," said Hiten with conviction.

AK hated to admit it but it was the truth.

"And…you get distracted very easily…I have to say this, you are gullible. You trust people easily. Not to worry, you have very few cheaters in your life. Most people will be friendly towards you and loyal," said Hiten. Leaning forward Bhavin stared at his own palms.

"I don't think I am gullible but yea maybe I do tend to trust people quickly," said AK. The palmist chuckled.

"You had quite a lot of health problems when you were a child. I mean, from the age of three to ten," said Hiten.

AK nodded "I had typhoid twice and jaundice once."

"I can see that you are distracted…but let me warn you…you have the tendency to be unlucky in love," said Hiten dejectedly.

"Will I become a CA?" asked AK, considering the war with Math he had all the time inside his head.

"To be honest with you…every human being can become whatever he wants provided he works hard at his goals with commitment and dedication," said Hiten firmly.

"Ok I get it…but will I really become a CA…tell me what you feel you know, what you can see, please," requested AK.

Hiten looked at his friend and smiled tolerantly at him.

"I clearly see that you are quite an analytical person and seldom give importance to feelings…see, you've a tendency to analyse and you do possess a fairly high level of intelligence. It clearly means that you are capable of being a CA or an MBA. I feel that you will choose some other career and not CA. I see that you have a natural flair for public speaking and engaging the audience. You also tend to win friends easily because of this," said Hiten.

"Dude, honestly, I think this is where you missed. I am sure that I will complete CA, and man, I have never tried public speaking. The very thought terrifies me," said AK, shaking his head, staring at his palms.

"Bhavin, you want to know?" asked Hiten with a smile.

"Later on, Hiten *bhai*, we have classes now," said Bhavin timidly. AK glanced at his watch and he was right, they had to hurry.

CA classes were a four-hour marathon session of Trigonometry. It was a nightmare and he did not understand any of it. These mathematics problems reminded him of his ineptitude, sapping away his mood completely.

"Really, I am not in the mood today," he told Nehal as they walked towards the station after the classes.

"Uff, you sound like you are on your…" she paused. Dimple laughed while Bhavin and AK looked on clueless. "So much drama this boy! Uff, my God!" she continued.

"Trigonometry is easy, I can teach you," she said "Maths is my subject."

"Today Shikha did not come, so no mood, eh?" teased Dimple, chuckling. He shook his head.

"Today is Saturday, I should go and chill," he replied.

"Alright! *Chalo*, let's have some dhokla! I am in the mood for it," Dimple said. Nehal and Bhavin happily agreed. AK, although reluctant, decided to go with the flow. They sauntered into a shop near the station and had dhoklas. AK loved them. Over dhoklas he told the girls about their new friend, Hiten, and his palm reading skills. Nehal told him many Gujjus value such knowledge. Dimple and Bhavin agreed. This was news to AK. That day he understood that Gujratis were culturally strong. Bhavin quickly mentioned that Garodia Nagar was one of the locales where the rich Gujjus of Ghatkopar stayed.

Their discussion diverted back to food again.

"Hmm, yummy! The sauce is very nice," said AK licking his fingers, as he finished. "I cannot believe I never had this before," he added in disbelief. He began to realize he enjoyed the company of his new-found friends. Without them, CA classes would have been boring.

Scent of wet earth hung in the air, thanks to generous morning showers. The earthly fragrance energising him as he strode towards Sanjay's apartment on a lazy Sunday afternoon. Surprised that there was no call from his buddy regarding any weekend plan, he decided to check on him. AK was glad to see Mukesh and Pratap there when he entered his room.

The two of them were in a celebratory mood with the good news Pratap gave them. Well, it so turned out that there was no Abhay, the birthday card was in fact a 'Love You' card meant for Pratap. Thus, Pratap and Nivedita were now officially and happily an 'item'.

"Party, boss! Today is full on your treat!" Mukesh said enthusiastically. Pratap kept nodding his head.

And so, their Sunday evening came alive at Pravin da Dhaba. Amidst the drinks and smokes, the boys were congratulating and teasing Pratap.

"*Bhai*, Pratap, this is great news but please don't hurry and give us a 'good news' soon. We can wait," teased Mukesh, winking at him.

"No way man, please use a condom! And yea, don't listen to this fool." AK quickly reacted and turning to Mukesh, exclaimed, "You can't be serious?"

"AK! Come on *yaar*, the beer already hit your head so quickly. He was joking," Sanjay shot back. Pratap and Mukesh chuckled.

Both Tanya and Shikha were on and off his mind. AK needed some relief. He grabbed his beer bottle off the table and guzzled it down at one go much to everyone's amazement.

"*Yaar, bhaisaab*, please take it easy eh…we'll find a cop's bike to puke on for you this time," Mukesh winked, smiling.

"Don't worry *yaar*, I will make do with his UNO," retorted AK and everyone laughed.

"Aww here is another fellow who is very happy. Tanya called him," announced Pratap.

They all began teasing AK. He was blushing. He raised his arms in surrender and said "It was a very casual call."

"AK, with her, you know…she is my Nivedita's best friend," added Pratap "She called because we requested, we said that you kind of like her. Let me warn you, she is not the serious types, but still take it slow."

"Chill dude! I have it all under control," AK said, patting Pratap's shoulder.

Sanjay chuckled. Mukesh shook his head, disenchanted.

CHAPTER 10

*M*id-July rains regularly affected mobility and traffic in the city. For a few hours, each day of the week, most parts of Dombivli faced power shut down. Tonight, the sky appeared darker than it had ever been. Like a shroud, the sky looked gloomy, and the lightening ominously attempted to tear apart the clouds.

It was at such times that people needed to know their loved ones were safe and sound. Those with mobile phones were the lucky lot. He and his friends regretted that mobile phones had just been launched, and were expensive. They could only dream of affording one. *Until then, we tolerate land line phones going dead in the monsoons,* sighed AK. He was glad his uncle had reached home early.

The phone rang, disrupting his musings, and he deftly walked over with emergency light from the balcony. Certainly, it was Sanjay to inform him of their night's plan.

"Let's cancel the plan, the weather doesn't look good," answered AK as soon as he picked up the phone.

"AK, hi!" said the caller amidst a lot of disturbance on the line.

"Oh Tanya, Hello! Yea, it's me AK. I am so sorry, I thought it was Sanjay," replied AK.

"Ok, I called…*fizzzfizzfizz*…Nivedita…*fizzzfizz*…" the disturbance in the phone line made these jumbled words confusing for AK as Tanya continued talking.

"Tanya, I can barely hear you. There is a lot of disturbance on the line," replied AK. It was ruining her sensuous husky voice. *Damn these rains!* He cursed.

"Can you hear me now?" asked Tanya.

"Yea, now I can," he replied assured.

No matter how disturbed the phone lines were, this question always came through clearly.

"Yea, I can now. That's cool. So, what you been up to?" enquired AK.

"M...*zzfizz*...not...*fizzfzz*...well...." she replied again with the usual cacophony of a disturbed phone line to fill in the blanks it had conveniently created. In between it sounded like someone was using a driller over the phone lines. Usually, one would continue the call later when the phone lines get clear. But then every moment spent with Tanya was precious for AK, and so he decided to defiantly challenge the noise created by the monsoon's fury with his smartness. The camouflage of smartness an immature mind creates is unshakable to any teenager in the throes of adulthood, and AK was no exception!

Oh, poor thing she is not too well, worried AK.

"Why, what happened? Everything alright?" he asked, concerned

Tanya replied again, barely audible, and AK was utterly clueless now. Hope always made one look forward to life. He waited, hoping the line would get better immediately somehow.

"Did you see the doctor? What did he say?" asked AK assuming that she had been to the doctor. He pushed the phone tightly to his ear.

"N...*f i z z z f i z z*...i n...*f i z z z f i z z*...c l i n i c... *fizzzfizzfizzzfizz*...Kro...*fizzzfizz* ni*fizz*les...izzarnia..." she replied through the chaos and the line went dead.

He pressed the dialler on the phone and the familiar dial tone was back. He did not have her number to return the call. He thought it wise to ask her phone number the next time they spoke, helped by the increasing comfort of familiarity. But today was their second call.

The problem is with her phone line, he lamented. AK relied on his intelligent guess and he was a bit shaken, both by the boldness and the trust she placed in him.

He thought, *Tanya must really think the world of me to confide this to me…that she is unwell…that her "Nipples have hernia". How in the world does one get hernia in the nipples? What the hell is hernia anyway?*

That a girl would reveal to him such confidential information spoke volumes of how she considered him worthy to confide in. And that too in such a short span of knowing each other. He felt manly, responsible, and proud. Now, he felt more attached to her. *Poor thing! Damn! It must be hurting her a lot! But what sort of an illness is this? Is it permanent? Temporary? Is there a cure?* His thoughts pondered around.

This time the phone rang again and it was his best friend on earth, Sanjay. He had buzzed in to inform that their night outing plan was cancelled.

"Sanjay, there is something I am worried about," said AK pausing, the line sounded very clear now.

"Yea, yea, go on," coaxed Sanjay, wondering as he chuckled within. The list could be endless with AK 'cause of the cultural shocks the guy kept getting from time to time.

"But promise me this will be our secret," said AK, worried about his dear crush, but concerned and wanting to know more about this disease. After repeated promises from Sanjay, he finally relented.

This time it was the boys who easily broke the promise unable to stomach this saucy secret. Like spicy chutney on a hot vada, it was flaming on every tongue that knew Tanya. It broke through the town like wildfire braving the rains and broken phone lines, in the darkest monsoon night. Whoever said boys don't gossip – Lied!

The CA classes were cancelled because of unexpected leakages and AC maintenance work due to heavy showers. He wouldn't have known had it not been for Bhavin who was informed via phone by the administration, before he left for college. After a quick snack of samosas and cola with his friends, Bhavin and Hiten, in the college canteen, he rushed to the station to get back home. He was eager to find out about Tanya and find a cure.

Scurrying up the stairs of the foot bridge, he ran into Shikha at Vidyavihar station. They greeted each other and stepped aside.

"The classes are off today...eh, some ac work going on," said AK.

"Acha. (Good) They know without AC no one will sit," she chuckled "Eh, you had lunch?" she asked him.

"No, just a samosa," he replied honestly.

"You?" he asked. She shook her head, "Not yet."

Should I go for lunch with her? Now? No, maybe not. Have to check on Tanya, he checked himself. The brief awkward silence prevailed. While she stood there with a smile that enthralled him.

"Nice weather, eh," he said trying to keep the conversation on. She smiled again, nodding her head. The cloudy sky cleared briefly and the sun rays glistened on her light brownish hair forming a silhouette like a golden halo. Her pretty smile, her figure hugging white salwar kurta with gold shimmery dupatta pushed Tanya out of his mind. *And again she takes my breath away...pure heaven!* She sent his heart pounding and his tongue knotting.

The siren of the approaching train saved him from further embarrassment. Waving her bye wordlessly, he rushed on. *TANYA! I am coming dear! Don't worry!*

Descending at Mulund from the fast train he had taken from Ghatkopar, he decided to take another fast train from Mulund to Dombivli. Meanwhile, hunger beckoned him to buy a bottle of *Energee* at the station cafeteria.

A Kalyan fast was expected at 2 p.m., so he sauntered on. He suddenly felt a tug on his right shoulder, his bag being pulled from behind. He turned to see Tanya and broke into a wide grin unable to believe the coincidence and relief. The person he was worried about was right there in front of him.

"Tan –"

THWACK! In a flash, the hot burn of a slap landed on his left cheek before he could complete her name. His neck nearly snapped at the force.

THAAP! Before he could react, another landed on his right cheek. His face burning with pain as the blood rushed to his face.

"TANYA!!! Whaatt??!!" exclaimed AK in shock.

"YOU MISERABLE PERVERT! WHO THE HELL DO YOU THINK YOU ARE? YOU WILL TELL SOME LIES AND RUMOURS TO RUIN ME AND GET AWAY WITH THAT? WHAT WRONG DID I DO TO YOU?" she screamed, with tears in her eyes, as she pulled at his T-shirt, tearing it like a tissue paper. A crowd gathered around them.

AK, reeling in fear, was unable to fathom what had gone wrong.

"*Kya hua* sister? *Yeh aapko chhedd raha tha kya*?" (What happened sister, was this guy trying to harm you?) asked a stranger from the crowd. The crowd fast turned into a mob.

Tanya was fuming but she remained quiet. Her nostrils flaring, her eyes red with rage, and rivers of tears flowing down easily.

The crowd was swelling up profusely. Pushing AK amongst the crowd, he heard his own heart pound in his chest amidst that noise. Which man would want to miss an opportunity to prove his heroism to a young buxom lass? And in this crowd all men were eyeing him like hyenas eyeing a carcass.

"*Arrey gheun taak tyaala*," roared another stranger in Marathi. (Hey, take him apart)

Panic gripped him, turning his feet cold as he was being pushed around by the crowd. *I AM SO SCREWED! I AM SOO DEAD!*

It was now clear. First the thrashings and then the questions! And after the beatings, he hoped his brain would be in a position to process their questions.

People kept asking her, and she kept quiet. AK prayed hard. She thundered, *"Iss KAMINEY se poochlo?"* (Ask this SCOUNREL?)

The train to Kalyan arrived.

Tanya and the crowd, young and old alike, were still staring daggers at him. His mind reeled back to the thrashing the thief had got. Strangers in the crowd were staring and cheering each other to land the first punch.

Realizing the situation could embarrassingly get out of hand, Tanya turned and rushed into the train and it immediately chugged off.

"ABBEY BATAA TUNE KYA KIYA?" bellowed a burly, tall man. (HEY, TELL US WHAT YOU DID?) There was no way out. AK was thinking fast.

"Woh meri ex-girlfriend hai. Hamara break up hogaya, maine uspe cheat kiya," (She is my ex-girlfriend. We broke up because I cheated on her) replied AK in one breath, panic-stricken, hoping this lie would spare him broken bones.

Amidst a few gasps and sighs from the crowd, they looked around for her to verify his statement. She was gone. The crowd started dispersing away--some laughing, some heckling him, while some shaking their heads in sadness and some shaking their head in shame.

He bent down to pick his bag. A stinging slap blessed his face as he arose picking his bag. He cursed within as he blinked, shaking to clear his head, expecting to look back at Tanya, but it seemed like some random woman came into focus as his eyes formed the image in front of him.

The middle-aged woman yelled in her shrill voice *"Besharam kahinka. Tum sab mard ek jaise hi hote hain!"* (Shameless fellow. All men are the same!) She walked away in a huff. AK turned around and walked over to the footbridge, eyes downcast, pride slapped out, with low self-esteem and humiliation generously gifted.

He stared at his watch--2:15 pm, July 14, 1998. *I can never forget this date,* he rued shaken as he trudged over to another platform and climbed into a slow Dombivli local. He stepped in and the train moved. He stood on the footboard. Breezy winds offered no help in drying his tears. He kept wiping them from the corner of his eyes.

Why? How? Slowly, his sadness and confusion faded away and was replaced with anger when he guessed what could have happened. He resolved to get to the root of this.

Sanjay was preparing to go to his NIIT coaching classes. He was dressing up when the doorbell started ringing continuously. Irritated, he opened the door.

"AK, hi! I am-" He punched and pounced upon Sanjay like a wounded lion attacking his hunter. Sanjay landed on his back, senseless, pinned to the ground. AK knelt across his chest and shook him violently and ferociously by the collar, growling and grunting.

"You sick psycho! It's all because of you!" AK growled shaking him. Sanjay was taken aback by his friend's behaviour. He pleaded to spare him and tell him all. AK sat up slowly on a chair and told him everything. Sanjay was bewildered.

"I…I told this to Mukesh that day and today morning…Pratap," he confessed and then as an after-thought added apologetically, "But I told them to keep it a secret."

"You bloody rascals! I am done with you guys and all your BULLSHIT! I don't want to see any of you psychos ever again." He retorted and left wiping his tears. Sanjay felt terrible seeing him this upset. He rushed to the phone.

For the next three days, the city had neither seen the sun nor had it seen AK. During the day, his friends rang his doorbell, his phone, but there was no answer. There was only one way to find out. The trio landed up at his flat after dinner and his uncle answered the door.

The trio entered AK's room cautiously. AK was at his study table, the books were strewn over the table and the bed, some clothes strewn across the bed. Unshaven, unkempt hair, he was a mess.

"We are all extremely sorry *yaar*," said Sanjay coming straight to the point.

"I am very busy. I will catch you guys later, yea," AK dismissed their presence coldly. They all sincerely apologized and professed promises of friendship. AK looked on coldly. Pratap and Sanjay quickly blamed Mukesh, who stood there quietly.

He sat down next to AK at the foot of his bed, and said, "Boss, I am very sorry, *yaar*! Almost a year back I asked her out for coffee and she not only rejected me but also taunted me as a classless bumpkin…so *bhai*…this illness was a…you know, right…perfect chance for me."

"But AK, it is not entirely his fault," interrupted Pratap, checking AK's rising temper. "Actually, mate… she said something and you understood something else only," said Pratap as AK looked on silently. "I got the true picture only after you left Sanjay's apartment. We never bothered to check with you either about how you arrived at that conclusion? And…we also fuelled the fire by discussing with others. We know our mistake now and we are here because we are really sorry mate…for not being good friends to you."

"*Yaar*, totally *yaar*!" said Sanjay, raising eyebrows apologetically.

"But that bloody Tanya! What she did was not right *yaar*," said Mukesh sheepishly in a soft tone, before casting his eyes downwards after a stern stare from Sanjay.

"Pratap…what did she say?" AK asked him curiously.

"Look Nivedita told me…Tanya actually said…her mom had gone to the clinic coz she was not well… fever...she said that she told you that she was reading a book called *Chronicles of Narnia* and…AK, pal, you…I don't know how you imagined such things man…you created an illness, and thought that her nipples had hernia," sighed Pratap helplessly, shaking his head and suppressing his laughter.

"*Yaar*, AK, you did something amazing. You broke her arrogance. She acted like a princess everywhere. But now…" said Sanjay, chuckling.

AK was still dazed at what he had heard.

"Whaat? I mean the phone line was bad and I did not hear most of it…so…so…what the HELL!" he grunted, slapping his forehead in horror.

"I heard *Chronicles of Narnia* as…Nipples have Hernia…SCREW ME!" he growled. His friends were in splits.

"Mate, I love your imagination! Thanks to you the entire city is laughing at her! And yea, she is too busy clearing the rumour and so meddling less between Nivedita and me now," said Pratap between his laughs.

"*Yaar*, but please do tell her sorry! I mean it is a mistake and you know Nivedita will feel bad *rey*, please," Sanjay suggested to AK. "Please help this guy clear it out," Sanjay suggested to Pratap, who nodded gravely.

I am a genius! It is all sinking into me now…only NOWWW! AK cursed himself.

"*Bhai*, AK," said Mukesh, standing with folded hands, in front of him, "All those guys she flirted and dumped, rejected and insulted have now found their peace. Thank you." He looked at AK like a serene devotee.

Annoyed, AK pushed him away. Sanjay slapped Mukesh at the back of his head.

"Tomorrow, I will talk to her. Guys, please leave. Please, leave now," he requested. They were taken aback by this request. But Sanjay understood and agreed. He knew AK was not being impolite but he just wanted to be left alone.

After they left, he sat on the floor dejected, burying his face in his hands. The enormity of his foolishness outweighed the burden of his intelligence, scaring him. Embarrassed, he shook his head in disbelief.

With a sense of complete loss sinking in, he got up and went to the mirror. Staring hard, examining every inch of his face, his frame. He massaged his slapped cheeks.

Speaking aloud in hindi *"Tujhse bada chutiya nahin dekha!"* (Never seen a bigger idiot than you!) He slapped himself hard on his face.

CHAPTER 11

*R*ecovering from an injury is easier for the body, but how does the heart recover from the scars of humiliation? It's even worse when it is self-inflicted. He was gutted. His stupidity hurt Tanya and nearly got him mobbed. He wouldn't wish that for anyone, any girl. Recollecting Mukesh's statement made him feel even worse. *It didn't matter to me what people thought of her. She had done me no harm...yet my stupidity,* he sighed as he mused.

AK learnt it the hard way and so he needed time.... time to forget and time to heal, and the courage to face the world again. But how was his uncle to know. Suspecting that his nephew had bunked CA classes and college for close to a week, he enquired of his nephew's well-being. His nephew had been irritable for the last few days, and it showed no signs of waning.

Mumbai has been a nightmare for me so far! He rued. After a brief pause, he corrected himself, *no, I have become my own nightmare. I should stop all these nonsense fantasies. I am not meant to date. I suck at this. I don't understand women. I am a major screw up in that department! I best focus on studies and it is best I be more respectful towards women...just don't think! Hiten was right. Oh my goodness! My other friends must never know,* he concluded.

The phone rang with the same distinct ISD ring. It was his parents. They enquired about his well-being, he lied. They enquired about how his studies and classes were going, he lied again. They spoke for a bit longer. They told him that he should call his sister at least once in a month. She had sent him a rakhi by post from her boarding school. He promised to call her and kept the phone. He missed his sister, and their sibling quarrels and chats.

It's easy to lie, but they just want to believe lies as the truth, he sighed. He had barely sat down on his chair when the phone rang again. It was his friends from the classes. He gave them an excuse of fever and food poisoning.

"If I am ok tonight, then I will come tomorrow. Else I will be there day after," he said to Bhavin. He wanted to keep the phone soon.

"Er, Nehal wants to talk," said Bhavin, handing the phone to her.

"I am getting a second call," he made an excuse and cut the call. He was still in no mood to talk to anyone. He knew Nehal would be upset by this, but he just wanted to be away from women.

The phone rang again. He did not answer it. After two minutes, it rang again. He had no hope that Tanya would call him. Ever. The continuous ring beckoned, forcing him to answer the call.

"Hello?" he answered.

"Hello, AK! Been trying since long mate…you ok?" enquired Pratap.

"Yea I was out…eh, just got home," he lied.

"I am at Nivedita's house…eh, you remember what we spoke about right?" Pratap asked him.

"Hmm, yea."

"She is here…I will pass the phone to her, ok?" said Pratap, and handed over the phone to Tanya.

AK pursed his lips and closed his eyes tight shut, expecting another barrage of abuses.

"Hello," she muttered.

"Tanya, I am extremely sorry. I am terribly, terribly sorry. Please forgive me, I deserve the worst. I am the biggest idiot alive. Your anger is justified. I hope you can forgive me with time," he spoke in a soft tone with his eyes tight shut as if she stood in front of him. He had never felt this humbled in his entire life. He heard some minor noise in the background.

"Pal, AK!"

"Pratap? Was I talking to her?"

"Yes, you were. Ok then, I will keep now."

"I am really sorry, *yaar*! Please tell her," said an apologetic AK.

Pratap agreed and kept the phone. AK sat on the edge of his bed and let out a heavy sigh.

Yea, I never thought I will be ruining her peace of mind this way. And ruining my name too...I jinxed my own chance with a hot chick and told her sorry at the end! I am an idiot of epic proportions! AARRGHH! He growled.

Apprehension and anxiety kept him company for the week and so did insomnia. On Monday morning, he left home for college. Hopefully, time would help him heal. Bhavin had rung the night before, informing him that Nehal was upset with him for rudely cutting the call. AK felt bad about it but couldn't care less. He was yet to get over his recent bad news.

On reaching college he learnt it was friendship day!

His two friends explained it to him. Yellow was for just friendship, pink was for special friendship, while red was for dearest friendship.

"Good, I am not buying any of it. Not needed!" AK announced curtly.

"What are you saying? Not for Shikha?" asked Bhavin curiously.

"Forget it, man! I am here to study...eh, so are you. So, forget it," said AK curtly.

"*Wah*! Determination boss!" smirked Hiten. The peon came and announced that there wouldn't be classes for the rest of the day.

"*Chalo*, let us go!" said Hiten (Come on, let us go!). Excitedly, the duo rushed down to the campus. AK reluctantly followed. Many girls and guys were dressed their best. While AK, compared to most of the others, wasn't. Hiten and Bhavin were not only well dressed but well prepared. They also had friendship bands.

As they ambled along the campus, they bumped into Sanjay and Mukesh. Hiten introduced Bhavin to his cousin and Mukesh introduced them to Sanjay.

"Unbelievable!" remarked AK, hiding his irritation. They nodded. Sanjay felt guilty about the whole episode with Tanya. He pulled AK aside and assured him the entire embarrassment would remain a secret for life.

"Don't worry, Mukesh won't tell anything to Hiten. Please *yaar*, we are all really sorry. Don't be so upset. Cheer up," said Sanjay, trying to console him.

"Here," Sanjay thrust the ribbons into AK's hand. AK looked away, disinterested. "Look, we are engineering guys and friendship day is the worst day of our lives... our college is like a desert compared to this oasis," said Sanjay smiling.

Someone tugged at AK's shoulder bag. He turned around, she looked ever so beautiful.

"Hi! The classes are on today, right?" Shikha asked him, extending her hand with a pink ribbon. She tried tying it around his wrist before he could say anything. It didn't fit. She chuckled and tied it on his ring finger.

"Em, yea, I guess so," replied AK, breaking into a smile.

"Happy Friendship Day!" she said and smiled. *Ah, that smile! Takes my breath away...again! She has a tiny beauty spot above her upper lip...wow! She is such an angel,* he mused.

"Hey, just a second!" AK quickly tied a pink ribbon to her finger and wished her too.

"You have a very pretty smile!" he murmured, innocently, complimenting her. She blushed. Some distance away, her friends were waiting for her. "Eh, ok, I will see you," she waved. He too pointed at his friends and smiled, and said a bye.

AK's friends flashed their naughty smiles and began teasing him. As they kept walking, many girls tied pink and red ribbons to AK, girls he had barely seen in the college, and he too reciprocated. He was pleasantly surprised.

Hiten and Bhavin had no such luck. They ended up giving theirs to AK. All his fingers were covered to tip with pink and red ribbons.

I did not get a single yellow ribbon. Good, I don't like yellow! Perhaps, AK, you are not such a bad guy after all. Today was a welcome change. Forget the Tanya incident like a bad nightmare, AK! Apologize to her again if that helps! He consoled himself.

Later on, he removed all friendship bands, except Shikha's, and happily put them in his bag.

It was routine to do combined studies at Sarvodaya after their CA classes finished for the day. Dimple and Bhavin were happy to see AK back, but Nehal looked upset.

AK assumed she was faking it. The plan was to practice 'Functional Derivatives'.

"So, how you all been?" asked AK as they made their way to the hall.

"We are all ok!" said Dimple but raised her eyebrows and pointed to Nehal, she was quiet all this while.

"What happened to her?" asked AK, "How are you? No friendship bands today, eh?" he teased.

"You are such a child!" she retorted.

"Yes mummyji," he replied, "That I am." He pointed to one pink ribbon.

"Guess who?" he asked playfully, raising his eyebrows.

"Bhavin, of course," replied Nehal. He shook his head.

"Shikha?" asked Dimple. AK blushed and nodded. "Really?" she asked, looking at Bhavin. He smiled.

"No way!" remarked Nehal, shocked. "*Waah*! That's a huge progress. Congrats!" she added.

AK threw his hand over himself and patted his own back. Dimple and Bhavin laughed. Nehal pinched his arm.

"You owe me a treat mister! This is all because of me," she demanded.

"Come on! No way! Ask Bhavin, he was there," smiled AK. Both the girls turned to look at him and he nodded and narrated what happened.

"Oh by the way…" he handed out two dairy milk chocolates to both the girls, "Happy Friendship Day!"

Nehal shook her head and withdrew and folded her hands behind her back.

"What? You don't want it?" asked AK, surprised.

"No!" she replied snobbishly, "Shikha must have given it to you." "You keep it," she added.

"Stop being silly Nehal. I wouldn't give that to you. I already had it. I got these for you two. Ask him," he said stubbornly. Dimple winked at AK hinting that Nehal was just pulling his leg.

"I am still angry with you," she said. He sighed with indifference. She pinched his arm.

"You were so RUDE! You cut the call when I came on the phone to ask you about your health," she said slapping his back. He grimaced in pain.

"Oh that! I am sorry about that," he apologized and he meant it. It occurred to him how comfortable he was around Nehal and Dimple. He liked their company.

"I was not…feeling well…you know," he said softly.

"Why do you think we called?" she shot back, grunting and twisting her lips. He acted indifferent but he was touched by what she said. He immediately checked his feelings and mused, *only if she knew the truth!*

"Oh, break it you two," said an annoyed Dimple. "She is being childish as always," she complained.

They reached Sarvodaya hall and sat down to study Math. Functional Derivatives were malfunctioning his brains. AK couldn't understand these complex problems but Nehal was patient with him. He envied her prowess in Maths. He noticed her nurturing and caring attitude towards him as she patiently taught them. He considered himself lucky to be her friend. He could just be himself with her.

He wondered, *why the hell am I after all that love and other nonsense with other girls? It's just better to be friends. It is much better. This moment, right here, feels real, feels good.*

It was close to 8 p.m. and the girls had to head home. Sauntering towards the auto stand near the station, AK told them about his three friends in Dombivli who spend time with him on weekends. Only Nehal seemed interested in listening to him, while Bhavin was chatting away with Dimple in Gujarati. When Nehal interrupted Dimple, the topic of discussion changed to Bollywood.

"Tell me…who is your favourite actress?" Dimple asked AK and Bhavin.

"Aishwarya Rai, she is gorgeous!" exclaimed AK, breaking into a wide smile.

"For me, Kajol…she is beautiful, but yes, Aishwarya is more beautiful," said Bhavin.

"Aishwarya is not an actress," grunted Nehal, "Stop drooling, please! It is cheap."

"*Acha*, you feel Shikha looks better than Aishwarya Rai?" said Dimple. (Acha - Alright). Nehal and Bhavin looked at him for an answer.

He said with a smirk, "She is my Aishwarya Rai."

"Oohh, what an answer," said Dimple, shaking her head. Bhavin and Nehal chuckled.

"By the way, I am sure Shikha likes you a lot. I have seen the way she looks at you. I will tell you when to ask her out," said Nehal. Hearing this, AK was quiet.

AK looked at her wondering if pursuing Shikha was the right thing to do. Considering his recent experiences, it was dangerous. He had almost made up his mind, no girl was worth pursuing anymore. He had to focus on his studies but he decided to break that news to her some other day.

"Eh…sure thing, I will wait for your cue," said AK with a wink and a smile.

They reached the auto stand and climbed into the first auto in the stand as per the norm. Before leaving, Dimple and Nehal both gave them pink friendship bands and wished them. The boys were surprised. Bhavin put it in his bag, while AK slipped it into his denim pockets.

CHAPTER 12

His gaze fell on the shops selling rakhi paraphernalia. Raksha Bandhan beckoned his brotherly affections. He missed his younger sister, Akhila, and felt a trifle guilty for not calling her. As soon as he alighted from the auto, below his apartment, he made his way to the nearest STD booth. He phoned her boarding school and spoke at length to her heart's content.

Nothing like hearing the voice of your loved ones after a hard day, smiled AK as he made his way home. Her handmade rakhi had reached him a day before Raksha Bandhan.

He loved the rakhi. Made with thick red and saffron threads, it felt strong. He missed her. He missed their silly fights and their late-night horror movie sessions. Terrified, she'd hide under the sheets, while he sat upright pretending to be brave watching the scary parts with his eyes closed.

Sanjay rang to enquire about AK's knee, he had slipped and fallen on the Dombivli station platform and hurt himself. Luckily, fellow onlookers took him to a nearby clinic. AK escaped with minor bruises and a swollen right knee. So he took a day off to recuperate. Sanjay promised to meet him by noon. "What brings you here? Skipped college today? Where's Mukesh?" enquired AK. His friend rolled up his sleeve and showed him the rakhi on his hand.

"Ah, Raksha bandhan! Yea...good, please help tie that rakhi on my hand," said AK pointing towards the rakhi on the table. "Akhila sent it for me," he smiled. Sanjay tied it on AK's wrist.

"Mukesh is a Gujju, *bhai,*" he sighed. "He has enough real sisters to tie him rakhis. I have only one real one, Gayatri, Mohan *chitappa's* daughter, but the rest, friends turned rakhi sisters, I am cursed! That's why I came to hide at your place today" he lamented, shaking his head with a shrug. Mohan *chitappa* was Sanjay's dad's younger brother.

"Come on man! How can you say cursed? You are very mean. They really respect you and want you as a brother for life," snapped AK, offended by Sanjay's response.

Sanjay jumped off his chair "Boss! Enough of respect! NRI heroes like you will not understand the pain we *desi* engineering guys go through, Bloody hell! As it is, college is dry. There are only some 3 or 4 girls in class who get treated like royalty by everybody. And the worst part! Even there you get bro-zoned! Not even friend-zoned, bloody hell, bro-zoned! This screw up is only in our country. Bloody nonsense *yaar*, just because there is one Raksha bandhan. These cunning girls think that they can make guys their brothers! And BOSS then there are guys like you...'NRI boyfriend material with that English accent and that cool factor'. No girls want to make you their brother EVER! Why? Because they are plotting to catch you through idiot rakhi brothers like me!" ranted off Sanjay in one breath, waving his hands wildly in the air. He sat back on the chair, grumbling.

AK threw up his hands in surrender. Laughing quietly, not wanting to offend him.

The phone rang and AK answered it. Sanjay was gesturing, waving his hands. AK paid no heed. It was Lakshmi aunty, Sanjay's mom.

"He is here only aunty," said AK, handing over the phone to Sanjay. He looked at AK angrily.

He told his mom not to tell anyone where he was today. He told her in plain Tamil he was hiding at AK's place and he did not want to be disturbed. She handed over the phone to his friend who had come home.

"You! Come over, I am here at AK's," said Sanjay, relieved. "Yea, just a sec," Sanjay passed the phone to AK. It was Mukesh.

"Hi dude," greeted AK

"Hey, Tanya wants to tie you a rakhi," Mukesh said seriously. "You are at home, right? Pratap will come home with her."

"Shut up idiot! Now I will tell everyone she has HIV!" irritated, AK shot back instantly. Mukesh couldn't stop laughing at the other end. He confessed that he was pranking AK and they hung up.

The four boys were chatting away undisturbed at AK's apartment on various topics like IT and how upcoming technologies like mobile phones becoming affordable would make pagers obsolete. How electronic mails would increase the workload on the new generation. Most importantly, they were eagerly waiting for the first cyber café to open in the city.

The phone rang, interrupting their banter. Mukesh and Sanjay frowned and looked at Pratap, worried.

"*Arrey* I did not tell anyone...even Nivedita doesn't know I'm here...I swear," said Pratap, pinching his adam's apple. AK chuckled as he leaned over from the bed and picked up the phone on the table.

"Hello," she greeted.

"Hello, hi Nehal," he answered, "Hey, what a surprise!"

"You didn't come today?" she asked, concerned. He told her briefly about his accident.

"Ahh nice excuse! Bunking classes on Raksha Bandhan, eh?" she teased him. He chuckled. In the background, he could hear Bhavin and Dimple chuckle.

"It is ok! Shikha will get the rakhi tomorrow," she said in a serious tone. He could hear their other two friends laugh again.

"Heh," he grunted, "Nice joke!"

"We are serious! Even we are bringing our rakhis tomorrow," she teased.

He drew a long breath and sighed, "Alright, cool but hey expect no gifts." He heard them laughing on the other side. He chuckled with relief. Sanjay, sitting there, figured and guffawed in anticipation of AK joining him in the 'bro-zone' creed. Nehal heard it and upon enquiry was told by AK that the trio were at his home. He passed their regards to the trio and theirs to his friends in Ghatkopar.

The interesting statistics lecture in college finished by midday. The friends were in mood for some coffee. *Statistics looks easy, phew!* AK mused with relief.

Craving for cold coffee, they went to their 'adda' (Hangout). Unexpectedly they were there, "What the hell? You both are here every other day!" exclaimed AK in surprise.

"*Yaar* we missed you so much, so…" replied Mukesh with a smirk and half a shrug. Sanjay smiled at AK.

"Come, let's go," said Sanjay getting up from the stool and straightening his pants.

"Hiten, you also come along. We are going to get some *gyan* for AK," said Mukesh, winking and chuckling. Bhavin looked on clueless. He assumed this wasn't for him, but they insisted he join them. Bhavin wiggled out with the excuse of 'work at home' and avoided '*asli gyan*' (true knowledge). Mukesh asked Hiten to come along, he declined citing work but after some insistence he agreed. Mukesh clarified the address of the place from Hiten before entering the auto. And then the four of them hailed two autos to Chembur.

They got off on the main road beside a crowded street. Mukesh signalled them to follow him. Their final destination was through this teeming crowd. People were brushing past each other as they walked by. The chaos did not seem to bother him anymore. He periodically checked his back pocket to ensure his wallet was still with him. He was relieved but cautious. Mukesh and Sanjay lead the way, with AK and Hiten trailing behind them. Towards the end of that chaotic crowded street on the right-hand side corner, the four boys stopped. AK would never have come to this side of town without his friends. Unfamiliar places made him uncomfortable, yet here he stood with his three friends.

"Sirjee dus rupaye ka show aur tees rupaye ka show aiye dekhiye!" (Sir, a show for Rs.10 and a show for Rs.30, come and see) announced the man. He was a scrawny man with a baked complexion and scruffy hairdo calling out to people standing outside what looked like a normal shop. He wore a thin, wrinkled red tie, a stained off-white shirt, faded brown trousers, and worn out brown shoes that looked older than him.

AK, who had a taste for finer things in life, detested his appearance. The scrawny man's gaze fell upon the four of them through his cheap, tinted, large imitation shades. Like a hawk that saw its prey, he grinned at them showing off his *paan-ghutka* polished teeth. *I am sure we don't have to go there,* mused AK.

"This is the place...follow me," said Mukesh, pointing at the shop. AK complied, hiding his reluctance. As he entered he noted the name on the aged name board 'Saraswati Devi Video Parlour'. They entered the shop.

At the entrance stood an unmanned counter--a four feet high dark brown wooden podium that looked like it had seen the history of the pre-independence era. Up on the wall there were photos of three Goddesses and Ganapati with incense sticks lit in front of them, a common feature in most shops run by Hindus.

At the far end of the counter was a door that was slightly ajar. A foot away from the door was a flight of aged and creaky wooden stairs alongside the door. AK tried but couldn't see anything. He could faintly hear some music and noises. The cheaply attired scrawny man who greeted them outside came up from behind them.

"*Kya saab, bahut dino ke baad dikhe. Sirjee char* balcony? English?" (What sir, seeing you after so long. Sir, four balcony seats? English?) he enquired enthusiastically. Mukesh agreed and dropped the money on the table. He opened a small booklet, half the size of his palm and scribbled something on four pages. Tearing these off, he handed them to Mukesh. He clasped them in his hand and ran up the creaky stairs behind the usher, who went in first, and the others followed him. Upon reaching atop the short flight of stairs, they found a dozen people sitting quietly on the floor like comfortable strangers. The four were guided to their seats by the usher.

The 'balcony' seats were actually a bench. The only bench in the room! They sat down and placed their bags on their laps. He looked around. There were no posters or any imagery on the walls. A minute later, a few more people walked into the room and joined the others on the floor. Mukesh enquired when the show would start. The man gestured five minutes with his palm. AK sat and surveyed the place. Gloominess hung heavy in the air. The crowd on the floor looked like ruffians and manual labourers to AK.

Light flickered from the TV set as it turned on inside the dark room. The dimly lit bulb was switched on and promptly switched off after a quick head count. There was a 30-inch magnifier attached to the TV. The show started. It took AK completely by surprise. The movie was called 'Naughty Girls'.

"*Yaar*, AK, this is *gyan, asli gyan* for you," whispered Sanjay, nudging AK. (Asli Gyan - Real Knowledge)

"Enjoy the show pal, any doubts we'll discuss after the show," whispered Mukesh with a chuckle.

"After this you should not have any doubts!" chuckled Hiten.

"Thanks guys," said AK in a hushed tone. He couldn't believe his friends would do this for him.

He was surprised to know that the movie dived straight into the plot. AK's excitement and interest were reaching higher planes with each passing minute. He experienced surprise and shock. He had heard of sex and discussed sex but never seen it. It was the first time he was watching all kinds of sexual activities, and the girl looked pretty. She was going on with one man first, then another man joined in, then another woman joined in, and very soon the entire screen had several men and women doing it in a park. His jaw dropped open, his mind was going haywire. He did not know whom to look at and where. It was a full-blown orgy. *Porn is awesome!* He could feel the stiffness in his jeans.

Men sitting on the floor got up and went through a door in the corner of the room. The pungent smell shot through the room and AK's nose squirmed on his face. But the interesting screenplay of the movie fixed his attention back to the screen. The odour did not distract him anymore. AK was so engrossed in the movie that time went by quickly. The movie finished in an hour. The four boys were the last to leave since they were sitting in the 'balcony'. And of course, AK's high interest levels that kept him glued to his seat even after the credits rolled, expecting something more.

CHAPTER 13

"**M**an, it was amazing *yaar*! I feel like going again," said AK, recalling his first porn movie experience. Hiten smiled.

"Ok, after the next lecture," said Hiten.

"*Yaar*, can I come? Please?" requested Bhavin. AK shook his head, teasing Bhavin. "Not for kids!" he said, chuckling.

"Let him come! Let's see if this baby can become a man or remain just a boy!" said Hiten, chuckling.

After the lecture finished, Hiten insisted that they go for a coffee. Bhavin readily agreed. As they got up to leave, AK's eyes met Jasmeet's, she smiled. Jasmeet was tall at 5'9" and always elegantly attired and graceful.

There is some sincerity in her smile He smiled back too.

"Going?" she asked.

He nodded in reply. She raised her hand gesturing him to wait. Stepping over to his side and placing her notebook on the table.

"Show me your proxy sign on this and I will try to copy it...to sign your attendance for you," she smiled. AK gladly signed on her book.

"Hmm...looks easy," she smiled.

"Thanks, eh...really, I mean it," said AK, smiling gratefully. Hiten and Bhavin were watching all this from near the door.

"Hey! Just thanks won't do. Take me for coffee someday," said Jasmeet smiling.

"Of course, I would love that. I am going now. Bye," smiled AK, waving her bye, and quickly dashed out to join his friends who soon began teasing him.

Wriggling and crawling through the traffic and human crowd they reached the spot. The boys stepped out.

"AK, you go buy the tickets for all, I'll settle the auto," suggested Hiten.

Bhavin looked at the name board written in bold red letters in Hindi and below that in English, 'Saraswati Devi Video Parlour'. He looked at Hiten with curiosity who was flipping through his wallet. AK explained to Bhavin about the visual treats available inside. Bhavin chuckled eagerly, ready, and told him this was his first experience.

"I am happy to hear that. I thought I was the only one," teased AK.

AK walked into the video parlour, Bhavin followed. The two stepped inside. He ordered three tickets for an English show. They turned around to see Hiten, but could not spot him. They finally saw him, and he gestured them to go upstairs and he would join them soon. AK told the man in the red tie about Hiten's ticket, gesturing towards Hiten who was outside.

"*Aap ticket leke jao, unko bhejdenge hum…no pirablem,*" said the man (You take the ticket and go, he will be sent upstairs…no problem).

AK and Bhavin climbed up the stairs and took their seats on the 'balcony' while the poorer mortals sat on the ground. Before light flickered on the magnified TV screen, a sudden burst of commotion downstairs distracted them from the screen.

"*Tumhi bharatmaatechya sanskrutichi vaat lavtaay!! Kiti vela sangitla naav badla!*" (You are trying to ruin Bharatmata's sanskriti! How many times have I told you to change the name!) thundered someone in Marathi.

"*Heech shikwan milali ahey ka tumhala?*" (Is this how you were brought up?) screamed another.

Blows, punches, and kicks rained on some helpless pleading souls.

"*Nalaayaka…tujhi himmat kashi jhali devanchi naava vaaprun ashya goshti chaalavnyachi…dharma aani tarunaahi cha satyanaash!"* (Bloody scoundrel! How dare you run such things in holy names...corrupting religion...corrupting youth) growled the man.

"Maaf karo humein...please maaf kardo iss baar," (Please forgive me... please forgive me this time) pleaded someone. The meek voice throbbing with tears and fears was instantly recognizable – the man in the tie! AK and Bhavin looked at each other in fear. Where was Hiten? They knew he wouldn't be able to survive it.

Overwhelmed by the sounds coming from below, some people took the risk and ran down the stairs. It is true what they say—a picture speaks a thousand words when you see it, but who knew the reverse could be frighteningly true—a few pleading words could summon a thousand horrifying pictures too.

AK looked at Bhavin, words stuck in his throat with fear. Had the moral police stomped the yard? Something was terribly wrong at the entrance. They were terrified. A few men got up and ran down the stairs to safety. There was some commotion, they could hear people getting beat up. But where was Hiten? AK prayed for his friend's safety.

Tension darted in the air and so did their anxieties. Within seconds the crescendo of violence was interrupted by thuds of feet running upstairs. The dim light that cracked from the smelly toilet door helped them see the silhouettes of three burly men, armed with sticks, in the dreaded darkness of the room.

"Tumhi ikdech basla aahat! Bekaar kuthle! Thamba... daakhavtoch tumhala aata!"

(You are all sitting here only! Bloody losers! Wait, we'll give you a free show!) he roared in Marathi. This was the same voice they had all heard before.

They rained blows on people sitting there. The victims' cries for help and forgiveness only fuelled hatred from the attackers. The two boys were horrified.

They certainly had not expected a live entertainment where they themselves were about to end up as victims any second. Bhavin resigned to being beat up.

Bhavin and AK were seated in the corner near the semi-open stairs fenced by a short wooden railing, in a reflex move AK nudged him and JUMPED! Luckily landing on even steps. Bhavin followed but nearly lost his balance because of his bag and fell on AK. Quickly, gaining composure, they burst open through the door and ran out, knocking down an armed man guarding the entrance of the parlour. He fell, screaming and hurling abuses at them, clutching his right ankle.

Running from a dark room into the sunlight nearly blinded them. And for almost two seconds, AK slowed down, squinting his eyes, unable to see. In that moment of vulnerability, someone grabbed his bag, and pulled with such mighty force that his right shoulder and neck felt like it would snap at the whiplash and he almost lost his balance. He turned around to look. He glimpsed Bhavin struggling to get free from the ruffian's grasp.

The next moment, a slap exploded in AK's ear and another one made his right cheek burn as he felt his head turn with the impact. The intensity of this unexpected attack muted AK. Half blind, and in terror, he swung his left arm wildly. His fist jabbed into his assailant's neck. He was free now.

AK paused, gathering his wits, looked around, and saw a guy yelping on the floor. That was his assailant. Desperation of self-defence had driven that punch effectively!

AK rushed over to Bhavin's assailant and pushed him with full force. The guy stumbled and fell. AK's powerful kick on his face snapped his head back and the man fell lifelessly. Bhavin broke free. He immediately gathered courage and kicked his assailant in between the legs. Regaining consciousness, instantly, the fallen assailant squealed in pain.

They picked the rest of their belongings strewn about due to the scuffle and dashed into the crowd. They nearly knocked off some onlookers. They ran as fast as their legs would carry them. The entire crowd on the street gathered outside the parlour watching the ruckus like a street play. This made it easier for them to flee.

AK and Bhavin now reached the end of the crowded street and slowed their pace, gasping for breath. AK's bag strap snapped. He quickly prevented it from hitting the ground. Bhavin and AK surveyed their damages. Bhavin's glasses were broken at the bridge, left lens cracked, but his bag was fine, just some minor scratches. There was a good three-inch long tear near the shoulder strap of AK's bag. The goon had pulled hard. Fortunately for him, his WESTAR wrist watch was fine, not a scratch!

"Baap, rey baap! Aa su thayu?" (Father, Oh father! What was that?) exclaimed Bhavin, bewildered, panting and his hands on his hips.

"That's a joke isn't it?" scorned AK, equally indignant.

Bhavin lowered his head. "Hiten?" Bhavin asked, gesturing with his open palm, realizing their friend was not around.

"Damn! I hope he is not held there with them." AK was dismayed. They glanced around for their friend. He was nowhere to be seen.

"He is there?" asked Bhavin, concerned.

"Maybe…but I am not going back there ever in my life, eh," said AK, shaking his head and waving his hands in desperation.

"Yes, me too," nodded Bhavin.

"Bah…leave it, he will come…maybe they will tear his clothes," said AK, contemplating sadly.

"Break his hands or legs, er…and he will come," added Bhavin, still panting with his hands on his hips.

"Yea, we just wait here," agreed AK showing a thumbs up. They looked at each other and gazed back into the street and again reluctantly.

AK decided, as friends, he had to go back inside for their friend. Bhavin would wait at this spot, in case Hiten turned up. But if AK were to get injured in the process of rescuing a battered Hiten, at least, that way, there would be one guy in good health to get the other two guys to the hospital or call for help if required. Bhavin agreed to the plan. As AK started to head back into the street, a familiar voice called out loudly them, "AK...Bhavin...AK...Bhavin!"

Both of them looked around to see where Hiten's voice was coming from. Like a white flag on a stick, a fair palm on a thin hand was waving at them. He was far across, on the opposite side of the road, inside an auto.

Bhavin and AK quickly ran across the road and jumped into the waiting auto.

"Where were you huh?" asked Bhavin, concerned, as the auto drove off.

"The auto guy had no change. So, I went from shop to shop and finally got it," replied Hiten innocently.

"Really? That's it?" asked AK in disbelief.

"Yea...that's it," said Hiten nodding vigorously and he cast his eyes downwards. Bhavin and AK both sat alongside in the auto, with Hiten sitting between them. AK and Bhavin sat silently with sullen faces.

"So, what really happened guys?" asked Hiten.

"Nothing much re...one of those guys owned the shop. So, he just came to inspect his business," said AK in a casual tone.

"And thank his customers...he thanked us," added Bhavin.

"Oh really? Nice! How?" said Hiten, bursting out with laughter.

"Like this!" said AK, and WHACK! WHACK! Both of them gave him two tight slaps.

Hiten went home immediately after they returned to college, while AK and Bhavin made their way to Bharat

Café in Ghatkopar. Bhavin walked in first, with AK behind him. Bhavin sat down at the first table, while AK went straight ahead towards a door written 'AC Dining'. Bhavin was surprised that his friend always preferred the chill of an air-conditioned room to everything else.

"What is this *yaar*, there you sit in smelly place with no AC and watch movie…and here you want AC?" Bhavin jibed at him.

Leaning over from across the table, AK whispered, "After getting so royally thrashed in full public view…I can't believe you are asking me this. At least for today, I hope somehow I can hide my face some place where people will not see me so easily."

Bhavin knew his friend had a very valid point. However, keeping an eye on cost was his second nature. He was already worried about the bill, even though his friend wouldn't let him pay.

"From today onwards we will never mention this incident ever again and never go to Chembur, ever again," AK said, and repeated himself again. Bhavin nodded. AK settled the bill. The food cost twice more than the non-AC food menu.

They both inspected their damages. Bhavin's shirt had a coin sized hole near his right ribs. AK suggested it would be best to skip classes for that day. Bhavin rejected the idea.

"It is ok. I am not skipping classes for this," Bhavin spoke with resolve. AK noted his friend's English had improved considerably, minus the accent, the grammar was often correct.

"You shouldn't, else Dimple will go crazy missing you," teased AK. He jabbed at AK playfully.

"I need to tell you something first," said Bhavin.

"Ok, shoot," said AK

"I talk to Dimple in the evenings," said Bhavin.

"You mean after the classes too?" exclaimed AK. He nodded.

"Dare you say anything about today! I will beat you to pulp," AK warned. Bhavin assured him of their promise.

He told AK that they had been talking on the phone in the evenings for a few minutes before going to bed. AK was surprised to know this development. They stepped out of the restaurant and paused in front of a nearby *paan beedi* shop. AK ordered his cigarette.

Bhavin informed him that she suggested that he try out casual clothing such as denims and cargos, and change his glasses to a metallic frame.

"I see, that's… interesting!" said AK, stroking his chin.

"So, what else did you guys discuss, eh?" he teased.

"Come on, *yaar*…nothing," replied Bhavin, blushing.

"Does Nehal know this?" he asked.

"I don't know…but I don't think so," replied Bhavin with half a shrug.

AK lit up and puffed his cigarette.

"Let's go to their college," Bhavin suggested sheepishly.

"Their college?" asked AK, checking if he heard right.

"*Arrey*, please *yaar* she told me to come…you also come please," requested Bhavin. (Arrey –Hey)

AK declined, he was fed up of being slapped around and now the last thing he wanted was to get slapped in front of a girls' college by some cruel act of fate. Bhavin kept insisting and AK stubbornly refused.

"Please! I am begging you my friend," said Bhavin, and proceeded to bend down.

"Stop it! Why today? Look at you…me…your glasses are broken, my bag torn and you want go there?" AK asked him, frustrated. Bhavin removed his glasses and put them in his bag.

"I don't know…she said some surprise," replied Bhavin, gesturing with half a shrug and open palms. He kept on insisting. Finally, AK agreed and they decided to cover the distance on foot since college was a walkable distance from the Café.

As they reached the college, the name board read SPN Doshi College. He pointed this out to Bhavin and he reminded him that the girls had mentioned SNDT. Bhavin told him the college affiliation was to SNDT University, hence the reference. The explanation and name did not matter anymore to the duo. They could see plenty of young women decked up in sarees and jewellery.

"Huh, I think their saree day is today," said Bhavin.

They decided to stand near the juice stall, adjacent to a small café, which was diagonally opposite to the gated entrance of the college. Hopefully, they would be spotted by their friends here.

Interesting, mused AK, *looks like this is one day where all plain Pavitras look like lovely Leenas! Quite good! I am glad I followed him!*

A tap on his shoulder broke his reverie, he turned to see a gorgeous lady smiling at him. His mouth gaped and he quickly checked himself. Her dimpled smile was unmistakable.

"Hi Dimple!' he mumbled. She greeted them both. Attired in a shimmery burgundy chiffon saree with gold sequins, make up, and matching gold jewellery, her hair flowing straight and left open. She was stunning!

"You look –"

"Beautiful!" said Bhavin, interrupting AK, and he merely nodded, stepping aside and allowing her to move closer to Bhavin.

"Nehal?" asked AK, and a familiar playful slap on his arm forced him to glance to his right. In a black and ashen silver coloured chiffon saree with silver sequins and matching silver jewellery, her magnificent radiance froze his eyes to this very moment that took his breath away. Straight open hair curling only at the ends, partly falling over her shoulder, dropped his jaw open. This gorgeous beauty nearly buckled his knees, mesmerizing him.

Raising her hand and swiftly snapping her fingers twice in front of his face embarrassingly snapped him back to reality.

"Uh hi," he greeted her meekly, "We were just eh –"

"Ahem…so, how am I looking?" asked Nehal, blushing.

Forcing himself to speak "Oh amazing! Both of you," he replied, showing a thumbs-up, raising his eyebrows in amazement. Nehal had taken him by surprise, so much so that his breath almost failed him and words refused to drift from his lips.

AK found his breath and quickly relaxed himself. Both the boys complimented the ladies on their exquisite taste and appearance. AK could only mumble while Bhavin generously complimented.

The girls told them they would be skipping CA classes that day, as they were hanging around with their college friends, a few of whom were introduced to AK and Bhavin. Post some small talk, they bid the girls farewell and left.

On his way back, in the train, AK couldn't help wondering the start and the end of his day. *Phew! Today Nehal ben became Nehal BABE! My goodness! And how? My heart stopped beating…I couldn't speak! Wow! Still can't believe it!* A smile played on his lips. He was glad that his two female friends were not merely pretty but also intelligent and elegant. He had a new found admiration for them.

A few days later at the classes AK stepped out during the break while Bhavin stayed indoors chatting with a friend. AK greeted Shikha and spoke to her as she stood with Nehal and Dimple. With Nehal around the awkwardness of starting a conversation was absent. Shikha hung around with them briefly and went back to her bench mate.

"Why do you get tongue tied?" asked Dimple. AK shrugged.

"You feel guilty...that what you are doing is not right?" asked Nehal.

"No...not that. I fear that I will lose this ability to talk to her...you know, like now. We won't be friends if she rejects me," he said.

"You are shy, AK," said Dimple, holding out her hand and resting another on her hip.

"What do you expect? Besides my sister and cousins and a few friends...you are the only girls I have actually spoken to," said AK, sitting on the parapet wall, folding his hands on his lap.

Nehal gasped and covered her mouth.

"School?" asked Dimple.

"Boys only," replied AK.

"Our schools were co-ed but college only girls," chuckled Nehal. Another girl approached them and began chatting to Dimple in Gujrati. AK's gaze wandered off and fell on Shikha. She was sitting next to a lanky guy he had seen around the classes a few times before, surrounded by a few of her female friends.

Helplessly envy pricked him like a needle. He reminded himself of his pledge, he sighed. *Why am I not able to forget the feelings I have for her? I need to let go of it! For good.*

Phone calls between Nehal and AK became a regular feature around thrice a week. She expressed her displeasure at AK's lack of interest in Math. He sighed and listened. She reminded him of the Math test that had been announced.

"Oh yea, that...I don't know how that will go," said AK, hoping for some miracle.

"It will be good. You will do well," she whispered. It was close to midnight.

"Ok then, I will keep. Is there anything else?" she asked before she kept the phone.

"Eh yea! You think I should propose to Shikha?" asked AK sincerely.

"No," pat came the reply "I think she will reject you...now is not the time," she added.

"I just want to be over and done with," he said with a sigh.

"Don't be silly! Listen to me and study for tomorrow's test," she said.

"Yea I will…hey, listen, both of you looked gorgeous on saree day...really, I mean...I was speechless!" he said, changing the topic. "There, I said it! I am not going to compliment again," he added quickly. He couldn't forget Nehal after that day. She was often in his thoughts.

"How come you are telling this now? All of a sudden?" Nehal chuckled "Dimple and I thought you know…you were quiet and not your usual self."

"I didn't say it then...but yea. Ok, now enough…I will see you at the classes tomorrow," said AK hurriedly, before hanging up.

The rest of the class was excitely solving the Derivatives Functions and Integral Calculus problems, but he could not understand how to proceed with the answer to the problems in the first place.

Just do it AK, just do it! Finish it somehow! He motivated himself.

After an hour, he handed over the paper and came out of the class. He was relieved. Standing there in the premises, leaning back against a wall, he mused, *at least the weather has gotten better in September.*

He saw the door open and out stepped Shikha. She smiled at him. He waved, and smiled back. She was walking towards him. Unbelievable!

"How was it?" he asked as she neared him.

"Don't ask…all I know is it came and went like the wind," she sighed, rolling her eyes and folding her hands against her midriff.

"Yea, it was tough! I mean Math is tough for me," he said dejectedly.

"So, how's college?" he asked changing the topic.

"Good," she replied, "I don't see you around much."

"Ah well…sometimes I am in classes, sometimes at home," he replied. *This is not going anywhere AK,* he chided himself. Then he saw a familiar lanky figure coming from the other side of the road. He had been hanging around with her friends from the classes quite often. *Is he really her guy?* He wondered.

"Hey, I think your boyfriend is here," said AK. A sudden rush of envy spiked inside him. She turned around.

"Na, he is a friend," she responded, turning back towards AK.

"Is it? You know I really, really like you a lot Shikha," he said, impulsively. *Ouch! What timing! Why did I do this?* He cursed himself.

"AK, eh sorry, what did you say?" she asked, leaning closer.

Damage done! No point holding back now, he scolded himself.

"I really like you a lot. I think you are very beautiful. Drop dead gorgeous actually! And I really like you a lot!" he muttered in a single breath, in a soft tone. His heart pounding hard and loud. She blushed, her cheeks went red. She smiled looking downwards.

"AK no…" she said softly, turned around and walked away.

The door opened and several students poured out. His three friends spotted him and rushed over to him. They began animatedly discussing the Maths paper. It occurred to him he had feared Shikha's rejection more than the Math paper. Now that fear was gone!

Finally, I am happy! Now, no more crushes! He mused, inhaled deeply, and smiled.

A few evenings later, Nehal called him. In the middle of their conversation about studies and other things, he felt the need to tell her.

"I want to tell you something, you must've heard it?" he asked.

"Heard what?" she asked concerned.

"Er...eh, I...you know that day after the Maths test?"

"Hmm...ok, what?"

"Did you see me talking to Shikha?" he asked.

"Ehh no," she replied casually.

"I actually spoke to her and I proposed," he confessed.

"WHAT? What?" she repeated in a hushed tone.

"Yea but like you said, she was like no," he replied sheepishly, "You were right! But you know...it doesn't matter-"

"Wait wait...did she say NO-no or no-YES?" she interrupted him.

"What the hell is that supposed to mean?" he asked.

"*Arrey*, uff you duffer...you don't know?" she exclaimed in disbelief.

She explained to him that a no-YES meant for now she means NO but if he pursues her then she will say YES, while the NO-no is a direct NO.

"This is all very confusing! Don't need this," he said firmly. "I am going to take her NO as a NO, got no time for pursuing her and all that nonsense."

"Really? I think you should –"

"No, not at all, and we are not discussing this ever again...really, it is not worth it," he said dismissively.

She agreed. She reminded him about Navratri and Dandiya, and said that she would not call him for two weeks.

"Cool, enjoy garba," he said smiling.

"Come once *na*…please," she requested.

The distance and the fact that he had two left feet when it came to dancing forced him to reject the idea. He politely refused. She requested him to observe a few days of fasting for Navratri. He assured her he would try but somewhere being an atheist and an agnostic he was least interested.

Upon Nehal's insistence, over the next two weeks he visited garba in Dombivli as a spectator for a few minutes. He was awed by the revelry, colourful clothing, folk music, the rhythmic way they moved to the beats playing with the colourful sticks.

Days after Navratri ended it was time for Durga Puja followed by Saraswati Puja. He gladly attended these at Sanjay's house, and how could he ever miss a chance to feast on Lakshmi aunty's scrumptious food. The disbeliever in him didn't keep his books for Saraswati puja.

CHAPTER 14

he Math lecturer called out the names of each student and personally handed out the Math test papers to them. AK quickly peeked at his paper, smiled, and swiftly kept it inside his bag. Bhavin looked visibly upset, so did Dimple, while Nehal looked pleased.

AK stepped out of the classes during the break with dread. Someone tapped on his shoulder from behind. It was Nehal.

"So…?" she asked excitedly.

"Eh, what?" asked AK.

"How much did you get?" she asked. Soon Dimple and Bhavin joined in.

"*Yaar*, I am so mad! I made a silly mistake and I got only 15 out of 25," lamented Bhavin slapping his fist on his palm.

"I got only 18," said a dejected Dimple, "Nehal got full marks!"

"Huh? Really?" exclaimed AK. *No way!* He mused. "Show me the paper?" he asked, holding out his hand. She fetched it and handed over the paper to AK. He unfolded the sheet and in red ink it was written 25/25.

He looked at her bewildered. Bhavin too went through the paper. "Wow! Congratulations! You are… a…scholar!" he exclaimed.

"I love Math but why are you looking at me like that?" she asked him with her hands on her hips.

"I am...er...shocked...surprised, congratulations!" he said, giving her a salute. Bhavin too followed. Nehal kept insisting that he show his paper but he kept refusing.

"I got only 12 out of 25," said AK "Happy? There, I said it!"

139

After some more discussion on studies, the topic changed towards a light hearted subject – Shopper's Stop. Several hoardings across the city welcomed people to their newly opened outlet in Amrut Nagar, Ghatkopar West. Nehal and Dimple were eager to go there. Organized retail was becoming the trend and the girls were keen to explore the new attraction in town. AK insisted they go immediately. He wanted to be away from classes for a while.

Bunking the last accountancy lecture, the four friends took two autos to the venue. The ambience inside the store screamed 'premium'. While the two girls were excited, curious, and cautious, Bhavin was a trifle uncomfortable. But AK was easily at home. For AK, the outlet evoked memories of his shopping experiences in Dubai. He missed Dubai. Interestingly, the store had a counter of *Hidesign* leather goods. AK longingly beheld the identical wallet he so foolishly lost. He vowed to buy the same someday.

Economics lecture was AK's favourite, although Bhavin always fell asleep. But today, both AK and Bhavin had a tough time staying awake. After two hours, they came out for a break.

"Bhavin, when will you change your broken glasses?" asked Dimple. He had replaced the broken lens but glued the bridge and tied it up with a black thread. It was visible when people stood close to him.

"Today! AK is coming with me after classes," he replied.

"Please get him some metal frame," she said, folding her hands to her chest.

"Yea, we will get a gold one," Bhavin replied.

"We can all go together," suggested Nehal. The rest agreed and Nehal suggested that they all should make a weekend plan.

AK was unhappy with the idea. Sunday was the only day he spent with his friends 'The Rascals'.

After classes, the two girls joined AK and Bhavin in choosing spectacles for him. After much deliberation Bhavin settled for a silver frame that Dimple liked.

"I want new clothes. I was thinking of Heera Panna," said Bhavin.

"Sounds like a plan!" grinned Dimple, and Nehal too smiled.

They planned for the coming Sunday. AK suggested that they go without him. He told them he had a few chores and errands to attend to. Nehal furrowed her brows at him.

Ambling towards Sarvodaya, she walked closer to him and nudged him.

"Come na…I will get bored, these two will be into each other only," she said.

"I'll see, I'll let you know," responded AK, disinterested.

Bhavin was evidently happy about their Sunday plan.

All of Saturday had been boring, despite the monsoons having fully cleared and giving way to the Diwali season. AK was bored and dejected. He was confident that he would fail in Math if they got Derivatives and Calculus in the CA exam, while his other friends stood a good chance of clearing it.

He had reluctantly agreed to Bhavin's repeated requests of accompanying them on Sunday but he was unhappy within. He lay down to sleep when the expected caller rang.

"Hey, had dinner?" he asked.

"Yea I did, and you?" asked Nehal in a soft tone.

"Yea of course, long back," he replied.

"Why are you so quiet? You are not yourself lately. What happened?" she asked.

"Nehal…I have not been honest with you…there is something I have been hiding from you," he said, "And I am not happy about it."

"What is it? Go on," she said in hushed tones, curious.

"Look I…eh…I really like you for all that you do and did…but," he said, and proceeded, "I mean helping us with Math, but it is not going anywhere with me… you know."

"Oh, go on," she said cautiously.

"I got ZERO in Maths test…I am a total failure," he said, smacking his forehead.

"I am terrible at this…I will disappoint my parents! I know it," he said.

"AK, relax…Maths is just for filtering out candidates in CA Foundation…don't worry so much…you can even do CA after B. Comm," she consoled him.

"But you are a genius…I am sorry, I really am…I hate to admit this…but I didn't think you would get full marks…I mean, please don't feel offended…but you are way better than anyone I know…and congrats!" he said.

"Ohh so you are a typical male pig! You thought I couldn't score in Maths! How disgusting! That's it, I am keeping the phone…bye, I am never going to talk to you ever again," she said sternly.

Sitting up on the bed instantly, "Hello, hello, hello… hold on…I said sorry *na*…I told you honestly…I am sorry, I really am," he apologized.

She was breathing heavily. *Is she really angry?* He pondered. The brief silence was becoming longer by the second.

"Look, I am really very sorry! You tell me what you want? I will get you a Dairy milk –"

"Tomorrow at 10 a.m., Ghatkopar station, be there!" she kept the phone.

Incredible woman! He mused and a smile escaped his lips. She knew exactly what to demand from him.

AK met the trio at Ghatkopar station. Nehal gave a high five to Dimple and said "Bhavin, you lost the bet! He is here! You owe me a Dairy Milk," she giggled. AK chuckled. He had expected the girls to be in their usual salwar suits, but he was in for a surprise.

Dimple wore blue denims and a white kurti with self-print on them. She looked pretty. AK had never paid attention to her looks before, but today it was difficult to ignore. She was an image of simplistic elegance. *No wonder Bhavin fell for her,* thought AK.

Nehal wore light blue stretch denims with a snug fitting dark blue short sleeved t-shirt, accentuating her curves. She quickly undid her pony tail and shook out her hair and tied it back into a pony. He saw men pause to look at her as they walked by. He stepped over to her side and stared down at some men.

Both girls wore lipstick and make up, but Nehal caught his eye. He never knew there was a glamorous side to her. Standing next to her, he could breathe in her fragrance all day. Nehal appeared more and more beautiful each time he saw her.

They bought tickets to Mahalakshmi and went via Dadar. Soon, they hopped into a taxi. AK sat in the front while Bhavin sat next to Dimple and Nehal sat on the other side. On the way, they noticed the famed Haji Ali *dargah*. They decided to visit it someday.

Splitting the fare equally, they alighted from the taxi and walked into Heera Panna. The entrance buzzed with people going in and out. A few months back, this sight of chaos would have deterred AK but not anymore. Now he had become a Bombay bloke as the other NRIs put it or a Mumbaite or Mumbaikar as the locals would say. He preferred 'Mumbaikar'.

Inside the shopping centre, it was a young adult's dream. It had electronics' shops, clothing and apparel, books and magazines too. *Aah Playboy magazines too! Hmm! No way can I pick one now! Damn it,* he cursed himself.

They scouted for clothing and apparel for Bhavin. Dimple and Nehal bargained for t-shirts and cargos while AK looked on. For whatever price the shopkeeper quoted, the girls were willing to pay only half the price. *Thank God, I am not the shop keeper. These girls and their bargaining can be quite insulting*, he mused.

AK realized these girls are tough customers. Bhavin too was feeling dejected because the girls rejected a t-shirt he liked, and pulled them into another shop.

They began the same drill again.

"Nahin boss, in donon ke liye 300 rupaiye theek hai, bas final kardo boss," haggled Nehal (No Boss, Rs.300 for these two, that's final)

"Kya behen tum bhi sawere mood kharab karte ho," said the shopkeeper. (What is this sister, you are ruining my mood in the morning).

"Hum log dobara bhi aake yahin se kharidenge na, mujhe ye bhi de do," added Dimple taking the cargo trousers Bhavin held in his hand (We will come again to buy it from here, and give me this too).

Nehal also picked two cargo trousers and two t-shirts for AK. She placed the cargos on his hip and turned him around and placed the t-shirt on his back turn by turn, and told the shop keeper to pack it.

"Haan aur yeh sab ab milake Rs.1000 mein bas," insisted Dimple. (Yea and this for Rs.1000 only)

Oh God! We are out again! AK quietly slipped out, sure that they would be out of this shop too like the five previous ones.

"Theek hai, chalo, purey 1000 rupaiye de do," said the defeated shopkeeper. (Ok now…give me Rs.1000) And he proceeded with packing the goods.

Incredible! AK looked at Nehal and Dimple with renewed respect. *Beauties with brains! Indeed!* He mused in admiration.

The respect-o-meter went a few notches high for Gujjus. They valued money and spent it wisely. He also learnt nobody could dissuade them from bargaining. They could nag, nag, nag and finally buy the devil's soul for half a rupee.

Bhavin and AK were impressed. They got four T-shirts, and three cargo trousers, all for Rs.1000/-. To AK this was all surreal. He quickly stepped into a shop and bought two dairy milk chocolates for the girls.

"Thank you, *devis*!" said AK bringing his palms in prayer towards both the girls. Bhavin too followed suit. The girls blushed.

"My Diwali shopping and birthday shopping are both done," announced AK.

"Oh yea, it will be your birthday soon," repeated Bhavin.

"Let's plan to go somewhere nice eh…AK, we need a grand treat from you," said Dimple happily. Nehal smiled at AK.

"See, aren't you happy that you came today?" Nehal asked. He nodded with a smile.

AK and Bhavin held their shopping bags as they came out of the shopping centre. The girls did not buy anything for themselves. The boys wanted to give them something in return and insisted on it.

"*Arrey*, just buy us some lunch! Very hungry!" said Dimple, while Nehal mocked a frown and rubbed her hand on her petite stomach. For the first time, AK noticed the shape of her breasts. He felt guilty. Immediately, his eyes scanned the vicinity and moved closer to her to keep lechers away.

AK couldn't help but feel protective about the two ladies, Nehal in particular. She was a Maths genius, tutor, friend, naughty, witty, charming, confident and… beautiful. *She is beautiful.* This thought had been crossing his mind again and again since morning.

Sauntering across the road, they hopped into Haji Ali Juice centre. Ordering sandwiches and juices, they decided to visit Haji Ali *dargah* soon after. Their order was served soon, service was quick and food delightful.

"Oh God! That's a big bite!" exclaimed Nehal as she watched AK bite into the sandwich. Dimple chuckled. Bhavin was not surprised at all. AK was perplexed.

"Idiot share it with me *na*," she said, taking a bite out of AK's club sandwich. He observed the bite marks, her lipstick marks over her small bite was cute.

"Here you go, genius!" said AK handing over the rest of the slice to her. He smiled as he watched her eat. She raised her brow in a questioning manner.

"Nah, I am just amused watching you nibble away at the sandwich like a squirrel," said AK, shaking his head in amusement. In reflex, she instantly slapped him on his shoulder.

"You are putting evil eyes on me while eating…see you will have stomach pain today!" Nehal frowned. *She looks cute when she frowns,* he observed.

"We did not have breakfast, we are hungry," said Dimple conscious and now eating slowly.

"You are fine, you eat," said Bhavin.

After settling their bill, they decided to go to Haji Ali *dargah*.

Bhavin and Dimple walked ahead, while AK waited for Nehal who smoothed down her denims as she got up.

He smiled at her.

"What?" she asked softly, "You have something on your mind…tell me?"

"You…look very nice today," he smiled "Yea and I can't believe it."

She grunted, "Can't believe it!" she playfully pinched him.

AK chuckled and moved his arm away. A big group of boys approaching from the opposite side halted her on her tracks, she changed sides and went to his left. She came very close to him. He felt empowered and very protective of her.

The wide pathway and the *dargah* were hugged and touched by the sea on both sides serenely.

"Don't walk so fast...wait," she said, grabbing and pulling his arm towards her. His elbow touched her right breast, he could feel the softness, and yet he couldn't pull his hands away. *Damnn! This is so awkward! Don't think wrong things! RESPECT HER!* he admonished himself.

She kept walking with him in close contact. *Doesn't she feel it?* he mused. He glanced at her, as the wind gently played with a lock of her hair, the noon sun gently kissing her skin. She turned and their eyes met.

"Your light brown eyes!" he said softly, surprised, "They are beautiful." She blushed.

She raised her eyebrows towards Dimple and Bhavin.

"Wonder what they must be talking about?" she asked. AK shrugged and they debated that their two friends are probably interested in each other. Although AK knew he was unsure if he should tell her, but he was tempted to.

At the *dargah*, they prayed. AK being disinterested, he spent more time observing how other devotees offered their prayers. Dimple informed them devotees who sought divine help and had special requests would tie a '*dhaga*' (thread). Nehal tied one.

AK was curious, "So what did you ask for?" She smiled but did not reply. He couldn't tell for sure if her eyes were moist. *Maybe it is the dust,* he thought.

The four friends walked back to the main road making small talk. On the way, he noticed a chap that resembled Pratap. He shared Pratap and Nivedita's interesting love story with his friends. They were all awed by it.

They decided to call it a day. If they left now they would reach by 6 p.m. at Ghatkopar, and it would take AK another hour to reach home.

They caught a taxi. This time, Bhavin sat in the front while the other three sat in the back, with Nehal in the middle. Congestion in the Fiat Padmini was a good excuse for AK to keep his arm over the seat to play with Nehal's pony tail. She sensed it and nudged him playfully. He could sit next to her and breathe in her perfume all day.

Paying off the taxi driver, they made their way. An empty Kalyan local beckoned them at Shivaji Terminus. The boys got into the gent's compartment while the ladies got into the ladies compartment.

The boys kept their packages atop the carrier rack and took their seats by the window. Bhavin smiled with contentment.

"What happened? You look like you proposed and she accepted!" said AK. Bhavin gave a happy dismissive wave of his hand.

"Kind of...I almost told her, she smiled and you saw the interest with which she got stuff for me," said Bhavin happily. AK agreed.

"But hey I don't know about you...but I won't read too much into all this until you have said and she has accepted it," said AK crossing his leg.

"Why do you say that?" asked Bhavin curiously.

"My gut feel...besides," he shrugged, "If she was into you then they would have been here with us in this empty compartment rather than in that ladies' compartment," he added.

Bhavin looked at him, unsure. The train started to move and as if on cue, the two girls came running into their compartment. They were dumbfounded. AK got off his seat.

Nehal and Dimple came and sat down on the opposite seats panting for breath.

AK held out his palm and asked "Why? You could have climbed here at the next station?" Nehal caught his hand and helped herself from the seat, and walked over to the door. AK followed, while Bhavin and Dimple stayed back in their seats facing each other.

AK stood facing her and he looked at her face. She was still panting. He offered her his fresh hanky. She smiled and wiped her forehead with it.

"So, what did you ask for at the *dargah*?" asked AK.

She shook her head as she picked a piece of lint from his t-shirt. "AK, remember that whenever you pray at any place…you are not supposed to reveal what you are seeking till it happens," she said, wiping away lint from his chest.

And for a brief moment, the breeze played with her locks. Silence spoke more than words could say. In her eyes he saw tenderness, care, love and a hint of mischief. Orange hues of the setting sun kissed her face. He stood there wishing it was him.

The train braked hard, breaking the moment. He held on tight to the metal loops, instantly she was thrown against him. His body cushioned her and snapped her out of silence.

"You alright?" she asked "I am sorry, I was not holding anything," she added, embarrassed. AK smiled and shook his head. "It's ok, you can hold onto me," he winked. She blushed, playfully slapping his arm.

They went back in and took their seats next to each other. She took his palm and placed it on her knee next to her palm.

"Uff, it is so big!" she said, staring at his palm. While hers was small. AK smiled at her discovery. She turned his palm around and said, "Your nails are big too! How?"

Her new discoveries and baffled expressions kept him amused throughout their journey.

Diwali, the festival of lights blessed the city's night life with colourful lanterns and firecrackers. During day time too, there were intermittent bursting of crackers as schools and colleges were off for the holidays. Homes and shops throughout the state were decked up in Diwali revelry. Irrespective of religion people would burst crackers and join in the festivities.

AK was glad that his birthday was in the same month as Diwali. Today, 15th October, he walked the earth for 18 years. His parents rang him at the stroke of midnight to wish him. They spoke at length. He told them he would be treating his friends at a restaurant. His Dad typically reminded him to keep an account of his expenses for the month.

Sanjay met the birthday boy, AK, below his apartment early evening and conveyed his birthday wishes and followed it up with a hug. They happily proceeded to Dombivli station.

"*Yaar*, you are looking very dapper!" complimented Sanjay.

"Thanks dude…" said AK. Sanjay informed him that Pratap would meet them at Dombivli station. While Mukesh and Hiten would meet them at Ghatkopar.

"Alright…anyways…with my limited budget, it will be difficult for me to throw a separate treat after tonight," said AK in a serious tone.

"*Yaar*, don't worry, we will see that later…we can have a few beers anyways…" said Sanjay, twitching his nose and pushing up his glasses.

Soon, they met Pratap at the railway station and caught a slow CST local. His CA friends, Nivedita, and new movie releases were a part of their small talk.

They walked over to the eastern side of Ghatkopar. His friends were surprised that the restaurant was bang opposite the station. An auto stopped in front of them and out stepped Hiten and Mukesh.

"Arrey *Bhaisaab*! Happy birthday!" said Mukesh, giving him a bear hug.

"Thanks, *yaar*!" said AK.

"Happy birthday *yaara*!" hugged Hiten smiling.

"Hey, thanks dude," said AK.

"Looking smart!" complimented Hiten.

"Thanks buddy! Picked it last week," said AK blushing slightly. AK wore light beige cargos with a bright blue t-shirt. Nehal had picked these for him, and she had specially requested him to wear it on his birthday.

"Ok, now don't go overboard, we are supposed to lie to you on birthdays!" joked Hiten, everyone chuckled. Soon, another auto stopped on the opposite side of the road and out stepped Bhavin, Dimple, and Nehal.

Both the ladies were well dressed in traditional salwar kameez. Nehal was in a soft orange salwar kameez with a creamish dupatta and a thin golden border. Orange was not AK's favourite colour but she carried off the entire ensemble with the grace of a princess. It was another one of those moments that took his breath away and wowed him.

Dimple looked elegant in a sky-blue attire and a shimmery white dupatta. Bhavin evidently kept stealing a few glances at her.

Bhavin hugged him and wished him a happy birthday. The girls wished him with a handshake. They all complimented his attire, but Nehal just wished him and smiled.

Brief introductions and pleasantries followed.

"Shall we?" enquired Dimple, extending her hand towards the restaurant. She was conscious of time.

Bhavin was not surprised that AK chose the AC hall. They all joked and laughed and had their fill of the food. Everyone shared friendly banter and trivia about each other. Even in between all their friendly banter, AK's thoughts and glances went back and forth to Nehal.

Good moments always seem to end fast, an hour had passed by and it was almost time to leave. Dimple and Nehal nodded at each other. Dimple handed a neatly wrapped package and gifted it to AK.

They all sang the Happy birthday song to him in chorus. He blushed. They goaded him to open it. He ripped it open and it was a dark grey casual polo neck t-shirt. AK thanked them for the wonderful gift.

Sanjay and Hiten had carried some extra money with them, in case the bill was beyond AK's budget. However, AK comfortably settled the bill.

"Thanks AK for the treat! Happy birthday once again," Nehal smiled, tilting her head. Everyone followed suit and thanked him for the treat.

"Guys, no formalities please…thanks for coming and making it special," said AK happily. And they all bid each other farewell. Bhavin and Hiten promised to call him later and he left for home.

The four "Rascals" boarded a Dombivli local for their journey back home. They all took their seats. Amidst teasing Pratap with Nivedita, which was now the group's hobby, Mukesh asked AK, "That Dimple is pretty…cute smile…I don't know but Bhavin is surely crazy about Dimple, I think?".

"I don't know but I guess so," said AK with half a shrug. Mukesh moved closer to AK, playfully slapped his thigh and asked, "Nehal is single, right?" He asked with a smile in a soft but audible tone. For a moment AK pondered, *Is there any mischief behind that question?*

Sanjay and Pratap too heard it.

"Let it be, AK!" said Pratap shaking his head "This guy is never going to be serious," he chuckled.

"*Arrey*, what do you mean Pratap? Just because I keep cracking crazy jokes you think I am a bad guy… some flirt, eh," replied Mukesh, agitated.

"*Yaar* AK! I am serious…I am Gujju and so is she…we get married after graduation anyways…I am interested and my parents will be happy if I tell them…but anyways that's far too long…but I am really interested in her…*yaar*, I trust you, please tell her eh…" he paused scratching his head as if he was looking for an appropriate word, "Ah! I have infatuation on her… please tell her…rest is her wish."

"Hmm...I agree she is good looking, charming, witty...and she seems nice," said Sanjay, leaning back on his seat, slowly rocking his crossed feet.

"Sorry Mukesh...I didn't say it to hurt you...anyways, good luck," said Pratap, leaning forward and pinning his elbows on his thighs.

AK wondered, *I never asked her if there is anyone she likes! Why? Hell, I have never asked her anything much about her ever!*

"AK, you are lost now?" said Sanjay, breaking his chain of thought. AK dismissively shook his head, "No, I really don't know...I mean as far as I know, she is single."

"Seriously boss! Nehal is beautiful and intelligent... she dresses very nicely...super combination...just like how Gujju women are!" remarked Mukesh with a smile and a snap of his fingers. AK wondered, *does this guy really like her or is he just lusting after her? She is my friend, I will protect her!*

Like true friends who have known each other for long, Sanjay sensed the undercurrents under the façade of that calm demeanour that AK showed. "AK *yaar*, you have been keeping quiet...for some time, everything ok?" Sanjay asked. Pratap and Mukesh looked at him.

"I am fine," said AK and he kept quiet. Mukesh jolted upright and said, "*Bhai* AK! I am sorry *yaar*. I didn't ask...you both an item? You like her?" asked Mukesh. AK looked at him, surprised by his question. He could barely shake his head "No, no...not at all!" AK pondered at his question, *we are definitely not dating. We are good friends, but yes there are times I feel that I am happy when I am with her. I can be myself without feeling guilt or being conscious of any sort of judgement.*

"I will tell her about you," promised AK. Mukesh thanked him.

An outing at Pravin da Dhaba was confirmed for the same night after dinner. After all, how could the Rascals let that go. Mukesh promised to pick them all up.

AK's mom had phoned him to enquire about how his day had been. She was happy that it went well. His dad came on the line. "So, Happy birthday once again son! You are happy with your birthday party, eh?"

"Yea daddy! It was nice," he said sheepishly.

"Good…now don't waste time, eh! Start studying, eh, how much did you spend today?" he asked. He could hear his mom grumble in the background. He knew his bean counting dad couldn't help himself. He avoided the topic making the excuse of a disturbed phone line and kept the phone.

Hiten called soon after, he thanked AK for the treat and warned him against drinking too much that night. Then the topic changed.

"Nehal, I am seeing her for the first time boss! She looks very nice…she is beautiful! In a nice homely way," he said. AK couldn't believe his ears. *Hiten, you too! Damn it!*

"You interested in her? Don't worry, I will tell her you are," he replied nonchalantly.

"To me she looked like she is interested in you…or maybe I just felt that way…alright, bye…you enjoy," Hiten said, before keeping the phone. AK couldn't believe him. *We are just friends! And I don't want to spoil it,* he sighed.

After dinner, he waited for Mukesh's call. The phone rang as expected.

"Hello AK!" greeted the familiar feminine voice.

"Nehal, hi!" he answered, surprised.

"Hey, you were looking very nice today…very handsome!" she said.

"Thanks…you too," he blushed "You actually looked very pretty…you always do but today even more. My friends were complimenting your looks." He could feel her blushing.

"Listen, I am coming to see you tomorrow," she said.

"Ha nice joke! I seriously don't believe you. I am going out with my friends for drinks tonight. We will speak tomorrow, ok?" he said.

"Yes, yes, you enjoy! Please don't drink too much. Bye, I will call tomorrow morning," she smiled. They soon signed off.

Soon the awaited call came and he rushed, he rushed down to be with his friends. It became routine that every birthday treat would end with drinks at Pravin da Dhaba. The Rascals were a happy drunk bunch. Diwali season meant some of them had pujas at home, so continuing on with more than two beers was out of the question. Mukesh dropped them all home before things got any wilder.

CHAPTER 15

AK tidied up the house and began toasting some bread for himself. The phone rang. The absence of the ISD tone convinced him it wasn't his mom.

"Hello!" he answered.

"Hello, AK!"

"NEHAL! Hey, good morning! I did not expect you at this time," said AK, surprised, looking at the clock, which showed quarter past nine.

"I know…you won't believe where I am!" she said.

"Where?"

"I am in Dombivli," said Nehal, excited.

"WHAT? Rubbish…silly joke eh," said AK dismissively.

"*Arrey*! I am serious baba! I am here in Dombivli," said Nehal irately.

"Whom did you come with?" he asked, certain that this was one of her pranks.

"Alone! Am I a child? Ok, now come to the station and pick me…I am waiting outside the East exit, near some theatre," she retorted with a huff.

"NO! you are lying…hah, I know I will not fall for this today."

"*Arrey*! This is the limit…I swear I am losing my cool on you AK and I am alone here-"

"Prove it to me that you are here," demanded AK, still in a state of denial "How am I expected to believe you?" said AK, interrupting her.

"AK! You are DEAD! I told you yesterday, I will come *na*," retorted Nehal angrily "There is some Madhuban theatre, a bookshop and Monginis cake shop near an auto stand. NOW DO YOU BELIEVE ME?" she growled. The payphone beeped the last few seconds of the call.

"Oh shit! Ok, wait right there, I am coming!" he said, baffled that she came all the way to meet him. He rushed out to meet her.

He reached the spot impatiently in an auto. *This better be no joke! Oh my goodness! Indeed, there she is,* thought AK.

"Nehal! Here," AK called out to her, waving his hand. She spotted him and got into the auto.

I am glad uncle is at office. I wonder what he would say if I brought a girl-friend home, mused AK.

AK showed Phadke road and Tilak road to her as they passed by while she looked on like a tourist.

"AK! I am pleasantly surprised...Dombivli isn't as bad as I imagined," she remarked earnestly.

"They just fixed up the place overnight...just to impress you her highness," joked AK. She slapped his arm.

"See, I meant that after seeing Kalva, Mumbra, and of course Diva, I could never imagine Dombivli could be like this," she said seriously "It's vibrant and full of life...busy life," she added, glancing at the crowd busy doing their duties. The auto finally reached his stop.

"The next time you are coming tell the auto guy 'Tridev Vada pav center', and he'll drop you right here, behind this apartment is mine."

"Oh! So, you won't come to pick me, eh?" she asked, raising her brow.

"Ah! Of course, I will NOT your highness!" he replied, chuckling. She pinched his arm playfully.

As they climbed the steps of his apartment AK hoped that there wouldn't be any nosy neighbour there. *I wonder if anyone sees us what would they think? Single guy...parents in Dubai...he is enjoying life...hanging out with friends, partying, and now GIRLS!* Part of him wanted to climb up stealthily, part of him wanted to rush into the apartment. He looked at Nehal and smiled briefly. His face was an image of calm that hid his emotions underneath.

Reaching the door of his apartment, he quickly grabbed his keys and nimbly unlocked the door without a sound and they both stepped inside, and AK quickly closed the door behind them.

She glanced around the apartment quickly and asked him "Where is your uncle?"

"Are you enquiring genuinely or just making sure?" shot back AK, chuckling.

Nehal pinched him hard, "Naughty fellow! Always 'A' jokes...you have such a corrupt mind," she joked. "You told me to go back home!' she pinched him again. He pulled away his arm in pain, "I am sorry! I didn't expect anyone to come here!"

"My uncle has gone to office. He will come back in the evening by seven or so," said AK changing the topic.

"I see...AK, where is your room?"

"Here," said AK pushing ajar the closed door of his bedroom.

She stepped in and placed her bag on the table.

"What can I get you to drink?" asked AK. Just as she was about to answer. He remembered, "Well frankly there isn't anything much apart from water," said AK sheepishly remembering the silliness of his question.

"Water is just perfect," she said smiling.

He returned with a glass of Tang Orange. He forgot it was there in the kitchen. Adding to it good doses of sugar and Tang, he prepared for both of them and then decided as a good host to offer it to her entirely.

"Where's your glass? Aren't you drinking this? Didn't you make one for yourself?" she asked quickly.

"Look, I am not thirsty, and rather than giving just water I thought I should offer some juice at least...so that's all...and I didn't feel like having," said AK. Making him wonder if she was apprehensive, *doesn't she trust me? But then she walked into the house with me! Girls were confusing!*

She drank and placed the cup on the table.

This is weird, thought AK, *why do I suddenly feel like I don't have anything much to talk to her about. This is odd… but it just feels so right that she is here with me.*

"AK!"

"Yea?" responded AK.

"No questions please…close your eyes," she said softly. He complied, half willingly, lest she pull some prank on him. On opening his eyes, a neatly wrapped box was placed before him.

"WHAT? There was no need for this Nehal!" said AK, completely taken aback.

"Go on…open it," she said.

"No Nehal, you shouldn't have wasted your money you know...but why?" asked AK, concerned.

"Idiot! This is your birthday gift…and wouldn't you buy me a gift if it was my birthday?"

"Of course, I would!" said AK.

"No, you shouldn't because you are not earning yet, but I am," said Nehal authoritatively "Ok, enough now, open it quickly."

"You talk too much," grumbled AK, carefully unwrapping his gift.

"Just rip it open will you…" said Nehal impatiently.

He just tore the wrapping and opened the box. From inside it he pulled a cloth bag. It was familiar to him. He opened it.

"Oh my God! How come? How did you know?" he asked, looking at his gift—a black *Hidesign* wallet. Brand new. Not a crease on it. Same as the one he lost.

"Do you like this one?" she asked. He was overwhelmed, he immediately hugged her. He nodded.

"But how did you know that this was the one I…I mean the one I wanted?" he asked, surprised.

"You remember that once while we four were out to Shopper's Stop, you were looking only at this wallet in the entire collection!" she said.

"Yea how can I forget..." and AK narrated the incident where the wallet got picked, but he still left out the tranny part for obvious reasons.

"Really strange that you could never feel it in a crowded train! But hey, I am really happy I picked the right one...pun intended!" she remarked, and chuckled.

"I know...but stranger things happen," he said.

"How did you get the money for it?" asked AK, surprised.

"I work in my cousin's clothing store *na*...so, I get pocket money and managed to save some of that for your gift," she said with a smile. He was surprised out of his wits and speechlessly stared at her.

"Hey, AK I think I...I...should go now. It might get late to go back," she said, getting up.

"Really? But you just got here," said AK.

"I know...but..." Suddenly the phone rang interrupting their banter. This brief respite helped her out of her awkwardness.

"Shit! Some wrong no..." said AK, putting the phone down. And he turned around in time to face her. The sunlight gently shone through his bedroom window caressing her face and lighting up her eyes. The moment was perfect. *They are all falling for you...Do you know how much I am falling for you, babe?*

"AK...I..." Nehal started to say. He placed his finger on her lips. Mesmerized by her beauty, he pulled her close. She slid her arm smoothly on his. Their eyes locked briefly in a scorching embrace that said all that their hearts wanted to hear. Soon they were consumed by their overpowering desire. His lips met hers and they kissed and hugged passionately. He could contain no more. He swept her off her feet, carrying her to his bed.

As he placed her on the bed, a smile escaped her lips. She hugged him tight, their lips locked in eternal passionate kisses, satiating their forbidden thirst. Within seconds their outer clothes melted away. He slid his hand inside her bra and she helped him unhook it. Both his palms gently touched her soft breasts. She clasped her hands tight on his shoulders digging her nails in. Her eyes closed, her body gasping for his loving touch, tremoring with tiny explosions at his passionate kisses. He continued kissing her neck while his one hand caressed her soft breasts and the other caressed her back. She shivered at his touch. Kissing her beautiful breasts, lovingly relishing her nipples like they were dipped in milk chocolate. He was unstoppable.

"Sweetheart…feels so good…Oh…" words unwillingly escaped her.

His hand slid down inside her panty, searching for the joyous crevice. He felt the softness.

"Sweetheart…mm..." She moaned at his touch. She slid her hand down through his underwear and clasped his member, squeezing it tight and it responded with greater ferocity. She was taken by surprise. He moved away and immediately diverted his attention to her belly. The shivers made her bite her own lips. She pulled him up by his hair and kissed him again and again. AK released himself from his last constraint and he helped her off hers too. He placed his fingers on her thighs and she responded by opening them in reflex but immediately shut them close abruptly snapping AK's excitement.

"No AK, no, no, no, no," Nehal begged with reluctance at first and then she immediately grabbed his pillow and sheet to cover herself up.

"AK this is not right…I…I am sorry," she said, as a tear escaped her eye.

In few seconds, this blaze of passion subsided bringing AK to his senses. He realized he was the one who started it all. *I am such an idiot. I nearly ruined her.*

"I am so sorry, so sorry…it's all my fault…I shouldn't have...but I think…I know…I have fallen for you…I miss you when you are not around...and today, I just couldn't control myself…I am sorry about that…but I am proud that I love you…and that you love me too," said AK.

She smiled through her tears.

"I love you too," she said. He smiled and hugged her over the sheet and pillow. This loving embrace lasted a few seconds but assured a lifetime of togetherness.

"AK!" she called.

"Yea,"

"Please turn around, I need to dress up," she said shyly.

"Let me help you," said AK picking up her bra from the floor. She shook her head and gestured to leave it on the pillow.

"No please I…I need to get ready…please AK," she requested. He gave in. *She is feeling shy now…I don't want her to feel uncomfortable…man! How did this happen? This whole thing is weird,* he thought. He picked up his clothes and left the room closing the door behind him.

AK, you are so hyper, stupid, and crazy! Do you have any idea what would happen if things went out of control? He scolded himself.

He was finally ready. She came out of his bedroom fully dressed. There was an unmistakable glow on her face. She held her bag on her shoulder. Looking away from him she went towards the door.

AK rushed towards her.

"Dear, please don't go so soon. It's too soon," he said.

She looked into his eyes and he could sense her mind was trapped by awkwardness and shyness of all that transpired between them. Yet, he strangely felt alive like he was reborn by this experience. He fell more and more in love and felt intensely protective of her.

"AK, I have to leave now. It will take an hour roughly to reach, and I've to get home around the same time Dimple gets home, otherwise my *didi* will call up at Dimple's place to check on me," she said gently, her voice close to a murmur.

AK knew it was pointless to protest.

"Let me drop you to the station," he suggested. She didn't say a word.

They caught an auto and reached the station. AK walked with her to platform no. 5. *Say something AK! Why are you so quiet?* AK looked at his watch. The time was only 12:10 p.m.

'Listen, do you want anything to eat? Samosa or some biscuits?' asked AK, finally breaking their awkward silence.

She wanted to speak but she could only manage to whisper, "Yea, some biscuits…please."

"Sure, just a sec," said AK and rushed to the in-station shop to get it.

Oh God! Please let this weirdness pass off soon…I think it will be ok once she leaves and she is alone.

AK returned soon with a pack of Good Day biscuits.

"Here, this should last you the whole journey," he said, handing it over to her. She took it and gave him a weary smile. She looked lost. This disturbed AK.

"Is everything alright?" he asked gently, hoping to hear something audible from those sweet kissable lips.

She nodded. He could see the softness of her heart through her eyes. *Babe, I badly want to kiss you right now!* He mused. She rolled her eyes and blushed.

AK was surprised.

"What? Say something…why are you so quiet?" he asked in a low tone

"Nothing *rey*…just like that," she said with a smile, nudging his arm.

Just then the train arrived. She climbed in and caught a window seat in the ladies' compartment. She smiled at him and waved him a half-bye by only opening her palm, trying to be discreet. While AK responded with a wider wave and a generous smile.

Back home, her fragrance lingered in his bedroom. Standing in front of the mirror, he couldn't stop blushing at the turn of events. *This was so much like some movie scene! What if she felt offended? She would have slapped me. But she didn't and with all that loving! I never imagined I would fall in love that way!*

Walking over to the table, he looked at the wallet, felt the soft texture of black leather. He picked it up to smell it. *FRESH! Brand new!* It was identical to the one he lost. The fresh smell of un-creased leather was welcoming. He transferred everything from his worn-out wallet to this new one. *She really loves me! I love her too! Why did I not know this before? I hope I didn't cross the line today...was too much...now I feel guilty,* sighed AK.

This was his first Diwali away from his parents. And it was GRAND! AK was at the Lakshmi Puja at Sanjay's place. AK was happy, he was in love with the world, in love with life and loving Nehal made this all possible. The new lovers were talking every night now and sometimes during the day too.

He couldn't wait for the puja to get over and tell Sanjay about it. Finally, the opportunity came but so did Mukesh.

"Hey, Happy Diwali!" he wished Mukesh. His friend wished him back too and they walked into Sanjay's room. After indulging in some small talk, the duo planned to walk on Phadke road the next day and asked AK to join them. The friends explained to AK about the much-awaited yearly ritual of walking with their best friends on Phadke road dressed in their Diwali attires. AK readily agreed.

"Guys, I have something to tell you," announced AK impatiently.

"*Bhai*, you spoke to Nehal about me, eh?" asked Mukesh, smiling hopefully. "Yea, about that..." said AK exhaling deeply, "She met me a few days back and... she told me that she likes me a lot...you know, like love me...and I realized that I too love her," explained AK.

Sanjay and Mukesh exchanged glances at each other and looked back at him, again at each other, and back at him. Sanjay sat up on his bed. Mukesh stood up. AK was perplexed by their silence.

"So, you both are now official?" asked Sanjay.

"Eh...yea I…guess so," said AK, standing up. Mukesh hugged him and said "I knew I had no chance…congrats *bhai*!"

"Congratulations! *Yaar*, your Diwali and birthday have been very lucky for you, huh!" said Sanjay patting his shoulder. AK smiled and nodded with elation.

Hiten had invited Bhavin and him to visit his house on Puja day. They met up outside the railway station and took an auto to Hiten's house. In the auto, AK told Bhavin about Nehal and himself, of course sparing the spicy bits. But Bhavin guessed, and AK did not deny, only blushed.

They reached Hiten's home. The puja was almost over.

"I have some surprise to share with you too," Bhavin whispered to AK. He smiled and mused, *maybe Dimple and he are an item too*. They both sat there quietly through rest of the proceedings.

AK had atheistic beliefs but he liked festivals like Diwali, Holi, Eid, and Christmas as they spread joy amongst people. Besides he did not want to offend Hiten by declining such an invite. Moreover, AK knew that he would be the odd one out amongst his friends, and of course, at the receiving end of their ire if he ever told them, *'I am not biased. I hate all religions equally'.* He recollected how his friend Naeem, in Dubai, used to bring him mutton biriyani and sweets prepared during Eid.

AK was always fond of good food and festivals meant that the feast was delicious. These festivals formed a collection of fond memories of teen years well spent in friendships and culture.

Growing up, he felt that all religious teachings were bound to an era and time he did not belong to. For AK, they were just a little more than history books and nothing more. He found more interest in reading about inventions and innovators. Newton, Einstein, and Tesla inspired him.

The puja finished and the pujari stood up. Everyone offered their obeisance, took *prasad* and sweets. Everyone conveyed Diwali wishes to each other. And after a few minutes, Hiten took them to the terrace of his building where they were welcomed by the festive warmth of the mid-day sun.

"I have been up since five, I am tired," sighed Hiten placing his hand on his hips and arching his back, stretching and yawning.

"What were you doing since then?" asked AK.

"Had to get ready and go to temple and all *yaar*...and also had to help around the house," he said.

"Liar! No way you did all that. Your servant must have done that," said Bhavin. AK noted his friend's English grammar was much better than before, even the accent was improving.

"No...she came in late today, she also has Diwali, right? Anyways, you guys tell me," said Hiten.

"Yes, I have got something to share...friends...this is my first time," said Bhavin, pulling out a folded piece of paper from his pocket.

"What is it?" asked Hiten.

"Wait...listen I have written this in Gujarati...so I need your help in translating this in proper English," requested Bhavin.

"Ok, but what is it?" asked AK, leaning in. It was written in Gujarati.

"No wait *yaar*, please be patient AK," said Bhavin pushing him back playfully.

Hiten took the paper and glanced through it. He had a very blank expression on his face. He nodded. Hiten took his position one step behind Bhavin and shrugged, rolling his eyes, and looking at AK.

Bhavin prepped himself and began.

"Aa pavan moujona pacchhal ane tey ramta ramta maara paase avechhe."

Hiten didn't say anything. AK looked confused since he couldn't understand Gujarati.

Bhavin nudged Hiten, "Translate, *yaar."*

"Oh yea…I am sorry…I was so surprised by your…I forgot…please repeat again," requested Hiten surprised. Bhavin looked at the paper to read. Hiten gestured to AK wildly, waving his hands and shaking his head. *Now, somebody please help me understand that,* mused AK helplessly, supressing his chuckle.

"Aa pavan moujona pacchhal ane tey ramta ramta maara paase avechhe," Bhavin looked at Hiten.

"The air…no, no, no, the wind behind comes to me running."

What in the world is that supposed to mean? Mused AK.

"Hoon temna anandma maja lauch," recited Bhavin.

"I am very happy in their happiness."

"Oh ok, that's nice," said AK, thinking it ended there. Bhavin smiled. Hiten looked perplexed.

"Ane hoon ek mitrna saathe aa anand batwa manguchoo."

"I want a friend to share my happiness with."

"Hmm, impressive," muttered AK trying to be positive. *Ah it's finished!*

"Avechhe ane jaayeche jawaan ani buzurgo tensionwala chehrao."

Hiten scratched his head, "Coming and going, young and old tension faces."

"Yaar Hiten, please translate properly…you need to feel…FEEEEL!" said Bhavin, stressing. Hiten looked helplessly at AK, raising his eyebrows in confusion.

"Hoon temna dukhono sakishichu, temni aasha paida thai niraasha maathi."

"I see sorrows of theirs, their hopes born from sadness."

Hiten has to be awarded the best translator! He is trying real hard! Poor Hiten, pitied AK, suppressing his laughter.

"Ane hoon icchu ek mitra jene maari shanka aney udaasi bataavi saku."

"I too wish for a friend with whom I share…to whom I can tell my doubts and sorrows."

"Tena premma vadharo thai jem panchiyo samajna bandhan maathi unche ud jay."

"In your love, like birds, we want to fly high."

"Wah wah!" said AK, encouraging his friend. Hiten glared at AK.

"Ane icchu ek mitra jeni saathe aav aakashne sparsh kari jaoo."

"I wish for one friend with whom I can touch the sky."

"Thaam maro haath choddi aav aa joothi duniya."

"Take my hand and let's leave this fake world."

What the hell is he getting to? Leave the world! Suicide? wondered AK. Hiten rolled his eyes and raised his eyebrows, concerned.

"Banawye apni kismet navi."

"Let's make a new destiny."

"Jyarthi tane malyo chho aapne banawye chhe."

"Since I met you…I want to make you mine."

"Hamna ane hames maate tu mari valentine?"

"So, now and forever, will you be my valentine?"

"Did you guys like it? I suddenly woke up in the middle of the night and wrote this…I knew the minute I wrote it that this is super!" said Bhavin, all excited and grinning from ear to ear.

"Who are you proposing to in this poem?" asked Hiten, relieved. AK had a sheepish grin on his face. Hiten kept a straight face.

"Wow! I was…completely…stunned!" said AK smiling, grateful the painful ordeal was over.

"Yea, we had no idea you were such a powerhouse of talent," added Hiten.

"Man, you blew us away," said AK.

"Thanks, *yaaron*! I am hoping that Dimple likes it," said Bhavin.

"Are you planning to propose to her?" asked AK.

"Yea I can't wait any longer…I am losing patience," he said

"But why do you want to propose to her in October… valentine *na*…February is far away," said Hiten, confused.

"Think future *yaar*…if I propose to her now and she agrees…then we'll celebrate our valentine's day together *na*," said Bhavin, his eyes gleaming with confidence.

"Wow! I admit I never thought of that," said AK, flabbergasted.

"Please, *yaar*, next time you get ideas in the middle of the night…please go back to sleep…stop all this poetry business…doesn't suit you," said Hiten, chuckling.

"Why? What do you mean by that?" asked Bhavin, a trifle upset. "You didn't read with the feeling I expected!" he added quickly.

"You propose to her with this poem, that's the end of you…first, I thought you were writing about farting… then, I felt you were talking about suicide…then, in the end it is just valentine…No *rey*…you know…you concentrate on your studies…now," said Hiten, shaking his head and pretending to fall at his feet, "And hello! What feelings eh…because of all this feeling," Hiten pointed to the poetry, "I feel I have a headache now! Feeling, eh!" AK burst out laughing. Hiten chuckled too.

"Oh, so Gujju prince thinks romance is meant only for the rich, eh!" said Bhavin, irritated, snatching away the paper.

"Hey, what *bhaisaab*? You are blabbering anything that comes to your mind," retorted Hiten.

"Guys, please…calm down!" Turning to Hiten, he said, "He made a genuine effort…propose to her…she may like the effort," advised AK.

"May?" said Bhavin, catching on this probability.

"She may not like the poem but she will accept your proposal for sure," explained Hiten.

Bhavin's shoulders drooped.

"Hey, Bhavin…there is only one way to find out…do it," said Hiten, patting his shoulder.

Recollecting all that he heard of Dimple and Bhavin from Nehal, AK was sure that the embers were smouldering on either side. They only needed to be brought closer.

"Bhavin, trust me! I am sure of this…she loves you too…but, maybe, there is something that holds her back…and it's probably the fact that you are too shy to take the first step," suggested AK.

Bhavin looked away dejected.

"Forget all that…the poem was a…I fooled thinking myself that I am someone like some future Tagore."

"Relax *yaar*! You fooled us too," joked Hiten laughing away.

Bhavin smacked Hiten's back. AK too joined in and chuckled.

Their topic veered towards AK's recent developments with Nehal. Both of them hugged him congratulating and wishing him the best.

In the pitch darkness of his room, he lit the last Rothmans cigarette and waited longingly to hear her. What was taking her so long? Of course, maybe it was not possible to call tonight…there might have been guests…or maybe the phone is dead…maybe her naughty nephew hurt himself. Besides there is no commitment that she should call me every day but at least I would like to hear her voice once in a day…at least once in a day. His cigarette finished. He stubbed it on the outer side of his bedroom window. Having given up hope he retired back to bed.

The phone rang. Instantly he picked it up.

"Hello," he answered "What took you so long?"

There was a slight delay and disturbance at the other end.

"Hello Hello…hello," he said repeatedly.

"Hello! Can you hear me now?" asked the womanly voice.

Oh shit! Mom! Shit! I hope she didn't hear what I said! Where is Nehal?

"Hello mummy! Yea, I can hear you," said AK quickly, his face paled.

"You don't sound sleepy…were you awake?" she asked.

"I was studying all this time. I just got prepared to go to sleep," said AK.

"Ok…how are classes going on?" she asked, concerned.

"Classes are fine…going on. They are covering a lot of portions quickly," he said.

"Good, study well and make us proud…wait, I will give the phone to dad," said his beloved mom, passing the phone over to his dad.

AK could hear the call waiting beeps over the phone. At this time of the night, it had to be Nehal. He was sure of it. Oh dad! Please keep the phone now! His impatience was now inching out of bounds.

"Hello *mone*! How are you?" asked Dad softly in his deep baritone.

"Yea, fine, dad," responded AK. In the background, the gentle second call tone was increasingly drilling into his patience.

The second call tone came again. I have to get this now. Only this can work! He has to keep the damn phone NOW. Damn it, in every love story fathers are the villains, either the girl's or the hero's! Damn it!

"What? Hello, hello…hello…I can't hear you…can you hear me? There is some disturbance in the line," lied AK.

"Oh…hello, hello…ok then, bye," his dad said.

"Hello…ah ok, bye," and he cut the call nearly biting his tongue at the last goof up.

AK quickly answered the call. He heaved a sigh of relief when he heard her voice.

"Were you trying for a long time? I was on the phone with my parents," said AK.

"Hey, that's nice…how are they? Please, carry on talking to them…we can talk later on," she said.

"Hey, no…my parents finished for today and they will call me sometime tomorrow. Besides, when you were calling. I hurried and cut the call."

"Why did you do that?" asked Nehal, concerned.

"What do you mean? Look, I wanted to hear your voice…and my dad was lecturing me as usual," he said.

"AK, stop this habit…you can't take your parents for granted…why this kind of behaviour? If your dad was scolding you, it was out of concern," she said, sounding annoyed.

Wow! At this rate, she will definitely respect my folks a lot! That's nice! smiled AK.

"What happened? *Bolti bandh kya?*" she asked (lost your voice?)

"No! I was just listening to you…you sound cute when you are angry," he said, smiling.

"Silly boy…" she blushed.

"Yea I do feel silly…silly that I chased Shikha when it is you I should have been after…and it is also silly that I feel so good…the way I have fallen for you and all that," said AK.

"Really? Me too!" said Nehal, blushing.

A few brief seconds of pause went by.

"What happened? Why so quiet?" she asked him.

"Nothing…" he said.

"Liar…tell me," she said playfully.

"Eh, what does your name mean? Mine is Akashan, so easy—sky."

"Rain," she said.

"What? It's raining there?" he asked.

"No baba, Nehal means rain," she smiled.

"Nice…I am the sky, you are the rain…see, we are perfect for each other…sky loves the rain and rain loves the sky," he blushed as he said it. He could feel her blushing too.

"You know what I feel like doing now?" said AK.

"No, no, no, no. You naughty fellow, I don't want to know," said Nehal, blushing. AK blushed and chuckled at her reaction.

They indulged in their small talk for some time. He told her about Bhavin's poem and his plan to propose to Dimple. She expressed surprise. They indulged in some more small talk after. Changing topic, he asked about Nehal's parents and brother. She responded by saying they were fine and celebrating Diwali in Gujarat. She told him about the Lakshmi puja that was conducted in their shop. She also told him that they should announce to their friends later on in good time. AK agreed.

"Come on, I want your hugs and kisses so badly," said AK.

"Noooo," said Nehal "You naughty liar."

"Give me a kiss now," demanded AK.

"Now? People are sleeping here," said Nehal.

"Uff drama queen! I am not telling you to kiss them…come on now…else I will not keep and I will not sleep," said AK.

"OK baba. Here goes," said Nehal and she gave him three kisses in quick succession. It sounded cute, sweet, and funny much to his amusement.

"No, this isn't the way I want," he complained.

"Huh, then how?" she asked, surprised.

"It should be like this--SSMMMOOOCCHHH!" AK demonstrated.

"What sound effects!" she said, blushing.

"Liked it, eh?" he asked with a lopsided smile.

"Hmm, no," she replied.

"What?" AK was surprised.

"I didn't feel it was sincere," she teased him.

"Meet me now and I will show you," he said with a winsome grin.

"Acha listen! I've to keep soon, ok?" she said. (Okay)

"But-"

"Dimple and I were thinking of a movie outing tomorrow, so you also be ready in the morning and wait by the phone."

"When? What time?" he asked.

"I'll tell you...hmm, we'll call you after booking the movie show," said Nehal.

"But any idea what time the show will be?" asked AK, excited at the thought of meeting Nehal soon.

"I don't know...most probably afternoon. For sure, Dimple will check in the paper tomorrow and we'll call you, ok?"

"Ok, that sounds great," said AK grinning.

"Don't you want to know which movie?" she asked.

"Who said I am going to watch the movie?" quipped AK.

"Then..." she said surprised.

"I am coming to see you," he said coyly.

"Oh God! How cheesy can you get?" she retorted.

"What the –"

"I was joking baba," she replied instantly, interrupting his shock by her giggles "Of course, why do you think I am calling you at this time and why do you think I want to see you tomorrow because I am madly, crazily in love with you and want to see you every day MUUAAAH, I

LOVE YOU, sweetheart. Please be ready tomorrow and I will call you well before an hour. *Chalo*, then bye. I have to keep. BYE."

"Yea, ok, bye," he said, and waited for her to keep the phone. He waited to hear the familiar "click" of the line cutting and the upcoming dial tone.

"Hello," she said.

"Hello," replied AK

"Keep the phone *na*," she said.

"No, you first," said AK softly.

"Noo, you first," she said, blushing.

AK agreed.

"But first," said AK lovingly showering a load of kisses into the phone "Good night…sweet dreams and tight hugs."

"Hmm, good night," she said and showered her kisses back to him.

"Ok, I am keeping," said AK.

"Ok, keep," she smiled. And finally, he cut the call.

AK was relieved. *We both had nearly made love and that magical intimacy was so sublime. I want to hear it from her all the time. I hope I am not crazy and driving her crazy!* mused AK.

He considered himself lucky that he had found his soul mate, his future wife, his eternal love. He reflected back on those last words…eternal love.

Damn! My life would have been royally messed up if I had been stuck with Shikha or Tanya. I am not sure about Shikha though…They all say Tanya was a flirt…and a gold digger or as they say…who would stick with me only because I was an NRI, mused AK. He reflected on all events of previous months gone by and he felt great.

What he achieved was a miracle!! Nehal was an end to his loneliness and his eternal love, her presence filled him with strength. He had something to look forward to. His tomorrow looked brighter with each passing day.

Maybe this is what love does! He mused and drifted to sleep smiling.

As decided, AK reached Thane station. Bhavin met him there on the footbridge.

"They must be waiting there...let's go to the theatre," suggested Bhavin.

"Yes, yes...let's hurry!" replied AK, "Besides, Nehal would want to see me first," AK blushed.

"You are lucky, you have some love in your life," said Bhavin, giving a half-hearted smile.

"Dude, we are going for a movie and surely today you will get some time to talk to Dimple and then, you know, share your poem with her," suggested AK.

"You really think I should tell her?" he asked.

This is a difficult question. He thought for a bit.

"What if she really, really likes you! But…she doesn't know it yet."

"*Arrey* why can't she tell me this once at least…or show me some sign that she likes me NO…show me that she LOVES me," said Bhavin dismayed.

AK couldn't see his buddy dejected and then it struck him

"Look, Bhavin, you know what if we were going for some romantic movie today then that would actually work," said AK confidently.

"You don't know which movie we are going for?" asked Bhavin.

"No dude, no clue," said AK.

"I am sure you spoke to her last night."

"I did but I didn't ask her this."

Bhavin gave him a sarcastic smile.

"Come on man, there are so many important things to talk about," said AK defensively.

They reached close to Anand theatre. The teeming crowd was visible from a short distance.

"There they are," said Bhavin, pointing them out to AK.

Dimple and Nehal seemed lost in a discussion. Nehal was in light blue denim and a sleeveless black top.

The boys reached there.

"Yo! So, were you missing us?" asked AK, winking.

"Ah finally his highness has arrived," said Nehal with sarcasm and a mischievous smile.

They exchanged greetings and the boys complimented their attire. Nehal and Dimple complained about their lack of punctuality. AK blamed it on the railways. Bhavin changed the topic by asking about the movie. Nehal showed them the ticket – *Kuch Kuch Hota Hai.*

"What? Are you serious?" asked AK, baffled.

"Oh, this movie, my neighbour was saying, it's a good one," said Bhavin.

"Yes, of course. It's a Shahrukh movie *yaar,*" said Nehal.

"These romantic movies are not my thing," responded AK, dejected.

The girls had booked balcony seats for the four of them in the topmost corner. Dimple went in, followed by Bhavin, Nehal, and AK sat on the outer seat. *I am an opportunist for such strategic locations! I hope Bhavin keeps Dimple busy!* hoped AK.

The movie started soon. In between the romantic scenes AK and Nehal discreetly held hands, gently squeezing each other's palms. Whenever the screen went blank, assuming no eyes were spying on them, AK kissed her on the exposed shoulder of her sleeveless top. She would blush and gently nudge him, whispering, "No!"

He kissed her there again. She blushed and pinched his palm. AK loved being naughty. He teased her whispering in her ear *"Kuch kuch hota hai!"* (Something… something happens) and bit her ear lobe. He was thrilled by his own antics. She pinched him hard, he nearly jumped off his seat. They both were feeling more loved up than the actors in the movie.

In between, Nehal shed a few tears when the hero's wife passed away. AK didn't find the movie as engrossing as Nehal's expressions watching the film. The movie finished after three hours and it was a feel-good movie.

They had some friendly banter over the movie. The girls were going gaga over the actors--SRK, Rani, and Kajol. Bhavin too joined in but AK stayed quiet for a while.

"Why are you so quiet?" asked Bhavin.

"Nothing...I think the movie was good but too much of an emotional attack, man! So much wasn't required," he said

"Shut up AK! The movie was perfect! You are just jealous of SRK," teased Dimple.

"Yea I can't help thinking if I ever got into movies surely, he would be out of business," AK shot back and laughed. He quickly added, "Salman was awesome man! He had a small role, did a superb job."

"Stop flying AK...enough...and Salman cannot come close to SRK," said Nehal mocking him. This went on for some time and AK gave up.

At quarter past three, late noon, they were all famished. Dimple shot down Nehal's idea of dhoklas with her cravings for vada pav.

"If you have come to Thane then you have to go to Kunjvihar!" exclaimed Bhavin. They were all excited and walked over to the eatery in Thane West crossing over the foot bridge.

"I have heard of this before, vada pavs, right?" said Nehal.

"Yes, jumbo size vada pavs!" said Bhavin, his eyes widening, "After today, AK will never feel hungry."

"Have you been here before?" asked AK.

"No! This is my first time but I like knowing more about a place before I go there," said Bhavin.

Ambling, they soon reached the venue and enjoyed their piping hot jumbo spicy vada pavs. Bhavin was right. The vada pavs were indeed very filling. All of them enjoyed it. AK loved being in Mumbai. There was so much of life to explore in this city, especially when one was away from parents. *Of course, I have to stay within my limits! No sex! No drugs! But everything else was totally OK!* He mused.

At the first ring of the phone, AK threw away the cigarette and answered it. He could hear heavy breathing on the other side. AK feared to answer it.

"AK!" called the voice panting.

"Bhavin! Everything ok? You sound like the cops are behind you," joked AK. He laughed.

"She said YESSSSS! And so, I ran! I am very happy!" announced Bhavin.

"Hey! Congrats! Double congrats!" complimented AK, "This calls for a big party!!"

"*Arrey yaar* but one stupid thing…she said don't tell anyone now!" said Bhavin.

"What's with these two girls? Don't tell anyone, don't tell," sighed AK.

"*Nah yaar*, us Gujjus are very conservative *na*, that's why," explained Bhavin. AK disagreed, but he trusted his friend would know better.

CHAPTER 16

*I*t was a warm sunny morning after the Diwali holidays. AK broke the news of Bhavin and Dimple to Hiten. He was taken aback and his curiosity to know more drove them all out in the campus. The new lover boy blushed.

"Bhavin, *yaar*, I am very happy for you…tell me everything," said Hiten as he wiped away dust from the bench before they sat.

"Congratulations Bhavin!" said Hiten, giving him a handshake.

"Thank you Hiten *bhai*!" replied Bhavin, smiling.

"Forget congrats! Don't do any silly mistakes before the wedding, ok?" warned AK.

"You are forgetting I am not you!" pat came Bhavin's reply.

They all laughed.

"That's what I am worried about! You won't do anything, she will tie a rakhi on your hand and go away," AK shot back. They laughed and Bhavin proceeded to tell them how it happened. AK had heard this before, and so Bhavin continued to narrate to Hiten in Gujarati while AK listened on.

"Akash, hi," he heard a feminine voice call him. All of them looked up. Strolling over to where they sat, she looked alluring in her dark blue denim kurta and white salwar. AK knew her height would be an intimidating factor for most boys in the college, but not for him. He was nearly 6 feet while she was 5'9". Apart from her clear, sweet voice and charming smile, a calm aura of an early morning prayer that assures a devotee of a blessed day ahead defined Jasmeet Kaur.

"Hi Jasmeet!" waved AK. She waved back.

"Hey, how are you?" she smiled.

"Fine and you?" he asked getting up from the bench as he smoothed his jeans and ambled halfway towards her.

"Bored yea…Neena, my friend, is absent today," she said "Eh, coffee?" she said gesturing towards the café. AK smiled and nodded.

He bunked college lectures without a care since she signed attendance for him regularly. So, having coffee with her once in a while was obligatory! He sometimes wondered if what Hiten and Bhavin said was true. They had often spotted her staring at AK.

"You know, we never got to speak much…so tell me," she said. AK was a trifle surprised. He knew he was not a good conversation starter.

"Yea I know…you tell me," said AK. She eagerly took the lead. She asked him about his parents, siblings, and his place of stay. He answered.

"Dubai eh…that's why your mannerisms and English are different," she noted.

He learnt her family were devout Sikhs and she had two strict elder brothers. She lived in Thane.

"Well, your English is good as well. So, can I assume that you are from the US or something?" said AK sceptically. Jasmeet laughed at AK's cheekiness.

"Oh, come on now, you don't have to pull my leg so much," said Jasmeet adjusting her dupatta around her face, "There are a few friends of mine in the building who are NRI's and I do mingle with them. One of them is from Kuwait, so I think…I can spot NRI's easily."

They entered through the clearing which lead them to the campus crowd's fave joint 'The Nescafe coffee shop'.

"Coffee? Cold?" he asked her. She nodded. He fetched two cold coffees and came to her, "Here you go."

"My close friends call me Jas! You are close enough," she said inching closer to him almost brushing his shoulder with hers. He chuckled.

"Any more and it will be a scandal," he said chuckling at her flirtatious wit. Her boldness surprised him.

"Ok, so I am a close friend now, eh?" he said, amused, with a lopsided grin.

"Hmm, ok, you are my close friend now, so...tell me REALLY. Do you have a girlfriend, A LOVER?" she asked curiously, biting her lower lip.

"Hmm...guess," suggested AK with a lopsided grin. "Hmm, you are a smart woman, right?" added AK.

"Of course," Jasmeet nodded.

"Guess...am I hitched, ditched, or never pitched?" asked AK smiling.

"What's with you? Even girls don't act this over smart," said Jasmeet, pulling her face, as she crossed her leg and stood there.

"I am seeing someone. I really like her a lot," said AK softly. He watched her eyes change from limpid white to a tinge of pink.

"Hmm, I knew it...congrats!" she said as her eyes moistened. One look at her and he knew today's sorrow would last longer than a month of joy. He understood her turmoil but words failed him. She stared into the cup of cold coffee and kept sipping it as if it were piping hot.

Where are your friends when you need them? He mused, *help me out, it is getting awkward.* Luckily for AK, two familiar faces walked in, Hiten and Bhavin. *Speak of the devil...These two will live a hundred years.*

She saw his distraction and she turned and waved at them, and after some brief banter she excused herself.

"Ok guys, bye...I will go for the next lecture," she said softly and turned away. AK and the two boys bid her bye.

He told them everything that had transpired. "There goes my fake attendance!" sighed AK.

Hiten looked at him and joked, "Phew huh... we saved you from that *sardarni*...she carries a *kirpan*!

(dagger) If we had been late then by now at knife point she would have made you Akashdeep Singh Kartar."

"Oh, shut up! Racist!" shot back AK. Bhavin laughed with Hiten.

"*Yaar*, if you had said single...she would have proposed to you today 100%, *pucca*," said Bhavin.

"Nehal is lucky she is not here! She would have known what that *kirpan* feels like," joked Hiten.

"You are not worried about that, I know," said Bhavin, leaning his arm on AK's shoulder, "*Yaar*, she will keep signing for you...she is a nice girl."

AK had felt a tinge of guilt for having hurt Jasmeet, but what could he do? He now belonged to Nehal and no one else. He didn't want anyone else either.

"Huh, nice girl!" smirked Hiten "Yea you will know when you cheat on her...she will bobbit you!" he joked, the other two stared at him clueless about what he meant. Hiten began explaining how the term came about. Apparently somewhere in the West an adulterous man named Bobbit cheated on his wife, when she found out, she thanked his manhood with her kitchen knife. In a reflex, AK quickly crossed his legs.

November evenings were blessed with a pleasant breeze. It was a good time to be outdoors. At Sarvodaya, the two couples put up a fine act of being the usual "good friends" after class hours. They kept learning and practising Math. Only Calculus and Derivatives seemed to worry AK, the rest appeared manageable.

AK was tempted to steal a few winks and some pecks from Nehal, but she didn't oblige. He was reprimanded for this in their late-night call.

"Don't create trouble for me AK...you don't understand how rumours work in our community," said Nehal, irritated.

"Ok, ok…hmm, I am really sorry," he apologized. He wanted to gauge her temper and envy. He told her about the events that played out with Jasmeet, and added his own spice.

"And she proposed to me…" he said. He could hear her grunt.

"I couldn't say NO because just then Bhavin and Hiten walked in…you know it would have been awkward so…" he said, biting his lips to suppress his chuckle, "She said we'll talk tomorrow."

A deafening silence prevailed, he pressed the receiver hard to his ear.

"Liar! I will slipper you and claw her," she fumed under her breath. AK suppressed his laughter. Abruptly she cut the call only to call back after a few minutes and inform him that she was coming over to meet him the next day.

On the way home from Dombivli station, in the auto, she kept quiet and did not even say 'Hi'. AK kept smiling naughtily. They quickly got off the auto. He could sense several prying eyes and eavesdropping ears around them. On the way, he quickly checked the mailbox. There was a letter for *Aji*, he dropped it in through the outer lattice door. He could hear the door open and he quickly gestured Nehal to move up the stairs and out of sight. *Aji's* maid opened the door and he pointed out that he had just dropped their letter. He enquired about their well-being and knowing all was well he took their leave.

The lovers rushed up to his flat. The sullen look on her face gave way to concern that neighbour's tongues would wag, but AK was least bothered. As soon as they got in and closed the door, she unleashed a volley of scolding's, pinches and slaps on AK.

"Ok, OK, OK, I am sorry! I am! I was just joking!" he said in between laughs.

"Was Jasmeet a lie?" she asked, irritated. He shook his head. "Then?"

"Just a friend, that's all!" he said.

"Liar!" she raised his hand and AK caught it mid-air and pulled her towards him. Hugging her tight, he gave her a long deep kiss on her lips and several more kisses melting her envy, insecurities, her worries and their clothes away.

In the comfort of his warm embrace, Nehal felt loved and protected. She lay with her head on his chest gently breathing. Her breath tickling his skin. She looked up. Their eyes met, he ran his fingers through her hair. Her hair was perfectly straight, soft, only slightly curly and wavy at the ends. He pulled her towards him, her soft naked skin brushing against his. Gentle kisses steadily lead to another wave of tremulous passion with welcome sighs and gasps.

In the clutches of these moments of breathlessness, AK loved and adored every facet of her body. He worshipped her every curve, her every turn. She too returned the favour, her coyness long beaten by intense craving.

Their bodies wrapped around each other like bandages on unseen, unspoken wounds healing each other every time they touched. And nothing mattered anymore.

After a while they lay beside each other, spent.

"It's natural isn't it...rain falls from the sky...and here the sky—Akash is in love with the rain—Nehal," he said, blushing, pointing at both of them.

"Poetic," she smiled, and quickly pinched him.

He protested, rubbed his arm, and asked, "Why?" She stared at him. "Next time I hear about that Jasmeet again...that's it," she warned him, raising her finger.

"What are you going to tell her?" she asked him immediately. He noticed her frown but he kept quiet. He tucked his arms behind his head and crossed his legs rocking them slightly.

"You better tell me…else I will bobbit you," she said. Taken aback, he shot back "What is that? Where did you hear it?"

She explained it.

"So, how do you know this?" he asked, curious, and pushing himself up on his elbows.

"Dimple told me!" she replied instantly.

Idiotic Bhavin! cursed AK.

Sanjay rang AK in the evening and warned him that his neighbours' tongues were wagging about a certain girl visiting AK at home.

"These crazy people have never bothered to check on me if I am dead or alive but they know that a girl is visiting me…funny," AK retorted.

"I just told you what I got to know from Patel uncle of B Block, I can manage it if my mummy asks me something…this should not reach your mummy…so you chill…enjoy life!" assured Sanjay. AK thanked him.

A while later, Mukesh phoned AK to ask him out for pool club and drinks. He declined and was met with complaints that he had no spare time for his friends. He jokingly blamed it on Nehal.

AK had a renewed purpose in life. He had to become a CA soon so that he could marry her someday. He knew it was too early to think of marriage but he couldn't help it. He had fallen madly in love with her and now there was no turning back.

CHAPTER 17

*F*alling on a Saturday, Sanjay's birthday was convenient for all of them. AK was excited for his best friend. The gang reached AK's apartment when he was on the phone with Nehal. He passed on the phone to Sanjay and she wished him too.

"The Rascals" went to their usual haunt. At Pravin da Dhaba, they all had their share of food and drinks and were laughing away pulling each other's leg.

Sanjay was the designated driver so he didn't have any whiskey but he had three beers and shared the fourth beer with AK at his insistence.

"Mate, you drank a lot...It's better if Mukesh drives," suggested Pratap.

"Chill, *yaar*! It's just beer," said Mukesh.

"Yea, man! You are simply getting worried for no reason," said Sanjay. AK too agreed with Sanjay and said, "We've been drinking for a few months now, our capacity should have increased."

They settled the bill and left.

Sanjay took to the wheel with Mukesh sitting next to him, while AK and Pratap sat behind. The Fiat UNO was cruising on the MIDC road under the night sky. Bryan Adams blared through the car stereo, Pratap's favourite number 'Summer of 69' played and they were rocking to the tunes. With Mukesh and AK playing the air guitars, Pratap playing the air drums and Sanjay lip syncing.

THHUUDDD! A stray dog that lay moon-bathing lazily was whacked on its butt by the Fiat UNO. It flew away spinning and fell onto the other side of the road howling in pain. The victims' brethren chased the car barking ferociously. Sanjay drove along, unfazed, as cool as a cucumber.

Mukesh, Pratap, and AK were shocked. They quickly exchanged horrified glances at each other. AK and Pratap strapped their seat belts. Mukesh stopped the tape. There was pin drop silence in the car for a brief moment. They were stupefied by Sanjay's composure. He appeared unnervingly calm, disturbing them immensely.

"Sanjay, I think you had too much to drink…please slow down," AK spoke as calmly as he could, trying to keep the tremor out of his voice.

"*Yaar*…didn't you see the dog? You could have avoided it *na*…the road is empty," said Mukesh, concerned. Pratap agreed.

"*Arrey*, calm down fellows! You all had whiskey, I only had beer. I am fine guys, I am perfectly alright… besides it is my *pucca* belief, no matter how much ever you hit stray dogs…damn it, they just don't die," said Sanjay casually, shaking his head as he slowed down the car from 80kph to 50kph.

They exchanged uneasy glances. None of them had heard Sanjay speak this way before. Ever!

"*Yaar*, I think I don't want to die so young! Or even go to jail so young…I don't even have a girlfriend, man! So, Sanjay let's pull over for a bit and smoke a cigarette *na*, please…what, you guys support me, man," said Mukesh, turning to AK and Pratap.

"Yes, Sanjay, please let us," said Pratap and AK insisted.

"Come on guys, I am the birthday boy," said Sanjay "I am perfectly fine and I want to drive my car," insisted Sanjay looking at Mukesh.

"*Yaar*, Sanjay! Forget us, think about them. Their marriage is close to being finalized," said Mukesh, pointing to their friends in the back seat. "They are wearing seat belts already…we both will end up as naked virgins on post mortem tables…please, please, drive slowly," requested Mukesh. Pratap and AK burst out laughing.

"Rascals! Laugh, laugh…yea, what a miserable death! Virgin! Shit!" chuckled Mukesh. They all laughed their hearts out again.

"*Haan*, coincidentally I am Gujju so I have to marry some other Nehal, Dimple –"

"Yea, yea…or you might marry some Kinjal who looks like a round Brinjal," interrupted AK. The guys laughed.

"What a pj! Thank God, we don't have any girls amongst us, they would've felt so bad the way we talk about them," said Pratap in retrospect.

"Huh, how do you know? Your Nivedita's best friend, Tanya, that gold digger flirt! She told you?" Sanjay jibbed.

"*Bhai*, you are in form…true…she dreams of a Mercedez Benz but her daddy can't even afford a Bajaj scooter! Mr. Nivedita is talking with too much respect, eh!" Mukesh said, turning around to face Pratap. He looked at AK and said, "AK, BSNL saved you!" They all laughed again.

"Huh, what BSNL? Give credit to his kidney," said Sanjay, tapping his finger on his own temple. They all laughed hard. AK showed him the finger.

"*Yaar*, don't be such a *despo*…you will definitely get someone to marry soon," said Sanjay, turning to Mukesh and comforting him by patting his shoulder.

Sanjay reached for an audio tape in the glove box. Unable to find it, he asked Mukesh to play Engima's music.

"Sanjay! Please look ahead and drive," pleaded AK.

"Don't irritate me! What is wrong with you Mr. Nehal?" said Sanjay, turning around, irritated.

"Hey, this turn," pointed Pratap and Sanjay realizing he nearly missed the turn, quickly swerved left into the dimly lit lane.

BANG! THUDD! PFFTT! Loud noises filled the air. The crazy swerve by Sanjay threw Mukesh against the windshield. In the backseat Pratap's head collided against the window and against AK's head. They all winced in pain as they sat back upright on their seats, their dazed eyes refocusing back to reality. The car had stopped and Sanjay sat in the driver's seat, pale as death itself, his hands tightly gripped on the steering wheel, his shoulders and lips trembling.

They all stepped out of the car dreadfully and slowly one after the other. Sanjay stepped out at last. Pratap's knees buckled under fear, he was down on the road. AK stood petrified. Mukesh held his head in his hands in despair. The car's head lights showed the damage that lay in front of them. The man was underneath the motorcycle, there was blood all over him.

Exchanging panic-stricken glances amongst each other, Sanjay staggered towards the victim. After a few seconds, he turned and ran unsteadily, pulling himself away from the scene. Tears, fuelled by guilt and fear, streaming down his face.

Pratap got up and he too tried to run but Mukesh stopped him. Pratap was crying like he lost his kin. "Nivedita was telling me she had a bad feeling about tonight!" He slapped his own head "I should have listened to her."

AK was transfixed to the spot, gazing at the body lying still. Mukesh knelt down and quickly checked the body while AK staggered over to Pratap to pacify him. Hastily, Mukesh rushed over to AK, gripped his shoulders and shook him up.

"*Bhai*, we've to act FAST! Don't call out any names," warned Mukesh. AK felt life crawling into his legs in the dead of the night.

"Shit! Man, we are so SCREWEDD!" cried Pratap.

Mukesh said nothing. He quickly walked over to the car and turned off the headlights. Sanjay was still running as far as his legs would carry him. Pratap and AK looked at Mukesh. He gestured with his finger to his lips indicating silence and pointing towards Sanjay. He gestured towards AK to run and catch him.

AK ran behind Sanjay faster than he could think. He caught up with the birthday boy just as he was about to collapse.

"Sanjay, please, calm down! It's ok! No one saw us…there are no proper street lights here. We'll take him to the hospital. We'll save him. He will be fine. Don't worry," assured AK, hugging his dearest friend.

"I am a murderer," whispered Sanjay amidst his uncontrollable tears.

"No, no you are not," said AK, trying to pacify him. AK felt guilty too. They looked over at Mukesh and Pratap. They both kneeled over the body and quickly got into the car and sped over to AK and Sanjay. Strangely, Mukesh didn't turn on the headlights.

Mukesh flung open the back door of the car as soon as they neared them. "Get in quick!" he demanded.

"Is he dead?" asked Sanjay, standing outside the car.

"No…not yet," replied Mukesh.

"Then, let's take him to the hospital," said AK placing one foot in the car.

"Yea, we will…trust me, he will live. I have already checked him, he will live. I know what I am talking about…but first we got to do something else," said Mukesh confidently.

"What? No, let's get him there NOW!" insisted AK.

"Guys, no names…he's alive, he is breathing…and he smells heavily drunk," said Pratap.

"Listen, trust me guys…I have a plan…let's pray this works, just get in QUICK!" summoned Mukesh. AK and Sanjay complied.

Mukesh quickly drove the car through the inner streets of MIDC area with street lights showing the way. As he entered the city he turned on the headlights. He demanded Sanjay and Pratap wait in AK's flat until further orders. AK handed them his keys requesting them to tiptoe into his room without waking his uncle. They drove to Sanjay's apartment and parked the car below his building and pulled out the car cover from the trunk and covered it fully.

Rushing from below Sanjay's building and jumping behind the alleyway adjacent to the building's water pump room, Mukesh jumped over a few walls and crossed the back alleys of a few buildings. AK was nimbly following Mukesh through these dimly lit paths, mice and stray cats scurried away hearing their approaching footsteps.

Soon, they reached Mukesh's apartment.

"Wait here. I will be back," whispered Mukesh, panting. AK nodded. Tensed, the wait felt longer than an hour. AK glanced at his watch as Mukesh hurried down the stairs. He was barely gone for five minutes. Soon he reappeared with his stuffed college bag and the Omni's keys. Cold sweat glistened on their foreheads.

"You better have a good plan," said AK in hushed tones as he got into Mukesh's Omni.

"There are some clothes inside, wear them...NOW! Do as I say," he ordered.

"I don't know what you are up to," muttered AK and quickly removed his shirt and changed into one of Mukesh's t-shirts. It fell loosely on him. Mukesh too changed into a t-shirt.

Mukesh pulled out a small pack of Wills cigarettes and offered a cig to AK.

"Light up," he ordered "Now!"

"It will smell in the car dude," protested AK.

"I'll explain later...do it," ordered Mukesh. Obediently AK lipped one and lit up both.

They were smoking and driving. *What is this guy up to?* wondered AK.

AK's stomach churned as the Omni entered the ill-fated street. Mukesh and AK quickly exchanged glances at each other in panic. They gasped.

"Oh SHIT!" they exclaimed aloud. Up ahead, they saw another bike parked nearby and two men engaged in a fist fight. As they reached closer, they saw that their fallen victim was being pummelled.

Stopping the car, they both jumped out, threw their cigs and charged at the assaulter unrestrained, raining punches, blows and kicks on him to save their wounded victim. The assaulter now lay on the floor defending and abusing them. Hearing the abuses, Mukesh and AK hurtled blows at him with renewed vigour and intensity. Their concentration broke on hearing the drone of a bike engine. They saw their victim speed off in a jiffy.

Before they could turn, they were kicked hard into the tarmac biting humiliation, pain, and dust in an instant. Turning around under the dim street light they saw his tall panting frame with devilish fury burning through his eyes and death aimed from his pistols.

AK and Mukesh stared back in surrender raising their hands.

We are dead, mused AK.

Suddenly, the grunt of a Sumo filled the air. In a twist of fate, they were now the hapless victims. Few men jumped out and roughed them up with punches and slaps. Throwing them inside the vehicle they drove off. The pistols still aimed at them.

They reached a remote area in MIDC and their kidnappers threw them on the road.

"*Nahin, please, nahin nahin!*" (No, please, no, no!) pleaded Mukesh. The men approached them. AK begged in tears, "Sorry, sorry! You were beating up that guy so we −"

Another burly man came over quickly and shook him up, slapped him hard, and pushed him to sit on a boundary wall. He cocked his gun and aimed it at AK, who raised his hands up. The stench and sound of gutter water convinced him he would soon be washed away into the dirt.

"*Bhaisaab aap jo bhi hain. hume maaf –*" (Sir, whoever you are, please forgive-) Mukesh's tearful begs were abruptly interrupted by a strong kick to his gut. AK couldn't watch this anymore. He had enough.

"Who are you people? What do you want? What are you doing at this time of the night?" AK asked.

"Oh, *angrezi babu*! James Bond, eh?" (Oh, English Sir! James Bond, eh?) exclaimed one.

"Who are you fucking idiots?" snarled the man who looked like their boss.

"I am Akash! He is Mukesh, my friend. Sir, we were just out for a drive and we saw you beating up a man... he was bleeding, we thought you were trying to kill him so we wanted to help him...who are you?" he asked. He quickly added, "I mean...sir, please tell us who you are? Why are you roughing us up, we just thought of helping a man in distress...please forgive us!" he pleaded.

They pulled Mukesh up from the ground. One of the men checked his wallet and verified Mukesh's name on his driving license.

The same man walked over to him and checked AK's back pocket, they found his college id and verified his name.

"Sir, please may we know who you are?" asked AK. Discomfort and fear were writ large on Mukesh's face. AK understood he should have kept quiet, but curiosity got the better of his fear.

"Special Police!" said their leader staring sternly at them.

"ID?" asked AK. The other men were annoyed and stepped forward.

"*Samant tyala ID dakhav,*" (Samant, show him the ID) he ordered. A slightly stocky man rushed forward. Expecting the worst, AK shut his eyes but his wrists were roughed into a handcuff. He expected to be slapped again, but luckily, he wasn't.

"Now, do you want ID?" asked Samant in his English laced with Marathi accent.

"Sorry, sir, please, very sorry sir!" cried Mukesh.

THWACK! He was smacked hard at the back of his head. The cops were irritated.

"Sir, really, we are so so so sorry! We thought we were helping that man!" cried AK, tears flowed from both of them.

"What made you think that he was the victim and not me? Generally, public watches a fight and goes away but they rarely come to stop it unless there is something in it for them. Something doesn't add up here," said the man, exchanging glances with Samant and the two boys.

AK and Mukesh shook their heads.

"Sir, you are not in uniform! How were we to know that you are a police officer...actually none of you are in uniform," said Mukesh softly.

He stared coldly at them, "You want to be a part of his gang? You two helped Bhaskar Lokhande escape!" he snarled. "We have been trying to nab him for so long! and just when we got him you two fucking idiots come along," he added, slapping the Sumo's bonnet.

"Sir, we are sorry, sir! We didn't know he was that gangster!" pleaded Mukesh with folded hands. He was notorious for extortion from builders and other wealthy business owners. He carried a prize on his head. It had often been mentioned in newspapers.

"You are not in his gang now! But his men will come to thank you by offering you jobs or favours! But when they know that you spoke to us..." said Samant, shaking his head.

"I think you can guess that it won't be easy for you both. You must alert us as soon as they contact you, Samant will give you our number. Now, we will drop you off at some quiet spot. Don't roam around at night and get back home," said the chief.

And so, yet again, I am the biggest idiot on this earth! My saga of slaps and idiocy never stops, mused AK helplessly as his tears flowed.

The four cops put their guns back into their holsters. Samant un-cuffed AK. The friends wiped their tears with their bruised hands.

Their banter was interrupted by some quick chaotic messages on their radio device. Their chief rushed to attend it. The duo soon learnt his name was SI Mandar Mhatre.

They had just begun to breathe freely when they were ordered to jump back in the Sumo. The police decided to drop them back to the same road where Mukesh's Omni stood. Both of them were relieved to hear it.

The Sumo took a sharp turn off the highway road and entered into a small lane. Suddenly, the silence was disrupted by frantic chaotic exchanges over their radio. They turned around and went back to the highway. AK and Mukesh sat clueless in the third row.

Out of nowhere, gun shots hit the Sumo and four guys on two bikes whizzed past them from the opposite direction, continuously firing. In reflex, AK and Mukesh ducked, squeezing themselves onto the floor of the Sumo. SI and his team quickly retaliated and fired at will. Turning the Sumo around, they accelerated hard and were hot on their tails. The goons on the bike speeding deftly avoiding the volley of bullets.

The Sumo's tyre, punctured by a bullet, lost control and hit a wall. The bikers turned around and charged shooting at the police. The cops jumped out and took cover behind the Sumo and fired on while the boys were stuck inside, petrified of everything going on around them. The bullets were now piercing the vehicle's doors, shattering the windows! The windscreen! In this menacing symphony of death and power their miniscule courage vanished.

The gun shots fell silent. Mukesh turned around and locked the Sumo's door. Someone was punching the door and pulling the handle trying to yank it open. No luck! AK and Mukesh looked at the silhouette with bated breath. *Is it one of the cops?* AK mused, quickly opening the door. It was the SI, he pulled out two loaded guns from under their seat and fired. He fell screaming in pain. A bullet had lodged into his thigh and blood gushed out.

Samant ran and gave him cover with his last round as Mandar threw the other gun at him. While he lay on the ground and kept firing back. The sounds of the incessant gunshots had paralyzed the teenage duo. They shut their eyes and covered their ears. They heard some running footsteps approaching the rear of the Sumo adjacent to where Mandar lay. AK and Mukesh opened their eyes, shaken. They saw a silhouette outside the door and it was not a cop. They saw Mandar's face go pale.

Instantly, Mukesh kicked open the rear door, hitting the attacker and throwing him off balance, but the gun was still firmly in his hand. Samant was in a fist fight with another attacker. AK burst out and lunged at the assailant wildly swinging his right hand, landing a brutal punch on his eye. Nearly flipping the gun, dislodged off his grasp. AK quickly grabbed it wanting to throw it to Mandar but the assailant instantly jumped on him and was trying to wrench the gun off his hand, while repeatedly punching AK on the chest with his free hand.

But AK held the gun tight, the gun slowly kept turning towards him. Mukesh charged and hit the assailant with a rock on his head. The assailant was still not down after Mukesh's swift assault. He jabbed Mukesh sending him doubling over. Turning back to AK, just as he was wrenching the gun off his grip. BAANGG! it went off. Both the bodies slumped motionless on the road.

Samant staggered up on his feet. The goon he choked to death was the least of his worries. He rushed over to the two boys, pulled them apart. He was dead. Bhaskar Lokhande was killed in an encounter. He glanced at

Mandar, who lay immobile in a pool of blood. Their other two colleagues also finished their assailants with whatever they could use as weapons.

They shook the boys. AK and Mukesh opened their eyes and quickly checked themselves. They were perfectly fine.

"Oh god!" AK and Mukesh groaned with pain as they got up. The sight of Bhaskar's blood splattered head made their insides turn and they puked.

AK trembled with tears at what he had done. One of the cop's shook his head and silently raised the gun he held indicating that he had done the job and not AK. This consoled AK and he stopped crying.

Mandar needed help. He had to be rushed to the hospital. Mukesh and Samant took one of the fallen bikes and fetched his Omni. They soon managed to get Mandar to a nearby hospital. He had lost consciousness on the way due to blood loss but doctors assured them he would be saved.

They bid byes to three cops—Jadhav, Datta and Samant and a few other policemen and climbed into the Omni.

Upon reaching a safe distance from the hospital,

"OH My God! That was HELLL!" said AK, heaving a sigh of relief, placing his hand on his chest. Mukesh too breathed heavily.

"*Jai Sri Krishna! Bach gayo re!*" (Saved by God!) said a relieved Mukesh.

"THAT'S IT! Never EVER! No more! No more drinking and driving! We went through hell!" announced Mukesh, shaking his head. AK nodded.

"Dude! We lived through a nightmare that ended well…I am exhausted! My hand, wrist, and the whole arm hurts, my entire body hurts!" said AK.

"I don't have any energy any more…give Sanjay a slap from me, will you?" asked Mukesh. "I'll give him two solid kicks," grunted AK.

Mukesh left his Omni below his own apartment and they walked over to AK's place cautiously.

AK rang the door-bell. His uncle answered the door. He enquired about Pratap and Sanjay. He informed them that he saw them leave. His sleepy uncle walked back to his bed and slept off. The duo quickly got into AK's room. Assuming the other two would have gone to their homes, they crashed onto the bed.

"*Bhai*! Bro! What happened today will remain with us! Not good to share man! I nearly peed my pants! I don't think I can sleep for a few days," said Mukesh.

"Same here! I thought I was going to be buried in the gutters," said AK. Soon, weariness pushed them off to a disturbed sleep.

The phone rang frightfully waking them up. Both jumped off the bed and recoiled on the floor. Relieved it was just the phone and not gunshots. He answered, hoping it was Nehal. He missed her. Last night, he was sure he would never see her again.

It was Lakshmi aunty, she called to enquire about Sanjay. Through her, he learnt that Pratap was missing from his home too. AK panicked but he lied to assure her that both were sleeping away at his house.

Soon, Mukesh and he scurried down the apartment and made their way to the Ganesh temple. They weren't there. They quickly called a few of their known friends. None had heard of them. Mukesh called up Nivedita and even she hadn't heard from him.

"You think they went to the police?" asked AK.

"Feeling guilty...maybe," said Mukesh. They sped off to the police station and they saw Samant. After explaining the entire set of incidents to him. They requested his help in finding their friends. Samant chuckled and thanked them for their honesty and everything they did for the police team.

He called on his colleague and gave him instructions. Soon, to their utter surprise a weeping Pratap and Sanjay were brought to them.

"They came and surrendered today morning!" said Samant chuckling, "You boys did a good job even though it was by accident!" he winked. He tore up the confession letter and set them free.

Upon enquiry, he informed them SI Mandar was recovering well. He also suggested they keep the details of the encounter a secret for their own safety and they couldn't agree more.

Later on, at AK's home, they divulged the details of their deadly misadventure. Pratap and Sanjay were flabbergasted. They all vowed to keep away from drinks for a while.

"There is one thing left though," said AK.

"Oh, yes *bhai*!" recollected Mukesh snapping his fingers. Swiftly pulling Sanjay off the chair, the trio generously gifted him with birthday bumps.

CHAPTER 18

The beautiful breezy winter of December was lost on the four Rascals. Over the next week they were below the radar. Sanjay, Pratap, and Mukesh were coping well from the aftershock of the previous week's incident. Staying with family meant one had less time to ponder over this issue. However, this wasn't the case with AK, he was alone most of the time and the fear that some goon from the gang might definitely come after them was constantly haunting his mind.

These worries plagued him for most part of the day. AK's subtle inattentiveness in the Law class caught Bhavin's eye.

In between the breaks, AK would be lost in thoughts even when he was with his trio of friends. After the classes, Nehal, Dimple, and Bhavin suggested they meet for combined studies on accountancy. AK declined.

"You guys carry on, I am not in the mood today," said AK.

"AK, please, you are supposed to teach us shares and debentures today!" insisted Dimple "You can't ditch us at the last moment," added Nehal. He conceded and agreed to teach them.

As they sauntered towards Sarvodaya, they stopped by a small shop to grab a cola and share. Lost in reverie, AK walked on ahead.

Nehal hastened behind AK. Adjusting her dupatta sideways, she paced ahead making her way through the crowd and tugged his arm snapping him out of his thoughts. Turning around, AK looked at her dazed.

"What happened? Which world are you in? I've been watching you…what is it? You are so lost!" remarked Nehal, concerned, "Anything you want to tell me?"

"Oh no, not at all," AK dismissed it with a wave of his hand. She didn't buy it and shook her head.

"No, I am fine…I just got carried away…a bit. Where are the other two?" asked AK, looking for Bhavin and Dimple. He couldn't see them behind her.

"Come now…they have gone inside to catch a table for us all…I wanted to have paav bhaji," said Nehal excitedly.

"Oh great! I have not tried that since coming to India," said AK broodingly. They walked over to the gate of the restaurant. Nehal nudged his arm and stopped him outside.

"AK, what is it? You aren't yourself…tell me," said Nehal, her brown eyes searching for an honest answer from him.

"It's nothing, really…let's go inside," said AK, and walked in and she followed.

"Hey, the name of this place is Achija? What kind of surname is that?" asked AK.

"Guess what it means?" prompted Nehal smiling. This guessing game was the last thing he needed. He frowned.

"I don't know," he muttered, "And I am really not bothered."

"Come again," said Nehal.

"What? See…look I didn't mean to be rude –"

"Achija means 'come again'," she said in a huff and walked over to her friends.

"Oh! I see," muttered AK and walked over to join them.

AK was apologetic, but he was confident of talking to her later on and sorting it out.

They had a gala time there. Each of them had their share of Paav Bhaji and Coke They were joking away, pulling each other's legs over trivial things. This lightened AK's mood.

Happy moments such as these came as brief interludes in an anxiety filled day and soothed his worried mind like an elixir. Basking in her smile, he knew he was lucky to be Nehal's lover. He was destined to be with her and she was the reason he survived.

Soon, after the girls left in an auto, Bhavin persistently asked AK to confide his worries but AK didn't relent and made some excuses.

Late at night, AK was tossing and turning. The phone rang. AK jumped out of bed. Fear gripped him faster than reality. *Could it be anyone from the gang? No, this should be Nehal.* He hurriedly picked up before it rang a second time.

He held the phone with bated breath. There were no utterances from either side apart from deathly silence. After a long pause, "AK…hello," said the caller.

"NEHal!" he almost yelped in shock when his tormentor revealed herself.

"You sound like you wanted it to be someone else," said Nehal curtly.

"What? No. Is everything ok with you?" he asked, concerned.

"Yea it is…" she said, and after a brief pause, "No, it isn't," she added.

"Really? Why? What happened?" asked AK quickly. *Man, what can happen to her? Surely, nothing as bad as what we went through.*

"AK why do you get angry with me? Almost all the time! I don't like it…I feel very bad when that happens," said Nehal, sounding upset.

"Oh! I am never angry with you…Nehal, why would I be?" asked AK genuinely.

"I don't know…only you know better…and I don't know why I get bugged with whatever little thing you say…and I know you are not telling me the truth now…I know you are hiding something from me…and I don't like it…I don't like being this vulnerable," said Nehal, he could almost hear her sob.

"Darling, I am very sorry if I ever sounded rude…I really didn't mean to…I really mean it when I say I am SORRY…today, I was just tensed, dear," said AK. *I can't tell her this. It has to be a secret. What will she think of me. I am such a reckless guy with a bad set of friends,* he deliberated.

"Tensed about what AK? Tell me…maybe I can help…you used to tell me everything before…what food you had, what you drank, everything…and about what you do with your friends and all…but now I feel you are pushing me away…you aren't talking properly even when we meet," said Nehal. *No way can I EVER TELL YOU,* vowed AK.

"Listen, this whole Maths subject has got me all wound up. I don't think I can clear this foundation course…all because of Maths…I regret not taking Maths in my 11th-12th," said AK. Hoping to change the topic and convince her with this lie. She was quiet.

"You are lying AK. I know you. I can feel it," she responded.

"What? What makes you think that?" he asked, surprised by her reaction. He thought he heard some sniffles.

"Umm, Nehal…what are you doing? Are you ok?" he asked. Her sniffles were more audible now.

"You are lying to me…I know there is some other girl…you are avoiding me…now you have had your fun and you want something new…all you guys are like this only," she said sniffling.

"Are you that experienced? All you guys? What the hell!" he shot back indignantly, getting off his bed and standing.

"Oh, very nice! You have focused only on those words!" she retorted.

"Look, you are…" he rubbed his forehead and grunted, "Look, you are over thinking….don't…NO, there is NO OTHER GIRL apart from you in my life…

and yes, I am worried about something and it is not YOU! It is something that happened with my friends…a small argument…it will be sorted out! And I will tell you that later on. Alright?" he placed his hand on his hip. His speech was met with silence.

"Promise?" she said.

"Huh?"

"Promise you will tell me later?" she asked. He agreed and tried to reassure her that she was the only one and true love of his life. "Tell me NOW! I won't tell anyone...what is this, AK?" she complained. He found it cute, but he was bound by the words he gave Mukesh.

"Darling, please don't…maybe, I will tell you tomorrow," he said. She kept insisting he tell her then and share his worries with her.

Her concern for him gently tugged his heart. *I am very lucky to have her…she cares for me so much.* His mind went on a flashback mode recollecting their first meeting and her willingness to help him with Shikha.

He loved the sweetness with which she scolded him.

"Promise me you won't tell anyone," said AK. She agreed and for over an hour narrated the entire incident.

"Phew! And so we are lucky to be alive," he said.

"AK, you liar! You wasted so much of my time telling the story of some B grade film," she responded with a smirk.

"What the…? You are incredible," said AK, slapping his forehead in frustration. And after some more banter AK gave her the excuse of drunken driving Sanjay's car onto a traffic divider. Much to his disappointment she believed him.

"AK, there is something else I want to tell you," she said, changing the topic.

"I am all ears and I am all yours," smiled AK. She blushed and told him about Dimple's sister, Sheetal, being involved with a Maharashtrian boy, and that her father came to know about it.

205

"I think her folks are being too strict! Times have changed…it doesn't matter, we are all Indians, after all, there shouldn't be an issue with all this," said AK.

"Ah my idealist man! You will make a good father," she said. "And yet you don't want to reveal anything to Dimple about us. Beats me!" he complained.

"Dear, we will tell everyone in due time. It is not even a year since we are going around," she said. He loved her too much to be upset with her. He agreed, although he wanted to shout it out from his building terrace and announce it to the world that they both belonged to each other.

"Yea, ok…some other day," he smiled. She reiterated his promise, and urged him not to drink and smoke anymore. She insisted he prevent his friends from drunken driving.

CHAPTER 19

ecember was nearing its end and Y2K was fervently discussed everywhere. AK couldn't care less, he was relieved that the coming New Year's Eve, he and his friends would usher it in a safe manner, away from any trouble. Since the incident, the Rascals hardly met, but now he spent most of his time with his beloved.

Nehal and he were playing under the sheets rock, paper and scissors, in their bare essentials. Each time the winner's demands had to be met. AK lost several times and his punishment was to kiss his palm plus pinches from Nehal. Sensibly, 'No touching the panty' rule applied, and AK wanted to break the rule today but for that he would first have to win.

Victory nowhere in sight, he grew impatient and he forcefully pulled her closer to him. Surprised by this sudden move, she giggled and resisted by hiding her face with her palms, exposing her top. He unhooked her bra swiftly and caressed her breasts with his lips, his tongue softly loving her nipples. Her hands tugged at his hair, her legs entwined with his, opening at his will. Their every touch electrifying, their kisses magnetic, his body athletic, her body gorgeous, his charm dominant, her charisma devilish, and their energy sinful, wild, and indulgent. Every passing moment, they pushed themselves to breathlessness with passionate abandon they couldn't tame.

Close to an hour later, they lay exhausted in each other's arms, cooling their bodies under the fan. Nehal turned to him and said, "Your wife, she is going to get screwed in the first night," she chuckled.

He laughed, "Darling, this is just the trailer for you!" He got up from the bed and from his almirah he pulled out a magazine and tossed it on the bed. She picked it up and gave a mischievous grin. He had managed to get a copy of Penthouse couples. She blushed and they flipped through the pages together. This was the first time she had seen a porn magazine. Their mood and energies were recharged for another round of loving indulgence. This time, they were slow and took their time.

"It is the perfect way to celebrate the new year, isn't it?" he joked.

"Much in advance, yes!" she smiled and hugged him.

Abruptly their loving deeds came to an end when they realized it was well past lunch time. It was time for Nehal to head back.

Late evening, AK's uncle appeared a bit uneasy and fidgety at the dinner table. AK noticed it and enquired. His uncle's reply was unexpected, "People in the neighbourhood are talking a lot. If they misjudge your friend as your lover...then so may your parents," he said. "Avoid complicating your life...you know your dad will become stricter," he added.

AK merely nodded and muttered, "She is a friend and we do combined studies sometimes." He quickly added, "She has come here only twice!"

His uncle smiled, "I trust you son."

Soon, Nehal called him the same night and after their usual lovey-dovey small talks, he told her about the diplomatic warning from his uncle.

"Ahh hmm...see, you are quite popular there," she said, "Definitely must be a girl who spread this."

"Yea right! You will know better!" AK replied sarcastically. He added, "I think this is a hint that we should make our relationship public now."

She was quiet and exhaled deeply.

"Err...why the silence?" he asked softly.

"You know my answer," she replied. He didn't want to upset the apple cart. He let go of this topic.

"Tell me, AK, if you were in my position…a girl who is staying away from her parents to study and is also helping out her cousin sister's textile store and who also gets food from this house…what would you do?" she asked. He was quiet. "Imagine, what would my cousin *didi* tell my papa if they came to know his daughter is going around with some guy…AK, I study in a girls-only college not because I want to but because they want me too. I am a Jain and my people are very conservative, but I am not like that. Did I ever tell you to stop having non-veg food?" she added softly.

Realizing AK was quiet for a long while, she asked, "Why are you so quiet now?" Swallowing the lump of guilt on hearing all this he said, "I was just lost hearing your voice."

"Liar," she smirked, "AK, sometimes I think it is not possible for us to work out…maybe, we are not meant to be."

"What? Please stop thinking negatively…what makes you think such things?" he enquired regretfully.

"Never mind, just ignore me when I say that…I can't resist you…never could…I say all those things and yet here I am talking to you every other night," she smiled. He smiled too.

"Forget all this…hey, will you take me to Bandra church? Let's go *na* this week…please," she said mushily.

"Hmm, a Jain girl wants to become Christian, I know why, because you want to have non-veg," he chuckled. She chuckled too. They indulged in small talk and bid each other good night.

Pleasant weather in January made the mornings and evenings easy, while mild humidity made its presence felt during mid-day. Sanjay, Pratap, and Mukesh were busy with their college and studies. Mutually, they had all decided that it was best to let January pass before they ventured to Pravin da Dhaba again.

January was also a busy time for AK with his CA classes in full swing. But they didn't let that get in the way of their romance. Nehal and he had their late-night chats but after his uncle's warning they decided against meeting in his apartment.

"Hey, you are not taking me to Bandra. I have been asking since when, AK."

"Yes, we will go, just you and me," said AK. She declined. She wanted Dimple and Bhavin to come too.

"Let them go somewhere else on their own, they need to be alone too," he said. Quickly realizing his slip of tongue, he added, "I mean they act like a couple…so we should leave them alone and see, you know."

"No, we all four should go together! How many times should I make you understand?" said Nehal, sounding dejected. AK immediately agreed to avoid any quarrel. However, he never gave up and he tried each day.

Hence all of January went in each other's thoughts. And now February had begun and he couldn't wait to be in her arms. He was hopeful of stealing a few moments even when Bhavin and Dimple were with them.

On Sunday morning, he woke up to his mother's phone call.

"Why is the phone always engaged AK?" she demanded as soon as he picked up the phone. He was still sleepy and yawning away.

"Hello mummy! So early?" he said, bleary eyed, checking his wall clock. It was only 7 a.m.

"Whenever I call you, your line is engaged," she admonished him. She told him the times she called and those were the times he was busy with Nehal. But he feigned ignorance and acted naive.

She warned him she would fly down if this continued. Alarmed, he wished this would never happen. He had to be more cautious. She enquired his weekend plans. CA classes were his immediate excuse.

They reached Dadar station and they both stepped off the train and made their way to the over bridge above platform no. 2.

"Can you see your Dimple anywhere?" AK teased Bhavin.

"*Arrey, yaar*…your Nehal and my Dimple are waiting on the footbridge somewhere," said Bhavin.

"She isn't…if at all they are here somewhere then your lover's eyes would have definitely spotted her by now, isn't it?" asked AK.

"I don't know…but it's silly, I feel every other girl passing by is her," smiled Bhavin, pining. AK chuckled.

"Listen, what about that one there?" asked AK pointing to an overweight middle-aged lady in a Gujarati sari. *She looks Gujju. This will be fun.*

Bhavin blushed, "My Dimple would probably look like that when she reaches that age. But I guarantee you, I will still love her more." He playfully slapped Bhavin on his back.

Nearing the platforms of western Dadar, they spotted each other. The girls beaming waved out to the boys. They rushed up to meet their ladies. AK only had eyes for Nehal. They quickly rushed over and caught a train to Bandra.

They got off at Bandra station and caught two autos from outside the station since no autos were legally allowed to ferry more than three passengers at once. AK and Nehal were in the same auto. Their auto was following behind Bhavin and Dimple's. They were on their way to the famed Mount Mary Church.

AK was engrossed in the fleeting sights of Bandra. Nehal pinched him.

"Ouch!" he responded by rubbing his arm.

"I am sitting here and you are staring outside," she made a silly upset face. He mocked her with a sorry. She gestured that the auto driver was watching them. AK tickled her and she nearly laughed out loud and then she resisted him. Their auto then turned to a road where the seaside was visible at a distance.

"Tell me something about this church," said AK.

"Have you seen the movie *Amar Akbar Anthony*? The Amitabh, Rishi, and Vinod Khanna movie?" Nehal asked.

"Of course! I don't think there is any Indian who has never seen that movie," said AK.

"Of course, there are...the ones who died before the movie released," said Nehal and chuckled. AK laughed too.

"AK, you know...Dimple and Bhavin were holding hands in the train for some time" said Nehal.

"What? No way...I never saw that," said AK, since he hadn't noticed anything.

"Well, they did...that's when I pinched you and ran to them," said Nehal.

"What? So, you pinched me because you saw them holding hands?" said AK, realizing his scream was their warning bell.

"Yea...it was like Dimple and Bhavin were lost in each other for some time" said Nehal.

Damn! I should inform Bhavin about this lady Sherlock Holmes!

Their auto stopped on the roadside near the church. AK settled the fare. They were looking at the other auto in front of them, waiting for Bhavin and Dimple to step out. Instead two strangers, two boys, alighted from it and went in to the church.

"Where are these two now?" asked AK, surprised.

"I hope they didn't elope," said Nehal giggling.

"You are very broad-minded. Thanks!" said AK sarcastically. "Yea…I thought so too," said Nehal chuckling.

"You think we've to elope?" asked AK in jest. She elbowed him playfully. "Maybe," she said with a shrug and laughed.

Just then another auto came from the bend. They could see Bhavin and Dimple inside there from a distance.

"Phew! There they are…I was getting worried," said Nehal.

"Aren't you sad? They didn't elope," said AK chuckling.

"Shut up now. Don't even mention it," said Nehal.

The auto stopped in front of them and Bhavin and Dimple got out and settled the auto fare.

"What took you guys so long?" asked AK.

"We stopped by a petrol bunk to fill up," said Bhavin.

They all hastened and entered the church. At a quick glance, the style of architecture resembled closely to the CST railway station building. Perhaps, this was even older.

"It has a nice old-world charm to it," said AK. The rich history of his country swelled his heart with pride.

"Yea, it looks beautiful," said Dimple. The other two were too awed to say anything, they simply nodded in agreement. They walked into the church quietly. There were a few devotees engrossed in reading the bible. The four friends sat on a bench there for a while and prayed.

Nehal went to the altar, lit a candle, went down on her knees, bowing down her head and gently closing her eyes, she prayed. Bhavin and Dimple went ahead and did the same. Being the atheist, AK quickly pretended to pray and walked over to the right and watched them. The rest were still engrossed in their prayer.

AK walked back towards the exit, Bhavin followed him. Dimple got up and waited for Nehal to finish. He particularly noticed Nehal. This time after she got up, her eyes looked moist again, similar to their Haji Ali outing.

Ambling over to her, he whispered, "I think you are allergic to such places, dust often seem to go in your eyes whenever you visit such places." She smiled and playfully hit his forearm.

An elderly gentleman who overheard AK gestured politely with a smile to be quiet by placing his finger on his lips. AK felt a trifle ashamed. Bhavin and AK stepped out of the church, within seconds Dimple and Nehal followed. The girls giggled at AK's embarrassment.

"Come now, let's walk towards the bandstand area," said Dimple.

"Shahrukh's house is here, in Bandra," said Nehal. Her eyes sparkled.

"Yes, I heard that too," said Bhavin.

"Wow! You guys are updated on all the Bollywood info!" remarked AK.

Sauntering around the place, one was filled with a feeling of contentment. It was a beautiful sight – lovers, friends and several others always came to bandstand. Friends waiting to become lovers, lovers waiting to become spouses, and other youngsters all eagerly working towards their destiny to carry out their self-fulfilling prophecy. They all spent a few hours of their Sundays in Bandra Bandstand promenade. The only nuisance were beggars, eunuchs, and hawkers always interrupting the lovers with their pleading and smiling like some irritating toothpaste commercials.

"What a cynical world we live in…our society blames people for falling in love and expressing love? Like these very same elders were born out of anger, guilt or hatred. How cynical of them to blame youngsters of ruining our country's culture as if to love and to be loved was never a part of our culture ever. Our ancestors wrote *Kamasutra*," said AK thoughtfully.

"It's not that AK. Our elders have a problem with public display of affection, and I think that's right. Keep everything to the bedroom," said Dimple.

"Come on *yaar*! Look around you and tell me which one of these couples are doing *it* in public?" asked AK.

"Huh…well no one…but you know, it's not right," said Dimple.

"And yet we are here watching all of them here. If we get a chance we might also be sitting here like these couples," said Bhavin. *Poor Bhavin must not be getting any action*, AK mused.

"Of all the people sitting here, I frankly don't know how many people would get married," said Nehal.

"Majority of them will, but will all of them get married to each other, that I can't say," said AK.

"You believe in marriage?" asked Bhavin to all of them.

"Of course, we do," said Nehal.

"Why?" asked AK.

"Because that's how it has been for centuries and we know our parents will choose the right person for us and that's how society works," said Dimple.

"I don't agree with all of that," said Nehal.

"I think it's dumb," said AK.

"Ok, let me ask you two questions. A – Are you not capable of choosing someone for yourself? B – Are you sure you will not regret after marriage, if the man you married changes drastically after wedding?" asked Bhavin.

"I know I am capable of choosing someone on my own, but I don't wish to hurt my daddy and I want this to be his choice," said Dimple. Bhavin accidentally stepped on a crushed plastic bottle crushing it further.

"So, you are ok to pay dowry and have an arranged marriage but you are saying NO to love marriage and ZERO dowry?" asked AK, surprised.

"Very good point, AK! He should be a lawyer *na* Dimple," said Nehal, chuckling.

"Times are changing Dimple. They are changing rapidly. There were no mobile phones earlier…now there are. I think in the future these tariffs would reduce and we will all be having mobile phones. And even then, we would be seeing that in our society certain traditions and systems don't change soon," said Bhavin.

"You see Dimple, if your parents chose the guy for you and your marriage didn't work out then they would feel it is their fault…but if you chose the guy and your marriage fails then it is your fault," said AK.

"Why marry to break it in the first place?" she asked.

"Exactly! So, what would change if you marry a guy of your choice?" asked AK, as they ambled on.

"I can't hurt my papa," she said.

"Maybe your guy, whenever you have one, can convince your papa that he will keep you happy always," said Bhavin.

Dimple paused for a bit. The breeze from the sea side grew stronger as the truth of Bhavin's words sank in.

"Guys, stop all these silly talks, *yaar*," said Nehal.

"I have to agree with Bhavin on what he said…and yea, let's chuck this philosophical chat dude," said AK. He understood where Bhavin's thoughts came from. He was sure he would know something new later.

The four of them sauntered around bandstand, had some sev puri from a hawker. Later, AK had some tender coconut juice with relish. Nothing could quench thirst better. As they walked AK noticed two guys sitting very close to each other.

"Hey, see that…they must be gays," said AK nudging Nehal and pointing to two guys sitting very close to each other.

"Dumbo! Don't point, have some manners," retorted Nehal seriously.

"Look, there are girls just like the movie *Fire*," said Nehal quickly pointing at them and withdrawing her finger.

"Dumbo! Have some manners," AK mocked her back.

"Ok I know…sorry," Nehal said playfully.

Since Nehal and AK were brisk walkers, they were several paces ahead of Dimple and Bhavin. They glanced behind to check where these two friends were and slowed down their pace.

"Have you seen the movie *Fire*?" asked Nehal.

"No, I haven't. I never will. Have you?" asked AK.

"Yea I did and I think the story was a good one," she said.

"I didn't see the movie and I don't plan to either because I can't relate to this concept of homosexuality. I can't get my head around it and I think it's wrong," said AK trying to justify his dislike for the movie.

"AK, I am not saying that it is right or wrong, But I am saying that I understand it. And I don't think it's a problem like an illness or something. I think it's normal to be gay," Nehal replied with a calmness he couldn't place.

"What's wrong with you Nehal? I mean…are you?" mocked AK.

"Just because I support it doesn't mean that I am a lesbian…it only means that I feel compassion for them," Nehal retorted back.

"Huh, like Jesus Christ?" mocked AK, bewildered.

"What? Why did you say that?" asked Nehal, surprised.

"Nothing, I meant like Jesus Christ, you are 'compassionate'. I am sure your touch can heal them," AK was all smiles, as he stepped out of reach of Nehal's kick.

"I can't believe you are such a bigoted racist, AK!" Nehal replied.

"Imagine, tomorrow if your son were to turn out gay…would you kick him out of the house? Would you love him less than your other children?" fumed Nehal.

"Chill! Don't get so serious! Gosh! Are you listening to yourself? Listen, Nehal. I don't want to start an argument. I would love my son or daughter whoever it is. It's not possible to take that kind of offensive stand against my own flesh and blood. But, on second thoughts. What the hell? They would NEVER be like this! NEVER. Well, if they do turn out to be like that, then, yea, I would accept them also," AK replied back sternly.

"I don't blame you…you just cannot understand certain things!" Nehal said as she shook her head, mumbling something in Gujarati. The unspoken words echoed louder through their eyes. They realized that opening their mouths could create more pandemonium so they continued in silence.

Standing by the window of his bedroom, puffing his cigarette, he contemplated about the day that went by and how to plan Nehal's birthday, on 11 February 1999, which was a Thursday, apart from organizing a treat with the group. Valentine's Day was falling on a Sunday. He had to discuss the plan of their first valentine's day too. He was glad that she was born in 1981 and younger to him by a few months.

I have to make it special for her! He mused with a smile as he glanced at the landline phone next to his bed. The phone rang. Stubbing out his cigarette, he jumped at the phone before it could complete the ring.

"Hello!" he answered.

"Hey, the phone didn't even ring once…you just answered?" she responded in surprise.

"Telepathy darling…telepathy," he said as he lay down on the bed.

"Hmm…today morning what debate, uh, between Dimple and Bhavin uff…sometimes, I think there is something going on between them…sometimes, I think there is nothing," she said.

"Never mind them…let's focus here where we've everything! Shall we?" said AK chuckling. She smiled.

"So, tell me what does my darling want on her birthday? Hmm?" asked AK. He was ready to move mountains for her.

"Nothing...just nothing," she said sternly.

"Hey come on –"

"Noo, no AK, dear, please don't…you are not earning, you are just a student…you shouldn't be spending your parent's hard-earned money like this," she said.

"Huh, shut up! Then why did you gift me? You shouldn't have," he retorted.

"Uff, you know I am working in my cousin sister's shop *na*. I make 1500 rupees every month plus I also get to wear clothes from there," she giggled.

"So, what? You could've saved it for yourself," he said, "Don't buy anything for me anymore...ok?" he added.

"Ok, by the way, after your birthday I have not got you anything at all," she said.

"Hmm, I don't want you to waste your hard earned money!" he said.

"I have decided to get you something. I hope you like it," he said.

"Don't, I may not like it," she said.

"Ok then give it someone else," he said seriously.

"No, I was just joking. I will like it, I am sure you will pick something nice for me…but I am thinking what will I tell at home?" she asked. He suggested that she make an excuse that she got it herself. She agreed.

"For valentine's we can't go anywhere, eh?" she said.

Unclear if she was asking or saying, he asked her "Are you asking me or telling me?"

"*Arrey*, dear, I am telling you it would be very silly to go on valentine's day...people at home would know… and you know, can't take the risk," she said.

"This is our first valentine's together!" remarked AK "Then when should we celebrate? You know I miss you…It's been so long since we spent time with each other! I want to…you know…do all lovey dovey things with you," he said mushily.

"AK, I know what you mean…naughty fellow!" she chuckled, "Look, Valentine's is on a Sunday, I cannot go out that day…hmm, yea, let's go to Maratha Mandir on Monday."

"What sort of a temple is that?" he asked, surprised.

"You are such a duffer! That's the temple where you will see the God of romance, Shahrukh – *Dilwale Dulhaniya Le Jayenge*!" she said excitedly.

"Oh, you mean the film…it's a theatre?" he asked, surprised.

"AK, you are such a fool! How come you don't know this?" asked Nehal, offended.

"What to do, darling? If it hadn't been for you I wouldn't have known anything about Mumbai," he replied sarcastically.

"Yea I know that…but you don't have to thank me… it's ok," she giggled. "Ok, so plan confirmed, huh?"

"Yea, I am cool with it but won't Dimple know? What excuse will you give her?" he asked.

"I don't know but I will think of something then," she said.

Time went by as they discussed their itinerary and attires for valentine's day and a host of other sweet nothings. As was ritual, they closed their call by showering kisses on each other.

AK's night was never completed without speaking to her, and his sleep never peaceful without hearing her voice and his ears yearned to hear her soft kisses. And his dreams only about her and their life together.

CHAPTER 20

Ambling into their college cafe, AK told Bhavin of his plan for her birthday and their Valentine's day plan. Hiten listened in with keen interest.

"Bhavin, your plans?" asked Hiten.

"Nothing, *rey*! Nothing at all...because my girl is planning her best friend- Nehal's- birthday!" he said, a trifle annoyed.

"I can suggest an idea...you both get out at the same time but don't cross paths," said Hiten.

"For the day, after Valentine's, you are going to be in Central Mumbai," he said looking at AK, and turning to Bhavin he said, "You go to Bandra side...just make sure that Nehal tells Dimple that she is not coming to college on Monday...then your plans are on."

AK admired Hiten's sharpness.

"Easy for you to say...I don't have an empty house for everything," regretted Bhavin.

"Go for some stupid movie, *re*...why do you think flop movies are promoted in the morning? A lot of lovers...married and unmarried...go for these shows to spend time together!" said Hiten "You'll be lucky if you don't run into your in-laws there," he added quickly.

"But hey, avoid any new movie, eh, she will not even look at you but watch the movie instead," said AK. They all chuckled.

Bhavin knew this idea was worth a try. So, he later bought a Mid-day tabloid to see movie listings.

Days quickly passed and Nehal's 18th birthday arrived on 11th February. The trio took her to her favourite snack joint and got her dhoklas, which she loved. They gifted her a dress material which was of Dimple's choice. She remembered that Nehal had seen it in a shop once and wanted it for herself.

AK did not want to give his gift to her in front of them, it would be too obvious. So, he got her a small eggless cake from monginis. At Sarvodaya, she cut the cake to their chorus of 'Happy Birthday'! Her eyes welled up. Dimple hugged her. Nehal thanked each of them. She promised to treat them all later. She suggested that AK bring his friends for her birthday treat.

"This Saturday, by 6, after classes," she said, "*Arrey*, call Hiten also, the full gang," she added. When AK conveyed this to his friends, they agreed happily.

Relaxed and happy, he lay on his bed, sleep wouldn't come till he spoke to her. She called much later than usual, he could see the hands on the alarm clock glow 1 a.m. in the darkness.

"Hey, I thought you forgot me!" said AK playfully.

"No, I was missing my parents and here people were awake and they took me out for dinner," she said.

"That's sweet of them...so what did your folks say?" he asked.

"What will they say?" she asked him sarcastically.

"Well," he chuckled, "They are all good, I hope?" he added.

"Hmm, yea," she said "I wish I could be with them."

"You can visit them during the summer holidays," said AK.

"Hmm."

"Come on, now cheer up! You were looking very pretty today," he said and quickly added, "I mean you look pretty every day." She chuckled.

"I don't fight or nag you! Do I?" she asked.

"Eh, is it a trick question?" he asked in jest.

"Idiot!" she chuckled.

"No, you don't," he agreed, "Except for telling me to keep away from cigarettes."

"Were you happy with your gift?" he asked, switching to a more interesting topic.

"Yea it is very nice! Everyone here also liked it," she said. "Eh, look I am really sorry I couldn't get you anything...I just contributed with Dimple," AK said apologetically.

"*Arrey*, this is more than enough...I really like it...good, you didn't waste money," she said, assuring him.

"Hey, come on, you bum…I got you something nice, I don't know when to give it to you...it is something to wear...and show," he said naughtily, with a wicked smile.

"AK!" she said sternly, "AK you know...we can't meet at your flat anymore...your neighbours," she said and chuckled.

"What did you think I got you?" he asked, surprised and feeling naughty. "Err, I don't know," she said playfully, "AK, I assumed...never mind…you have such a dirty mind."

"Yea, now blame me, eh! Nice, nice…I will give it to you when we meet after Valentine's day," he said.

"So, tell me what else you want?" he asked.

"Nothing…I just can't wait to watch DDLJ with you," she said.

On Saturday, the day of promised treat with AK's friends, they all met up. Hiten and Bhavin arrived together in the same auto while AK, Sanjay, Pratap, and Mukesh arrived from Dombivli. They all were having a fun time in the AC hall of Samrat Café in Ghatkopar.

After they ordered their drinks and food from the menu, AK gestured his assurance to Nehal that he carried extra cash in case of a short fall, but he knew her pride wouldn't allow him to pay.

Cutting the cake was a predictable affair. And since she already cut the cake with AK, Dimple, and Bhavin before, AK wanted to do something else. After much thought an idea clicked, and the waiter agreed.

Nehal was engrossed in chit chat with friends and she did not see the waiter until he kept the dish in front of her. It was her favourite Medhu wada sambar. The wada and the sambar were both in separate dishes. The waiter had lit a small candle atop the wada.

The presentation wowed everyone. Other couples in the AC hall too smiled at the ingenuity. When the boys wished her 'Happy Birthday' and sang in chorus, the entire audience present there joined in.

Surprised and speechless she blew the candle and cut the crispy hot wada with her spoon. She was grinning from ear to ear. She gave a piece to everyone and there was only one small portion left for her. AK had considered this and soon there was another hot wada that dived into her sambar.

AK knew this was the right time to give his gift because it could pass off as a gift from the group.

In order to keep up the façade of not letting Dimple and Bhavin know about them, Sanjay decided to help with the gifting ritual.

"Here, Nehal, a little something from all of us!" he said as he placed the envelope and the small box on the table in front of her.

She pressed her hands to her cheeks, "This is very sweet! Thank you guys! But actually, there was no need."

"Please open it!" requested Pratap. She began neatly and patiently unwrapping the box. Dimple lunged to tear apart the wrapping. Nehal swiftly pulled away the box.

"Nooo Dimple! I want to savour every moment of this," she said and stole a quick glance at AK.

"Do it fast!" said Dimple impatiently. Finally opened, she pulled out a glistening blue flower pendant with a white crystal stone in the centre on a shiny thin silver chain with matching earrings.

"Wow! It is beautiful!" she gasped in awe. Dimple couldn't take her eyes off it.

"Whose choice was this? Superb selection!" exclaimed Dimple.

"We all chose it," said Pratap casually.

"Yes, *yaar*, with a little help from the lady at the store," said Sanjay. AK was quiet and happy to see Nehal's expressions of joy. There were no tears this time. She opened the envelope and was pleased by the card too.

She admired the gift and kept it back in the box. Mukesh immediately said, "*Arrey, yaar*, please wear it now...just because we guys gifted you this...don't feel shy like Draupadi!" Everyone laughed. AK mused, *bloody Mukesh!*

"Of course not, Bhishmaji!" pat came her reply. All of them laughed at him. She took it out of the box and adorned it around her neck and ears. AK couldn't hide his smile.

"See, Pratap...I told you this will look nice on her!" remarked Mukesh.

"Of course, elders know best," said Sanjay, ribbing Mukesh further. They all chuckled again. After some small talk Dimple and Nehal decided they had to leave. After thanking them all for coming, she asked the waiter for the bill.

The waiter agreed and left only to come again with a big chocolate cake, and placing it in front of her he lit the candle. Dimple and Nehal were both surprised. Bhavin and Hiten had ordered this from Monginis on AK's request and pre-arranged the timing with the waiter. They all sang and wished her 'Happy Birthday!' again.

The smile on her face made it clear that this was the most surprising birthday treat she had. It was already late evening, so the girls had to rush. AK thanked his friends for helping him out with the arrangements and they all went home.

The following Sunday being Valentine's day, AK spent it at home, his suspicious mom called him a few times during the day to check on him. He was glad to be at home to placate her worries.

CHAPTER 21

Alighting at Ghatkopar station in the morning rush hour on a Monday was not ideal but AK now managed like a pro. Besides, what could ever keep him away from his lady love.

His eyes searched for hers amongst others in the crowd. He couldn't find her. Waiting for her on the overbridge, a few minutes passed by like hours. He kept a steady gaze at the west side of the bridge, glancing at his watch from time to time losing patience slowly. He wondered, *will she be able to come?*

A pat on his back and he turned around. There she stood in a three-fourth beige capri pants and a figure hugging white top with black embroidery designs around the neck. She smiled and tilted her head to show the ear rings.

"You look gorgeous! I will always be in love with you!" he muttered amidst the din of the rush hour crowd. She blushed and dragged him by the arm. They rushed into a waiting CST local. They climbed into the same compartment.

After Dadar, they sat together. Public display of affection was something Nehal was averse to. So, when they held hands, she placed her bag as a cover to hide.

AK mused, *this is love…I feel so loved up and this is cuteness overloaded. She looks stunning! Those rich honey brown eyes… she is my angel! I want these moments to last for life!*

Upon reaching CST station, they both had some biscuits and Energee flavoured milk. As soon as they stepped out, McDonald's across the road beckoned them. She gladly feasted on two softies and half a veg burger, while he satiated himself with her leftover burger and his full veg burger.

They bought a mid-day tabloid and checked the timings of the show. "Yea, 11:30, this is perfect I can get home on time too!" smiled Nehal.

"We still have two hours...shall we go to Marine drive now?" he asked. He wanted to be with her by the sea.

"After the movie?" she suggested, "Now, let's roam around the city in the bus and get to the theatre." He agreed.

"Hey, but I really am not sure about the travel time," he said with a shrug.

"Don't be silly, we will reach the theatre somehow... let's enjoy the day," she smiled, holding his hand.

Boarding a double-decker, they took their seats at the top deck, in the front. They sat next to each other. The breeze, the fleeting scenes from the bus, her head on his shoulder resting peacefully, the aroma of her hair, her arm in his, a moment so perfect that a smile lit up his face naturally. He leaned and kissed her on the forehead.

"Happy Valentine's day, darling," he whispered.

"Happy Valentine's day," she blushed and kissed his shoulder.

They passed by Marine Drive and other prominent places of Mumbai like Colaba and Flora Fountain. They later stepped off the bus and made their way to the theatre by taxi.

AK bought two tickets for balcony and they were ushered in. To his surprise, the theatre was sparsely filled here and there and the only occupants were couples.

"I am glad it is so full," he said to her, winking. She smiled.

"I have seen Titanic 6 times, and DDLJ 11 times, today will be the 12th," she grinned in excitement.

"I have seen Titanic only once and this also I will see only once!" assured AK "Because I get them in the first go easily," he mocked.

"It's the best romance movie, dumbo! You have to watch it multiple times," she protested. "You men watch news multiple times," she added.

"Relax babe…maybe others…not me," he said raising his hands.

"Ssshh the movie is starting," she said, pointing at the screen. AK turned to the screen.

Twenty minutes into the movie, AK turned to look at her and she was lip syncing every dialogue of Kajol and Shah Rukh. He was amused by the sight. She was the first movie fanatic he had ever seen.

He grabbed her and kissed her lips quickly. She slapped his arm in reflex and rolled her eyes at him in surprise and blushed.

"What? I am sitting here with my babe and I am watching this movie on our belated valentine's day! When I feel like doing so many other nice, nice things… with you," he mumbled.

"Sshh!" she pressed her finger to his lips. "Not now…please watch this movie for me *na*, please! Every time you are in the same mood!" she said with a naughty grin.

AK conceded defeat. He slouched on his seat and fixed his bored eyes on the screen. From time to time, he would look at her in amusement. Her cuteness in all she did was hard to resist. Ten minutes later, he stealthily kissed her neck. Gently, she pushed him away from her neck.

"AK!" she whispered. Her eyes met his, and then gently she pulled him closer. They kissed. Stealing kisses, hugging, and holding hands in the darkness of the theatre was more thrilling than the movie itself. Their only intervals were when they felt someone would notice them. Seated at the top most balcony seat AK pointed out many young couples like them.

"Secret public display of affection! Hmm, ok, I feel…" she smiled and kissed him on his cheek. They kept stealing and giving kisses to each other until the movie ended. Soon they proceeded where most lovers go.

Alighting from the bus they sauntered on to Marine Drive where the scent of sea salt and rushing waves beckoned. Nehal and AK strolled on, the breeze of the sea gently caressing them.

"Feels like the wind is pushing you to me," remarked AK. She smiled.

"Nah I am just drawn to you...like a magnet," she smiled playfully.

They walked past a few couples sitting on the wall facing the sea. On finding a long empty area on the marine drive wall, with no lovers on either side, Nehal tugged AK's arm.

"Let's sit here for a while," she said. He smiled. They climbed up the wall, she smoothed down her pants and sat next to him.

"This feels so nice," she said, resting her head on his shoulder.

"Hmm...everything with you feels magical, darling... we are magic," he said with a smile. "Feels like the waves are pushing the wind towards us," he added.

"Today is just perfect. Thank you dear...this is the best gift I've ever had! And yes, that party too," she said, stroking his hand gently.

"Anything for you, love," he whispered.

They sat there, staring at the sea, doing sweet nothings.

After a while, AK decided to seriously ask her the question that nagged him.

"Sweetheart, you know you are my first love," he said, smiling.

"Hmm?"

"You know...it's no big deal...but...am I your first boyfriend? I am just curious," asked AK with some hesitation. She smirked.

"I have never asked you this question...and it took so many months for you to ask me this," she said. Her reply made him wonder, *did I say something wrong?*

"Well, you know I always wondered how come a girl as pretty as you was never chased by guys. So, I asked," he said with half a shrug.

She smiled "Of course there were two who really liked me. One guy who met me at my friend, Sheetal's, wedding and the other was a friend," she said.

Ok...a friend? Interesting! Bells rang in his head.

"I see...and they were?" he asked.

"The first one was a smart, fair, and cute looking chap with silky straight hair with middle partition, Nikunj."

AK keenly noted the brief clear description. In an instant, he realized that he was exactly the opposite. He felt jealous but he controlled himself.

"The second one?"

"Well that...was Sailesh, Sheetal's cousin brother. He really likes me a lot but I don't...of course, I like him as a friend but not more than that."

"You know he is also my friend's brother. Sheetal is very close to him. She is very fond of him as her older brother...and you know even amongst us girls, we don't date our friend's brothers...it's an unforgivable sin," she said casually.

Immaturity is when the brain cannot reign the tongue. AK immediately asked "So, if he wasn't your friend's brother, would you have said yes to him?"

She looked at AK. He couldn't tell anything from her eyes. She turned to look at the crashing waves as the wind tried to soothe him.

"Honestly, I like him but there wasn't anything much between us, besides I want to marry the guy my parents tell me to," she said.

"So, do you think your parents will agree to our marriage?" asked AK seriously.

231

"I will ask them in time," she replied "But first we need to stand on our own feet. We need to make a career and earn money…then everything will be easy."

"Yea, you are right about that," quipped AK.

"You think your parents will say yes to us?" she asked, playing with a lock of her hair. He shook his head and said, "Not so easily...not anytime soon."

"But there is something else I need to tell you, honestly…I am in touch with Sheetal and Sailesh since we have all grown up together. Sailesh sometimes write letters to me…and I reply back to him. Please do trust me when I say this, I do love you for who you are AK," she said, twirling a lock of her hair.

Unhappily, AK was discreet about his discontentment, "Did you ever tell Sailesh that you and I are going around?"

She slowly shook her head.

"Why?" he asked. Immediately regretting his question as her expression changed. *I shouldn't have… maybe she will tell him when we tell the world…later.*

"Enough, AK! You are in my thoughts all the time and almost every week…we are doing something together," she said, her voice softened by sadness. "And I love you so much that I..." tears streamed down her cheeks.

"Yea, right…now cry…you are the victim! I am the bad guy in all this!" AK said.

She looked into his eyes, "AK, a woman will bare her heart, her soul, and her body ONLY to a man she loves just like I love you," she said. She stood up to get down from the short wall.

"Look, I am sorry," apologized AK, getting up.

"NO, NO, Move. I am going. I said MOVE, AK! Forget it! I don't think it will work between us," she said, climbing down.

AK was shocked to hear this. His heart sank.

"Why do you have to get angry over this? We will be fine," asked AK, bewildered. "Ok, fine, we won't tell anything to anyone now. Only when you want…ok?" said AK, desperate to pacify her.

"AK, I am sorry. I know I am not being easy either… but these friends of mine have taken very good care of my brother and me. They have really helped my family a lot. So, please, understand," she said and collapsed into his arms.

He held her as she sobbed.

"Can I know helped in what way?" asked AK curious.

"AK, later…please," she pleaded amidst her sobs.

He nodded and hugged her close hoping to calm her down, and raising her chin he kissed her gently on the lips and cheeks.

AK kissed her on the forehead and whispered, "I love you, babe." She looked at him with those loved up brown eyes and said, "I love you too." She gently kissed his shoulder.

A few minutes passed by the serene seaside. Like the waves of the sea hitting the rocky shores, AK's insecure thoughts were lashing his heart. He couldn't pacify his worries.

He muttered, "I have decided to tell Dimple about us. Imagine, she will be so thrilled! And super excited for us!" said AK happily. Her face sank and then she got irritated.

"How many times? How many times do I tell you NOT now! What did we just talk about?" she shot back, her temper rising under her breath.

He had had enough. "You know this whole damn act of yours is BULLSHIT," said AK, his voice raising in public, strangers looked at them.

"Stop it, AK! We are in public, behave yourself!" she said firmly, her eyebrows tensing and arching in anger.

"I am not your bloody child! So, stop treating me like one. I can't understand why you don't want to tell them and keep it hidden. It makes no sense at all," growled AK.

"Keeping it hidden? Yea, go on and tell everyone about it. It is my request that you respect my feelings and my privacy," said Nehal.

"Oh really! YOUR feelings! YOUR privacy! What about MINE? They don't mean anything, isn't it?" he almost bellowed to which she got up and walked off. He caught up and pulled her by her arm.

"Look, I want people to know that we are a couple. Is that ok with you or not?" asked AK.

"Leave my hand! You are hurting me!" He let go of her arm. "No, I don't want them to know, at least not now. AK, please!" growled Nehal, albeit in a softer tone.

"To hell with you! This proves that you are hiding something...you are definitely lying to me about something. Are you two-timing me? Of course, you are, damn it! It might be more than two, three, four-"

"Yea, that's all you can think of, huh! If there is any doubt it should be on my character never yours. Your Highness is squeaky clean. Mr. Goody two shoes, who was this little baby that I morally corrupted! Oh my God! I will be damned because you think I am a slut!" erupted Nehal, interrupting him.

"We are officially finished! Oh wait! We were officially never on. So, that does it. Good bye, nice knowing you...GET LOST!" snarled AK, and turned around.

"Fine! It's better this way," said Nehal "Our relationship has run its course anyways!"

"Of course, someone with experience would know it better!" snarled AK, walking away. Her words stung him. He turned to glimpse, she didn't turn back, he strode on. She turned and looked over her shoulder. She couldn't believe he was walking away without a second glance.

She turned around in a huff and walked on. She did not bother looking behind her again. AK had turned around and saw her walking on. *How can women be so irritating? Is it like this everywhere? I am freaking annnggggggryyy! Grrr! But damn it, I just can't do without her! Why does happiness last so short in love and the pain…it just doesn't seem to end. There she is walking without even looking back!* Wondered AK in dismay. AK decided to follow her. He wanted to be sure she got back home safe.

A small crowd of boys near a tender coconut stall stepped aside to let Nehal pass through. A stranger, a dark skinned young chap in a lime yellow fluorescent t-shirt and grey jeans, coming from the opposite direction, deliberately brushed against her and with his right hand quickly pinched her behind. She turned around in disgust and snapped angrily back at him but immediately let go, hoping to avoid attracting attention to herself in public.

The bunch of boys who saw this paused their conversations and looked on like mute helpless spectators when this lecherous creep passed by.

AK was horrified by what he saw. *I shouldn't have left her alone. It's all my fault. I should have been with her.* His guilt gnawing him as he walked towards him. Every step, every second, they were coming close. In a few seconds, AK and that lecher's paths would cross. They were only a few paces away and AK could now clearly see his face. He was stunned, *what a decent looking chap! What irony! And he is smiling at his achievement! And those pansy boys saw it all happen shamelessly and did nothing!*

The lecher approached and seeing AK he veered slightly off AK's path but AK deliberately collided with him.

"*Eh paagal, dekh ke nahin chal sakta hai kya?*" said the irritated groper. (Hey psycho, can't you see and walk?!)

"*Toh tujhe dikhaye diya na aur phir bhi ladki se takraaya!* BASTARD!" yelled AK. (You could see and yet you collided with the girl! BASTARD!) The groper staggered back and turned to run. AK lunged at him, caught him by his collar, and pulled him hard. The guy lost his balance

235

and swung his arm wildly, missing AK completely. AK aimed a punch at his abdomen and kicked the man between his legs with all that he could muster. He was gratified with a yelp that saw the guy buckle down to eat the pavement. AK couldn't control himself. He aimed another punch into the guys face as he lay sideways with one hand on his stomach and the other in between his legs. Enraged by his failure to protect Nehal and fuelled by frustration, AK unleashed rage he never knew he was capable of. He threw several kicks in quick succession and the lecher was screaming in pain. The other boys who stood as mute spectators joined him on the action while the rest of the public gathered around them.

One of the guys crashed the coconut on his ribs.

"*Arrey abhi bas bhi karo,*" said an onlooker, "*Marjayega!*". (Hey, enough now, else he will die). The punishment didn't stop despite seeing his tears and bloodstained t-shirt.

Suddenly, AK was pulled back, sensing a threat AK swirled around to jab and he stopped in time from giving a bloody nose to Nehal, who only managed to feebly shake her head in shock.

She ran, dragging AK by the hand, and jumped into the waiting taxi. Consumed by his act of street justice, AK had not expected Nehal to come back for him. The taxi drove off.

"Darling, next time don't do such things! Don't try to be a HERO, what if he had a knife or something and what if you got hurt?" sobbed Nehal, checking him quickly. AK looked on and quickly checked himself. He was alright except a few dirt stains.

"If something bad happened to you how would I ever face your parents?" she exclaimed.

"If they ever ask, tell them I hammered an eve teaser," said AK, "Besides what did you expect? That I act as if nothing happened and move on. Or should I think, this is India, *sab chalega* (It's alright)...nonsense! You have come out with me and it is my responsibility to make sure you reach home safe. That's all I tried to do."

"Thank you, AK! I know you are a nice guy, but really I did not expect you to do what you did out there," said Nehal.

Getting off from the taxi, they quickly settled the fare and rushed onto the platform and got into a Kalyan local train.

AK took his seat in the gent's compartment, next to the window. "AK," said Nehal sitting next to him, "Thank you and…I am very sorry for being rude to you earlier. Please forgive me…please."

"It's ok, forget it…I am sorry too, you know. I shouldn't have quarrelled with you," said AK. She pulled out a Dairy milk chocolate from her bag and offered it to AK. Happily, they shared the chocolate.

Cautiously, AK glanced around the thinly crowded train compartment. Hoping they were not followed by the ruffian's friends, AK bit into his piece of chocolate.

Nehal too looked around like AK and said, "You are famous now! I am just looking around to see if your fans will come for autographs!"

He grinned, shaking his head.

"Too bad, we ran too fast," she winked and chuckled. A smile escaped him too. Indeed, laughter is the best medicine. Laughing, AK began to feel much lighter. Quickly, he stole a kiss as the train started.

CHAPTER 22

Bhavin and Dimple had a rather interesting Monday, unlike AK and Nehal.

"So, as soon as she got to know that Nehal is not in college she called me and we met. I rushed and booked the tickets." They went for the movie show of a film called *Gunda* (Gangster). "Seriously, *yaar*, we both were not interested in watching it at all and the theatre was empty too…just a few people here and there. So, we had a nice time," said Bhavin, blushing.

Hiten raised his eyebrows at AK. "Hmm, looks like his day ended more happily than the movie producers," chuckled Hiten. AK chuckled too.

"Oye but the best is yet to come," said Bhavin in jest.

"Really?" asked AK in excitement.

"We just got out of the theatre and there right in front of us…is her elder sister… with her boyfriend," said Bhavin, folding his hands and puckering his lips.

"Oh shit! And then?" asked AK. Hiten held his head in his hands. "Her elder sister jumped in excitement! But Dimple was shocked to see her! Then, in that excitement she forced us to watch the movie again…and this time we watched the film seriously! *Baap re* what dialogues *yaar*! We all must watch this mad film," said Bhavin, shaking his head, laughing. He narrated a few dialogues from the film. They all laughed.

Hiten asked, "What about you AK?" AK remained silent, not knowing where to start.

"Nothing good or you are confused on where to start from?" asked Hiten.

"It was ok, dude...except for some annoying bits," he replied.

"You tell *na*...leave that for us to decide," said Bhavin. And so, AK narrated every detail of their intimate conversations, the eve teasing, his resultant outburst. He glossed over details of their romance in the theatre.

"*Yaar*, AK, you are a half mad guy! Don't quarrel with her in public and then walk off!" said Hiten patting his back.

"AK, it is not just that don't fight with strangers! You never know who is connected to whom...but what you did is right," said Bhavin. AK agreed and so did Hiten.

"*Yaar*, Hiten! I really don't understand these girls and their secrecy of not telling anyone," sighed Bhavin.

"Simple! Boss, even they don't trust each other with each other's secrets!" he said, and they all laughed.

"In my case…she only wants to hide me from her papa!" laughed Bhavin. "The way she talks about him," said Bhavin, shaking his head. "I am scared and I don't like him. All because of his daughter!" he said. They all chuckled.

"No man, jokes apart! I am really losing it with her! I have a feeling she is hiding something...but I don't know what," said AK.

AK and Nehal neither had friendly chit chats nor loving banters, instead only more quarrels. It was getting worse. He thought she was ignoring him, but according to her, she was merely focusing on her studies. Final year exams were a fortnight away.

After several nights, his phone rang at midnight. He picked it quickly. After a brief pause, he spoke, "Hello!"

"Hello, AK!" whispered Nehal, "I hope your studies are going well?" she asked.

"Not as genius as yours...but going on," he said and yawned.

"Look, I know it looks like I have not been spending time with you...just that I have too many things on my mind," she said.

"Like...anything I can help you with maybe?" he asked.

"Eh no...nothing really...It's just me...I've lots to catch up on with my studies," she said.

"Hmm, I can understand," he said.

"AK, for the summer I will go to my native town...I will send you a letter from there!" she said, smiling.

"Oh...I can suggest something better...there will be internet cafés opening up soon in the city. Sanjay will create an email id for me...and I will ask him to create one for you too...we could be in touch through that...it is much faster you know," assured AK.

"Hmm, I see!" she remarked.

"Yea, same day within the same hour you can get my email and vice versa," he added.

"Anyways, just give me your postal address *na*," she requested. AK agreed and dictated it to her.

They spoke for a bit longer and she hung up. There were no lovey dovey kisses or words of sweetness, only 'Byes and Good night'.

AK knew something was amiss, but he too wanted a break. The relationship was draining his energies. He too needed to focus on his studies.

By the end of February, combined study sessions at Sarvodaya had come to a complete stop. March welcomed the warmth of summer and the heat of final year exams. AK and Nehal's relationship too felt the heat, and they would speak on the phone once a week, mostly on Saturday or Sunday.

The incessant ringing of the doorbell at ten in the morning forced AK to rush and open the door. His friends – Sanjay, Mukesh, their brothers and other friends stood there excited, and they pulled him out and drenched him with coloured water and colours, and they burst water balloons on him. Multi-coloured from head to toe, they were a crazy, happy bunch!

"Happy Holi!" they screamed in chorus. They all laughed.

"Where is Pratap?" AK asked.

"We are going to his place now. Coming?" asked Sanjay. He agreed and they went to Pratap's place and made sure he too looked like a multi-coloured dyed wool. AK enjoyed Holi to the hilt. The stubborn stains of colour refused to go after a wash, but he did not care.

He decided to tuck away the t-shirt in a remote corner of his almirah, in a cover, as a symbol of one of the happiest days of his life. *Life is not just beautiful with love, it is colourful with friends too*, he mused.

Soon after Holi came Shivaji Jayanti which was celebrated with pomp and gaiety throughout the city by garlanding statues of Chhatrapati Shivaji Maharaj followed by speeches from various eminent personalities in public. For Maharashtrians, Chhatrapati Shivaji was a source of great pride. His presence was felt everywhere, in stickers, on vehicles, statues, and in naming of various places.

AK had grown to love festivals and celebrations as these spread much joy and happiness amongst people. These happy moments were slowly erasing his irreligious views.

In Dombivli, the Rascals met up during the weekend and visited Pravin da Dhaba. Their last outing before exams, resuming after the Holi week. Nothing like the festive spirit of colours that helps people see the brighter side of life and move on with optimism. The friends too recovered from that December incident and looked on to the future with hope.

Over drinks, their discussion veered around internet and how email would disrupt the postal industry. The boys all agreed, they were living in interesting times. Mukesh and Sanjay were dreaming away of meeting Sabeer Bhatia and his ilk at Silicon Valley someday.

Pratap was happy that he had chosen biotechnology while AK sat mute and confused, thinking he was into something boring, and after so many months becoming a CA did not inspire him anymore.

His friends noticed his silence and they enquired. He shrugged it off using 'listening to their conversation' as an excuse. After a while, on the way back, AK confided to them that Nehal and he were on the verge of breaking up or so he felt.

"Every relationship has to go through such things," said Pratap.

"The funny thing is...what I have noticed is all lovers somehow seem to like this love pain of anxiety and worry...but this is just temporary! *Yaar*, you don't worry for the time being. Just focus on your upcoming exams... this will all just pass by," said Sanjay. Mukesh agreed with the others.

"AK *bhai*, you should be least worried...if Nehal doesn't work out then you will get someone else, *yaar*!" said Mukesh, cheering him up. Mukesh was at the wheel of Sanjay's car and was the only one who did not drink beer, but Pepsi.

"AK, after your CA exams go for driving license. And you know you will fall in love with driving! That's what you need, *yaar*," said Sanjay.

"Of course, Sanjay will know better," chuckled Mukesh, "Every time *bhai* takes his car out, Swati from the neighbouring building gives him a smile," he added.

"Isn't she Satish's sister? That guy who used to play cricket with us long back?" asked AK.

"Yea, that psycho, Satish!" said Sanjay.

"Sanjay, don't push your luck! For all you know she might be thinking with a Rakhi brother I will get a driver free!" joked Pratap. They all laughed.

"I swear! This is one big reason why I want to get out of here and go to Silicon Valley...make my name there," said Sanjay.

"Thankfully, not as a Rakhi bro…but yea, please don't drive there!" joked AK.

"Eh, no way…that's why I am taking this driver with me!" said Sanjay as he slapped Mukesh on his shoulder. They all laughed.

Amidst all these jokes and fun moments AK couldn't help but wonder, *why did she ask me for my postal address? Is she going to send me a letter telling me about her life? Boyfriends? Stop thinking! But why do I feel this pain? Sanjay is right! I am a sucker for this pain! I am just overthinking… this will all pass.*

Strangely, there were no calls from Nehal during the night, and she rarely called during the day. Few times that she called their conversations were abrupt and they wished each other all the best for the exams. She conveyed she would be busy with her studies and hence her calls could be expected only after the college exams.

Final exams had begun and AK was fully engrossed with them. He was sure of passing these exams, but the impending CA Foundation exams in May worried him.

For many of his friends including, The Rascals, when exams got over it was a relief. But not for AK! The CA Foundation exams that seemed a distant speck in the horizon, several months back, now loomed over him like an ominous cloud.

AK's ever sharp dad decided of his own accord that it would be ideal if AK came to Dubai during this time and prepared for his CA exams. He felt his son would focus more on studies under their watchful eyes and away from any distraction. His mom jumped with joy at the idea. And so, when the suggestion was passed to AK, he tried his best to argue the demerits of this decision. Their son was eventually ordered to comply and the tickets booked.

After conveying the news to his friends—The Rascals—he spoke to Bhavin and Hiten too. He was a trifle worried about how Nehal would react. *I hope she will miss me, at least a bit or maybe sound like it, or at least just lie about it over the phone.*

Bhavin had already informed him that the girls knew that he was leaving for a study break to Dubai. Each time the phone rang he rushed to pick it hoping it was her. By now almost all his friends had called except Nehal and Hiten. He waited for her call. He reluctantly went out for last minute purchases and hurried back hoping to attend her call, yet there was none.

Enough was enough, his patience had worn off, and it was already quarter past five in the evening. He punched her number impatiently breaking the promise that he wouldn't call at her cousin's place. The phone rang a few times.

"Hello!" answered the receiver. No response, "Hello!" she said again.

"Hello! Nehal!" he answered after a pause assured it was her.

"Hi! How are you?" she asked with a smile.

"Good and you?" he asked.

"Fine…how were your exams?" she asked him.

"Sure of passing in these, at least! And yours? You must be topping for sure," he quipped.

She sighed, "Don't know, let's see, but I think I did well," she replied.

"I am leaving for Dubai," he said.

"Ah, I heard, when?"

"Flight is tomorrow evening," he replied.

"Happy journey…have a good break," she said casually. The formal tone and the detached behaviour throughout their conversation was inescapable. He gritted his teeth in irritation and soon slipped into sadness.

"What should I get you from there?" he asked, hoping for some semblance of care and love in her reply.

"Nothing…I don't need anything…you be happy and good, that's all…ok, bye," she said, proceeding to keep the phone.

"Nehal, what's wrong with you? Why aren't we talking normally like before? Why can't we just be us like we used to be?" he asked her, desperate for an answer.

"AK…somethings are difficult to explain," she paused and continued, "Maybe after you are back, we will talk…not now…concentrate on your studies, eh?"

"Difficult to explain?" he shot back, clenching his fist, and controlling his irritation.

"AK!" she sighed, "I am sorry, the fault is all mine… it is not possible for us to work in the long term…I am not easy."

"What are you –" interrupted AK, but she did not stop.

"My life is not easy…forget me, alright…we will not be meeting after this anyways. And please do not call…I am going out and I will not return home early. Bye," she kept the phone. AK was heartbroken.

He couldn't believe his ears. *She didn't even wait to hear a bye from me. Nothing! I can't believe this failed! Incredible! A relationship couldn't weather this…her issues? She doesn't even want to talk about it? This whole thing is a lie,* he chided and exhaled deeply. He opened his drawer and pulled out his pack, lit up a cigarette and puffed out his anger.

The phone rang, he didn't bother to pick it up, it rang until the caller gave up. It rang again. *SHE BETTER SAY SORRY!* He mused as he went to pick it up this time. To his surprise, it was Hiten, and he confirmed calling before too. They exchanged pleasantries. Hiten apologized for not calling before as he had to attend to his brother who had fractured his hand in a fall.

"I am sorry, *yaar,* I wish I could come to drop you off at the airport…what time is the flight today?" he asked.

"It's tomorrow, at 5p.m.," he said dejectedly.

"Good, boss! Call me after you reach Ghatkopar. Bhavin and I will drop you in my car," he smiled, "It will be my first time dropping a friend to the airport," smiled Hiten excitedly. AK merely mumbled in agreement.

"Hey, AK what happened? Fought with her, is it?" he asked. AK sighed.

"We broke up...just a few minutes ago," he said, sitting down on his bed and resting his head on his hand. Rubbing his temples, he said, "You were right! I am not meant for this."

"Relax *yaar*...everything will be fine," consoled Hiten. AK disagreed and narrated the conversation.

"Hmm, never mind...distance makes the heart grow fonder...so, just go and come back...and she will be crazily missing you," said Hiten.

AK chuckled, "I admire your positive spirit...I really do, but I think this won't work because...because she is not honest with me...and she doesn't want to... anyways...I will let you know when I start from here, ok?" said AK dispassionately.

"Cheer up *yaar*, everything will be fine," assured Hiten. AK agreed. After indulging in some small talk, they hung up.

AK proceeded with his packing and after about two hours finished. His uncle got him the air ticket in the evening. The rest of the Rascals visited him late evening and went for a drive. They had a few beers and Sanjay drove back carefully this time. He broke the news to them that Nehal and he had broken up. They all took it lightly and dismissed it off as a temporary snag in the relationship. Pratap assured him and confessed he too had such moments with Nivedita.

His friends suggested it was best that he focus on his CA studies for now, and ignore this distraction. AK agreed. He was left with no other choice.

The following day, Bhavin received AK at Ghatkopar station. On the way to Hiten's house, in the auto, AK told him everything.

"*Yaar*, these girls are mad!" complained Bhavin. "She was telling me that Nehal is acting different lately," he added.

"I wanted to tell her, so are you!" he said, shaking his head, "All will be ok. You told Hiten this?" he asked. AK nodded, "He had called."

Upon reaching his apartment, they found Hiten ready with his car. AK kept the bag in the trunk and they hopped in. They chit chatted about a lot of things and it was fun company till the airport.

They hugged him and he hugged them back. Bidding them byes and promising to be back soon he made his way with the luggage trolley. He would be gone only for a month. He felt a sense of comfort and peace in knowing that he may have loved and lost but he gained good friends.

It occurred to him, in this one year he had changed a lot. *If not a lot, at least a bit*, he mused with certainty. *I wish I could see her before I leave…I wish she was here…I wish we were still going strong…men don't cry! Boys do perhaps and I am just a boy madly in love with this girl… but does she even care?* he mused, fighting the ache in his heart. Turning back, hoping against hopelessness, yearning to see her, he found his two friends waving at him. He waved back, swallowing the lump of sadness rising within. Reality was indeed harsher than wishful thinking. He vowed to forget her.

CHAPTER 23

*R*udely, he was awoken by the chaotic rasp on the speaker. Hazily, his vision cleared and he watched the earth sliding by deceptively slowly. He had always been fascinated by this spectacle though he had travelled quite a few times before.

And he heard the rasp on the speaker again, "Ladies and gentlemen, this is your captain speaking, we have started our descent...in about 30 minutes, we will touchdown in Dubai International Airport. Please remain seated and kindly fasten your seat belts." The voice on the radio went off.

In between the whine of the engines, he heard a beautiful voice. He turned to see the owner, and there stood a gorgeous stewardess. He saw her pretty lips move and the words drifted to him, "I am sorry, sir... we are about to land, please keep your seat upright. You look tired. Can I get you anything to freshen you up?"

"Water...please," he replied back smiling, only to realize later, that this action was done unknowingly.

He had barely managed to catch a few winks in this two and a half hour journey. So, technically though he was up and awake, he still felt sleepy and tired. But she had caught his rapt attention.

By now, AK had already lost his staunch, and explored the unknown realms of feminism only to have his heart broken. A few hours back he had vowed to never think of love again. Yet, here stood another creation of the feminine world, beautiful, fascinating, charming, and mesmerizing him!

He was coming back to Dubai after a year. Flying from Mumbai after his freshman year exams, and now in the holidays, to study for his CA Foundation exams.

He needed a break, a good one at that, but that was impossible! He found himself slipping back into his memories. He tried not to relive it. *No! It is all over and done.*

"Here you go, sir. Will that be all?" The beauty interrupted his thoughts.

"Yea, thanks. Thanks a lot…your good name, ma'am?" even before he realized, he asked eagerly. With all the bitterness swelling inside him, he suddenly felt like a fool as he glimpsed the growing amusement in her eyes.

He cursed himself deep within. What was he trying to do? Maybe he needed to try and be "more cool" next time on? *The immaturity of my age! Oh God!* He mused and sighed.

"Nehal!" she replied, with an all-knowing smile and tilting her head.

"Thank you, Nehal! Have a nice day," he turned his face away wincing in disgust that he had even asked, only to be humbled.

It's so strange that what we try so hard to avoid so hard to forget, somehow comes back to tease us. *Why did her name have to be Nehal? It could have been anything else*, he mused, complaining to himself.

He hated the way their relationship had ended. He screamed within wanting this feeling of loss to disappear into the sky. Looking out, he saw the rush of his thoughts colliding with the rush of the land as the wheels touched the ground and the engines whined all so loudly.

As the plane slowed onto its embankment slot, he wondered, *things were perfect! Where did everything go wrong? It was good while it lasted! Maybe…we are not meant to last? I have to forget her! Let it go! But it hurts*, wearily, with a sigh, dismissing his reflections after a push and pull, he succeeded in entangling himself into that flowing mass of legs and hands, joining the furore of the human world, to see his loved ones too.

Bags were being dragged out of the overhead stowage, children gurgling, and everybody pushing forward to get off the plane. The pushes were creating a domino effect, similar to train journeys which he was now comfortable with. *Wow! We Indians really need to change this habit. We treat even planes like trains and buses,* he mused as he reached the exit.

The stewardess stood by the door, with an amused smile, that he hated to admit, made him melt and worse, feel 'childish' in front of her.

These were the times, frustrating as it is, when age and experience were at a disadvantage for you, making you feel powerless watching these beautiful beings of the opposite sex give you a sympathetic 'you are such a silly, cute puppy' look!

The crowd carried him forward into the airport, and he trudged on past the immigration queue, past the baggage counter, collecting his bags.

Pushing the trolley and nearing the exit, he found his thoughts turning to his parents. Had he missed his parents? He certainly had not thought of them as much as he thought of Nehal. He needed a change and that too desperately. But did he come here only for a change? Did he lose his connection with his family? Why did he feel aloof? Was it the spell of age or the magical touch of physical separation that created this distance? Or was it the heartbreak? A tap on his shoulder and a kiss on his cheek, knocked him out of his reverie to see his mom standing by!

5 feet tall, a bit plump, and as dark as himself, he looked at this stunning lady who had made him who he was. Those eyes filled with compassion, the smile and a warm hug, halted his philosophical trek as he dissolved into her arms.

A sudden rush of gratefulness enveloped him as he thanked his stars for having come home. Back home to Dubai!

Maybe you just don't tend to realize that you miss your near and dear ones until you see them! He had missed her, all of her love, pampering, and nagging! He hugged his mom back tightly.

At a distance, he saw a familiar stooping figure, with glasses, and a midriff that had started showing the signs of prosperity, talking over his mobile phone. He had the famous wrinkled furrow on his forehead when he normally went into a thinking spree, deliberating on premeditated calculations of numbers and words that had made him the successful businessman that he was.

"Mummy, when did he get the mobile phone?" asked AK.

"A week back!" she replied. The year 1999 was the year of a new era in telecommunications. AK was glad to be a part of the modish crowd too.

Mr. Krishnakumar, a self-made man, who fought tooth and nail to make his life, knew to take life only the hard way and that in course of time became a part of him and his ways of life. The father nodded curtly at the son, turned, and walked towards their car. He was internally happy to see his son, the torchbearer of his family name and hard built reputation.

Though AK had grown so much within and seen so much of life in Mumbai, though he felt a lot more matured than he had been a year before, his mom still spoke to him in the same old way, with the same old love, and for that he was grateful.

He smiled as he walked with his mother while she jabbered away excitedly about how she had been looking forward to see him and what all she had cooked for him back home.

Mothers! He sighed inwardly, happy just to be by her side. Their drive back home was incidentally peaceful, thanks to his mom.

Alighting from the car, Krishnakumar watched his son and wife walk into the apartment complex. He sighed, shaking his head, worried as usual about his son.

The tantalizing smells from the kitchen couldn't keep AK waiting. He changed, took a refreshing bath and rushed to the dining table; impatiently waiting to gobble up his mom's long missed tasty chicken biriyani.

As he was enjoying the bliss of his "Mother's Homemade food" she asked, "So, how are your friends there?"

"All good, mom!" he replied. She enquired about Sanjay and his parents too.

His father muttered something in between mouthfuls, and AK knew for sure it was some comment to aggravate him but he kept quiet.

He might as well get it out of his father right now itself, rather than keep playing hide and seek with him forever. *It must be about monthly expenses,* mused AK. He had neither kept one nor had he given his dad one…yet.

Mr. Krishnakumar looked at his son wanting to say something, but one glance from his wife and he understood – not now!

"Dad, what happened?" AK asked, "You want to ask me something?"

"Nothing," he replied, shaking his head.

He just sighed, wondering whether his son would ever realize that he was wasting his life doing some unwanted degree course while his sensible friends were getting far ahead of him because they took Engineering!

After lunch, the father and son sauntered off into their own rooms. The mother exhaled a sigh of relief.

She had specifically warned her husband not to speak to their son and spoil his mood. For the simple reason, she didn't want the house brought down from the first day of his arrival. Her darling son was home after a year. When would the father understand his son? She loved her husband and had seen him grow. But her implicit trust in her son, and her love for him, made sure that no matter what happened under the sky, she always stood by him.

But there was a nagging worry within her. She was worried for her son. There was a change, she had noticed, but she didn't want to broach the topic today, maybe later.

Krishnakumar changed his clothes wondering when she would understand that all he wanted was their son to be matured, responsible, and successful.

He was a self-made man, built by his tough past. From his humble beginnings to this day in a foreign land, Krishnakumar had come a long way. The road was tough, and there were days he had almost given up, but the sight of his family, memories of his past kept him moving forward. He vowed that his children would never undergo what he underwent. He would never want that for his son. He hoped that they would understand someday where he came from but he feared that his son would never understand.

Calculating the family expenses and tightening screws on the children's pay styles was where Krishnakumar and his son never got along well. The boy had no idea of the life his father had lead, and the extravagant life his son led made him feel that he had made his son neither responsible nor understand the importance and value of saving money. He sighed, turned, and drifted into a troubled afternoon nap.

In his own room, AK tumbled into bed, resting there, blinking at the ceiling and wondering how he loved the feel of his own bed, in his own room. The softness of the sheets, the cool breeze of the AC relaxing him. He stretched out on the bed and wondered about Nehal. He missed her, hopefully things would get back to how they used to be. With hope on his lips and Nehal in his heart, he soon drifted off into a troubled sleep.

Over the next two days, he began studying for his CA foundation exams, or so he tried. Nehal's memories kept haunting him. He tried brushing them off, with little success. Eventually, over the week he managed fine.

After a week, his mom asked him about life in Mumbai, about the places he visited. She noticed the grey polo t-shirt.

"You bought this?" she asked.

"No, it's a birthday gift from Sanjay and others," he said, lying convincingly.

She hoped that he was not spending money unwisely. He assured her that he was not into anything unlawful, immoral, and unnecessary.

She expressed concern over his studies like all mothers do. She hoped that he would clear his CA Foundation exams in the first attempt.

"If you do very badly in CA Foundation this time, please drop the idea and pursue something else...you can't afford to waste time, *mone*. I am telling you this for your own good," she said sincerely. (*mone* in Malayalam - son)

"I will become a CA, mom, you just chill, ok?" assured AK, though he himself couldn't believe it.

He knew soon, in a few days, his dad would come around to ask him about the expense statements. Sanjay had helped him with a few ideas to wriggle his way out of any 'suspense account'.

One Friday morning, it abruptly began. AK gave his own account of expenses, substituting alcohol expenses with medicines, fruits, dining out. His dad did not buy into it. No mother can see her son lose. She always came to his rescue. AK kept saying that, "5000 rupees is too less daddy! You talk as if it is 50 lakhs!" His dad walked away, annoyed and frustrated.

Over the next one month, AK had to endure lectures and advice especially whenever his dad walked in and caught him relaxing after his study break but suspecting the worst that he was whiling away his time.

There was silence for most parts of the day after such discussion and everyone kept to themselves. AK kept himself busy with his studies. He struggled with Math as usual and Math also reminded him of Nehal. She was a born Math genius!

Nehal was shaking AK, he looked directly into Nehal's desperate eyes as she said, "Darling, I need your help, save me please, save me, save me please…I love you and only you can save me," she cried.

He was flabbergasted.

Seeing his bewilderment, she giggled and started running away from him. He tried to chase her down, wanted to stop her, hold her, and ask her what it all meant. But he was frozen stiff and his legs were unwilling to obey his commands. His soul tore itself up, his mind was at war to obey or not obey, but his legs remained stuck to the ground. All he could do was watch her disappear into the crowds helplessly.

AK jumped out of the bed, shaking and sweating. *Why did it have to be him? Why did it have to be her?*

He looked around. It was still dark. 4:05 a.m., his watch glowed. It was too early to call Bhavin and check on her. He shrugged it off dismissively.

Perhaps, it was just a bad dream! He mused, and after a while he forced himself to sleep.

A few days later the same nightmare visited him again. This time he chased her, but he couldn't keep up. She was too fast for him. He assumed that she was leaving him for good. Their break up – final!

He called Hiten the following morning and asked him to check on Nehal through Bhavin. He got back to him the same day with the affirmation that everything was absolutely fine and she was hale and hearty at her cousin's home. AK felt relieved to know she was safe.

Such nightmares kept haunting him over the next few weeks but he kept his calm. Days were drawing closer and it was time for him to head back to Mumbai to face CA Foundation exams, Nehal, and life.

Perhaps it's because I am headed to Mumbai and I am worried about what she will say…maybe it will be the end of our relationship for good, he mused helplessly.

His mom helped him shop for his choice of clothes, perfumes, and new shoes—CAT steel toes—these were the new fad. This would guard his toes in the Mumbai train. He felt truly blessed and lucky to be her son.

Finally, the day arrived and he was ready to return to Mumbai. After some emotional goodbyes from his darling mom and stern warnings from his dad, AK pushed the baggage trolley into the airport. He had informed Hiten, Sanjay, and his uncle of his arrival.

In the flight, AK mused, *I can't believe I couldn't get Nehal out of my head even in Dubai but I did much better than expected. It's ok…there are so many gorgeous girls around. My time will also come…so I just need to chill!* He consoled himself. The plane landed bumping him back to reality, and his mind now raced to his CA foundation exams which were a week later.

CHAPTER 24

RRIINNNNGGG! Tring! A loud noise burst through the silence. The phone rang, waking him up, and fumbling, he reached for it, yawning as he picked it up, he wondered, *could it be her? Forget her! But did she miss me? I have been away for nearly a month.*

"Hey, AK! Welcome back!" Bhavin was happy to hear his friend.

"Hi, dude!" he answered sleepily. They indulged in some chit chat about flight and studies.

AK smoothed the t-shirt over his midriff. Hottest summers most of India ever experienced were in April and May. Seeing the ceiling fan in full speed, he already missed the comfort of his room and AC in Dubai.

"You must be missing your parents? Mummy definitely?" asked Bhavin.

"Well, kind of…but more than missing them, I miss the AC!" replied AK, rubbing his eyes. He felt a trifle guilty of his own feelings. Bhavin chuckled.

"*Arrey*, May will be very, VERY HOT!" said Bhavin, chuckling. "Our exams will be even HOTTER!" he added. AK noted his friend's English had improved and complimented him. Bhavin smiled.

"Hey, how are things with Dimple and you?" he asked Bhavin.

"Ok *rey*, going on…concentrating more on studies now," he replied. He added, "I spoke to her a few days back...Dimple called from a PCO booth and Nehal was with her…so she also wished me luck for the exams… that's all."

"Hmm…did she ever ask about me?" asked AK with some deliberation.

"Yes, Dimple did…but not her and eh…" Bhavin paused briefly, "We told Nehal about us and Dimple and I thought to tell you after you are back," he added.

"Tell me what?" asked AK

"*Arrey*, about me and Dimple…please behave like you never knew."

"Who could've guessed! What did Nehal say?" asked AK, his interest peaking.

"She said congrats and smiled but I know she was not happy, I felt so," said Bhavin. This irritated AK but he kept quiet.

"Did she say anything about us?" AK asked.

"See, Dimple thinks Nehal is behaving differently… but no she has not been saying anything about you," said Bhavin hesitantly, knowing that this would hurt his dear friend. "Hiten told me that you had some bad dreams about her, did it happen again?" he asked.

"No, I think it was just a silly dream!" AK replied. "I will never ask about her ever again! I too have some self-respect!" AK grunted. Bhavin agreed.

"I feel something is not right…but I don't know what! You don't worry about it," said Bhavin, consoling his friend. He concealed the annoyance he felt towards Nehal for hurting his dear friend.

Bhavin changed the topic and they spoke about their other friends Hiten and the rest of the Rascals and indulged in some small talk.

Over the course of the day he had spoken to his parents, Sanjay, and Lakshmi aunty over the phone, informing them about his arrival and conveying his parents' regards. But he was yet to hear from her.

Diverting his mind to unpacking and sorting out his clothes and placing the new ones in the almirah only eased him temporarily. *I shouldn't have asked Bhavin about her, makes me look weak…I hate being weak. I am*

STRONG! I AM STRONG! He mused and he kept telling himself aloud "I won't call her!" all the while until early evening.

His eyes fell on the phone and he reflected on his self-talks. Defeated by a sudden rush of impulse, love, and longing, he picked the phone and punched her number. The phone rang on the other side. Rang several times. He was about to disconnect when the familiar sweet voice answered, "Hello!"

"Hello, Nehal! AK here. How are you?"

"Hi! When did you come back?" she asked. He could feel the smile and warmth in her voice.

"I…today morning," he replied.

"How are your parents?" she asked.

"They are fine…err Nehal," said AK. He wanted to tell her how badly he missed her. *No, no, no, don't AK, self-respect! Damnn it! Out with it!* he mused.

"Good…listen I will be –"

"I love you Nehal. I love you a lot," said AK quickly, interrupting her.

"NOOO! AK, stop it!" she hissed and banged the phone down in disgust. He immediately felt guilty. He let it slip so badly, his willpower crushed out by his love for her. He did not know how to make peace with that. His heart never followed his own voice, never wanted to because he only needed to hear her sweet voice to soothe his aching heart. *Why do feelings overpower thoughts? Why?* He mused dejectedly, his shoulders drooping as he slowly sat down on his bed. He covered his face with his hands, hiding his humiliation, forgetting he was alone in the room.

AK quickly checked his line again. The dial tone returned and unhappily he kept the phone down. In that moment, like a lost weary traveller in search of a few drops of water, his heart sank.

Soon, like a dying ember invigorated by a sudden gust of wind, anger flamed inside him, slowly fanned by every memory of her recent denials to patch up, and her final insult – banging the phone down at him. He was enraged, he too banged the phone down. *That's it, there is never going to be US in the future! She has made it very clear! I am never ever going to talk to her ever again… This time it was far too much!* He reflected on his previous actions. Hurt, a few tears escaped him. *Damn! I say this all the time and never follow it but this time I WILL!* He washed his face and sat down to study for the CA Foundation exams.

He later spoke to Hiten when he rang in the evening and conveyed his disgust.

"Leave it *yaar*, she is not worth you at all," he said and added, "If, despite all that you have done for her, she still acts this weird then there is something wrong with her…maybe she definitely has something to hide you know…"

"Enough dude…frankly, I just told you all this…but please, please…don't analyse anything anymore…she is dead to me, that's it. Alright I'm keeping now…good night," said AK.

"Hey, please, I didn't want to make you feel bad *yaar* but-"

"I know pal, I know…thanks a lot for that," smiled AK.

"No worries *rey*…good night…bye," said Hiten.

After he kept the phone, he exhaled and inhaled deeply a few times. He was pleasantly surprised how liberating that was. He felt a sense of peace and happiness.

What the heck? She isn't the only woman in the world and I would be a fool to pine for her! AK was hoping that this sense of peace and liberation was not a false signal like before because this time he really wanted to mentally break away from her. He did not want even a shred of her thoughts to bother him anymore. He looked at his wallet, the one she had gifted him. It was the same as the one his mom gifted. He removed and transferred everything back to his old cheap wallet.

The CA foundation exams commenced on 2nd May 1999 and the papers were consecutive without any study leave. The good – it would be over fast, the bad – hardly any time to revise, the ugly – he had no hope of clearing it. AK's exam centre was Birla college in Kalyan West.

His Accountancy, Economics, and Law exams went well. Today was his last paper - Math. An hour into the paper, he realized it was neither worth wasting ink nor paper. Instead, he decided to take time to focus on life's bigger meanings. Auto piloting into dreamland, some turbulent revelations jolted him.

I don't think I want to be a CA. I would rather be something else...but why don't I want to be a CA? Because that would be a very boring job…and how many times would I keep writing and writing exams in the hope of clearing them? I think Hiten was right…I should do an MBA and try and join a job...and then become a businessman…or do something on those lines...but why this sudden change of plan? Just because of Maths? Damn it! Maths is my Achilles heel… always has been…But no, my heart isn't set on becoming a CA. How will I ever explain this to my parents? Mom will be heartbroken…she was when I didn't want to become a doctor! But this time CA...why do I find CA very boring? Is it because I don't know the job? Hmm...but I still think I would be able to manage and convince mom about it…but dad will breathe fire! Shucks, man! Anyways, there is time for all that until the results come. He let out a sigh. *Surely, Nehal must be topping this!* He scolded himself. *Avoid her! Focus back! There is more to life than her.*

The phone call from his parents woke him up from his afternoon nap. They enquired about his papers and AK convinced them that he had done his best.

261

"So, *mone*, do you think you will pass?" asked his mom excitedly. He noted that her excitement stayed at pass and not beyond that.

"Let's see, mom," he replied. His Dad overheard it on the speakerphone and grumbled.

"If you pass then good for you," he said. They spoke for a bit more over his future academic plans and they hung up. It was only around 4 p.m. Flopping back on his mat, he stretched himself out and quickly dozed off to sleep again.

Waiting for a CST local at Dombivli station, AK looked around in earnest like all the other commuters. A passenger train to Saurashtra was announced to pass by. Commuters stepped back as it approached the platform.

The engine passed by first followed slowly by the coaches one after the other. AK looked away.

"AK! AK! AK!" he heard a familiar voice calling out his name, the volume growing louder as the coach neared. He looked around bewildered, it was coming from this train.

"AK! Please save me! I am sorry! Please! Only you can save me!" she screamed as she stretched out her hands from the window. He ran and reached out to her. She immediately pulled her hands back in. Everyone in the train laughed but she was laughing, wiping away her tears. He ran towards the door of the coach. It was locked from the outside with a big brass lock. Shaken, he yelled, "Darwaja kholo! Darwaja kholo!" (Open the door! Open the door!). The train picked up speed and was gone. The railway police charged towards him waving their lathis in the air and blowing the whistle at him. The crowd clearing the way towards him. Their whistle sounded different! It sounded like a phone call.

AK opened his eyes. Rubbing his eyes, he jumped at the phone.

"Hello," he said in a hushed sleepy voice. He cleared his throat and said again, "Hello!"

"Hello, AK," replied the feminine voice.

"Nehal, you?"

"Hmm…how are you?" she asked. *This must be a joke,* mused AK.

"What happened? Why did you call? I mean, I wasn't expecting you at this time," he asked in a serious tone. He was in no mood to answer her previous question, but he was relieved to hear her voice. He was certain that his worrisome dreams about her were just silly dreams. *Why didn't she bother calling me before?* He mused.

"I just simply called…wanted to hear your voice," she said. No sooner had he heard this, dormant anger burst through like a volcano.

"ENOUGH! ENOUGH OF THIS BLOODY BULLSHIT, NEHAL!" he erupted, "Enough! Whenever it suits you, you can call me up and talk to me but if I were to do it then you bang the phone down…and God knows what goes on in your head? Do you know the amount of pain I have been through? GODDAMMIT! Did you even care to make our relationship work? NO! You were not bothered at all! You were in your own world always."

"AK, I am very sorry I –" He did not want to listen to her anymore.

He fumed, "NO, NO, NO, NO, I am not AK for you anymore. SO, PLEASE, don't ever call me ever again. I mean it. I don't want to talk you or know about you anymore, and you know what I DON'T CARE!" he roared and banged the phone down. The phone rang again but he quickly lowered the volume. The phone rang again. He stared at it in anger and adamantly didn't answer, it rang again a third time and then no more.

Furious, he got up, slowed down the fan and lit up his Wills cigarette. He threw the match out of his window. The flaming end was the only company he had now fuelling his thoughts *Incredible! So, what now? Did she tell them? She must've, let me see if Bhavin and Dimple call me? Nehal has definitely told them about us? Is she finally trying to patch up with me just before any meeting this week. BULLSHIT! Why complicate things in the first place then? Women know how to complicate things!*

He pulled the last puff off his cigarette and threw it out the window. Finally relieved of his angst, he walked over to the wash basin and splashed cool water over his face. If there was anything to hear from Nehal he would listen to it when they met, but not today.

CHAPTER 25

*P*reening in front of the mirror, AK checked himself and dabbed on his new CK One spray.

An hour earlier, Sanjay rang and asked him to join the gang for a drive to Navi Mumbai. It was a new planned township that was widely spoken about in the news and this drive would be an ideal getaway. Every 'Rascal' deserved a break!

AK got ready and left a note for his uncle on the dining table informing him that he would return late after dinner. He had just stepped out the door, when the phone rang again. *What would Sanjay want this time?* He mused as he walked over to answer it.

"Hello?" he answered.

"AK *yaar*, Bhavin..."

"Hi, how was your paper?" he asked Bhavin.

"Please meet us now," Bhavin said.

"Us? Who us?" AK asked "I am not interested in meeting Nehal...and I am going for a drive with Sanjay and our friends. I can't come now!" he added quickly.

"Dimple and I want to discuss with you, I mean we met up today after exams...Please come, *yaar*. It is urgent," requested Bhavin.

"Oh! *Waah*, Bhavin *bhai*, you are very fast nowadays! What's the plan? Register marriage, huh?" AK teased.

"No *rey*, please come *na*. It's about Nehal," said Bhavin in a sombre tone.

"AK!" Dimple said, snatching the phone from him.

"Hey, dude! How are you?" asked AK casually.

"Come now! It's very urgent! We're waiting for you at Sarvodaya...only Bhavin and I are waiting for you," she said and the phone call got cut. *What could be so urgent? Damn that woman!* AK thought over and decided to go. After all, it was his friends who called, and he still couldn't resist Nehal beyond a certain point. His anger stemmed from his pain and not hate. He sighed as he started towards Bhavin and Dimple.

Confusion reigned in his mind. He quickly rang Sanjay and apologized for ditching them. He explained briefly that Bhavin and Dimple wanted to meet him in Ghatkopar tonight. He was unsure why. Sanjay chuckled and teased him about Nehal and reminded him he was becoming Pratap version 2, annoying AK.

Traveling towards Ghatkopar, after 5 p.m., in the evening he found the fast train empty. He reached quickly and made his way to Sarvodaya. Upon reaching their usual meeting place outside the hall, he was greeted by Dimple and Bhavin.

"Guys, what's happening? Why do I feel like both of you are pulling a fast one on me?" said AK jokingly.

Dimple didn't respond but wore a solemn expression on her face. He glanced around, Nehal was nowhere in sight.

Bhavin looked at her and like a pre-decided meeting began, "*Yaar*, there is something you don't know…and also I got to know all this today…and…Dimple will tell you," The couple looked uneasy.

"*Moah kholo havey!*" (Open your mouth now!) scolded Bhavin in Gujarati.

"Hey, chill man!" said AK to Bhavin, "Talk softly… why get angry?" consoling Dimple.

"Nehal isn't here AK!" she said after a brief pause and lowered her head.

AK glanced around, leaned forward, and whispered "I can see that." He chuckled.

"So, what is she doing at home? Or at the shop, eh?" he asked.

"AK," said Dimple "Nehal is not in Ghatkopar anymore…I mean she is not in Maharashtra anymore… she left for Surat on 4th May, the night of our third exam."

"What? How is that possible? You mean to say she never wrote her exams?" he asked, bewildered.

Dimple nodded slightly and fixed her gaze to the ground.

"You guys are joking, right? No way in this world is this ever possible," he said in disbelief.

"Impossible! She spoke to me just today afternoon! But wait…hold on, when did you say she left?" asked AK in disbelief and confusion.

"This happened around two weeks after you had gone to Dubai. That day she called up and told us to meet her. She said she had some surprise for us. We all met up. Bhavin was there too and so were a few friends of ours from the locality. The surprise - her brother was in town. He had come to meet her in Mumbai." Dimple said.

"Oh ok! That's nice," said AK. Dimple raised her hand gesturing him to pause while she continued.

"Her brother was meeting her after three years!" she said. AK's brain ceased thinking the moment he heard it and from then on, he decided to only listen to her.

"He had gotten into wrong company. There were a lot of things. He was into gambling and drinking being the main vices. I don't know what else…even when we met him that day, we could tell that he looked so drunk or maybe he was sober then...but still that slight smell of alcohol was on him. I could sense it when I went near him," she said.

"AK, if you saw him that day you would also say the same thing, 100%," added Bhavin in his slight Gujjuish English.

"Why didn't she ever tell me about all this? She never told me about her brother being like this!" he muttered in shock.

"AK, except me there was no chance that anyone could have known. I was with her all the time and I knew about most of her life, and she swore me to secrecy," she said. "But, I can't sit idle any longer...AK, please don't get mad at Bhavin. He told me about you guys...but only after I told him about Nehal...and he insisted that I tell you everything today...because you deserve to know," she said, her voice choking with emotion.

Listening to all this overwhelmed AK. He shook his head and looked around to be certain this was no dream. AK slumped back against the wall for support. *Damn it! Why the secrecy? Didn't she trust me?* mused AK. With doubts ravaging him, he wanted to know more, wanted to know why was all this making Dimple so emotional. He sensed more bad news coming his way.

"What is he like?" asked AK slowly.

"*Yaar*, when he met us, he was in a white shirt and dark brown trousers. He is about my height, very thin and you know what?" he said "He is four years elder to her but he looked a lot older...his face had this old and tired look and he smelled like *paan, ghutka,* and beer, I think. My first impression - not good," said Bhavin, shaking his head in dejection.

"AK, I am sure that if you were to meet him then he wouldn't have impressed you...I know," declared Dimple. "In fact, even my sister didn't have a good opinion about him."

"When did she tell you that she is leaving for Surat?" asked AK.

Dimple shook her head, "Actually, she did not. She didn't tell me at all...she didn't tell anyone...that's what I feel terrible about...she knows I wouldn't have let her go," said Dimple and a tear slipped out the corner of her eye. "I used to share everything about myself with her... but she didn't treat me that way...she proved that."

"Dear, its ok...calm down now...go on, he needs to know," said Bhavin. Reaching out to console her, he gently held her hand.

AK was totally bewildered now. "Then who told you all this Dimple?" he asked curiously.

"Nehal told me a lot about her life before, but yesterday afternoon her cousin sister came to my house and she was talking to my mummy and me," she replied.

"Ok…and?" AK prodded Dimple gently.

"Her cousin asked me why I didn't stop Nehal from going? In fact, that's when I got to know that she left…it all happened so suddenly. She didn't even tell them but just left a letter for them thanking them for everything and saying that she was sorry for any pain caused but she has to go with her brother."

She looked at AK and paused for a brief second. AK was distraught.

"Her cousin sister warned her not to go with her brother if he came to Mumbai, it could be a lot of trouble but she didn't listen."

"What trouble?" asked AK, his brows shot up.

"Her cousin thinks since he kept wrong company there could be some trouble, you know, that's all I think but I don't know exactly," she said.

"I don't think there will be any trouble," said Bhavin "I think it's just fear."

"Yea, maybe…maybe, there won't be any trouble, let's hope," said AK, looking at Bhavin. Whatever Nehal told him didn't seem to add up. He decided now to verify all that Nehal told him with what Dimple truly knew about her.

"Wait a minute…her dad…I mean wouldn't they be able to stop her…her parents? Can't they do something?" asked AK, suddenly coming out of his reflections.

"Oh God!" said Dimple, grief stricken, and covering her face in her hands.

"What happened?" AK asked, more confused than shocked by her reaction. Bhavin looked away dejected.

"AK, they are dead! They both passed away three years back," she said softly in sadness.

"WHAAATT?" AK was shocked, "No, this can't be true, she told me her dad…she told me she spoke to her parents every week…isn't it?"

Dimple shook her head, "No, her brother has been her only family, she doesn't have parents, AK," she whimpered.

"I am sorry, *yaar*, I couldn't tell you this on the phone because I was worried as to how you would manage the whole news…I am feeling bad all this is hurting you," said Bhavin.

"No dude, no, only lies hurt, truths don't…in fact, reality doesn't hurt at all, if it's bad, it only makes us stronger because we have no choice. Besides, a lot of things happen in our day to day lives and we are still alive, right?" said AK, his eyes fixed to the floor for a few brief seconds. *She had called and I had slammed the phone down on her. Oh God! Only if I had known…what was she thinking? That I wouldn't want to be with her because she is an orphan!* Waves of worry began crashing on him. *Dimple hasn't finished yet…I got to know more.*

"Go on, please," he said, looking at Dimple sombrely.

"Her dad worked at a provision store in Surat, they were from a lower middle-class family, AK. Her mom was a housewife."

"How did they die?" he asked.

"Her dad had a heart attack and two months after his death her mom suffered the same fate," she said.

"And where was her brother in all this?" AK asked curiously, leaning forward.

"Her brother had left the family soon after…after… after a very, very embarrassing problem," she said and paused, she looked up at them both. AK looked on at her with rapt attention. She continued "He was in a relationship or something with some…guy in their neighbourhood," she said all this reluctantly. AK's face paled in shock. He couldn't believe what he had just heard. He waved his hands wildly, wanting her to stop saying anything anymore. He couldn't breathe, felt enveloped by vacuum. He couldn't believe all this, his feet finally found some strength and he staggered onto his feet and yet struggled to walk away.

No wonder Nehal had told me...that I wouldn't understand...He shook his head in sadness. AK understood how superficial he had been.

Bhavin jumped up instantly and reached out to him "*Yaar*, please be cool...please...please, be strong," he hugged a shaken AK. Dimple too got up, she too held him to console him. "She hated people looking at her with sympathy and not everyone she met had good intentions in mind...so please forgive her," she pleaded.

"I know that all this is too much for you...but AK unluckily, there is more...so please, listen...I know it hurts to listen but it's even more shattering for me...I am...carrying all this in my heart...dying inside, unable to...to help her...somehow. She is a very proud woman, she wanted to win on her own terms despite everything," she said gently. AK was still speechless, he sat down.

Dimple controlled her sobs and soon she continued, "It was one of the neighbour's children who saw Nehal's brother in a compromising position...and they alerted the neighbouring houses and they humiliated the two boys...her father came to know of this soon and he couldn't take the jolt of all this...he kicked her brother out of the house for being a homo...Nehal is four years younger to her brother and although she did not know the real reason why her brother was kicked out of the house, she soon learnt it from her friends in the school and neighbours in the locality, not to mention the ragging she received due to her brother's actions," Dimple paused.

"And then?" asked AK, a trifle impatient.

"And then they were hounded to shift from their locality for dishonouring their society and with his meagre earnings her father tried to but he couldn't, the shock and embarrassment of his son's scandal took a toll on his health and he died due to heart failure," she said.

"And her mom?" he asked.

"She died six months later...the heartbreak of her missing son, the death of her husband and family break up was too much to handle," said Bhavin softly. AK sighed in despair, he couldn't imagine all she had been through.

"It was during this time that she was getting a lot of help from her friend, Sheetal, and her family, and eventually in her vulnerability she got attached to Sheetal's cousin, Sailesh. He was around five years elder to her. They both were in love for some time...but they split...the reason is not clear," she said.

"Love? Really?" asked AK, trying not to sound surprised. He felt betrayed by Nehal's unwillingness to trust him. *I took everything for granted? I was also not sensitive enough for her to confide in me.* He despised himself.

"Ohhh! So...didn't she tell you this?" asked Dimple, exchanging surprised glances at Bhavin. She now felt guilty for divulging something that could betray her dear friend and hurt AK.

"Yea, I do remember...she told me about it...just that I forgot...today, it's been just too much for me already," said AK, trying his best to sound casual though the lump was turning out to be too huge to swallow.

He couldn't believe what he just heard. *She told me that he was the one who was interested in her but she wasn't...I can't believe she lied to me about it...but why?*

"Eh, Dimple, how long were they going around for? Nehal and that guy?" he asked with some deliberation.

"Not for long...maybe just a few months and then she came to stay here at her cousin sister's place," she said.

"Hmm...She told me her dad is a textile trader, they have a big house and all that," he said, *I can't believe*

I've been taken for a ride. He exhaled deeply, shaking his head.

"*Yaar*, it's ok she did not tell you because there may be nothing between them," Bhavin suggested.

"Yea, I guess so," said AK. *Or maybe there was too much.*

"Last I heard, Sailesh joined the army much against his family's wishes…but I don't know where he is," said Dimple.

"But the real concern isn't her brother now…it's her. I don't know how she is? What she is doing? Is she safe?" said Dimple, concerned. There were lots of thoughts, memories and moments whirling through AK's mind. He looked at Dimple, with hardened eyes, questioning her with his raised eyebrows.

"AK…eh, I know that you must be upset but please understand that right now as good friends we should at least try to help her…I know her…she is very proud, she doesn't like anyone knowing her problems and worrying about it…and thinking of her as the '*bechari abla naari*', (damsel in distress) and she knew I wouldn't let her go and she would never want to hear anything bad about her brother from me…she missed him…that Sunday she even tied a *dhaga* at the *dargah* for him, prayed at the church, visited temples every day," explained Dimple, wiping tears from the corner of her eyes.

"She has not betrayed my trust, AK. She never did… even if she did, I forgive her because that's what good friends do and if I was in her place…she would forgive me too," said Dimple, "Women try to avoid unpleasantness while men usually face it head on."

"Yea, and *yaar*, AK, we don't know what situations she is actually facing and what is forcing her to do things that she doesn't like to do," said Bhavin, placing an arm on his friend's shoulder.

"She could have told me all this before…I mean, about her family, her brother, and everything else…but she didn't. I feel like a fool! I mean, she didn't like me enough to tell me all about herself or she didn't trust me?" AK spoke out his confusion.

"Honestly, AK, it's neither of these. She never told these things to anyone…because the nice people give her sympathy while the bad ones only want to take advantage of her helplessness," she said with a sigh.

"SHE COULD'VE TOLD ME, DAMN IT!" exploded AK, shocking them. He could no longer bottle it in him. Realizing he was in a public place quickly, he chose to continue softly.

"She could've told me. No, in fact, she should have told me all this before…what was she thinking? That I would leave her or something?" he said in frustration.

"Please understand, AK. I am sure this would have crossed her mind and I am sure she would have wanted to tell you," said Dimple, hoping to console him. "I really don't know why she did not tell you. I wish she had…then, at least, you might have understood her better and maybe…maybe she wouldn't have left," Dimple added.

"*Yaar*, AK…please give her the benefit of doubt, please. You know she has seen bad times and think about it…I don't think any of us can imagine a life like hers right now. So, AK, please *yaar*, forgive her," said Bhavin, resting his hand on AK's shoulder, consoling him.

He took a deep breath and turned his face away to look at the street light filled night sky. "Oh, damn!" he cast his eyes downward. "Look, I can't blame her for her fate. She's been very unlucky much like a tragedy queen, but guys there is something you need to know," he said and explained to them about Nehal's phone call earlier at noon and what actually transpired.

"I told her never to bother me ever again! I feel so terribly guilty now," sighed AK, gulping the lump of sadness down his throat and wiping a tear that escaped his eye.

"Oh no!' sighed Dimple, with a dejected look on her face, soon she was sniffling again.

"Yea, I did not expect that at all," said Bhavin, upset.

He smirked, "Well, I assumed that she was here and that you guys were going to patch things up between us…how was I to know?" said AK, upset. His eyes welled up, he wiped them with his hanky. He couldn't hide he was feeling gutted about what he did.

Bhavin and Dimple decided to split since they had covered everything they had to say. They were feeling dreadful they did not convey this to AK before.

"*Yaar*, please don't feel bad! I am sure she'll call again. We should have told you all this before. It's my fault, I thought if I told you about her brother coming here...thought it might affect your mood for the exams," said Bhavin apologetically.

Bhavin blamed himself for AK's emotional outburst at Nehal when she called him. AK was quiet, he did not blame Bhavin at all, but he was feeling too overwhelmed to speak. Dimple knew that she needed to leave the boys alone. It was time for her to go home.

The two friends saw Dimple off in an auto rickshaw. Lost in his troubled thoughts, AK did not heed her byes. He looked at the world around him without Nehal by his side – Grim and devoid of love, laughter, hope and strength!

A clueless Bhavin did not know how to make his friend feel better, then it struck him, "*Yaar*, AK, do you want to smoke?" He did not respond. He asked again.

"Yea, why not?" AK responded. They crossed the road and he bought a Rothmans single for his friend.

"*Yaar apni bhadaas ko bahar nikaal…nikaal, yaar*. I know you are very upset, anyone would be," said Bhavin. (Mate, let your emotions out…even if it's an outburst of anger, let it out). He thought direct approach is the best. AK puffed his cigarette, his brows slightly tensed.

"She's gone now...don't hold it inside, let it out... meaning, Dimple has gone home now," Bhavin corrected himself. "I know...it's bad, Nehal should have said these things to you," Bhavin said.

"I can't blame her really…Hiten was right! I am not meant for this. I need to talk to him now. Let's call him and find out if he's at home," he said.

"Do you really want to call him?" asked Bhavin earnestly. AK nodded. Bhavin called Hiten and soon they reached his apartment.

Atop the terrace of his building they stood listening patiently while AK spoke. Hiten was stunned by the revelations.

"I feel so devastated…so betrayed…and so helpless, there's nothing that I can do!" said AK, as a tear escaped from the corner of his eye. He quickly wiped it off.

"Boss! I am completely shocked! I mean, you see such things in some movies sometimes but…but," raising his hands at the night sky, "It's impossible to think that such things could happen to someone we know," said Hiten. "Or someone we loved," added Bhavin dejectedly.

AK looked at him "Yea, true...and I still do," he said with some deliberation. He loved her and it now hurt more than ever before.

"Boss! So, what's your plan AK?" asked Hiten.

"What is there to do? What should I do?" sighed AK

"I mean *arrey, yaar*, don't you want to find out some answers?" asked Hiten.

"Whatever chance I had of doing that, I blew it away," he said.

"What? I don't get it!" Hiten replied.

AK explained how he assumed that she had called to patch up with him and he lost his temper at her.

"*Hare Krishna*! That's a tragedy! Shit man!" replied Hiten.

"But I am confident that she will contact you again... just wait and watch," assured Bhavin.

"How can you be so sure?" asked Hiten.

"Just my strong feeling," said Bhavin.

"Yea…I really hope she does," said Hiten.

"At least then I can know when she'll be back…and if she ever REALLY loved me or…was I just a roll in the hay?" said AK with a stoic expression.

"I don't think you were that," Hiten said, shaking his head.

"You mean roll in the hay? But what does that mean?" asked Bhavin.

"*Arrey*, meaning, did she consider him time-pass or serious?" clarified Hiten.

"Ah…no, I don't think she was like that," said Bhavin confidently.

"Anyways, now what is your next plan of action?" he asked AK.

AK stared, lost, at the night sky.

"*Yaar*, I meant how are you planning to get in touch with her? And you know, help her out?" asked Hiten.

"I don't know, man…I've not been able to think much today…frankly, it's been too much to take in. I don't know what I should feel bad about? For her? For me? For her cousin? For Dimple? I just don't know…all I know is that I feel bad about everything that's happened until now…and all this is shocking for me," said AK, and as he recollected he couldn't help wonder that tragedy was laughing at her and fate at him.

It was already 9:45 p.m. Hiten insisted that AK stay over at his house but AK insisted on going, "I've to be there in case she calls tonight," he said. Hiten agreed.

Hiten and Bhavin both accompanied him to the station. AK was quiet all along the way, he hardly spoke. He wore the look of a fatalist, devoid of expressions. His silence said it all.

AK went off in a 10:15 p.m. local. Bhavin turned to Hiten, "What's wrong with you? Action plan? Huh!" Bhavin scolded him. Hiten looked on stupefied.

"If he goes and any harm comes to him…will you be responsible?" Bhavin asked him sternly. Hiten apologized and conceded defeat, "*Yaar*, I did not think that way, sorry!"

AK reached Dombivli station later than usual due to some signal issues on the way. He couldn't help feeling the world was against him. He glanced at his watch, it showed 11:15 p.m. *I better get home fast! She might call me. Nehal, please, please, call me.*

Rushing down the stairs, he saw three girls sitting behind their baskets to sell flowers. He recalled seeing them almost every day. They were there during the day and at night but away only during noon. *They must be working so hard for their families, struggling hard to make ends meet.*

Any other day he would have passed by without a glance but today was different. He was weighed down by his thoughts about Nehal and all her struggles that she hid from him and the world. *Oh Nehal! Wherever you are come back please…and let me be there for you.* Reaching the end of the stairway, he paused as kindness summoned him towards the slightly older girl who sat amidst the other two flower sellers.

I might as well do some charity, at least that might help me find some peace tonight, hoped AK. He reached the spot and looked at the basket of flowers. His eyes fell on the inviting fragrance of jasmines.

"*Yeh dus ka diya, do le lo saab,*" said the dark-skinned girl. (Rs.10 for one, take two, sir) She looked fresh with a powdered face, lipstick, and flowers in her hair, as did the other two girls.

What will I do with these flowers? They are of no use to me. I won't wake up in time in the morning to hand these to Lakshmi aunty for her puja. It's no use really, he mused. Peering hard into his wallet under the dim street lights, he took out a Rs.50 note and handed it to her. She took it, lightly rubbing his palm with her fingers.

"*Yeh rakhlo, phool nahin chahiye,*" he said wearily. (Keep this, I don't need the flowers) She looked at him, for a bit longer and slipped the money into her small purse. AK wondered, *so much deliberation to accept the money! Perhaps no one has been this generous to her before… poor thing.*

He turned to leave.

"*Saab, ruko,*" she called out to him. (Wait, Sir)

"*Do sau aur do saab, main aati hoon na...aapke paas thakaan door karne!*" (Sir, give me 200 more and I will come with you to drive your weariness away) she said raising her brow, tilting her head and muttering in a husky seductive tone, and winking.

Her reply jolted AK.

"Eh, eh, nnn…nn…oo," he could only stammer. He dashed without looking back. After running for a while, he felt out of breath and looked over his shoulder.

Why? Why? Why did this happen? Is she so desperate? Dammn it! It's unbelievable. Nooo, this is just a bad dream. I have had too many shockers for today! This was even worse!

On reaching home, his uncle informed him that his parents had called, and also told him of an inland letter he had left on his study table.

Assuming it would be his younger sister, Akhila's, he promised to check it later. He dined and took a shower and lay down on his bed with the fan on in full blast.

Everything he heard today spinned around in his head banishing sleep away for the night. Thinking about Nehal and all that she had been through, a deep sense of anguish enveloped him. *Why was life so cruel to her? Why such a cruel fate? I was right! There is no God! This is so unforgivable. Why did I rant at her like that? I don't know what she must be going through...maybe, she called to tell me the truth, it was my stupidity that I didn't bother to listen.*

Damnit! His eyes were moistening often but he decided to stay positive.

He got up and paced his room to and fro, staring at the phone, hoping for a phone call from her. He was restless and unable to console himself. He ran his hand over his bed sheet, they had nearly made love here several times. He could feel her presence linger in this room. Her smile, her giggles, her witty retorts, the first day they met, and then her saree day. *My gorgeous Maths genius!* He sat down on the floor, despondent.

He recalled everything Dimple told him about her parents, her brother, and he sympathized with her. He recollected every time her eyes moistened at the *dargah*, the church was for her family. He forgave her because she was right. He was too shallow to ever try understanding her but she had understood him so well. She thoughtfully gifted him the wallet, her concern when he was stressed with the drunk driving accident that he hid from her. He felt ashamed of himself for all the things he took for granted. Tears trickled down his cheeks. *I am so sorry Nehal! I am so very sorry! You deserve the best! But you could've told me about your parents at least, if not about Sailesh.*

He couldn't shake these thoughts out of his head. *How come her brother was so irresponsible? What wrong company had he gotten into?* His musings about her brother reminded him of his own sister. He wiped his tears and was up on his feet.

The blue inland letter stared at him from the study table. Lifting it in his hand he noticed that the handwriting looked familiar but definitely did not belong to his sister. Quickly turning it over, he observed there was no name on the sender's address. Deftly tearing it on the sides, he opened it.

Dear AK,

I know I won't be around when this letter reaches you. I know I have hurt you a lot in the last few weeks. I am deeply sorry about it. But I believe we have given each other moments of fun, laughter, joy, and love too. Let us remember each other through those memories.

AK, you are right that you have the right to know everything about me. It is your right, as a lover and friend. But my life changed from simple to complex and to complicated in no time. It is not fair to burden you with my troubles. So, I never said many things that I should have. And I really don't wish to, it is difficult to explain and more difficult to understand. Please forgive me. Someday, when everything is sorted out, hopefully, I will tell you myself. I hope you will understand. But I want you to know, you were the only perfection in my imperfect life.

I know I have been rude and I have hurt you with my behaviour. The fault was never yours but completely mine. I wanted to keep you away from the sadness in my life. Because just like a smile, sadness can be contagious too and not in a nice way. I could not see that smile and that voice I fell for hurt any more. I am really sorry, AK. Please, forgive me.

I want you to know that in your own crazy ways you filled my life with lots of happiness. Thank you, AK! You had once said **the sky loves the rain**. It felt so natural. It was the sweetest thing I ever heard. I will always remember it. Unluckily, rain is seasonal. That's how it always is. But remember **this rain too loved the sky**.

Apart from our religions and food habits being slightly different, everything else clashes,

281

AK. In a few words – Us won't work. So, I think it is best we forget this part of our relationship. I am sorry to hurt you with these words but that's the harsh truth. You see, the clouds leave the rain naturally, and it falls on the earth. But the rain cannot fall on the sky, it is against nature.

AK, please, I am sorry for hurting you with all this. It is not easy for me. Please remember what we had was true, everything was true, what I felt for you was true. But now it's time to let me go. I know you will be angry but after a while you will be able to forget me for good, time will help.

I will call you one last time just to hear your voice and say good bye. You will be in my prayers always. Besides, a hot guy like you won't be single for long. I wish you a life blessed with love, happiness, and riches. Good bye.

Love always,
Nehal

He turned the letter over and checked the date, the postal seal on it read May 1, 1999. He recalled that Dimple had said she left on the night of 4 May. He looked at the letter carefully. The paper had patches where the ball point ink was slightly blotted. Running his finger over it, he wished to wipe her tears over the wrinkled parts of the letter. He read it again and again. 'I will call you one last time' screamed hoarsely at him in the eerie silence of the night.

So, she sent me this a few days before she left. She had been planning this all along...and that was her last call... Oh my goodness! How can I ever forgive myself? He cursed himself, flopping back on the bed, his tears flowed.

CHAPTER 26

He requested AK, "Please take good care of her. She can be safe only with you now." He hugged his dear sister and they left home in an auto. Upon reaching the station, they heard the announcement and bell. At a distance, they could see their hope ready to leave, their train to Mumbai began to chug away slowly. Clasping her hand tightly and the bag in another hand, they dashed.

"Run faster!" cried AK. They dashed up the overbridge and down, the train picked up speed, they ran faster, nearly stumbling. The train had almost left the station. AK did not give up the chase, he let go of her hand, she was panting for breath, he ran and caught it, jumping in through the open door he grabbed the nearest chain and yanked it hard to stop the train. The train did not slow down, instead the speed kept increasing and the alarm bell went off. He pulled harder and harder, the train did not stop. The bell still continued to ring much to his irritation, infuriating him.

SHIIITTT! He awoke and lunged at the phone and slapped it to his ear. The drone of the dial tone welcomed him. *Damn it! I was asleep! Did the phone ring? I can't believe I missed her call! Please call me back baby, please call me BAAACCK!*

He waited near the phone with bated breath. He glanced at the wall clock, it showed 10:05. *What the hell? Oh, the damn clock stopped working!* He looked around and picked his watch. *Oh no! It can't be…I woke up this late!* He squinted at the bright daylight from the frosted window pane. "WAKE UP!" He snapped his fingers and yelled at himself.

The phone rang, within two rings he picked it up.

"Hello!" he answered with hope, his morning voice slower than usual.

"AK, hello!" answered Bhavin. "Did she call you?" he asked. AK was quiet, he couldn't believe it was not Nehal.

"Hello! AK! Are you ok?" he asked.

"Yea, I am. I...I...slept really late, just woke up now...I can't believe I slept for so long," he replied, sounding slightly drowsy. "Ok, fine, come meet us now, will you?" asked Bhavin.

"You called me some time back?" asked AK, clearing his throat, unable to shake off the raspiness.

"Yea, just a minute back," affirmed Bhavin. *Oh, so it wasn't her!*

AK promised to be in Ghatkopar in an hour. He didn't want to ask him anything over the phone, even if it was not to talk about Nehal. He still wanted to get out of the house. He didn't want to be alone. Being alone meant Nehal was with him every second in his soul, heart, and head. And within him, his guilt of yelling at her. Would she call him again? Ever? The letter left no hope.

Alighting at Ghatkopar station, he met them just outside platform number 1. They quickly greeted each other and walked over to Bharat café. AK spotted a waiter and ordered three cokes as he sat down.

"*Yaar*, AK, eh..." said Bhavin, fumbling nervously and he paused. Turning to a worried Dimple, he said, "You tell him."

"Yesterday night, Nehal's cousin sister came home very worried. She said that in the afternoon three guys came to her place asking for Chandan, Nehal's brother. They looked like thugs, he owes them money from his gambling days. They said if their money is not paid back then..." Her voice broke. "They threatened that they will make Nehal work to pay it off!" said Dimple, her eyes swelling with tears and panic.

AK's mind reeled back to the flower seller girl he had seen the night before. The impact of Dimple's words crushed him.

"Shut up! This is all bullshit! Nothing is wrong! Everything is fine. She is there, safe in Surat. She has gone there for her holidays. This is all...all this is a huge LIE. You guys are lying to me about everything," cried AK. Indignant in wishful disbelief, he hurried out of the cafe.

The waiter saw AK leave and called out to him. Bhavin ran out behind him. Dimple stopped the waiter.

"AK, wait! Wait! Please!" called out Bhavin, chasing him. AK didn't heed him at all. He caught up with him.

"AK!" he tugged at his shoulder forcing him to turn around. AK's eyes were reddened, brimming with tears. "*Yaar*, please, I know all this is not easy at all. It's very tough for all of us and I know it feels very bad for you," he said, consoling his friend.

"I can't believe that in spite of being so close to her, she didn't tell me any of this...and she wouldn't have even if she called me again," he said, his voice nearly choking.

"Oh, come on, she will," said Bhavin, he wanted AK to let out his bottled up emotions.

They walked back across the road to the *paan beedi* stall outside the café and Bhavin ordered two Classic Menthol singles.

Bhavin knew that Dimple would be upset if he smoked but there are times when friendship supersedes love, and this was one such moment. They took the cigarettes. AK saw Bhavin picking up one for himself. AK lipped his ciggy.

"Here," said Bhavin, lighting a match. AK obliged and simultaneously took the other cigarette from him.

"Don't do it! I am not a believer of bad for health bullshit, but be honest to Dimple, she truly loves you," said AK and pulled in a short puff.

AK pulled out a folded piece of paper from his pocket and handed it to Bhavin. Curiously, Bhavin unfolded the inland letter and read it. His face paled and his shoulders drooped.

"See," he said, taking in a puff, "She wouldn't have told me! She won't call me again!" He blew the smoke away.

"Want to show this to Dimple?" asked Bhavin.

"Yea sure…like it matters now," he replied sadly.

"You slept last night?" Bhavin asked him. He shrugged, "Somehow, I did."

"Yaar you-"

"Leave it, dude," interrupted AK, "Please…now don't say anything, you know what…I am responsible for the way she behaved with me…if I had shown her that I was sensitive to certain things she said then I am sure she would have told me the truth," he said. AK explained about the gay incidents and discussions and how he poked fun at them. He regretted it.

"*Yaar*…look, even if Dimple had asked me something like that, I wouldn't have a doubt that someone in her family had that problem. I mean she cleverly asked that question because she had no other choice. Nehal had to test every person she met after all things went wrong in her life…I feel it's only natural for her."

"But still…I could have…I should have sensed something was wrong. I just didn't think properly," he said, wiping his tears with his hanky under the summer sun of May. "Let's leave all this. Dimple is waiting inside…let's go," he said, stubbing out his cig which he had smoked till the filter tip with a vengeance.

They both walked back in, sipping their colas while she read the letter. AK did not speak a word. Bhavin sat next to him, facing Dimple. As she finished, she sniffled. AK didn't want to say anything, he knew his voice would choke.

Their silence, in this din of Ghatkopar life, was discomforting Dimple. She wanted to break this, "Eh,

AK! We have to find some way to help Nehal. Please think of something."

"What do you mean?" Bhavin asked Dimple, concealing his irritation.

"I think one of us should go there and bring her here, right? Or find someone there who can go and check on her!" said AK pensively.

"It's difficult to make a choice," said Bhavin, sounding confused. He was certain he wouldn't let AK go.

"I think I should go there. At least, if I try hard begging her to return, there is a good chance she'll come back," said Dimple. "What about her brother, Chandan?" she asked.

"He can go jump off a bridge for all I care," said AK coldly.

"Shut up Akash! Don't talk this way. He is the only family she has!" Dimple shot back.

"Yea, that's why he screwed up so badly! Bloody idiot!" he retorted.

AK settled the bill. Dimple kept mute. After a while, she again broached the topic, "So, is anyone of you willing to go?" AK didn't utter a word. Dimple was concerned and she wiped her eyes in between her sobs.

Unknown to the couple AK had already resolved what he should do. Bhavin wanted to discuss this privately with AK after Dimple left.

"I would have gone if I could…but…but…I am a girl. It's not safe for me there and I don't have any excuses that I could give at home," she said, concerned. Bhavin nudged her and urged her in Gujarati to be quiet. AK remained silent like a fatalist. She finally gave up and took their leave.

After seeing her off, Bhavin and AK walked over to the eastern side of Ghatkopar. AK was in a pensive mood and Bhavin in a dilemma since yesterday.

"Look, *yaar*, AK, I know you want to bring her back…but I…don't think it's a good idea…there could be serious risk to your life. I mean, where money is involved goons will stop at nothing to get it back."

"That's why I am going there alone," said AK, stroking his chin.

"WHAAAT? *Yaar*, AK, please don't do this...please, *yaar*. It is dangerous, you have a family...your parents are not here...if something were to happen to you... then what? Please think of them first," he tried to reason with AK. Failing, despite repeated requests, Bhavin now begged with folded hands.

"Bhavin! I can't believe that you are saying this to me now. Oh! So, this is why you were quiet in front of Dimple, eh? You don't want her to feel bad that you don't want me to do anything," shot back AK vehemently.

"No, not that."

"Then, what is it, eh? Let me ask you this, if something like this were to happen to Dimple would you sit back like a coward?" asked AK, annoyed.

"AK! Please stop this, *yaar*...Dimple is saying all this so selfishly because she cares for her friend now...if she told me these things before, I would have stopped Nehal myself...but she didn't...she also waited for things to go this bad *na*...and just like her, I care for my friend too. I can't see you go in harm's way. Why aren't Nehal's cousin and her husband going down to Gujarat to get her back, huh? They can get some police help if they wanted...but, why aren't they? And as a son who is living away from his parents, someone like you should take care and not fall into trouble," said Bhavin, irritated.

"Dude, I can't let it happen...if she has a chance at a normal life with me or even without me...I think I should help her out... I owe it to her and myself, else I will go mad knowing that I stayed back and did nothing...that I did nothing for the girl I love! I am prepared to face the consequences. True love is the happiness of the beloved, and according to me she will be free to choose whoever she wants. Besides, haven't we all read it somewhere...

love is like a bird, set it free…if it's ours it will come back to us, and if it doesn't it never was," said AK.

"*Arrey*! But she run away from you and from here without any explanation…and she wrote a letter…she first break up with you...you are mad AK! Hiten was right, you not fit to fall in love. Please don't repeat same mistake again…what if you are rebound?" he said and turned his face away in disbelief. "Stop behaving like Mahatma Gandhi! What do you plan to do now?" he grunted and asked AK.

"Go home and sit on a hunger strike till she comes back," replied AK curtly.

"Huh, what?" asked Bhavin, and quickly realized his friend was being sarcastic.

"Don't worry, I will be going for all this alone. Money is the only issue for now…but I will make some arrangements," said AK. "And I will need to make arrangements for a new lease of life to help her forget her past," said AK with some deliberation.

"This is mad and you are totally mad! And you want to do this alone? Why aren't you thinking logically? It's impossible for you to do it, you are only 18!" said Bhavin, concerned, waving his hands up and down in frustration.

"Look, I understand why you were saying all that you were saying before," AK raised his hand to allow him to finish before Bhavin could say anything "Screw self-respect! I will do this because I care for her and I still have feelings for her, and Bhavin?" he said, gripping Bhavin's shoulders, "I would do this for you and for Dimple at any given opportunity."

"*Yaar*, AK, I know…you are a nice guy, I cannot forgive if something bad happens to you…you are my true friend!" said Bhavin thoughtfully. He had known it all along that AK had a good heart. He had seen his school friends who ditched him after they found a new friend circle in college. Unlike many other rich boys, AK remained Bhavin's friend not because he valued people by money or looks, but by their character.

"Shut up!" retorted AK, "Stay positive!"

"But I am serious! I not want you risk your life for your ex," said Bhavin. AK gave him one hard look. Bhavin knew that in his confusion and worry, he wasn't speaking English correctly but he didn't care.

"Shut up!" he said sternly "Don't interfere where you don't have to...she is risking it for her brother...I have a sister too."

Bhavin tried his best to make him understand the realities of a solo trip to an unknown place, fraught with unknown dangers, but AK wouldn't listen.

"Look, only I should go, I can't risk the others coming with me, I can't risk their lives to sort out this mess... besides, I can't have anyone slow me down either," he said intently. Bhavin knew any more discussion with AK was pointless. AK wanted to set his plans in motion. He left a dismayed Bhavin alone and headed back home.

As he climbed up the bridge at Dombivli station, he couldn't control his worries. *What would those people do to her brother if they don't get their monies? Will they kill him? No...he would be no good to them dead, then...he can't pay them back.* He walked, pondering over these things, and climbed down the steps. His eyes fell on the flower girl he had given money to the night before. *Ohhh Noooo! Nehal! They could use her! No, she will be fine and they won't harm her at all...but it's money these bloody goons are after and they won't hesitate to...DAMN IT! There is no time left anymore, I have to go and check on her...and if needed, bring her back...at any cost!*

With a decisive mind, he headed home, calculating monies that would be needed for the trip, train tickets required. He knew he must try and book train tickets that night, from Kalyan. AK reached home in time to pick a call. Hoping against hope, it was Hiten, they spoke briefly but AK didn't mention anything about his decision to travel.

AK quickly checked the monies he had, only Rs.4500. He felt this would not be enough but he had no choice. He began arranging his clothes for the trip.

After a few hours, the bell rang, and AK answered the door. Sanjay and Mukesh walked in. It had been almost a week since he had spoken to them. He had contemplated telling Sanjay about this, but he refrained, suspecting Sanjay would discourage him from taking a stand he felt was right.

Sanjay walked in to his room with Mukesh. They were surprised to see AK's clothes folded neatly and arranged on the bed.

"Are you going somewhere?" Sanjay asked, slightly surprised.

"No, just folding washed clothes," replied AK, looking away.

"Hi, AK *bhai*," said Mukesh. "Long time, huh?" he said.

"Not really, we spoke after I landed...we were anyways going to meet up over the weekend," said AK confidently.

Sanjay was quiet, he was lost with all that he heard from Mukesh and Hiten on the conference call. He was trying to make sense of the whole thing, and here was his childhood friend who hid every bit of pain from him and bottled it up inside. And he had already decided on travelling. He had to broach the subject quickly. Diplomacy be damned.

"AK, what are you planning to do? Answer me, honestly...please, at least respect my friendship and tell me the truth now. Your parents have entrusted us as your guardians and are staying in Dubai. So, please..." said Sanjay, raising his palm and pausing, "No matter how difficult it may be, please tell me the truth. I have the right to know," he looked at AK like an innocent man who had been defrauded out of his wealth by his trusted Chartered Accountant.

"I am going to meet Nehal, in Surat," said AK.

"How did she get to Surat?" asked Sanjay, trying to verify what he had heard from Mukesh and Hiten. He secretly hoped it was all a lie.

"She is from there. She has gone back there for her holidays and she invited me over, so I am going," he lied confidently. Had they not known these things through Hiten, they would have believed him. Sanjay and Mukesh exchanged glances. Mukesh felt that he had to make his point there and then, as blunt as it may be.

"Hiten *bhai* told me everything and we told him," said Mukesh, tilting his head and pointing towards Sanjay.

"Eh...we know that you are going to...kind of try... and bring her back," said Mukesh sheepishly, bracing for another retort.

AK frowned and quietly carried on with his packing. He pulled out his bag from underneath his bed and quickly dusted and unzipped it to pack. He took his jeans to pack them in. Sanjay jumped up and caught his arm, stopping him.

"Wait a minute, AK!" said Sanjay.

"Look, I can understand that you feel morally responsible but...don't you think you are taking an unnecessary risk?" he asked.

"I am 18, Sanjay. I know what I am doing," he shot back curtly and pushed his arm away.

"AK, I can't let you go...I am sorry...but I can't," he said with some reluctance knowing fully that his stand against AK was selfish but in the best interest of his childhood friend.

"Look, I know there could be a lot of risk considering that the people I have to face are probably armed and dangerous, but I have to do this…I need to do everything I can and know she is at least fine," said AK, sounding cold.

"Why you?" asked Mukesh.

"Because she doesn't have anyone else who will," he replied.

"*Yaar*, AK, this is crazy! Impractical! You both have broken up!" said Sanjay.

"AK, *yaar*, please no," requested Mukesh, looking sad with a puppy dog face.

"I can't believe this! You guys are trying to stop me? Bloody hell! No, it is not crazy. It would be crazy to sit back and not do anything," he replied.

"AK, there's probably no point getting her back. I don't think she is going to love you the same way as before," said Sanjay, trying to convince AK that he change his mind.

"Guys, what I know or what I feel is that true love is the happiness of the beloved and as much as I want to get out of all this, I can't…perhaps, if none of these things would have happened to her, then I would not have bothered at all. I would have definitely avoided her because we broke up, but now it's a different case altogether…I need to help her out and if I don't even try, I will never be able to forgive myself…If not as an ex-boyfriend…then at least as a friend…I still care about her and I still love her! and I don't care if she doesn't love me back…I want her to be safe…and to me, nothing else matters!" said AK, choking with emotion. "I am doing this alone. I don't want anyone else to come with me. It could get very risky," said AK, concerned.

Sanjay got off the chair and after some deliberation, he said, "I can't let you go, AK! *Yaar*, I can't, I am sorry, if anything goes wrong there…" Sanjay shook his head, "I will not be able to face your family, my family…myself for the rest of my life. None of this is PRACTICAL!" he finished, waving his hands in the air.

"SHUT UP, SANJAY!' thundered AK, jolting both the guys. "If something like this had happened to your cousin sister, Gayatri, what would you do, eh?' Sanjay was quiet and shifted his gaze downwards. Mukesh looked on in silence and he continued, "I would have done the same, I would have gone to bring her back. Now, both of you, please excuse me, I am busy," said AK curtly, raising his arm towards the door gesturing to leave.

Mukesh spoke, "It's so hard to believe! I don't know if my dad would have thrown me out if I were a homosexual! Thank God, none of us are!" he added "AK *bhai*, you are going to Gujarat, you need me. I am the only one who knows Gujarati inside out...I am coming and you don't have any say on that," added Mukesh with a wink and hugged AK. He was taken aback.

"No, I'll manage please," said AK, releasing himself.

"I'll make arrangements *bhaisaab* and come back... we will try to leave tonight," Mukesh said intently. AK and Sanjay were surprised.

"Mukesh! *Yaar*, what are you doing?" asked Sanjay, bewildered.

"AK is right! *Bhai*, Sanjay, listen very carefully... when that Tanya thing happened...we all were guilty of spreading rumours...but AK owned up...he took the blame and apologized to her! He did not retaliate with any crazy thing after that...even though he was not completely at fault...you and I never apologized for spreading the rumours...but we should have...agreed AK is crazy...we are all crazy but in a good way! He is a nice guy! He is a man who takes responsibility! In your case, when the accident happened...he stood by me every minute of that night to save you! That night I understood becoming a MAN is not about drinking, driving, watching porn and flirting with chicks and all that. Oh no! It's much more than that! It is about being brave, responsible and caring for oneself and others."

Glancing at AK he went on, "We became MEN when we bravely tried to save that fallen man not knowing who he was because we cared for him and more than that…we cared for you!" Sanjay fixed his gaze at the floor, speechless.

Mukesh added, "That night, running away, leaving him to die was more practical but we went back there to save him and…to save you! And we almost died saving you! You know that! AK has the guts to save Nehal! The woman, the lover, and the friend he loves! Great! Then I am with him all the way." said Mukesh curtly.

"You guys are watching too many crazy movies! IDIOTS!" cried Sanjay, dejectedly looking away.

"Things can get crazy out of hand! Whacked out crazy! We are just 18 year-old idiots who call ourselves Rascals for fun's sake! There is no guarantee that we may come back alive!" cried Sanjay.

"Terrible things can happen to Nehal! But she went for her brother! She has more guts being a girl! Then I am not going to sit back," said AK, determined.

After a few seconds of silence, Sanjay twitched his nose, stroked his hair. "There is no point being stuck here with Pratap, he will be too busy with Nivedita…I'll come too," said Sanjay, forcing a smile on his face.

Before AK could say anything, they hugged him. They promised to make the arrangements and return. AK looked on stupefied. He later continued with his packing.

In his hopelessness and vulnerability, he forgot his atheism. He knew they needed every higher power for courage, hope, and luck. By four in the afternoon, he visited the Ganesh Mandir to pray for Nehal, his friends, and himself.

The Rascals had planned everything, tickets were arranged and they were travelling that night. Visiting

Shirdi Sai Baba was the best excuse. AK's parents were unhappy with the decision but his dad assumed that fear of failure in exams was bothering his only son. His mom complained that he could go with his uncle to their native place. His uncle, Mahesh, was leaving in two days but he refused. AK's adamancy won and he was going to Shirdi, as they presumed.

Sanjay and Mukesh had it fairly easy, their parents were happy to see them go. Except, Mukesh's father asked him several times if Shirdi was an excuse for Goa. Mukesh tried to convince him but gave up after a point.

Hiten, Pratap, and Bhavin accompanied the brave trio to Mumbai Central station. Total money arranged, Rs. 55,000, generously contributed by Hiten. Everyone else put in whatever they had.

Bhavin told him, "I'll not be sad if you do not go! It's not too late!" AK shook his head.

"We are all coming back together!" AK said resolutely.

As they prepared to load their bags into the compartment, a porter rushed up and told AK, "*Saab, mujhe karne do,*" (Sir, please allow me) and quickly took the bags and climbed in to place it inside the compartment. AK and his friends hurried behind him. The porter turned around and standing in attention raised his hand in salute firmly and said, "Jai Hind!" AK surprised, returned the salute.

His friends watched this in stunned silence. The aged porter smiled with his *gutkha* stained teeth. Thanks to AK's summer haircut, he believed him to be a soldier. AK and his friends glanced around and saw several soldiers in similar haircuts on the platform.

Blindsided by Nehal's misfortunes, they had failed to notice everything else. Tensions prevailed high in Kargil and patriotism in the hearts of citizens.

The intensity of their impending adventure dawned on the trio when the departure was announced. They hugged each other and waved farewell. Mukesh promised to call Hiten every day. Bhavin promised to fast and devoutly pray for their safety.

The trio took their seats. Sitting by the window, AK's eyes fell on young trained soldiers, as the train chugged along. While the nation prepared for war with a known enemy, he knew that his friends and he were unprepared to face unknown enemies. *Hopefully, there aren't any...but if there are...I will risk it all! There will be no turning back!* Musing, he promised himself.

Determined and undaunted he muttered, "Nehal! Stay strong, darling! I'm coming babe, just hold on."

Stepping off the train at Surat station, AK looked fresh at half past four in the morning. He had barely slept throughout the journey but his friends were drowsy. He asked around in Hindi and walked towards the auto stand, while the sleepy duo dragged themselves behind him.

He handed over Nehal's address slip to Mukesh who spoke to an auto driver in Gujarati. He quickly negotiated the price and hopped in. AK and Sanjay followed. In about 20 minutes, they reached the area. The auto rickshaw driver slowed down as he entered a lane and halted in front of a house. Mukesh verified the address and confirmed it by reading the signposts in Gujarati. They had reached their destination. Settling the bill, they all stepped out.

Standing outside, they glanced at each other. The house looked the oldest in the area. Cracks on the outer walls revealed the owners couldn't afford to age it gracefully. Unlike other houses in the vicinity, there were lights neither outside the door, nor at the gate. The small rusted gate stood between them and Nehal's gloomy house.

AK slid the lock and pushed the rusty gate open. It creaked loudly as it opened reluctantly. As they approached the house, their gaze fell on the door and they exchanged uneasy glances with each other.

More than the brunt of time, the door seemed bruised by recent violence. The shoe prints on the door looked fresh. It must have taken several kicks to break it down but it seemed firmly in place.

Is she safe?
Are we late?

To be continued...

RAIN INFERNO

(Sequel - The Rain that touched the Sky)
Manoj N Premal

Fate betrayed her, but she stood relentless.
Unchosen by destiny, yet he went fearless.

A loan sharking money lender and his goons refusing
to give back her dad's property papers.
A don from whom her brother has stolen money.
A bunch of angry cops and a lone hitman.
Apart from Nehal and Chandan, these challenges await
AK & his friends.

Should they fear the unknown?
Will fortune favour the brave?
Or
Will she be unlucky?
Are they foolish to be brave?

It all ends here!

About the Author

Namaste / Hola!

To briefly introduce ourselves - We are sales and marketing professionals by day who have moonlighted as authors. We had each other to fight, discuss, and write with and phew! We are glad to have finally met you through this humble venture of ours.

We hope you like our debut effort. We assure you the successive part of this story will be more entertaining. We sincerely hope to raise the bar. We wish to hear your constructive feedback to help us grow into better storytellers.

So please reach us on -
Twitter: @AuthsmNp
Gmail: authormnp@gmail.com

Happy Reading!

Thanks a billion!
Manoj N Premal

Pen Name - <u>Manoj N Premal</u> is the registered copyright of Mr. Manoj Narayanan Nair & Mr. Joseph Premal Austin